He kissed her...

There. There it was again: that whirlpool pulling her in, sweeping away all the doubts and fears and sorrow, all her thoughts. Leaving in their place only *feeling*, pure and searing. He licked into her mouth with a hot, conquering tongue. Artemis stood on tiptoe, trying to get closer to him, spreading her fingers wide against the silk of his banyan. If she could, she would've crawled right into him, made a home for herself in his broad, strong chest, and never emerged again.

This man, she wanted this man, despite his wretched title, his money, his land, his history, and all his myriad obligations. Maximus. Just Maximus. She'd take him bare naked if she could—and be the gladder for it.

He pulled back, his chest heaving, and looked at her angrily. "Don't start something you mean to stop."

She met his gaze squarely. "I don't mean to stop."

D0180010

PRAISE FOR
ELIZABETH HOYT'S
MAIDEN LANE SERIES

Lord Of Darkness

"*Lord of Darkness* illuminates Hoyt's boundless imagination...readers will adore this story."
—*RT Book Reviews*

"Hoyt's writing is imbued with great depth of emotion... heartbreaking...an edgy tension-filled plot."
—*Publishers Weekly*

"*Lord of Darkness* is classic Elizabeth Hoyt, meaning it's unique, engaging, and leaves readers on the edge of their seats, waiting for the next book...an incredible addition to the fantastic Maiden Lane series. I Joyfully Recommend Godric and Megs's tale, for it's an amazing, well-crafted story with an intriguing plot and a lovely, touching romance that I want to enjoy again and again and again... simply enchanting!"
—*JoyfullyReviewed.com*

"I adore the Maiden Lane series, and this fifth book is a very welcome addition to the series...[It's] sexy and sweet all at the same time...This can be read as a stand-alone, but I adore each book in this series and encourage you to start from the beginning."
—*USA Today's* **Happy Ever After Blog**

"Beautifully written...a truly fine piece of storytelling and a novel that deserves to be read and enjoyed."
—TheBookBinge.com

Thief Of Shadows

"An expert blend of scintillating romance and mystery... The romance between the beautiful and quick-witted Isabel and the masked champion of the downtrodden propels this novel to the top of its genre."
—*Publishers Weekly* (starred review)

"Amazing sex scenes...a very intriguing hero...This one did not disappoint."
—*USA Today*

"Innovative, emotional, sensual...Hoyt's beautiful blending of the essential elements of a fairy tale into a stunning love story enhances this delicious 'keeper.'"
—*RT Book Reviews*

"All of Hoyt's signature literary ingredients—wickedly clever dialogue, superbly nuanced characters, danger, and scorching sexual chemistry—click neatly into place to create a breathtakingly romantic love story."
—*Booklist*

"When [they] finally come together, desire and long-denied sensuality explode upon the page."
—*Library Journal*

"With heart and heat rolled into one, *Thief of Shadows* is a definite must-read for historical romance fans! Hoyt really has outdone herself...yet again."

—UndertheCoversBookblog.blogspot.com

"A balanced mixture of action, adventure, and mystery and a beautifully crafted romance...The perfect historical romance."

—HeroesandHeartbreakers.com

Scandalous Desires

"Historical romance at its best...Series fans will be enthralled, while new readers will find this emotionally charged installment stands very well alone."

—*Publishers Weekly* (starred review)

"4½ stars! This is the Maiden Lane story readers have been waiting for. Hoyt delivers her hallmark fairy tale within a romance and takes readers into the depths of the heart and soul of her characters. Pure magic flows from her pen, lifting readers' spirits with joy."

—*RT Book Reviews*

"With its lush sensuality, lusciously wrought prose, and luxuriously dark plot, *Scandalous Desires*, the latest exquisitely crafted addition to Hoyt's Georgian-set Maiden Lane series, is a romance to treasure."

—*Booklist* (starred review)

"Ms. Hoyt writes some of the best love scenes out there. They are passionate, sexy, and blazing hot...I simply adore Ms. Hoyt's books for her sensuous prose, multifaceted characters, and intense, well-developed story lines. And she delivers every single time. It's no wonder all of her books are on my keeper shelves. Do yourself a favor and pick up *Scandalous Desires*."

—TheRomanceDish.com

"*Scandalous Desires* is the best book Elizabeth Hoyt has written so far, with endearing characters and an all-encompassing romance you'll want to hold close and never let go. If there's one must-read book, especially for historical romance fans, it's *Scandalous Desires*."

—FallenAngelReviews.com

Notorious Pleasures

"Emotionally stunning...The sinfully sensual chemistry Hoyt creates between her shrewd, acid-tongued heroine and her scandalous, sexy hero is pure romance."

—*Booklist*

Wicked Intentions

"4½ stars! Top Pick! A magnificently rendered story that not only enchants but enthralls."

—*RT Book Reviews*

OTHER TITLES BY ELIZABETH HOYT

ELIZABETH HOYT

DUKE *of* MIDNIGHT

GRAND CENTRAL
PUBLISHING

NEW YORK   BOSTON

Copyright © 2013 by Nancy M. Finney
Excerpt from *Wicked Intentions* copyright © 2010 by Nancy M. Finney

Grand Central Publishing
Hachette Book Group
237 Park Avenue
New York, NY 10017

www.HachetteBookGroup.com

Printed in the United States of America

First Edition: October 2013

10 9 8 7 6 5 4

OPM

Grand Central Publishing is a division of Hachette Book Group, Inc.
The Grand Central Publishing name and logo is a trademark of Hachette Book Group, Inc.

The Hachette Speakers Bureau provides a wide range of authors for speaking events. To find out more, go to www.hachettespeakersbureau.com or call (866) 376-6591.

The publisher is not responsible for websites (or their content) that are not owned by the publisher.

For my agent, Susannah Taylor: fifteen books, eight years, two unfortunate manuscripts under the bed, one novella, and innumerable moments filled with laughter, friendship, and chocolate. This one's for you.

$\mathcal{A}$cknowledgments

Thank you to my Facebook friend, Anna Carrasco, for naming Percy the spaniel!

As always, thank you to my wonderful agent, Susannah Taylor; my talented editor, Amy Pierpont; the glorious Grand Central Publishing art department; and my poor, overworked copy editor, Mark Steven Long, who has probably started involuntarily flinching at the sight of em dashes.

DUKE *of* MIDNIGHT

Chapter One

*Many a tale I've told, but none so strange as the
legend of the Herla King....*
—from *The Legend of the Herla King*

JULY 1740
LONDON, ENGLAND

Artemis Greaves did not like to think herself a cynical person, but when the masked figure dropped into the moonlit alley to confront the three toughs *already* menacing her and her cousin, the hand on the knife in her boot tightened.

It seemed only prudent.

He was big and wore a harlequin's motley—black-and-red diamond leggings and tunic, black jackboots, a hat with a wide, floppy brim, and a black half mask with a grotesquely outsized nose. Harlequins were meant to be clowns—a silly entertainment—but no one in the dark alley was laughing. The harlequin uncoiled from his crouch with a lethal movement so elegant Artemis's breath caught in her throat. He was like a jungle cat—wild and without a trace of compassion—and like a jungle cat his attack held no hesitation.

He launched himself at the three men.

Artemis stared, still kneeling, her hand gripping the little blade sheathed in her boot. She'd never seen anyone fight like this—with a kind of brutal grace, two swords flashing at once through the shadows, too swift for the human eye to follow.

The first of the three men dropped, rolling to lie still and dazed. On the other side of the fight Artemis's cousin, Lady Penelope Chadwicke, whimpered, cringing away from the bleeding man. A second man lunged, but the harlequin ducked, sweeping his outstretched leg under his opponent's feet, then kicked the man to the ground and kicked him once more—viciously—in the face. The harlequin rose, already striking at the third man. He hammered the butt of his sword against his opponent's temple.

The man collapsed with a squishy thud.

Artemis swallowed drily.

The dingy little lane was suddenly quiet, the crumbling buildings on either side seeming to loom inward with decrepit menace. The harlequin pivoted, not even breathing hard, his boot heels scraping on cobblestones, and glanced at Penelope. She still sobbed fearfully against the wall.

His head swiveled silently as he looked from Penelope to Artemis.

Artemis inhaled as she met the cold eyes glittering behind his sinister mask.

Once upon a time she had believed that most people were kind. That God watched over her and that if she were honest and good and always offered the last piece of raspberry tart to someone else first, then, even though sad things might happen, in the end everything would work out for the best. That was before, though. Before she'd lost both her family and the man who'd professed to love her more than the sun itself. Before her beloved brother had been wrongly imprisoned in Bedlam. Before she'd been so wretchedly desperate and alone that she'd wept tears of relieved gratitude when she'd been offered a position as her silly cousin's lady's companion.

Before, Artemis would've fallen upon this grim harlequin with cries of thanks for having rescued them in the nick of time.

Now, Artemis narrowed her eyes at the masked man and wondered *why* he'd come to the aid of two lone women wandering the dangerous streets of St. Giles at midnight.

She winced.

Perhaps she *had* grown a trifle cynical.

He strode to her in two lithe steps and stood over her. She saw those intense eyes move from the hand on her pathetic knife to her face. His wide mouth twitched—in amusement? Irritation? Pity? She doubted the last, but she simply couldn't *tell*—and bizarrely, she wanted to. It *mattered*, somehow, what this stranger thought of her—and, of course, what he intended to *do* to her.

Holding her gaze, he sheathed his short sword and pulled the gauntlet off his left hand with his teeth. He held out his bare hand to her.

She glanced at the proffered hand, noticing the dull glint of gold on the smallest finger, before laying her palm in his. His hand was hot as he gripped her tightly and pulled her upright before him. She was so close that if she leaned forward a couple of inches she could've brushed her lips across his throat. She watched the pulse of his blood beat there, strong and sure, before she lifted her gaze. His head was cocked almost as if he were examining her—searching for something in her face.

She drew in a breath, opening her mouth to ask a question.

Which was when Penelope launched herself at the harlequin's back. Penelope screamed—obviously nearly out of her mind with fear—as she beat uselessly at the harlequin's broad shoulders.

He reacted, of course. He turned, yanking his hand from Artemis's fingers as he lifted one arm to push Penelope aside. But Artemis tightened her hand on his. It was instinct, for she certainly wouldn't have tried to hold him back otherwise. As his fingers left hers, something fell into her palm.

Then he was shoving Penelope aside and loping swiftly down the lane.

Penelope panted, her hair half down, a scratch across her lovely face. "He might've killed us!"

"What?" Artemis asked, tearing her gaze away from the end of the lane where the masked man had disappeared.

"That was the Ghost of St. Giles," Penelope said. "Didn't you recognize him? They say he's a ravisher of maidens and a cold-blooded murderer!"

"He was rather helpful for a cold-blooded murderer," Artemis said as she bent to lift the lantern. She'd set it down when the toughs had appeared at the end of the alley. Fortunately, it had survived the fight without being knocked over. She was surprised to see that the lantern's light wavered. Her hand was shaking. She drew in a calming breath. Nerves wouldn't get them out of St. Giles alive.

She glanced up to see Penelope pouting.

"But you were very brave to defend me," Artemis added hastily.

Penelope brightened. "I was, wasn't I? I fought off a terrible rogue! That's much better than drinking a cup of gin at midnight in St. Giles. I'm sure Lord Featherstone will be very impressed."

Artemis rolled her eyes as she turned swiftly back the way they'd come. Lord Featherstone was at the moment her least favorite person in the world. A silly society gad-fly, it was he who had teased Penelope into accepting a mad wager to come into St. Giles at midnight, buy a tin cup of gin, and drink it. They'd nearly been killed—or worse—because of Lord Featherstone.

And they still weren't out of St. Giles yet.

If only Penelope weren't so set on becoming *daring*—loathsome word—in order to attract the attention of a certain duke, she might not have fallen for Lord Featherstone's ridiculous dare. Artemis shook her head and kept a wary eye out as she hurried out of the alley and into one of the myriad of narrow lanes that wound through St. Giles. The channel running down the middle of the lane was clogged with something noxious, and she made sure not to look as she trotted by. Penelope had quieted, following almost docilely. A stooped, shadowy figure came out of one of the sagging buildings. Artemis stiffened, preparing to run, but the man or woman scurried away at the sight of them.

Still, she didn't relax again until they turned the corner and saw Penelope's carriage, left standing in a wider street.

"Ah, here we are," Penelope said, as if they were

returning from a simple stroll along Bond Street. "That was quite exciting, wasn't it?"

Artemis glanced at her cousin incredulously—and a movement on the roof of the building across the way caught her eye. A figure crouched there, athletic and waiting. She stilled. As she watched, he raised a hand to the brim of his hat in mocking salute.

A shiver ran through her.

"Artemis?" Penelope had already mounted the steps to the carriage.

She tore her gaze away from the ominous figure. "Coming, Cousin."

Artemis climbed into the carriage and sat tensely on the plush indigo squabs. He'd followed them, but why? To discover who they were? Or for a more benign reason—to make sure that they had reached the carriage safely?

Silly, she scolded herself—it did no good to indulge in flights of romantic fancy. She doubted that a creature such as the Ghost of St. Giles cared very much for the safety of two foolish ladies. No doubt he had reasons of his own for following them.

"I cannot wait to tell the Duke of Wakefield of my adventure tonight," Penelope said, interrupting Artemis's thoughts. "He'll be terribly surprised, I'll wager."

"Mmm," Artemis murmured noncommittally. Penelope was very beautiful, but would any man want a wife so hen-witted that she ventured into St. Giles at night on a wager and thought it a great lark? Penelope's method of attracting the duke's attention seemed impetuous at best and at worst foolish. For a moment Artemis's heart twinged with pity for her cousin.

But then again Penelope was one of the richest heiresses

in England. Much could be overlooked for a veritable mountain of gold. Too, Penelope was esteemed one of the great beauties of the age, with raven-black hair, milky skin, and eyes that rivaled the purple of a pansy. Many men wouldn't care about the person beneath such a lovely surface.

Artemis sighed silently and let her cousin's excited chatter wash over her. She ought to pay more attention. Her fate was inexorably tied to Penelope's, for Artemis would go to whatever house and family her cousin married into.

Unless Penelope decided she no longer needed a lady's companion after she wed.

Artemis's fingers tightened about the thing the Ghost of St. Giles had left in her hand. She'd had a glimpse of it in the carriage's lantern light before she'd entered. It was a gold signet ring set with a red stone. She rubbed her thumb absently over the worn stone. It felt ancient. Powerful. Which was quite interesting.

An aristocrat might wear such a ring.

MAXIMUS BATTEN, THE Duke of Wakefield, woke as he always did: with the bitter taste of failure on his tongue.

For a moment he lay on his great curtained bed, eyes closed, trying to swallow down the bile in his throat as he remembered dark tresses trailing in bloody water. He reached out and laid his right palm on the locked strongbox that sat on the table beside his bed. The emerald pendants from her necklace, carefully gathered over years of searching, were within. The necklace wasn't complete, though, and he'd begun to despair that it ever would be. That the blot of his failure would remain upon his conscience forever.

And now he had a new failure. He flexed his left hand, feeling the unaccustomed lightness. He'd lost his father's ring—the *ancestral* ring—last night somewhere in St. Giles. It was yet another offense to add to his long list of unpardonable sins.

He stretched carefully, pushing the matter from his mind so that he might rise and do his duty. His right knee ached dully, and something was off about his left shoulder. For a man in but his thirty-third year he was rather battered.

His valet, Craven, turned from the clothespress. "Good morning, Your Grace."

Maximus nodded silently and threw back the coverlet. He rose, nude, and padded to the marble-topped dresser with only a slight limp. A basin of hot water already waited there for him. His razor, freshly sharpened by Craven, appeared beside the basin as Maximus soaped his jaw.

"Will you be breaking your fast with Lady Phoebe and Miss Picklewood this morning?" Craven enquired.

Maximus frowned into the gold mirror standing on the dresser as he tilted his chin and set the razor against his neck. His youngest sister, Phoebe, was but twenty. When Hero, his other sister, had married several years ago, he'd decided to move Phoebe and their older cousin, Bathilda Picklewood, into Wakefield House with him. He was pleased to have her under his eye, but having to share accommodations—even accommodations as palatial as Wakefield House—with the two ladies sometimes got in the way of his other activities.

"Not today," he decided, scraping whiskers from his jaw. "Please send my apologies to my sister and Cousin Bathilda."

"Yes, Your Grace."

Maximus watched in the mirror as the valet arched his eyebrows in mute reproach before retiring to the clothes-press. He didn't suffer the rebuke—even a silent one—of many, but Craven was a special case. The man had been his father's valet for fifteen years before Maximus had inherited him on attaining the title. Craven had a long face, the vertical lines on either side of his mouth and the droop of his eyes at the outer corners making it seem longer. He must be well into his fifties, but one couldn't tell by his countenance: he looked like he could be any age from thirty to seventy. No doubt Craven would still look the same when Maximus was a doddering old man without a hair on his head.

He snorted to himself as he tapped the razor against a porcelain bowl, shaking soap froth and whiskers from the blade. Behind him Craven began laying out smallclothes, stockings, a black shirt, waistcoat, and breeches. Maximus turned his head, scraping the last bit of lather from his jaw, and used a dampened cloth to wipe his face.

"Did you find the information?" he asked as he donned smallclothes.

"Indeed, Your Grace." Craven rinsed the razor and carefully dried the fine blade. He laid it in a fitted velvet-lined box as reverently as if the razor had been the relic of some dead saint.

"And?"

Craven cleared his throat as if preparing to recite poetry before the king. "The Earl of Brightmore's finances are, as far as I've been able to ascertain, quite happy. In addition to his two estates in Yorkshire, both with arable land, he is in possession of three producing coal mines in the West Riding, an ironworks in Sheffield, and has recently bought interest in the East India Company. At the beginning of the year he opened a fourth coal mine, and in so doing accrued some debt, but the reports from the mine are quite favorable. The debt in my estimation is negligible."

Maximus grunted as he pulled on his breeches.

Craven continued, "As to the earl's daughter, Lady Penelope Chadwicke, it's well known that Lord Brightmore plans to offer a very nice sum when she is wed."

Maximus lifted a cynical eyebrow. "Do we have an actual number?"

"Indeed, Your Grace." Craven pulled a small notebook from his pocket and, licking his thumb, paged through it. Peering down at the notebook, he read off a sum so large Maximus came close to doubting Craven's research skills.

"Good God. You're sure?"

Craven gave him a faintly chiding look. "I have it on the authority of the earl's lawyer's chief secretary, a rather bitter gentleman who cannot hold his liquor."

"Ah." Maximus arranged his neck cloth and shrugged on his waistcoat. "Then that leaves only Lady Penelope herself."

"Quite." Craven tucked his notebook away and pursed his lips, staring at the ceiling. "Lady Penelope Chadwicke is four and twenty years of age and her father's sole living offspring. Despite her rather advanced maiden status, she does not lack for suitors, and indeed appears to be only unwed because of her own...ah...unusually high standards in choosing a gentleman."

"She's finicky."

Craven winced at the blunt assessment. "It would appear so, Your Grace."

Maximus nodded as he opened his bedroom door. "We'll continue downstairs."

"Yes, Your Grace." Craven picked up a candle and lit it at the fireplace.

A wide corridor lay outside his bedroom. To the left was the front of the house and the grand staircase that led to the public rooms of Wakefield House.

Maximus turned to the right, Craven trotting at his heels. This way led to the servants' stairs and other less public rooms. Maximus opened a door paneled to look like the wainscoting in the hall and clattered down the uncarpeted stairs. He passed the entrance to the kitchens and continued down another level. The stairs ended abruptly, blocked by a plain wooden door. Maximus took a key from his waistcoat pocket and unlocked the door. Beyond was another set of stairs, but these were stone, so ancient the treads dipped in the middle, worn away by long-dead feet. Maximus followed them down as Craven lit candles tucked into the nooks in the stone walls.

Maximus ducked under a low stone arch and came to a small paved area. The candlelight behind him flickered over worn stone walls. Here and there figures were scratched in the stone: symbols and crude human representations. Maximus doubted very much that they'd been made during the age of Christianity. Directly ahead was a second door, the wood blackened by age. He unlocked this as well and pushed it open.

Behind the door was a cellar, long and with a surprisingly high ceiling, the groin vaulting picked out in smaller, decorative stone. Sturdy pillars paced along the floor, their capitals carved into crude shapes. His father and grandfather had used the space as a wine cellar, but Maximus wouldn't have been surprised if this hidden room had originally been built as a place to worship some ancient pagan deity.

Behind him Craven shut the door, and Maximus began taking off his waistcoat. It seemed a waste of time to dress and then undress again five minutes later every morning, but a duke never appeared in dishabille—even within his own house.

Craven cleared his throat.

"Continue," Maximus murmured without turning. He stood in only his smallclothes now and looked up. Spaced irregularly along the ceiling were iron rings he'd sunk into the stone.

"Lady Penelope is considered one of the foremost beauties of the age," Craven intoned.

Maximus leaped and clung to a pillar. He dug his bare toes into a crack and pushed, reaching for a slim finger hold he knew lay above his head. He grunted as he pulled himself toward the ceiling and the nearest iron ring.

"Just last year she was courted by no less than two earls and a foreign princeling."

"Is she a virgin?" The ring was just out of arm's reach—a deliberate placing that on mornings such as this Maximus sometimes cursed. He shoved off from the pillar, arm outstretched. If his fingers missed the ring, the floor was very, very hard below.

But he caught it one-handed, the muscles on his shoulder pulling as he let his weight swing him to the next ring. And the next.

"Almost certainly, Your Grace," Craven called from

below as Maximus easily swung from ring to ring across the cavernous room and back. "Although the lady has a certain amount of high spirits, she still seems to understand the importance of prudence."

Maximus snorted as he caught the next ring. This one was a little closer together than the last and he hung between them, his arms in a wide V above his head. He could feel the heat across his shoulders and arms now. He pointed his toes. Slowly, deliberately, he folded in half until his toes nearly touched the ceiling above his head.

He held the position, breathing deeply, his arms beginning to tremble. "I wouldn't call last night prudent."

"Perhaps not," Craven conceded, the wince evident in his voice. "In that regard I must report that although Lady Penelope is proficient in needlework, dancing, playing the harpsichord, and drawing, she is not considered a great talent in any of these endeavors. Nor is Lady Penelope's wit held in high esteem by those who know her. This is not to say that the lady's intellect is in any way deficient. She is simply not...er..."

"She's a ninny."

Craven hummed noncommittally and stared at the ceiling.

Maximus straightened and let go of the iron rings, landing lightly on the balls of his feet. He crossed to a low bench where an array of different-sized cannonballs lay. He selected one that fit easily in his palm, hoisted it to his shoulder, sprinted across the length of the cellar, and heaved the cannonball at a bank of straw pallets placed against the far wall especially for that purpose. The ball flew through the straw and clanged dully against the stone wall.

"Well done, Your Grace." Craven permitted himself a small smile as Maximus jogged back. The expression was oddly comical on his lugubrious face. "The straw bales are undoubtedly cowed."

"Craven." Maximus fought the twitching of his own lips. He was the Duke of Wakefield and no one was permitted to laugh at Wakefield—not even himself.

He picked up another lead ball.

"Quite. Quite." The valet cleared his throat. "In summary then: Lady Penelope is very wealthy, very beautiful, and very fashionable and gay, but does not possess particular intelligence or, er...a sense of self-preservation. Shall I cross her off the list, Your Grace?"

"No." Maximus repeated his previous exercise with a second cannonball. A chip of stone flew off the wall. He made a mental note to bring down more straw.

When he turned it was to find Craven staring at him in confusion. "But surely Your Grace wishes for more than an ample dowry, an aristocratic lineage, and beauty in a bride?"

Maximus looked at the valet hard. They'd had this discussion before. Craven had just listed the most important assets in a suitable wife. Common sense—or the lack thereof—wasn't even on the ledger.

For a moment he saw clear gray eyes and a determined feminine face. Miss Greaves had brought a *knife* into St. Giles last night—there'd been no mistaking the gleam of metal in her boot top. And what was more, she'd appeared quite ready to use it. Then as now a spark of admiration lit within him. What other lady in his acquaintance had ever displayed such grim courage?

Then he shook the frivolous notion away and returned

his mind to the business at hand. His father had died for him, and he would do nothing less than honor his memory by marrying the most suitable candidate for his duchess. "You know my thoughts on the subject. Lady Penelope is a perfect match for the Duke of Wakefield."

Maximus picked up another cannonball and chose to pretend he didn't hear Craven's soft reply.

"But is she a match for the man?"

THERE WERE THOSE who compared Bedlam to hell—a writhing purgatory of torture and insanity. But Apollo Greaves, Viscount Kilbourne, knew what Bedlam really was. It was limbo.

A place of interminable waiting.

Waiting for the restless moaning in the night to be over. Waiting for the scrape of heel on stone that heralded a stale piece of bread to break his fast. Waiting for the chilly splash of water that was called a bath. Waiting for the stink of the bucket that served as his commode to be emptied. Waiting for food. Waiting for drink. Waiting for fresh air. Waiting for something—*anything*—to prove that he still lived and was, in fact, not mad at all.

At least not yet.

Above all, Apollo waited for his sister, Artemis, to visit him in limbo.

She came when she could, which was usually once a week. Just often enough for him to keep his sanity, really. Without her he would've lost it long, long ago.

So when he heard the light tap of a woman's shoes on the filthy stone in the corridor outside his cell, he leaned his head back against the wall and found a smile to paste on his blasted face.

She appeared a moment later, peering around the corner, her sweet, grave face brightening at the sight of him. Artemis wore a worn but clean brown gown, and a straw bonnet she'd had for at least five years, the straw mended in small, neat stitches over her right ear. Her gray eyes were lit with warmth and worry for him, and she seemed to bring a waft of clear air with her, which was impossible: how could one smell the *absence* of stink?

"Brother," she murmured in her low, quiet voice. She advanced into his cell without any sign of the disgust she must feel at the uncovered slop bucket in the corner or his own damnable state—the fleas and lice had long ago made a feast out of his hide. "How are you?"

It was a silly question—he was now, and had been for the last four years, wretched—but she asked it earnestly, for she truly worried that his state might someday grow *worse* than it already was. In that, at least, she was correct: there was always death, after all.

Not that he would ever let her know how close to death he'd come in the past.

"Oh, I'm just divine," he said, grinning, hoping she didn't notice that his gums bled at the smallest motion these days. "The buttered kidneys were excellent this morning as were the shirred eggs and gammon steak. I must compliment the cook, but I find myself somewhat detained."

He gestured with his manacled feet. A long chain led from the manacles to a great iron ring on the wall. The chain was long enough for him to stand and take two steps in either direction, but no more.

"Apollo," she said, and her voice was gently chiding, but her lips curved so he considered his clowning a victory. She set down the small, soft sack she'd been holding in her hand. "I'm sorry to hear you've already dined since I brought some roast chicken. I do hope you're not too full to enjoy it."

"Oh, I think I'll manage," he said.

His nose caught the aroma of the chicken and his mouth began to water helplessly. There'd been a time when he'd never thought much about his next meal—beyond wishing vaguely that cherry pie might be served every day. It wasn't that their family had been rich—far from it, in fact—but they'd never lacked for food. Bread and cheese and joints of roast and buttered peas and peaches stewed in honey and wine. Fish pie and those little muffins his mother had sometimes made. Dear God, the first slurp of oxtail soup, the bits of meat so tender they melted on his tongue. Juicy oranges, roasted walnuts, gingered carrots, and that sweet made from sugared rose petals. Sometimes he spent days simply thinking about food—no matter how much he tried to drive the thoughts from his mind.

He'd never again take food for granted.

Apollo looked away, trying to distract himself as she took out the chicken. He would put it off as long as possible, the inevitable descent into becoming a ravening, mindless animal.

He shifted awkwardly, the chains clinking. They gave him straw for both settee and dainty bed, and if he rummaged a bit he might find some cleanish spot for his sister to sit on. Such were the only comforts he could offer a guest to his cell.

"There's cheese and half an apple tart I wheedled from Penelope's cook." Artemis's expression was gentle and a little worried, as if she knew how close he was to falling on her present and swallowing it all in one maddened gulp.

"Sit here," he said gruffly.

She sank gracefully, her legs folded to the side as if they were on some pastoral picnic rather than a stinking madhouse. "Here."

She'd placed a chicken leg and a slab of the tart on a clean cloth and held it out to him. He took the treasure carefully, trying to breathe through his mouth without seeming to. He clenched his jaw and inhaled slowly, staring at the food. Self-control was the only thing he had left.

"Please, Apollo, eat." Her whisper was almost pained, and he reminded himself that he was not the only one being punished for one night of youthful folly.

He'd destroyed his sister that night as well.

So he raised the leg of chicken to his lips and took one delicate bite, placing it back on the cloth, chewing carefully, keeping the madness at bay. The taste was wonderful, filling his mouth, making him want to howl with eager hunger.

He swallowed, lowering the cloth with its contents to his lap. He was a gentleman, not an animal. "How is my cousin?"

If Artemis were less a lady she would've rolled her eyes. "She's up in the boughs this morning over a ball we're attending tonight at Viscount d'Arque's town house. Do you remember him?"

Apollo took another bite. He'd never moved in the most elite circles—hadn't the money for that—but the name tweaked a memory.

"Tall, dark fellow with a bit of a manner? Witty and knows it?" *And a devil with the ladies*, he thought but did not say aloud to his sister.

She nodded. "That's him. He lives with his grand-mother, Lady Whimple, which seems a little odd, considering his reputation. The ball I'm sure is completely planned by her, but it's usually in his name."

"I thought Penelope went to balls almost every night of the week?"

A corner of Artemis's mouth quirked. "Sometimes it seems like it."

He bit into the tart, nearly moaning over the crisp-sweet apple. "Then why the excitement over d'Arque's ball? Has she set her cap at him?"

"Oh, no." Artemis shook her head ruefully. "A viscount would never do. She has plans for the Duke of Wakefield, and rumor has it he may attend tonight."

"Does she?" Apollo glanced at his sister. If their cousin finally settled on a gentleman to marry, then Artemis might very well be out of a home. And he could do absolutely nothing about it. His jaw tensed and he reined in the urge to bellow his frustration. He took another deep breath and drank from the flask of beer she'd brought him. The warm, sour taste of hops settled him for a moment. "Then I wish her well in the endeavor, though perhaps I should be commiserating with His Grace—Lord knows I wouldn't want our cousin's sights on *me*."

"Apollo," she chided softly. "Penelope is a lovely girl, you know that."

"*Is* she?" he teased. "Known for her philanthropy and good works?"

"Well, she is a member of the Ladies' Syndicate for the Benefit of the Home for Unfortunate Infants and Foundling Children," his sister said primly. She plucked a piece of straw and twisted it between her fingers.

"And she once wanted to put all the little boys at the orphanage in yellow coats, you told me."

Artemis winced. "She does try, really she does."

He took pity on his sister and rescued her from her doomed defense of their mercenary cousin. "If you believe so, then I'm sure 'tis true." He eyed the way she was bending the piece of straw into angular shapes between her fingers. "Is there something else about tonight's ball that you're not telling me?"

She looked up in surprise. "No, of course not."

He tilted his chin at the mangled straw in her hands. "Then what is disturbing you?"

"Oh." She wrinkled her nose at the bit of straw and threw it away. "It's nothing, really. It's just that last night..." One hand crept up to touch the fichu that covered the center of her chest.

"Artemis." The frustration was nearly overwhelming. Were he free he could question her, find out from servants or friends what was the matter, pursue and make right whatever troubled her.

In here he could but wait and hope that she would tell him the truth of what her life was like outside.

She looked up. "Do you remember that necklace you gave me on our fifteenth birthday?"

He remembered the little green stone well enough. To a young boy's eyes it had looked like a real emerald and he'd been more than proud to give such a wonderful present to his sister. But that wasn't what they'd been talking about. "You're trying to change the subject."

Her lips pursed in a rare expression of irritation. "No, I'm not. Apollo—"

"What happened?"

She huffed out a breath of air. "Penelope and I went to St. Giles."

"*What?*" St. Giles was a veritable stew of lowlifes. *Anything* could happen to a gently reared lady in such a place. "God, Artemis! Are you all right? Were you accosted? What—"

She was already shaking her head. "I knew I shouldn't have told you."

"*Don't.*" His head jerked back as if the blow had been physical. "Don't keep things from me."

"Oh." Her expression was immediately contrite. "No, my dear, I shan't keep anything from you. We were in St. Giles because Penelope had made a very silly wager, but I took the dagger you gave me—you remember the one?"

He nodded, keeping his anguish under wraps. When he'd gone away to school at the age of eleven, he'd thought the dagger a clever gift. After all, he'd been leaving his twin sister in the care of their half-mad father and a mother bedridden by illness.

But what had seemed a decently sized dagger to a boy was to a man a too-small weapon. Apollo shuddered at the thought of his sister trying to defend herself—*in St. Giles*—with that little dagger.

"Hush now," she said, bringing his attention back to the present with a squeeze of her fingers. "I admit we were accosted, but it ended all right. We were saved by the Ghost of St. Giles, of all men."

Obviously she thought this bit of information reassuring. Apollo closed his eyes. 'Twas said the Ghost of St. Giles murdered and raped and worse. He didn't believe the tales, if for no other reason than that no one man—even a mad one—could've done all that he was accused of. Still. The Ghost wasn't exactly a harmless kitten.

Apollo opened his eyes and took both his sister's hands in his. "Promise me you won't follow Penelope into another of her insane schemes."

"I . . ." she looked away. "You know I'm her companion, Apollo. I must do as she wishes."

"She's liable to break you like a pretty China shepherdess and then throw you away to find a new plaything."

Artemis looked shocked. "She'd never—"

"Please, my darling girl," he said, his voice hoarse, "*Please.*"

"I'll do my best," she whispered, cupping her hand against his cheek. "For you."

He nodded, for he had no choice but to be content with that promise. And yet he couldn't help but wonder.

When he was gone, who would worry over Artemis?

Chapter Two

Long, long ago when Britain was young, there lived the best of rulers. His name was King Herla. His mien was wise and brave, his arm was strong and swift, and he loved nothing better than to go a-hunting in the dark, wild wood....
—from *The Legend of the Herla King*

The Earl of Brightmore was many things, Artemis thought that night: a respected peer, a man very aware of his wealth, and—in his best moments—a Christian capable of adhering to the letter, if not the spirit, of compassion, but what he was *not* was an attentive father.

"Papa, I told you yesterday at luncheon that I was to attend the Viscount of d'Arque's ball this eve," Penelope said as her lady's maid, Blackbourne, fussed with the bow of her half cloak. They were in the grand entrance hall to Brightmore House waiting for the carriage to pull around from the mews.

"Thought you were there last night," the earl said vaguely. He was a big man with bulbous blue eyes and a commanding nose that rather overtook his chin. He'd just arrived home with his secretary—a withered little man with a frightening head for numbers—and was doffing his tricorne and cape.

"No, darling," Penelope said, rolling her eyes. "*Last* night I was dining with Lady Waters at her house."

Artemis felt like rolling *her* eyes but refrained, because of course last night they'd been busy being nearly killed in St. Giles and hadn't been anywhere near Lady Waters's dining room. Actually, she rather thought Lady Waters might not even *be* in town at the moment. Penelope lied with a breathtaking virtuosity.

"Eh," the earl grunted. "Well, you look exquisite, Penny."

Penelope beamed and twirled to show off her new gown, a brocaded satin primrose gown overembroidered with bunches of flowers in blue, red, and green. The gown had taken a month to put together and cost more than what ninety percent of Londoners made in a year.

"And you, too, of course, Artemis," the earl said absently. "Quite lovely indeed."

Artemis curtsied. "Thank you, Uncle."

For a moment Artemis was struck by how very different this life was from the one she'd known growing up. They'd lived in the country, then, just she, Apollo, Papa, and Mama. Papa had been estranged from his own father, and their household was meager. There had been no parties, let alone balls. Strange to think that she'd become used to attending grand soirees—that she was actually bored by the prospect of yet another one.

Artemis smiled wryly to herself. She was grateful to the earl—who was really a distant cousin, not her uncle. She'd never met either him or Penelope while Papa and Mama still lived, and yet he'd taken her into his house when she'd become a social pariah. Between her lack of dowry and the stigma of familial madness, she had no hope of marrying and having a household of her own. Still, she couldn't quite forget that the earl had refused—absolutely and without opportunity for appeal—to help Apollo as well. The most he'd done was make sure that Apollo was hastily committed to Bedlam instead of going to trial. That had been an easy enough job for the Earl of Brightmore: no one wanted an aristocrat hanged for murder. The elite of society wouldn't stand for such a thing—even if the aristocrat in question had never moved much in society.

"You'll turn every young gentleman's head at that dance." The earl was already talking to his daughter again, his eyes narrowing for a moment. "Just make sure yours isn't turned as well."

Perhaps he was more aware of Penelope than Artemis gave him credit for.

"Never fear, Papa." Penelope bussed her sire's cheek. "I only collect hearts—I don't give them away."

"Ha," her father replied rather absently—his secretary was whispering something in his ear. "See you tomorrow, shall I?"

"Yes, darling."

And with a last flurry of curtsies and bows from the gaggle of lady's maids and footmen, Penelope and Artemis were out the door.

"I don't know why we didn't bring Bon Bon," her cousin said as the carriage pulled away. "His fur would've quite set off this gown."

Bon Bon was Penelope's small, white, and quite elderly dog. Artemis wasn't sure how he would "set off" Penelope's gown. Besides, she hadn't had the heart to disturb the poor thing when she'd seen him curled up in the silly green-and-pink dog bed Penelope'd had made for him.

"Perhaps," Artemis murmured, "but his white fur would've stuck to your skirts as well."

"Oh." Penelope frowned quite becomingly, her small rosebud mouth pouting. "I wonder if I should get a pug. But everyone has one—they're almost common—and the fawn isn't nearly so striking as Bon Bon's white."

Artemis sighed silently and kept her opinions about choosing a dog by the color of its fur to herself.

Penelope began prattling about dogs and dresses and fashion and the house party at the Duke of Wakefield's country residence they would soon attend. Artemis merely had to nod here and there to help with the conversation. She thought about Apollo and how thin he'd appeared this morning. He was a big man—or had been. Bedlam had caved in his cheeks, hollowed his eyes, and made the bones at his wrists protrude. She had to find more money to pay the guards, more food to bring him, more clothes to give him. But all that was just a temporary fix. If she didn't discover some way to get her brother out of Bedlam, she very much feared he wouldn't live another year there.

She sighed softly as Penelope kept talking about Belgium lace.

Half an hour later they were descending the carriage steps in front of a grand mansion ablaze with lights.

"It's a pity, really," Penelope said, shaking out her skirts.

"What is?" Artemis bent to straighten the hem at the back.

"Lord d'Arque." Her cousin gestured vaguely at the stunning town house. "Such a beautiful man and rich as well—he's nearly perfect."

Artemis wrinkled her forehead, trying to follow her cousin's sometimes mazelike thought process. "But he's not?"

"No, of course not, silly," Penelope said as she sailed toward the front doors. "He's not a duke, is he? Oh, I say, there's Lord Featherstone!"

Artemis trailed after Penelope as she flitted up to the young lordling. George Featherstone, Baron Featherstone, had large blue eyes with luxuriant curling lashes and a red, full-lipped mouth, and had it not been for the strength of his jawline and the length of his nose, he might've been mistaken for a girl. He was considered very comely by most of the ladies in London society, although Artemis personally found the nasty glint in those pretty blue eyes distasteful.

"My Lady Penelope!" Lord Featherstone crowed, halting on the marble steps and making an extravagant bow. He wore a crimson coat and breeches with a gold waistcoat embroidered in crimson, purple, and bright leaf green. "What news?"

"My lord, I am pleased to report that I have been to St. Giles," Penelope said, extending her hand.

Lord Featherstone bowed over it, lingering a fraction of a second too long before looking up through his lush eyelashes. "And did you partake of a cup of gin?"

"Alas, no." Penelope flipped open her fan and turned her face into it as if abashed. "*Better.*" She lowered the fan to reveal a grin. "I met the Ghost of St. Giles."

Lord Featherstone eyes widened. "Say you so?"

"Indeed. My companion, Miss Greaves, can bear witness."

Artemis curtsied.

"But this is wonderful, my lady!" Lord Featherstone threw wide his arms, the gesture making him wobble, and for a moment Artemis worried that he might over-balance on the steps, but he merely braced himself by throwing one foot on the next step up. "A masked demon vanquished by the beauty of a maiden." He tilted his head and glanced sideways at Penelope, a sly smile on his lips. "You *did* vanquish him, did you not, my lady?"

Artemis frowned. *Vanquish* was rather a risqué word that could be taken—

"Good evening, my lady, my lord," a calm, deep voice said.

Artemis turned. The Duke of Wakefield appeared from the darkness behind them, his footfalls making no sound. He was a tall, lean man, dressed severely in black and wearing an elegant white wig. The lights from the mansion cast faintly ominous shadows across his counte-nance, emphasizing the right angles of his face: the stern, dark shelf of his eyebrows, the prominent nose positioned vertically underneath, which led straight to the thin, almost cruel line of his lips. The Duke of Wakefield was not considered as beautiful as Lord Featherstone by the ladies of society, but if one could look at his features apart from the man beneath, it was possible to see that he was in fact a handsome man.

Coldly, sternly handsome, with nary a trace of softness to relieve the harsh masculine planes of his face.

Artemis repressed a shiver. No, the Duke of Wakefield would never be a darling of the feminine members of society. Something about him was so opposite to female that he almost repelled the softer sex. This was not a man to be swayed by gentleness, beauty, or sweet words. He would bend—assuming he was even capable of bending—only for reasons of his own.

"Your Grace." Penelope made a flirtatious curtsy while Artemis dipped more sedately beside her. Not that anyone noticed. "How lovely to see you this evening."

"Lady Penelope." The duke bowed over her hand and straightened. His dark eyes betrayed no emotion, either positive or negative. "What's this I heard about the Ghost of St. Giles?"

Penelope licked her lips in what might have been a seductive movement, but Artemis thought her cousin was probably nervous. The duke was rather daunting at the best of times. "A grand adventure, Your Grace. I met the Ghost himself last night in St. Giles!"

The duke simply looked at her.

Artemis stirred uneasily. Penelope didn't seem to be aware that her lark might not be taken as an accomplishment by the duke. "Cousin, perhaps we should—"

"Lady Penelope has the wonderful courage of Britannia herself," Lord Featherstone trumpeted. "A sweetly brave bearing embraced by the beauty of her form and face, resulting in perfection of manner and grace. My lady, please, accept this bauble as a token of my admiration."

Lord Featherstone dropped to one knee and held out his jeweled snuffbox. Artemis snorted under her breath. She couldn't help thinking that Penelope had won the wager fair and square, at risk of both life and limb. Lord Featherstone's snuffbox wasn't the simple offering he was trying to make it seem.

Male ninny.

Penelope reached for the snuffbox, but strong fingers were ahead of hers. The duke plucked the thing from Lord Featherstone's hand—making the younger man flinch—and held it up to the light. It was oval, gold, and there was a tiny, round painting of a girl was on the top, bordered by pearls.

"Very pretty," His Grace drawled. He palmed the box and turned to Lady Penelope. "But hardly worth your life, my lady. I hope you'll not risk something so precious for such a mundane trinket again."

He tossed the box to Penelope, who simply blinked, forcing Artemis to dive rather ungracefully for the thing. She caught the snuffbox before it could hit either the ground or Penelope, and straightened to see the duke's eyes upon her.

For a moment she froze. She'd never looked into his eyes before—she was a creature relegated to the sides of ballrooms and the back of sitting rooms. Gentlemen rarely noticed a lady's companion. If she'd been quizzed as to His Grace's eye color, she would've had to reply simply that they were dark. Which they were. Very dark, nearly black, but not quite. The Duke of Wakefield's eyes were a deep, rich brown, like coffee newly brewed, like walnut wood oiled and polished, like seal fur shining in the light, and even though they were rather lovely to look at, they were as cold as iron in winter. One touch and her very soul might freeze.

"An adept catch, Miss Greaves," the duke said, breaking the spell.

He turned and mounted the stairs.

Artemis blinked after him. When had he learned her name?

"Pompous ass," Lord Featherstone said so loudly the duke must've heard, though he gave no sign as he disappeared into the mansion. Lord Featherstone turned to Lady Penelope. "I must give apology, my lady, for the ungentlemanly actions of the duke. I can only assume he has lost all sense of play or fun and has ossified into an old man before the age of forty. Or is it fifty? I vow, the duke might well be as old as my father."

"Surely not." Lady Penelope's brows drew together as if she were truly worried that the duke had suddenly aged overnight. "He can't be over forty years of age, can he?"

Her appeal was to Artemis, who sighed and slipped the snuffbox into her pocket to give back to Penelope later. If she did not take care of it, Penelope was sure to leave it at the mansion or in the carriage. "I believe His Grace is but three and thirty."

"Is he?" Penelope brightened before blinking suspiciously. "How do you know?"

"His sisters have mentioned it in passing," Artemis said drily. Penelope was friends—or at least acquaintances—with both Lady Hero and Lady Phoebe herself, but Penelope was not in the habit of listening, let alone remembering, what her friends said in conversation.

"Oh. Well, that's good then." And nodding to herself, Penelope accepted Lord Featherstone's arm and proceeded into the town house.

They were greeted by liveried footmen, taking and storing their wraps before they mounted the grand staircase to the upper floor and Lord d'Arque's ballroom. The room was like a fairyland. The pink-and-white marble floor shone under their feet. Overhead, crystal chandeliers sparkled with thousands of candles. Hothouse carnations in every shade of pink, white, and crimson overflowed from huge vases, perfuming the air with the sharp scent of cloves. A group of musicians at one end of the ballroom played a languid melody. And the guests were arrayed in every color of the rainbow, moving gracefully, as if to an unspoken dance, like a cohort of ethereal fairy folk.

Artemis wrinkled her nose ruefully at her plain gown. It was brown, and if the other guests were fairies, then she supposed she must be a dark little troll. Her gown had been made the first year that she'd come to live with Penelope and the earl, and she'd worn it ever since to all the balls she attended with Penelope. After all, she was merely the companion. She was there to fade into the background, which she did with admirable skill, even if she did say so herself.

"That went well," Penelope said brightly.

Artemis blinked, wondering if she'd missed something. They'd lost Lord Featherstone and the crowd was thickening around them. "I'm sorry?"

"Wakefield." Penelope waved open her elaborately painted fan as if her companion could somehow read her mind and thus complete the thought.

"Our meeting with the duke went well?" Artemis supplied doubtfully. *Surely not.*

"Oh, indeed." Penelope snapped closed her fan and tapped Artemis on the shoulder. "He's *jealous.*"

Artemis gazed at her beautiful cousin. There were several adjectives she might use to describe the duke's frame of mind when he'd left them: *scornful, dismissive, superior, arrogant* . . . actually, now that she thought of it, she was fairly sure she could come up with *dozens* of adjectives, and yet *jealous* wasn't one of them.

Artemis cleared her throat carefully. "I'm not sure—"

"Ah, Lady Penelope!" A gentleman with a bit of a tummy straining the buttons of his elegant suit stepped deliberately in front of them. "You are as lovely as a summer rose."

Penelope's mouth pursed at this rather pedestrian compliment. "I thank you, Your Grace."

"Not at all, not at all." The Duke of Scarborough turned to Artemis and winked. "And I trust that you're in the best of health, Miss Greaves."

"Indeed, Your Grace." Artemis smiled as she bobbed a curtsy.

The duke was of average height but had a slight stoop that made him seem shorter. He wore a snowy wig, a lovely champagne-colored suit, and diamond buckles on his shoes—which, rumor had it, he could well afford. Gossip also said that he was on the hunt for a new wife, since the duchess had passed away several years previously. Unfortunately, while Penelope could probably forgive the man his stoop and little belly, she was not so sanguine about his age, for the Duke of Scarborough, unlike the Duke of Wakefield, was well past his sixtieth year.

"I am on my way to meet a friend," Penelope clipped out, trying to dodge the man.

But the duke was the veteran of many a ball. He moved with admirable deftness for his age, somehow catching Penelope's hand and hooking it through his elbow. "Then I shall have the pleasure of escorting you there."

"Oh, but I'm quite thirsty," Penelope parried. "Perhaps you would be so kind as to fetch me a cup of punch, Your Grace?"

"I'd be most delighted, my lady," the duke said, and Artemis thought she saw a twinkle in his eye, "but I'm sure your companion wouldn't mind the chore. Would you, Miss Greaves?"

"Certainly not," Artemis murmured.

Penelope might be her mistress, but she rather had a fondness for the elderly duke—even if he didn't have a prayer of winning Penelope. She turned sedately, but fast enough to pretend not to hear her cousin's sputter. The refreshments room was on the other side of the ballroom, and her progress was slow, for the middle of the floor was taken up by dancers.

Yet, her lips were still curved faintly when she heard an ominously rumbling voice. "Miss Greaves. Might I have a word?"

Naturally, she thought as she looked up into the Duke of Wakefield's cold seal-brown eyes.

"I'M SURPRISED YOU know my name," Miss Artemis Greaves said.

She wasn't a woman he would notice under normal circumstances. Maximus gazed down at the upturned face of Miss Greaves and reflected that she was one of the innumerable female shades: companions, maiden aunts, poor relations. The ones who hung back. The ones who drifted quietly in the shadows. Every man of means had them, for it was the duty of a gentleman to take care of females such as she. See to it that they were clothed and housed and fed and, if possible, that they were happy or at least content with their lot in life. Beyond that, nothing, for these types of females didn't impact on masculine issues. They didn't marry and they didn't bear children. Practically speaking they had no sex at all. There was no reason to notice a woman like her.

And yet he had.

Even before last night he'd been aware of Miss Greaves trailing her cousin, always in concealing colors—brown or gray—like a sparrow in the wake of a parrot. She hardly spoke—at least within his hearing—and had mastered the art of quiet watchfulness. She made no move to draw any attention to herself at all.

Until last night.

She'd dared to move to draw a *knife* on him in the worst part of London, had stared him in the eye without any fear at all, and it was as if she stepped into the light. Suddenly her form was clear, standing out from the crowd around them. He *saw* her. Saw the calm, oval face and the entirely ordinary feminine features—ordinary save for the large, rather fine dark gray eyes. Her brown hair was pulled into a neat knot at her nape, her long, pale fingers laced calmly at her waist.

He *saw* her and the realization was vaguely disturbing.

She raised delicate eyebrows. "Your Grace?"

He'd been staring too long, lost in his own musings. The thought irritated him and thus his voice was over-harsh. "What were you thinking, letting Lady Penelope venture into St. Giles at night?"

Many ladies of his acquaintance would've burst into tears at such an abrupt accusation.

Miss Greaves merely blinked slowly. "I cannot imagine why you would think I have any control at all over what my cousin does."

A fair point, yet he could not acknowledge it. "You must've known how dangerous that part of London is."

"Oh, indeed I do, Your Grace." He had intercepted her meander about the edge of the ballroom and now she started forward again.

He was perforce made to stroll by her side if he didn't want her to simply walk away from him. "Then surely you could've persuaded your cousin to refrain from such a foolish action?"

"I'm afraid Your Grace has an overly optimistic view of both my cousin's docility and my own influence over her. When Penelope has an idea in her head, wild horses couldn't pull her away from it. Once Lord Featherstone mentioned the words 'wager' and 'dashing,' I'm afraid we were quite doomed." Her dulcet voice held an amused undertone that was unreasonably attractive.

He frowned. "It's Featherstone's fault."

"Oh, indeed," she said with unwarranted cheerfulness.

He scowled down at her. Miss Greaves didn't seem at all worried that her cousin had nearly caused both their deaths in St. Giles. "Lady Penelope should be dissuaded from associating with gentlemen like Featherstone."

"Well, yes—and ladies, too."

"Ladies?"

She gave him a wry look. "Some of my cousin's most harebrained ideas have originated with ladies, Your Grace."

"Ah." He looked blankly at her, absently noting that her eyelashes were quite lush and black—darker than her hair, in fact. Did she use some type of paint on them?

She sighed and leaned closer, her shoulder brushing his. "Last season Penelope was persuaded that a live bird would make an altogether unique accessory."

Was she bamming him? "A bird."

"A swan, in fact."

She looked quite grave. If, in fact, she was playing some type of silly game with him, she hid it well. But then one such as she had innumerable occasions to learn to hide her thoughts and feelings. It was almost a requirement, in fact.

"I never noticed Lady Penelope with a swan."

She glanced swiftly up at him, and he saw the corner of her lips curve. Just slightly, and then it was gone. "Yes, well, it was only for a week. As it turns out, swans hiss—and bite."

"Lady Penelope was bitten by a swan?"

"No. Actually, I was."

His brows knit at that bit of information, imagining that fair skin darkening with a bruise. He didn't like the image. How often was Miss Greaves hurt whilst carrying out her duties as companion to Lady Penelope?

"Really, sometimes I think my cousin should be locked up for her own good," Miss Greaves muttered. "But that isn't likely to happen, is it?"

No, it wasn't. Nor was it likely that Miss Greaves herself would find some other source of livelihood— somewhere *away* from her dangerously feckless cousin.

That simply wasn't the way the world worked, and even if it was, it was no concern of his.

"Your tale makes it even more imperative that you find a way to persuade Lady Penelope out of the more dangerous of her ideas."

"I have tried—I *do* try," she said in a low voice. "But I am simply her companion, after all."

He stopped and looked at her, this woman more self-possessed than her lot in life gave her any right to be. "Not her friend?"

She turned to glance up at him, that nearly invisible smile at the corner of her lips again, tiny and discreet, almost as if she'd learned not to smile very widely, not to acknowledge strong emotion too soon. "Yes, I am her friend. Her relative and her friend. I care for Penelope quite a bit—and I think she loves me as well. But first and foremost I am her lady's companion. We will never be equals, because my position will always be lesser to hers. So, although I may *suggest* we not enter St. Giles at night, I can never order her."

"And whither she goes, so do you?"

She inclined her head. "Yes, Your Grace."

His jaw tightened. He knew all this, yet still he found the information...irritating. He looked away. "When Lady Penelope marries, her husband will rein her in. Keep her safe." *Keep* you *safe*.

"Perhaps." She tilted her head, gazing at him. She was an intelligent woman. Surely she knew his intentions toward her cousin.

He looked at her hard. "He will."

She shrugged. "That would be for the best, I suppose. Of course if Penelope were reined in, we wouldn't meet such interesting people as the Ghost of St. Giles."

"You make light of the danger."

"Maybe I do, Your Grace," she said gently, as if he were the one who should be reassured, "but I must admit it was exciting to see the Ghost."

"That ruffian."

"Actually, I'm not sure he is." They had started strolling again and he finally realized that she'd been making for the refreshments room. "May I tell you a secret, Your Grace?"

Usually when ladies offered such a thing to him, they did it in the interest of flirtation, yet Miss Greaves's expression was straightforward. He found himself curious. "Please."

"I believe the Ghost might be of high birth."

He was careful to keep his face blank even as his heartbeat began to speed. What could he possibly have let slip? "Why?"

"He left something with me last night."

Dread wrapped itself about his chest. "What?"

That hidden smile played about her lips again. Mysterious. Captivating. Utterly feminine.

"A signet ring."

THE DUKE OF Wakefield's face was as still as stone. Artemis wondered what he thought and, rather disconcertingly, what he thought of *her*. Did he disapprove of her levity regarding the Ghost of St. Giles? Or did he find it offensive that she thought a costumed footpad might be an aristocrat?

She searched his face for a second more and then faced forward again. She supposed it hardly mattered what he thought of her—besides being an adequate lady's companion for Penelope. He'd never before sought her out specifically to talk to her. She doubted he would ever do so again. They, simply put, didn't move in the same orbits. She smiled wryly to herself. They didn't even move in the same *universe*.

"Are you going to fetch refreshment for Lady Penelope?" he asked, his voice rumbling pleasantly at her shoulder.

"Yes."

She saw him nod out of the corner of her eye. "I'll help you bring it back." He turned to the footman ladling glasses of punch and snapped his fingers. "Three."

To her amusement, the man leaped to provide three glasses of punch while the duke simply stood there.

"That's very kind of you, Your Grace," she said, all trace of irony carefully erased from her voice.

"You know that's not true."

She glanced at him quickly, startled. "Do I?"

He bowed his head, murmuring quietly, "You seem an intelligent woman. You know I'm courting your cousin. Therefore, my offer is but a way to gracefully meet her again tonight."

There didn't seem much to say to that, so Artemis remained quiet as they gathered the three glasses of punch.

"Tell me, Miss Greaves," the duke said as they began the trek back across the ballroom. "Do you approve of my courtship of your cousin?"

"I can't imagine that my approval matters one way or the other, Your Grace," Artemis clipped out, unaccountably irritated. Was he patronizing her?

"Can't you?" One corner of his mouth flicked up. "But you see I grew up in a house full of women. I don't discount the weight of a whispered confidence in a feminine boudoir. Several judicious words from you in your cousin's ear could scupper my suit."

She looked at him in astonishment. "Your Grace assigns me more power than in truth I have."

"You're modest."

"Truly I am not."

"Hmm." They were nearing Penelope who was still in conversation with Scarborough. Wakefield's eyes narrowed. "But you haven't answered my question: will you back my suit?"

She glanced at him. In her position she ought to tread carefully. "Do you have an affection for Penelope?"

"Does that matter to Lady Penelope?" He arched an eyebrow pointedly.

"No." She lifted her chin. "But I find, Your Grace, that it matters to me."

Penelope turned and, catching sight of them, broke into a gorgeous smile. "Oh, Artemis, *finally*. I vow I'm quite parched." She took her cup from Artemis's hands and looked up through her eyelashes at Wakefield. "Have you come to scold me some more, Your Grace?"

He bowed and murmured something over her hand.

Artemis took a step back. Then another. The tableau— Penelope, Wakefield, and Scarborough—were the players in this theater.

She merely swept the stage.

She tore her gaze from the trio and looked about the room. Several chairs had been set against the wall for the older guests and such. She caught sight of a familiar face and began moving in that direction.

"Would you like some punch, ma'am?"

"Oh, how kind!" Bathilda Picklewood was a stout lady with a round, pink face framed by gray curls. In her lap was a small black-white-and-brown spaniel, alertly watching the room. "I'd just begun to think that I ought to go in search of punch."

Artemis held her hand out to the spaniel—Mignon— as Miss Picklewood took a sip. Mignon licked Artemis's fingers politely. "Lady Phoebe isn't here?"

Miss Picklewood shook her head regretfully. "You're

aware that she doesn't attend crowded events. I'm here tonight with my good friend Mrs. White—she's gone to repair a bit of lace on her costume."

Artemis nodded as she settled next to the older lady. She did know that the duke's youngest sister didn't usually attend crowded events, but she'd hoped anyway. A sudden thought occurred to her. "But Lady Phoebe will be at her brother's house party, surely?"

"Oh, yes, she's quite looking forward to it, though I'm afraid the duke isn't." Miss Picklewood chuckled. "He hates house parties—really *any* party. Says it takes him away from more important things. I saw you with Maximus earlier."

It took Artemis a moment to remember that Maximus was the Christian name of the Duke of Wakefield. Funny to think of a duke having a Christian name, but it suited him. She could see him as a ruthless Roman general. But of course Miss Picklewood would call Wakefield by his given name. She was a distant relation to the duke, and she lived with him and Lady Phoebe as a sort of companion for the young girl.

Artemis looked at the other woman with new interest. Miss Picklewood must be one of the women his house was full of. "He was helping me bring the punch to Penelope."

"Mmm."

"Miss Picklewood…"

"Yes?" The older lady looked at her with bright blue eyes.

"I don't think I've ever heard how you came to live with the duke and Lady Phoebe?"

"Oh, that's simple enough, my dear," Miss Picklewood said. "It was after the death of both of their parents."

"Yes?" Artemis frowned at her lap. "I didn't remember that."

"Well, it was before your time, wasn't it? Seventeen twenty-one, it was. Poor Hero had just turned eight and Phoebe was only a babe, not quite a year. When I heard— I was staying with an aunt of mine—I knew I had to go. Who else would look after those children? Neither the duke nor poor, dear Mary—Maximus's mother, you know—had living siblings. No, I came down at once and found the house in chaos. The servants were all in shock, the men of business were nattering on about the lands and money and succession and not noticing that the boy had hardly risen from his bed. I took charge of the girls and helped Maximus as best I could. He was stubborn even then, I'm afraid. After a while he said he was the duke now and didn't need a nanny or even a governess. Quite rude, but then he'd lost his parents. Awful shock."

"Hmm." Artemis looked over to where the duke was standing near Penelope, his eyes half hooded and impossible to read. "I suppose that explains quite a bit."

"Oh, yes," Miss Picklewood said, following her gaze. "It does indeed."

They sat for a moment in silence before Miss Picklewood roused herself. "So you see, it can be quite a good life, nonetheless."

Artemis blinked, not following her companion's train of thought. "I'm sorry?"

"Being a lady dependent on the kindness of relatives," Miss Picklewood said gently and quite devastatingly. "We might not have children of our own blood, but if one is lucky one can find others to help through life." She patted Artemis's knee. "It'll all come right in the end."

Artemis held very still because she had a quite mad urge to tear sweet Miss Picklewood's hand from her leg. To stand up and scream. To run through the ballroom, out the front door, and keep running until she felt cool grass beneath her feet again.

This couldn't be her life. It simply couldn't be.

She did none of that, of course. Instead she nodded pleasantly and asked Miss Picklewood if she'd like another glass of punch.

Chapter Three

❦

Now one hot day whilst hunting, King Herla came upon a clearing with a cool, deep pool. He dismounted and knelt to drink from the pool, and as he did so he saw reflected in the water a strange little man riding on a billy goat.
"Good day to you, King of the Britons,"
called the little man.
"And who might you be?" asked King Herla.
"Why, I am King of the Dwarfs," said the dwarf, "and would like to make you a bargain." …
—from *The Legend of the Herla King*

Artemis drifted up into consciousness from a dream of a dappled forest and lay remembering. It had been cool and quiet, the moss and damp leaves under her bare feet muffling her footfalls. A hound or maybe several padded behind her, keeping her company. She'd come on a clearing through the trees, and anticipation had made her breath catch. Something was there, some creature that really shouldn't have been in any English forest, and she wanted to see—

Someone was in her room.

Artemis froze, listening. Her room at Brightmore House was at the back of the house, small, but comfortable. In the morning a maid came to light the fire, but otherwise no one disturbed her here. Whoever was in her room was not the maid.

Perhaps she'd imagined it. The dream had been quite visceral.

She opened her eyes. Faint moonlight from the one window showed her the familiar shadows of her room: the chair by her bed, the old dresser by the window, the small mantelpiece—

One of the shadows detached itself from beside the mantel. The shadow coalesced into a figure, large and looming, his head distorted by a floppy hat and the outsized nose on his mask. The Ghost of St. Giles.

He was rumored to rape and ravage, but bizarrely, she felt no fear. Instead a strange elation filled her. Perhaps she was still enthralled by her dream.

Still, best to make sure.

"Have you come to kidnap me?" Her voice emerged a whisper, though she hadn't consciously thought to lower it. "If so, I hope you'll do me the courtesy of letting me put on a wrap first."

He snorted and moved to her dresser. "Why are your rooms apart from the family?" He, too, whispered.

He hadn't spoken in St. Giles, and she really hadn't expected him to answer. Curiosity made her stir from her nest of covers, sitting up.

It was chilly with the fire dead and she shivered as she wrapped her arms about her knees. "Room."

He paused in whatever he was doing at her dresser and his head turned, the mask a menacing profile. "What?"

She shrugged, though his back was to her and *she* at

least could hardly see in the dim light. "There's only the one room."

He turned back to the dresser. "You're a servant, then."

Hard to tell from a whisper, but she rather thought he meant to provoke her.

"I'm Lady Penelope's cousin. Well," she amended, "first cousin twice removed, strictly speaking."

"Then why do they put you here, away at the back of the house?" He crouched and pulled out the bottom drawer of her dresser.

"Haven't you heard of a poor relation?" She craned her neck, trying to see what he was doing. He appeared to be pawing through her stockings. "You're a fair distance from St. Giles tonight."

He grunted and shoved the drawer in, moving to the one above it. That one held her chemises, all two of them; she wore the third.

She cleared her throat. "Thank you."

He stilled at that, his head still bent over her drawer. "What?"

"You saved my life the other night." She pursed her lips, considering. "Or at the very least my virtue. And that of my cousin's. I can't think of why you might have done it, but thank you."

He turned at that. "*Why I might have done it?* You were imperiled. Wouldn't any man help?"

She smiled ruefully—and a little sadly. "In my experience, no."

She thought he'd simply go back to searching her room, but he paused. "Then I'm sorry for your experience."

And the odd thing was that she thought he meant it.

She pleated the coverlet between her fingers. "Why do you do it?"

"Do what?" He rose and began on the top drawer.

That held her few personal possessions: old letters from Apollo from when he'd been sent away to school, a miniature of Papa, Mama's earbobs, the gilt flaking off and one of the wires broken. Nothing of interest, except to her. She supposed she should feel resentment that a stranger was laying hands on her meager possessions, but really, in the larger scope of all the things that had happened in her life, this was quite a small indignity.

He stilled. "You've half a loaf of bread in here and two apples. Do they not feed you that you must steal food?"

She stiffened. "It's not for me. And it's not stealing—not really. Cook knows I took them."

He grunted and resumed searching.

"Why do you don the disguise of a harlequin actor and run about St. Giles?" She cocked her head, watching him. His movements were economical. Precise. Yet, strangely graceful for a man. "You know, there are those who think you a ravisher of women—and worse."

"I'm not." He shut the drawer and glanced about her room. Had years spent hunting in the night made him able to see in the dark? She could hardly make out the outlines of her room and it was her own. He chose the old wardrobe next, a piece that had been replaced with something newer and finer in one of Brightmore House's guest rooms. He opened the door, peering in. "I've never violated any woman."

"Have you killed?"

He paused at that, before reaching into the wardrobe to move aside her spare day gown. "Once or twice. The men deserved it, I assure you."

She could believe that. St. Giles was a terrible place. A place where people were driven by poverty, drink, and despair to the depths of a human soul. She'd read reports in her uncle's discarded news sheets of robberies and murders, of entire families found starved to death. For a gentleman to venture into St. Giles night after night for *years* to confront the demons unleashed by man's worst state... he must have more than a trifling reason. She very much doubted he did it for excitement or on a dare.

Artemis inhaled on the thought. What sort of man acted as he did? "You must love St. Giles very much."

He whirled at that, and an awful, loud laugh broke from his lips. "*Love*. Dear God, you mistake me, ma'am. I do it not for love."

"Yet the citizens of St. Giles are the ones who benefit from your..." She trailed off, trying to think of how to describe what he did. Hobby? Duty? Obsession? "Work. If, as you say, you don't harm except those who deserve it, then those who live in St. Giles are the safer for what you do, surely?"

"I care not how my actions affect them." He closed the door to the wardrobe with finality.

"I do," she said simply. "Your actions saved my life."

He was standing, looking about the room. There wasn't much left: the mantel and her bedside table, both without anything to hide something in. "Why are you so concerned with my actions in any case?"

Even in his whispered voice he sounded irritable, and she supposed he had a right. "I don't know. I guess that you're a... novelty, really. I don't usually have the occasion to talk to a gentleman at length."

"You're Lady Penelope's relation and companion. I

would think between balls, parties, and teas you'd have more than ample opportunity to meet gentlemen."

"Meet them, yes. Have a true conversation?" She shook her head. "Gentlemen have no reason to talk to ladies such as I. Not unless their intentions are less than honorable."

He took a step toward her, almost as if the movement was involuntary. "You've been accosted by men?"

"It's the way of the world, isn't it? My position makes me vulnerable. Those that are strong will always go after those they think are weak." She shrugged. "But it isn't often, and in any case I've been able to fend for myself."

"You aren't weak." It was a statement, final and without doubt.

She found his conviction flattering. "Most would think me so."

"Most would be wrong."

They stared at each other and she had the idea that they were both somehow taking stock of the other. She certainly was. He wasn't what she would have expected, had she bothered to think about what to expect from a masked harlequin. He seemed to be truly listening to her, and that hadn't happened to her in a very long time. *Well, except with the Duke of Wakefield last night*, she silently amended.

The Ghost had understood her truth in a shockingly short period of time.

Then there was his *anger*—the underlying pulse of suppressed rage that seemed to vibrate through him. She could feel it, almost a living thing, pressing against her.

"What are you looking for?" she asked abruptly. "It's rather rude for a gentleman to enter a lady's room without permission."

"I'm not a gentleman."

"Really? I thought otherwise."

She'd spoken without thinking and immediately regretted it. He was beside the bed in an instant, large, male, and dangerous, and she remembered at this inopportune moment what the creature had been in that clearing in her dream: a tiger. In an English forest. She almost laughed at the absurdity.

She was forced to tilt her head up to see him, baring her neck, which was never a good idea when in the presence of a predator.

He bent over her, deliberately planting his fists on the bed on either side of her hips, caging her in. She swallowed, feeling the heat of his body. She could *smell* him: leather and male sweat, and it should have repelled her.

Except it did the opposite.

He thrust his masked face into hers, so close she could see the glint of his eyes behind it. "You have something that belongs to me."

She held very still, breathing in his exhalations, sharing the same air as he, like a very dear enemy.

His face dipped toward hers, angling, and her eyelids fell. For a very brief moment, she thought she felt the brush of something warm across her lips.

Footsteps sounded in the hall outside her room. The maid was coming.

She opened her eyes and he was simply gone.

A moment later Sally the upstairs maid came in the room with her coal shuttle and brushes. Sally started when she noticed Artemis still sitting up in bed. "Oh, miss, you're up early. Shall I send for some tea?"

Artemis shook her head, inhaling. "Thank you, no. I'll go down for some in a bit. We came in late last night."

"That you did." Sally clattered at the hearth. "Black-bourne says as her ladyship didn't get in until past two in the morn. In a right mood she is, too, for having to wait up so late. Oh, and how did the window get left open?" Sally jumped up and crossed to the window, slamming it shut. "Brrr! 'Tis too early for such a draft."

Artemis's eyebrows rose. Her room was on the third floor and there was no convenient trellis or vine on the wall outside. She hoped the silly man wasn't lying dead in the garden.

"Will that be all, miss?"

A fire was crackling on her hearth and Sally was already by the door, pail in hand.

"Yes, thank you."

Artemis waited until the maid had closed the door behind her before drawing the thin chain around her neck out from under her chemise. She wore it always because she didn't know what else to do with what hung on it: a delicate pendant with a glittering green stone. Once she had thought the stone was paste, a pretty ornament Apollo had given her on their fifteenth birthday. Four months ago she'd tried to pawn it for more money to help Apollo—and found out the horrible truth: the stone was an emerald set in gold, which made it a treasure too dear, for ironically she couldn't sell such a fine piece without awkward questions about its provenance. Questions she simply couldn't answer. She had no idea where or how Apollo could've gotten such an expensive piece of jewelry.

She'd worn the emerald pendant for months now—too afraid to leave the damnably expensive thing alone in her bedroom—but yesterday she'd added something else to the chain.

Artemis fingered the Ghost's signet ring, the red stone warm under her thumb. She should've given it back. It obviously was important to him. Yet something had made her want to conceal it and keep it a little longer. She examined the ring again. The stone had once had a crest or other insignia carved into it, but it was so battered by age that only vague lines remained, impossible to decipher. The gold, too, had the matte patina of age, the band worn thin on the underside. The ring, and thus the family it belonged to, was very old indeed.

Artemis frowned. How had the Ghost known she had his ring? She hadn't told anyone besides Wakefield, not even Penelope. For one wild moment she imagined the Duke of Wakefield donning the motley of a harlequin.

No. That was just absurd. More likely the Ghost had either known he'd dropped the ring in her hand or simply guessed by process of elimination.

Artemis sighed and tucked the ring and pendant back under her chemise. Time to dress. The day had begun.

MAXIMUS CROUCHED ON the sloping roof of Brightmore House, fighting the urge to reenter Miss Greaves's room. He hadn't found his ring—his *father's ring*—and the insistent beat to return was strong in his chest. Under the impulse to take back what was his, there was a subtler, softer cadence: to speak again to Miss Greaves. To look into her eyes and find out what made her so strong.

Madness. He shook off the siren's call and leaped to the next house. Brightmore House was in Grosvenor Square; the white stone buildings around the green in the middle were new and close together. It was child's play to travel by rooftop to the end of the square and then slither down a gutter into an alley. Maximus kept to the shadows for the length of the short alley and then once again took to the rooftops.

Dawn was near and people rarely looked *up*.

Had she pawned his father's ring? The agony of the thought made him gasp even as he ran along the crest of a roof. He'd searched her room and meager possessions and the ring hadn't been there. Had she given it away? Dropped it somewhere in St. Giles?

Surely not, for she'd made a point of boasting about having it in her possession at the ball. But she was poor—that much at least was starkly evident after seeing the room her cousin had gifted her. A gold ring would fetch enough money for some small luxury.

He waited at the edge of a crumbling building, watching as below a night soil man labored with two foully full buckets.

Then he jumped to the next roof.

Maximus landed silently, despite the distance across the alley, the only sign of his exertion the slight grunt as he rose. He remembered his father's hands, the strong, blunt fingers, the dark hairs on the backs, and the slight curve of the right middle finger, broken as a child. His father might've been a duke, but he always had a healing cut or abrasion or bruise on his hands, for he used his hands without any regard for his rank. Father had saddled his own horse when he'd been too impatient to wait for a groom, sharpened his own quill, and loaded his own fowling piece when hunting. Those hands had been broad and scarred and had seemed, to Maximus as a boy, to be utterly competent, utterly reliable.

The last time he'd seen his father's hand, it had been covered in blood as Maximus had removed the signet ring.

He dropped to the street and saw that his feet had brought him to St. Giles. To the spot where it had happened.

To his left a worn cobbler's sign squeaked over a door so low that all but children would have to duck to enter. The sign was new as was the shop—it had been a tavern selling gin all those years ago, beside it a narrow alley where barrels of gin had once stood. Maximus flinched, glancing away. He'd hidden behind those barrels, and the stink of gin had filled his nostrils that night. When he'd taken the mask as the Ghost, this had been the first gin shop he'd shut down. To the right was a teetering brick building, the upper stories wider than the lower, every room let and relet until it might as well have been a rat warren—only one inhabited with humans instead of animals. Near his feet the wide channel was so blocked with detritus that not even the next rain would clear it. The very air hung thick and wet with stink.

To the east the sky had begun to pinken. The sun would soon be up, clearing the sky, bringing the hope of a new day to every part of London, save this one.

There was no hope in St. Giles.

He pivoted, his boots scraping against the grit underfoot, recalling Miss Greaves's comment. Love St. Giles? Dear God, no.

He loathed it.

A faint cry came from the narrow alley where the gin barrels had once stood. Maximus turned, frowning. He couldn't see anything, but daybreak was coming. He needed to return home, get off the streets before people noticed him in his Ghost costume.

But then the cry came again, high and nearly animal

in its pain, but most definitely human. Maximus strode closer to peer into the alley. He could just make out a slumped form and the glint of something wet. Immediately he bent, catching an arm and pulling the figure into the relatively better lit lane. It was a man—a gentleman, by the fine velvet of his coat—with blood on his bare, shaved head. He must've lost his wig.

The man groaned, his head sagging back as he looked up at Maximus. His eyes widened. "No! Oh, no. Already been robbed. Don't have me purse anymore."

His words were slurred. The man was obviously drunk.

"I'm not going to rob you," Maximus said impatiently. "Where do you live?"

But the man wasn't listening. He'd started wailing weakly, his entire body thrashing rather like a landed flounder.

Maximus frowned, looking around. The people of St. Giles had begun to creep from their houses in preparation for the day. Two men scurried by, their faces averted. Most here knew better than to show interest in anything resembling danger, but a trio of small boys and a dog had gathered at a safe distance across the lane, staring.

"Oi!" A little woman wearing a tattered red skirt advanced on the boys. They made to run, but she was quick, grabbing the eldest by the ear. "What did I tell you, Robbie? Go'n fetch that pie for yer da."

She let go of the ear and all three boys darted off. The woman straightened and caught sight of Maximus and the wounded man. "Oi! You there! Leave 'im alone."

Tiny though the woman was, she was brave enough to confront him, and Maximus had to admire that.

He ignored the man's continued moaning and turned to her, whispering. "I didn't do this. Can you see him home?"

She cocked her head. "'Ave to see to me man, then start me work, don't I?"

Maximus nodded. He dipped two fingers into a pocket sewn into his tunic and came out with a coin, which he tossed to her. "Is that enough to make it worth your time?"

She caught the coin handily and glanced at it. "Aye, 'spect it is."

"Good." He looked at the wounded man. "Tell this woman your place of residence and she'll see you home."

"Oh, thank you, fair lady." The drunken man seemed to think the little woman was his savior.

She rolled her eyes, but said with a sort of gruff kindness as she came over and bent to take his arm, "Now what mess 'ave you gotten yerself into, sir?"

"'Twas Old Scratch, plain as day," the man muttered. "Had a great big pistol and demanded my purse or my life. And then he hit me anyway!"

Maximus shook his head as he moved off. Stranger things had been imagined in St. Giles than highway robbery by the Devil, he supposed, but he hadn't time to stay and learn more about the matter. It was already far too light. He swarmed up the side of a building, making his way to the roof. Below he could hear the clatter of hooves and he swore under his breath. It was early yet for the Dragoons to be about St. Giles, but he didn't want to take the chance it might be they.

He ran across the angled rooftops, leaping from building to building. He had to descend to the ground twice, each time for only a short run before he was back traveling by London rooftop.

Twenty minutes later he caught sight of Wakefield House.

When he'd first started his career as the Ghost of St. Giles, he and Craven had very quickly realized that he would need a secret means of access to the town house. Which was why, instead of approaching the house directly, Maximus slid into the gardens in back. They were a long, narrow strip of land between the house and the mews, and at one side was an ancient folly. It was small, little more than a moss-covered stone arch enclosing a bench. Maximus entered and knelt to sweep aside a pile of dead leaves by the bench. Underneath was an iron ring set into the stone paving. He grasped it and lifted and a square block of stone pulled back on well-oiled hinges, revealing a short drop to a tunnel. Maximus lowered himself inside and pulled the covering stone back on top. He was in complete and utter blackness.

Wet blackness.

Maximus crouched, for the tunnel was only about five feet high—not nearly tall enough for him to stand upright—and began crab-walking through the cramped space. The walls were barely wider than his shoulders and he brushed against them often. Water dripped in a slow lament, and he splashed through stagnant pools every third step. He could feel his chest tighten, his breath coming too light and fast, and he fought to breathe deeper, to lay his hand against slimy brick without flinching. *Only a few feet further.* He'd used the tunnel for years. He should be resigned to its horrors—and the memories they evoked—by now.

Even so, he couldn't help but draw a deep, relieved breath when he came to the wider entrance to his underground exercise room. He felt carefully along the wall as he stepped down, searching for the small ledge that held tinder and flint.

He'd only just struck a spark when the door that led to the house opened and Craven appeared with a candle in hand.

Maximus exhaled in relief at the light.

Craven advanced toward him, holding his candle high. Maximus had never told his valet his feelings on the tunnel, yet as in innumerable times past Craven was lighting the candelabras set into the walls as swiftly as he could.

"Ah, Your Grace," the valet drawled as he worked. "I'm gratified to see that you've returned in one piece and with barely any blood about your person."

Maximus glanced down and saw the rusty stain on his tunic sleeve. "Not mine. I found a gentleman who'd been robbed in St. Giles."

"Indeed? And was your other mission fruitful?"

"No." Maximus stripped off the tunic and leggings of his costume, swiftly donning his more usual breeches, waistcoat, and coat. "I have a task for you."

"I live to serve," Craven intoned in a ponderous voice so solemn it could only be subtle mockery.

Maximus was tired, so he ignored the response. "Find out everything you can about Artemis Greaves."

Chapter Four

"What bargain might that be?" asked King Herla.
The dwarf grinned. "It's well known that you've betrothed
yourself to a fair princess. As it happens, I, too, will
soon be wed. If you will do me the honor of inviting me
to your wedding banquet, I in turn will invite you to
my wedding festivities."
Well, King Herla thought deeply on the matter, for 'tis
known that one should not enter a pact, however innocent,
with one of the Fae without due consideration, but in the
end he saw no harm in the invitation.
So King Herla shook the Dwarf King's hand and they
agreed to attend each other's weddings....
—from *The Legend of the Herla King*

Three days later Artemis Greaves descended from the Chadwicke carriage and looked up in awe. Pelham House, the seat of the dukes of Wakefield for the last one hundred years, was the largest private residence she'd ever seen. A massive yellow stone building with rows upon rows of windows across the facade, Pelham dwarfed the numerous carriages drawn up at its front. Twin colonnaded arms reached out from the central building, embracing the huge circular drive. A tall portico dominated the entrance, four

Ionic columns holding aloft the triangular pediment with wide steps across the front leading to the drive. Pelham House was majestic and daunting and didn't look particularly welcoming.

Rather like its owner.

Artemis was conscious that the Duke of Wakefield stood at the center of the portico, wearing a blue suit so dark it was nearly black, his immaculately white wig making him look austere and aristocratic. Presumably he was there to welcome his guests to the country party—although one would never know it from his unsmiling face.

"Do you see *she's* here?"

Artemis started at the hiss at her shoulder, nearly dropping poor Bon Bon, asleep in her arms. She juggled the little dog, a shawl, and Penelope's nécessaire box before turning to her cousin. "Who?"

There were three other carriages in the drive beside their own, and "she" could've been any number of ladies.

Still Penelope widened her eyes as if Artemis had become suddenly dimwitted. "*Her.* Hippolyta Royale. Whyever would Wakefield invite her?"

Because Miss Royale was one of the most popular ladies of the last year, Artemis thought but of course did not say out loud—she wasn't *actually* dimwitted. She glanced to where Penelope indicated and saw the lady descending from her carriage. She was tall and slim, dark haired and dark eyed, a quite striking figure, really, especially in the dull gold-and-purple traveling costume she wore. Artemis noted that Miss Royale appeared to be arriving unaccompanied, and it occurred to her that unlike most ladies, she'd never seen the heiress with a particular friend. She was friendly—or at least she seemed so, for Artemis had never been introduced—but she didn't link arms with a bosom bow, didn't lean close and giggle over gossip. Miss Royale appeared eternally alone.

"I knew I should've brought the swan," Penelope said.

Artemis shuddered at the memory of the hissing fowl and hoped she didn't look too wild-eyed at her cousin. "Er...the swan?"

Penelope pouted. "I have to find some way to make him notice me instead of her."

Artemis felt a pang of protectiveness toward her cousin. "You're beautiful and vivacious, Penelope, dear. I can't imagine any gentleman not noticing you."

She forbore pointing out that even had Penelope been plain and retiring, she would still have been the center of attention at all times. Her cousin was the richest heiress in England, after all.

Penelope blinked at her words and almost looked shy.

Miss Royale murmured a "good afternoon" as she crossed in front of them on the way to the portico entrance of Pelham.

Penelope's eyes narrowed determinedly. "I'll not let that upstart steal *my* duke away from me."

And so saying, she marched off, evidently with the idea of reaching the Duke of Wakefield ahead of Miss Royale.

Artemis sighed. This was going to be a very long fortnight. She crossed to the side of the gravel drive, almost in back of one of the long colonnaded arms, and set Bon Bon gently down on the grass. The elderly dog stretched and then toddled, stiff-legged, to a nearby bush.

"Ah, Miss Greaves."

She turned to see the Duke of Scarborough striding

toward her, looking rather dapper in a scarlet riding habit. "I hope your journey was a comfortable one?"

"Your Grace." Artemis dipped into a low curtsy, a little confused. Dukes—or indeed any gentlemen—rarely sought her out. "Our journey was quite pleasant. And yours, sir?"

The duke beamed. "Rode my gelding, Samson, with my carriage behind, don't you know."

She couldn't help smiling just a bit. He was such a jovial gentleman—and so pleased with himself. "All the way from London?"

"Yes, indeed." He puffed out his chest. "I like the exercise. Keeps me youthful. And where is Lady Penelope, if I might enquire?"

"She's gone ahead to greet the Duke of Wakefield."

Artemis bent to lift up Bon Bon and the little dog sighed as if in gratitude. When she rose the Duke of Scarborough's eyes were narrowed. She turned to look where he was gazing. Penelope was leaning close to Wakefield and smiling up at him as she let him kiss her hand.

Scarborough caught Artemis's curious stare and his expression relaxed into another cheery smile. "Always did like a challenge. May I?"

He took the nécessaire from her hand and offered his arm.

"Thank you." She laid her fingertips on his arm, reminded again of why she rather liked the elderly duke. In her other arm, Bon Bon laid his little chin on her shoulder.

"Now Miss Greaves," he said as he led her slowly toward the front doors, "I'm afraid I have an ulterior motive in seeking you out."

"Do you, Your Grace?"

"Oh, yes." His eyes twinkled at her merrily. "And I think you're a bright enough lass to have an inkling of what it is. I wonder if you might tell me the sort of things your cousin likes most in the world."

"Well..." Artemis glanced at her cousin as she thought about the matter. Penelope was laughing prettily at something the Duke of Wakefield had said, though Artemis noted that the gentleman himself wasn't smiling. "I suppose she likes the same sort of things most ladies do: jewels, flowers, and beautiful objects of all kinds." She hesitated, biting her lip, then shrugged. It wasn't as if it were a secret, after all. "Beautiful, *expensive* objects."

The Duke of Scarborough nodded vigorously as though she'd imparted some wonderful wisdom. "Indeed, indeed, my dear Miss Greaves. Lady Penelope should be showered with all that is most lovely. But is there anything else you might tell me? Anything at all?"

They were nearly to the portico and on impulse Artemis ducked her head to murmur, "What Penelope really adores is attention. Pure, undivided attention."

The Duke of Scarborough just had time to wink and say, "You're a marvel, Miss Greaves, truly you are."

And then they were climbing the steps to where the Duke of Wakefield stood with Penelope beside him.

"Your Grace." Wakefield's bow was curt enough to nearly be insulting. His cold eyes flicked between Scarborough and Artemis and one corner of his mouth crimped. "Welcome to Pelham House." He merely glanced at a waiting footman and the man promptly stepped forward. "Henry will show you to your rooms."

"Thank you, sir!" The Duke of Scarborough grinned.

"A nice little house you have here, Wakefield. I confess it quite puts my own country seat, Clareton, to shame. Of course I've recently built a music room at Clareton." Scarborough's eyes widened innocently. "Pelham hasn't been updated since your dear father's time, has it?"

If Wakefield was bothered by the rather obvious jab, he didn't show it. "My father had the south facade on the opposite side of the building rebuilt, as I'm sure you remember, Scarborough."

Artemis realized with a start that Scarborough was of an age to have been a contemporary of Wakefield's father. What did Wakefield feel, welcoming his father's friend to his home? Seeing what his father might've looked like had he lived? She examined Wakefield's face. Nothing at all, if one were to go by his expression.

For a moment the Duke of Scarborough's face softened. "Had all those windows put in to overlook the garden for your mother, didn't he? Mary always did like her gardens."

It was slight, but Artemis thought she saw a muscle tic underneath the Duke of Wakefield's left eye. For some reason the small reaction prompted her into speech. "What sort of instruments have you in your new music room, Your Grace?"

"I confess, none at all."

Artemis blinked. "You haven't *any* musical instruments in your music room?"

"No."

"Then what's the point in it?" Penelope asked rather irritably, joining the conversation for the first time. "'Tisn't a music room without musical instruments."

Scarborough looked suspiciously crestfallen. "Oh,

dear, I hadn't thought of that, my lady. I confess I was so interested in hiring the most talented Italian artist to paint the murals on the ceiling, finding the best imported pink marble, and making sure that the workmen used enough gold to gild the walls and ceiling that I forgot all about the musical instruments themselves."

Lady Penelope turned, almost as if against her will, to the Duke of Scarborough. "Gold..."

"Oh, quite." Scarborough leaned forward earnestly. "I do think one shouldn't stint on gilding, don't you? Makes one look so damnably *frugal*."

Penelope's perfect pink lips parted. "I—"

"And now that you've pointed out my folly in neglecting actual instruments for the music room, perhaps you could give me your opinion." Somehow Scarborough had tucked Penelope's hand into the bend of his elbow. "For instance, I've heard that Italian clavichords have the best sound, but I confess I do enjoy the look of some of the French painted ones, even if they cost nearly double the Italian. I think in some ways taste should precede art, don't you?"

Scarborough turned and guided Penelope into the house as she answered. He was so adroit that Artemis wondered if her cousin even realized she was being managed. She glanced at the Duke of Wakefield, expecting him to be frowning after the odd couple, and she was indeed right about one thing: he was frowning.

But it was at her rather than Penelope.

Artemis inhaled, feeling a strange tightness in her chest. He stared at her so intently, as if his entire focus was upon her. Those sable eyes were stern and dark, but there was a spark of something hidden away at the back of them that she suddenly wanted to discover.

"Your Grace."

Artemis nearly jumped at the words. More guests had arrived, drawing the duke's attention. She turned swiftly to go inside, but as she entered the cold marble hall, she thought she knew what she'd seen in the duke's eyes.

A spark of warmth.

She shivered. The thought shouldn't have filled her with dread, but it did.

ARTEMIS WOKE BEFORE dawn the next morning. She'd been given a room next to Penelope's, smaller than her cousin's but far grander than the ones she usually stayed in.

But then everything about Pelham House was grand.

She stretched, remembering the long table in the immense dining room where they'd eaten dinner last night. Besides herself and Penelope, Miss Royale, and the Duke of Scarborough, the guests included Lord and Lady Noakes, a couple in their fifties; Mrs. Jellett, a well-known society lady with a penchant for gossip; Mr. Barclay, a male version of Mrs. Jellett; Lord and Lady Oddershaw, political allies of the duke; and finally Mr. Watts, also a political ally. Artemis was glad to see Lady Phoebe and Miss Picklewood, who were in attendance as well. Unfortunately, she'd not had the opportunity to talk to Phoebe last night. They'd sat at opposite ends of the table during dinner, and Phoebe had retired shortly after the meal ended.

Artemis rose and dressed in her usual brown serge. It would be hours yet before Penelope would wake and need her. In the meantime, there was something Artemis longed to do.

She slipped quietly from the room, glancing up and down the wide corridor outside. A maid was walking away from her, but otherwise the hallway was deserted. Artemis picked up her skirts and ran lightly to the back of the house. There was a staircase here—grand, but not the overwhelming monstrosity at the front of the house. She crept down it carefully. It wasn't as if she was doing anything wrong, but she liked the idea of moving unseen. Of not having to answer to anyone.

A door nearly as tall as the front one led to the south side of the house. She tried the handle, holding her breath. It turned beneath her fingers, but then she heard footsteps.

Quickly she opened the door and was out onto the back terrace. She stood beside the door, breathing quietly, and watched through the windows beside the door as a footman hurried by.

When he was past she slipped down the wide steps into the garden. Trimmed hedges stood severe and dark in the grayish pink light of dawn. She ran her hand over the prickly leaves as she padded down a gravel path. She'd worn neither hat nor gloves, a terrible breach of etiquette. Ladies never went outside without both for fear of freckling in the sun, even when the sun wasn't out.

But then she'd never been much of a lady.

The hedges ended at a wide, cut grass lawn and Artemis bent on a sudden impulse, pulling both her slippers and stockings from her feet. Holding them in one hand, she ran for the stand of trees, the dewy grass making her feet wet.

She was panting by the time she'd made the edge of the trees, her heart beating faster, a grin stretching her lips. It had been so long since she'd been in the country.

Since she'd been herself.

The Earl of Brightmore had a country residence, naturally, but neither he nor Penelope ever went there. They were much too enamored of the city. Artemis hadn't been back to the country in years, and she hadn't had a proper run on grass since...

Well, since she'd been forced to leave her childhood home.

She shook the dreary thought from her mind. This time was precious and there was no point in using it to mourn past sorrows. The sun was up now, the light fresh and delicately new, and she tiptoed into the trees, placing her steps carefully, for her feet had become tender since she'd last walked barefoot on a forest floor.

This wasn't really a forest, she knew—it was a carefully cultivated copse, made to look wild by expensive gardeners—but it would do. Overhead, the birds were waking, singing their joy at the new day. A squirrel ran up the trunk of a tree and then paused to scold her as she glided past. Soft leaves rustled underfoot, and every now and again she stepped on bare earth, cool and welcoming.

She could lose herself here. Cast off her clothing and become a wild thing, escaping civilization and society, another animal in the woods. She'd never have to go back, never have to bow to those who thought her inferior or simply looked through her as if she were the paper on the walls.

She could be free.

But who would care about Apollo, then? Who would visit him, bring him food, and tell him stories so he wouldn't truly go insane? He'd rot, forgotten in Bedlam, and she couldn't let that happen to her darling brother.

Something moved in the trees up ahead. Artemis

stilled, flattening herself to a broad trunk. It wasn't that she was frightened of whoever it was, but she liked her solitude. Wanted to enjoy it a little longer.

She heard a panting and then all at once she was surrounded by dogs. Three dogs, to be specific: two greyhounds and a hunting spaniel with a lovely plumed tail, wagging briskly. For a moment she and the dogs merely took stock of each other. She looked around, but no one else seemed to be in the woods, as if the dogs had gone for a jaunty ramble all on their own.

Artemis extended her fingers. "Are you three by your lonesome, then?"

At her voice the spaniel sniffed interestedly at her fingertips, his mouth hanging open as if he were grinning. She fondled his silky ears and then the greyhounds bounded forward to give their approval.

A corner of her mouth curved up and she stepped out, continuing her own walk. The dogs ranged in front of her and to the sides, loping ahead before circling back to snuffle her fingers or butt against her hand as if to receive permission before trotting off again.

Artemis meandered for a bit, not worrying about their destination, she and the dogs, and then, suddenly, the trees parted. Ahead was a pond, the morning sun shining off the dappled water. At the far side of the pond was a clever rustic bridge that led to a small, artfully tumbling tower at the other end.

The two greyhounds went immediately to the pond's edge to drink while the spaniel decided simply to wade in until he could lap the water without bending his head.

Artemis stood at the tree line, watching the dogs, tilting her face to scent the woods.

A shrill whistle broke the tranquility.

All three dogs lifted their heads. The taller greyhound—
a brindled brown-and-gold female—took off toward the
bridge, the other greyhound—a red female—right behind.
The spaniel bounded to shore in a shower of water, shaking vigorously before barking and following.

There was a figure on the other side of the bridge, drawing closer. A man in worn boots and an aged coat that
once had been of exquisite cut. He was tall, with broad
shoulders, and he moved like a great cat. A floppy hat
covered his head, obscuring his features. For a moment
Artemis inhaled in shocked recognition.

But then he stepped into the light and she saw that
she'd been mistaken.

It was the Duke of Wakefield.

MAXIMUS SAW MISS Greaves standing at the edge of
the woods like a suspicious dryad and thought, *Naturally*. What other lady would be up and about so scandal-
ously early? What other lady would make his dogs desert
him?

Those same dogs ran to him as if to share with him
their new friend. Belle and Starling milled around his feet
while Percy planted muddy paws on his thigh and drooled
upon his coat.

"Traitors," Maximus murmured to the greyhounds,
not bothering to reprimand the disheveled spaniel. He
glanced across the pond, half expecting Miss Greaves to
have disappeared, but she was still watching him.

"Good morning," he called.

He approached her as he would a wild, woodland creature: gingerly and with an attempt to appear harmless,

but she didn't start. He amended the analogy as he drew closer: a wild animal would show fear.

Miss Greaves merely looked a little curious. "Your Grace."

Percy, who had been investigating the tall reeds by the edge of the pond, lifted his head at the sound of her voice and appeared to take it as invitation to run to her and attempt to hurl himself against her legs.

Miss Greaves gave the dog a stern look before he'd even reached her, and said simply, "Off."

Percy collapsed at her feet, his tongue hanging out the side of his jaws, ears back as he gazed up at her adoringly.

Maximus shot the dog an irritated look as he turned and began walking back around the ornamental pond. Miss Greaves fell into step beside him.

"I trust that you rested well last night, Miss Greaves?"

"Yes, Your Grace," she replied.

"Good."

He nodded, unable to think of anything else to say. Usually he disliked company on his morning walk, but for some reason, Miss Greaves's presence was almost…soothing. He glanced sideways at her and noticed for the first time that her feet were bare. Long, elegant toes flexed against the ground as she walked. They were quite dirty from the forest floor and the sight, if anything, should've filled him with disgust for such a shocking display of impropriety.

Yet disgust was the exact opposite of his reaction.

"Did you build this?" Her voice was low and rather pleasing as she gestured to the tower folly they were approaching.

He shook his head. "My father. My mother saw something similar on a trip to Italy and was quite taken with the idea of a romantic ruin. Father had a tendency to indulge her."

She glanced curiously at him, but continued walking.

He cleared his throat. "We spent a great deal of time here at Pelham House when they were alive."

"But not afterward?"

His jaw tightened. "No. Cousin Bathilda preferred London for raising my sisters, and I thought I should remain with them as the head of the family."

He caught her odd look out of the corner of his eye. "But...forgive me, but weren't you a boy when the duke and duchess died?"

"Murdered." He couldn't quite keep the rasp from his voice.

She stopped. "What?"

Her naked toes were curled into the loam, white and soft and strangely erotic. He raised his eyes, looking at her plainly. It was useless to try and avoid pain. "My parents were murdered in St. Giles nineteen years ago, Miss Greaves."

She didn't give him any useless platitudes. "How old were you?"

"Fourteen."

"That's hardly old enough to become the head of a family." Her gentleness made something bleed inside of him.

"It is when one is the Duke of Wakefield," he said curtly. Odd that she bothered arguing with him over this *now*. No one had at the time—not after he'd started talking again—not even Cousin Bathilda.

"You must've been a very determined boy," was all she said.

There was nothing to say to that, and for a minute they tramped through the woods companionably.

The greyhounds bounded ahead, while Percy flushed a frog and began a rather comical chase.

"What are their names?" she asked, nodding at the dogs.

"That's Belle"—he pointed to the slightly taller greyhound bitch, her coat a lovely gold and russet—"and that's Starling, Belle's daughter. The spaniel is Percy."

She nodded seriously. "Those are good dog names."

He shrugged. "Phoebe names them for me."

Her odd little half smile appeared at the mention of his sister. "I was glad to see she was here. She does so enjoy social events."

He glanced at her swiftly. Her tone was neutral, but he felt the implied disapproval in her words. "She's blind— or as near to as to make no difference. I'll not see Phoebe hurt—either physically or emotionally. She's vulnerable."

"She might be blind, Your Grace, but I believe she's stronger than you think."

He looked away from her alluring bare toes. Who was she to tell him how to take care of his sister? Phoebe was barely twenty years of age. "Two years ago my sister fell because she didn't see a step, Miss Greaves. She broke her arm." His lips twisted at the memory of Phoebe's face white with pain. "You may think me overprotective, but I assure you I *do* know what is best for my sister."

She was silent at that, though he doubted she'd changed her mind over the matter. He frowned, irritated, almost as if he regretted his cold words.

The folly loomed in front of them and they stopped to look at it.

Miss Greaves cocked her head. "It's rather like Rapunzel's tower."

Big blocks of artfully weathered dark gray stone made a round tower with a single, low arched opening.

He raised an eyebrow. "I'd always imagined Rapunzel's tower taller."

She tilted her head back to eye the top of the little building, and the long line of her pale throat was caught in a beam of sunlight. A pulse beat delicately in the soft juncture of her neck and collarbone.

He looked away. "Certainly this would be no obstacle for a fit man to climb."

She glanced at him, and he thought he saw that tiny smile at the edge of her lips. "Are you saying you'd scale these walls for a damsel in distress, Your Grace?"

"No." His mouth tightened. "Just that it's possible."

She hummed under her breath. Percy romped up and dropped a sadly mangled, dead frog at her feet, then backed away and sat proudly by his prize, looking at Miss Greaves as if expecting praise.

She absently ruffled the spaniel's ears. "You'd leave poor Rapunzel to her fate?"

"If a lady were so silly as to get herself locked in a stone tower," he said drily, "I'd break down the door and climb the stairs to help her from the building."

"But Rapunzel's tower had no door, Your Grace."

He kicked aside the dead frog. "Then, yes, I suppose I would be forced to scale the tower walls."

"But you certainly wouldn't enjoy it," she murmured.

He merely looked at her. Was she trying to make him into some romantic hero? She didn't strike him as a silly chit. Her eyes were a dark, soft gray, lovely and alluring, but her gaze was as steady and bold as any man's.

He glanced away first, his lips twisting. "Anyway, it's not Rapunzel's tower. It's the Moon Maiden's."

"What?"

He cleared his throat. What had possessed him to tell her that? "Mother always said that this was the Moon Maiden's tower."

She looked at him with those bold gray eyes. "Well, there must be a story in that."

He shrugged. "She used to tell it to me when I was very young. Something about a sorcerer who fell in love with the Moon Maiden. He built a tower to try and be closer to her and walled himself inside."

She stared at him for a moment as if waiting for something. "And?"

He glanced at her, puzzled. "And, what?"

She widened her eyes. "How does the story end? Did the sorcerer win his Moon Maiden?"

"Of course not," he said irritably. "She lived on the *moon* and was quite unattainable. I suppose he must've starved or pined away or fallen off the wall at some point."

She sighed. "That's the least romantic story I've ever heard."

"Well it wasn't my favorite," he said, sounding defensive to even his own ears. "I liked the ones about giant killers much better."

"Hmm," she answered noncommittally. "Can one go inside?"

Instead of answering he strode to the arched entryway, a bit hidden by briars. Ruthlessly, he pulled them aside, ignoring the scrapes on his fingers, then gestured for her to walk in ahead.

She glanced at his hands, but made no comment as she passed him.

There was a spiral staircase immediately inside, and he watched as she lifted her skirts to climb it. A bare ankle flashed and then the dogs pushed past him to follow her eagerly.

He followed her as well, but naturally not as eagerly as the dogs. At least that was what he told himself.

The staircase opened onto a small stone platform. He made the last step and joined her by the low wall, which was crenellated like a medieval castle's battlements.

She braced her hands straight-armed on the wall and leaned over to look. The folly wasn't high—no more than a single story—yet one had a nice view of the pond and the surrounding woods. Belle reared up on her hind legs beside her to look as well, while Percy whined and paced, unable to see. A gentle breeze teased a few strands of hair at Miss Greaves's temple, and he couldn't help but think she looked like a ship's figurehead—proud and somewhat wild and ready for adventure.

What an extraordinarily foolish thought.

"It's quite silly, isn't it?" she said after a moment, almost as if speaking to herself.

He shrugged. "A folly."

She cocked her head, looking at him. "Was your father a man given to amusements?"

He remembered the strong hands, the kind but somber eyes. "No, not much."

She nodded. "Then he loved your mother quite a lot, didn't he?"

He caught his breath at her words, the loss as bleak and frozen as if it'd happened yesterday. "Yes."

"You're lucky."

"Lucky" wasn't an attribute most people assigned to him. "Why?"

She closed her eyes and tilted her face to the sun. "My father was mad."

He looked at her sharply. Craven had made his report last night. The late Viscount Kilbourne had been estranged from his own father, the Earl of Ashridge, and the rest of his family, and had been known for making wild, unfortunate investments—and, at his worst, raving in public.

He supposed the normal thing to do would be to offer some word of sympathy, but he'd long ago used up all his tolerance for polite, meaningless phrases. Besides. She'd been brave enough to forgo the usual false comfort when he'd told her of his own loss. It seemed only just to offer her the same dignity.

Still, he couldn't help a small frown as he thought of her as a small girl, living with an unpredictable sire. "Were you frightened?"

She glanced at him curiously. "No. One always thinks one's upbringing—one's family—is perfectly normal, don't you think?"

He'd never considered the matter: dukes weren't, generally speaking, considered normal. "In what way?"

She shrugged, her faced tilted toward the sun again. "One's own family and situation are all one knows as a child. Therefore they are, by default, normal. I thought *everyone* had a papa who sometimes stayed awake all night writing philosophical papers, only to burn them all in a rage in the morning. It was only when I was old enough to notice that other fathers didn't act like my own that I realized the truth."

He swallowed, oddly perturbed by her recitation. "And your mother?"

"My mother was an invalid," she said, her voice precise, unemotional. "I rarely remember them in the same room together."

"You have a brother," he replied, testing.

Her brow clouded. "Yes. My twin, Apollo. He's in Bedlam." She turned to look at him, her eyes wide open and sharp. "But then you already know that. My brother is notorious and you're the type of man to find out all he can about a prospective wife."

There was no reason to feel shame so he neither denied nor confirmed that he'd had her investigated along with her cousin. He simply held her gaze, waiting.

She sighed, turning away from the wall. "Lady Penelope will want me soon."

He followed her down the short staircase, watching her level shoulders, the vulnerable angle of her nape as she bent her head to watch her steps, the companionable bump of Percy against her skirts. It would be the height of idiocy for the Duke of Wakefield to pursue the cousin of the woman he wanted as wife. And yet, for the first time in his life, Maximus wanted to let the man rule him instead of the title.

Chapter Five

King Herla was married a fortnight later, and a grand affair it was indeed. One hundred trumpets blared the news from the castle rooftops, a parade of dancing lasses led the procession, and the feast that followed became one of legend. Princes and kings journeyed from all corners of the earth to witness the nuptials, yet none compared to the Dwarf King. He arrived with his retinue, all dressed in fairy finery, riding on goats, and bearing a great golden horn filled with rubies and emeralds as a wedding gift....
—from *The Legend of the Herla King*

Artemis had long ago come to terms with her life and her fate. She was an acolyte, a handmaiden subject to the whims of her cousin. Her life was not her own. What might have been—what she had once dreamed of so long ago, late at night in a young girl's bed—would never be.

That was simply how it was.

So there was no percentage in watching that afternoon as the Duke of Wakefield tucked Penelope's hand into the bend of his elbow and led her from the dining room where they'd all just partaken of luncheon. His head was bent solicitously toward Penelope's, dark to dark. They made a lovely couple. Artemis couldn't help wondering if, when they were married, he'd ever let his wife know that he liked to walk his woods as the dawn lit the sky. Would he tell her the silly story about the Moon Maiden's tower?

She looked at her hands, twisted together at her waist. Petty, jealous feelings weren't for women such as she.

"I'm so glad you came!" Lady Phoebe Batten interrupted her thoughts by linking arms and said in a lower voice, "Maximus's guests are so very *ancient*."

Artemis glanced down at the other woman as they strolled from the dining room. Phoebe wore her light brown hair pulled back from her softly rounded face and the sky blue of her gown set off her pink cheeks and large brown eyes. Had Phoebe been allowed a coming out, Artemis had no doubt she would've been one of the most popular of the young ladies in society—not for her looks, but rather for her kind disposition. It was quite impossible not to love Phoebe Batten.

But Phoebe had an unbreakable fate just as Artemis did: her near blindness had kept her from the usual balls, soirees, and courting a lady of her rank and privilege should've had by right.

Sometimes Artemis wondered if Phoebe was as sanguine about her situation as she was with hers.

"Penelope is closer in age to you than me," she pointed out as they neared the doors to the south terrace. Most of the guests had decided to stroll the garden after luncheon. "Watch the step here."

Phoebe nodded in thanks, carefully placing her slipper-clad foot on the marble step. "Well, but Penelope hardly counts, does she?"

Artemis threw her companion a quick, amused glance.

She wasn't used to *Penelope* being the one disregarded between the two of them. "What do you mean?"

Phoebe squeezed her arm and lifted her face to the bright sunshine outside. "She's nice enough, but she has no interest in me."

"That's not true," Artemis said in shock.

Phoebe gave her a world-weary look that certainly did not belong on her girlish face. "She pays attention to me only when it occurs to her that it might help her campaign for Maximus."

There wasn't much to say about that since it was uncomfortably true. "Then she's more foolish than I thought her."

Phoebe grinned. "And *that's* why I'm so glad you're here."

Artemis felt her lips lift. "Here are the steps down to the garden."

"Mmm. I can smell the roses."

Phoebe turned her head toward a trellised rose a few yards away. Unlike the rest of the primly pristine garden, the rose was rather wild and weedy looking, more suited to a cottage garden than a formal one. There was no reason for it to be here . . . except for the near-blind girl beside her, happily scenting the air.

"Can you see anything?" Artemis asked low.

The question was so intimate it verged on the rude, but Phoebe merely tilted her head. "I can see the blue sky and the green of the garden. I can see the shape of the rose bushes over there—but the individual flowers are lost to me." She turned to Artemis. "I'm much better in bright light. For instance, I can see that you're frowning at me right now."

Artemis hastily put a more pleasant expression on her face. "I'm glad. I'd thought that you'd lost more."

"Indoors and at night I have," Phoebe replied matter-of-factly.

Artemis hummed to show that she'd heard. They started down one of the graveled garden paths. She'd bypassed the garden in favor of the woods this morning. Now she found it pleasant to meander in the afternoon sunshine—though of course she was properly gloved and bonneted.

A peal of laughter turned heads.

"Lady Penelope?" Phoebe asked, leaning close to Artemis.

"Yes." Artemis watched as Penelope tapped Wakefield flirtatiously on the arm. He was smiling down at her. "She's getting on well with your brother."

"Is she?" Phoebe asked.

Artemis glanced at Phoebe, wondering. Phoebe had made it plain in the past that she didn't think Penelope the best choice for her brother, but of course she had no say in the matter. Was Phoebe worried that she'd have to move out of her brother's house if Penelope married Wakefield?

"Here's Miss Picklewood," Artemis told her companion as they approached two ladies. "She's in conversation with Mrs. Jellett."

"Oh, Phoebe, dear," Miss Picklewood called. "I was just telling Mrs. Jellett that you're the one who manages the garden."

Phoebe smiled. "I only *maintain* the garden. Mother was the original designer."

"Then she had quite an artistic hand," Mrs. Jellett said promptly. "I do envy you the space you have to work with.

My Mr. Jellett left me only a small garden at our country house. Now can you tell me what this elegant flower is? I don't remember ever seeing the like."

Artemis watched as Phoebe bent and felt the flower before giving a quite academic lecture about the plant, its origin, and how it had come to be growing here at Pelham. Artemis was a bit bemused. She hadn't known her friend was so interested in gardening.

A wet nose thrust itself into her hand and at the same time Miss Picklewood chuckled. "Percy seems quite taken with you. Usually he never leaves Maximus's side."

Artemis glanced down at the hunting spaniel's adoring brown eyes and ruffled his soft ears. She was surprised to see that Bon Bon was by the bigger dog's side, pink tongue hanging out as he panted happily. She looked up. The duke was escorting Penelope on the far side of the garden. "Where's Mignon?"

Miss Picklewood pointed to where the little spaniel was nosing under a boxwood. "She doesn't much like the larger dogs, unlike Bon Bon."

"Mmm." Artemis crouched to give the little white dog a pat as well. "I haven't seen him so active in years."

"I must show Lady Noakes," Mrs. Jellett was saying in a rather-too-loud voice. "She's such a keen gardener, though she doesn't often have the funds to indulge." She tucked her chin into her neck and whispered, "Noakes *gambles*, you know."

Miss Picklewood shook her head. "Gambling is such an evil." She sent Mrs. Jellett a significant look. "Have you heard the story about Lord Pepperman?"

"No!"

Phoebe gave a small groan. "If you'll excuse us, Cousin Bathilda, Mrs. Jellett, Artemis expressed a special interest in the espaliered apricot trees."

Artemis dutifully took her friend's arm and waited until they'd walked out of earshot before leaning close. "Espaliered apricots?"

Phoebe stuck her nose in the air. "Something *everyone* should take an interest in. Besides, I'm not sure I could take the Pepperman story again."

A shrill whistle rent the air. Percy, who had been trotting along beside them, lifted his head alertly before racing to Wakefield's side. Bon Bon scrambled on short little legs to keep up with his new friend.

Artemis watched the dogs go and found herself staring at the duke. He was looking in her direction, and even at this distance he was commanding, almost as if he were demanding something of her.

She felt light-headed.

Then Penelope tapped him on the arm and he turned to the other woman to smile and make some comment.

Artemis shivered despite the bright sunshine.

Phoebe bumped at her shoulder. "I've been thinking."

"Have you?" Artemis said distractedly. Wakefield and Penelope had met up with Lord and Lady Oddershaw, and even at this distance she recognized the slight stiffening of the duke's shoulders. He seemed displeased by something Lord Oddershaw was saying.

"Wouldn't it be lovely if all the ladies from the Ladies' Syndicate for the Benefit of the Home for Unfortunate Infants and Foundling Children went together to see the theater at Harte's Folly?"

Artemis blinked and looked down at Phoebe. "That

does sound lovely—I'm sure Penelope would like to attend. She likes any sort of public event, even if she doesn't always follow the play."

Phoebe smiled up at her. "And you, too, of course. You're rather an honorary member, don't you think? Since you attend the meetings with Penelope?"

"I suppose." Artemis's lips twisted wryly. She certainly would never be a real member since the Ladies' Syndicate existed to help the Home for Unfortunate Infants and Foundling Children in St. Giles. Money was a rather large prerequisite for becoming a member.

"Oh, do say you'll come," Phoebe said, hugging Artemis's arm close. "They're doing *Twelfth Night* with Robin Goodfellow playing Viola. She's always so funny in her breeches roles. I quite love her low voice and the droll way she speaks her lines."

Oh, Artemis thought with a pang. Phoebe probably couldn't actually see the actors on the stage when she attended the theater. It would all be about the speeches of the actors for her.

"Of course I'll come," she said warmly to the younger woman.

"That's settled, then," Phoebe said with a little skip. "I'll ask the other ladies if they can attend, too."

Artemis felt the corner of her mouth curl at Phoebe's infectious joy. They were nearing the end of the garden and a stone seat set against the wall, and Artemis now saw that a solitary figure sat there, gazing into the distance as if deep in thought.

"You know," she said impulsively, "I've heard that Miss Royale is an heiress in her own right."

Phoebe's brows knit slightly. "Yes?"

Artemis squeezed her arm significantly. "There's always room for one more member of the Ladies' Syndicate."

"*Oh!*" Phoebe said.

Artemis patted her arm and raised her voice just a bit. "And here's Miss Royale."

That lady swung her head around as if she hadn't noticed their approach. "Good afternoon." Her voice was low for a woman, her expression cautious.

Phoebe smiled innocently. "Are you enjoying the gardens, Miss Royale?"

"Why, yes, my lady," Miss Royale replied. "Er... will you both join me?"

Her words were a trifle belated as Phoebe had already settled on one side of her while Artemis had taken the other.

"Thank you," Phoebe said sweetly. "I was just telling Miss Greaves that I do hope all the ladies of the Ladies' Syndicate for the Benefit of the Home for Unfortunate Infants and Foundling Children can join me at Harte's Folly when we return to town."

Miss Royale blinked at this information, but politely replied, "I don't believe I've heard of the Ladies' Syndicate for the Benefit of the Home for Unfortunate Infants and Foundling Children."

Phoebe opened her eyes wide. "*Haven't* you?"

Artemis privately hid a smile as Phoebe began expounding on the St. Giles orphanage and all the good works it did for the most vulnerable of children. She glanced up as she did so and saw Wakefield, still strolling with Lady Penelope and Lord Oddershaw. His face was creased in an irritable frown.

What had Lord Oddershaw said to him?

*   *   *

MAXIMUS WOKE FROM dreams of work unfinished and bloody tresses shining dully in the moonlight. He'd been awake until well past two of the clock in polite argument with Oddershaw. Maximus didn't mind the intrusion of politics into his house party, but he didn't like the other man's insistence on bringing up the matter when Maximus had been in the garden with Lady Penelope. But, although Oddershaw was an uncouth blowhard, he was also an important political ally in order to build a strong backing for Maximus's newest Gin Act.

Thus the dreary duty of debating the man into the small hours.

He rose and quickly donned his old coat and boots and strode through Pelham to the back of the house. Even having slept later than usual, he met only a few servants, and they were well trained enough to simply bow or curtsy without speaking as he passed by.

Mornings were the one time of day that he kept to himself.

Outside, he strode around Pelham in the direction of the long stables. Usually the dogs were waiting for him in the stable yard, eager for their ramble, but today the yard was empty.

Maximus frowned and set off for the woods.

The sun was already up as he crossed the wide south lawn, and the sudden darkness of the canopy when he entered the woods made him blind for a moment. He closed his eyes, and when he opened them again she appeared before him like some ancient goddess, calm and otherworldly, standing under the tall trees as if she owned them, his dogs at her side.

Percy broke the moment first, naturally, rushing from Miss Greaves to him, muddy and excited. A small, formerly white dog darted out from behind her skirts, barking madly as it chased after Percy.

"You're late today, Your Grace," Miss Greaves said, almost as if she'd been waiting for him.

Foolish notion. "I talked long into the night with Lord Oddershaw," he said. "Is that Lady Penelope's dog?" He looked down at the dog sniffing around his ankles. He didn't remember ever seeing the animal so muddy—or so active.

"Yes." She fell into step with him as easily as if they'd been doing this for years. "What were you talking to Lord Oddershaw about?"

He glanced at her. She wore a brown dress he'd seen innumerable times on her before and he remembered her wardrobe with its three dresses: two for day and one for evening balls. "We discussed politics. I doubt a lady such as yourself would be interested."

"Why?"

He frowned. "Why what?"

"Why wouldn't a lady such as myself be interested in your political discussion, Your Grace?" Her tone was perfectly correct and yet somehow he thought she was mocking him.

As a result his voice might've been a trifle brusque. "It had to do with canals and a proposed act of my own to eradicate the gin trade in London amongst the poor. Fascinating stuff, as I'm sure you'll agree."

She didn't rise to the bait. "What do canals have to do with the gin trade?"

"Nothing." He picked up a stick and threw it rather

overhard for Percy, not that the silly spaniel minded. The dog took off, barking joyfully, as Lady Penelope's pet tried gallantly to keep up. Apparently the odd pair had become friends. "Oddershaw is angling for me to back his act opening a canal in Yorkshire that will benefit his mining interests before he'll throw his support behind my Gin Act."

"And you don't want to support his canal?" She picked up her skirts to step over a tree root and he saw the flash of her white ankle. She'd taken off her shoes again.

"It's not that." Maximus frowned. The intricacies of parliamentarian politics were so twisted that he didn't often like to discuss them with ladies or men uninterested in politics. Everything built upon another thing, and it was rather hard to explain the entire tangled mess. He glanced again at Miss Greaves.

She was watching the path, but she looked up as if she felt his gaze and met his eyes, her own impatient. "Well? What is it, then?"

He found himself smiling. "This is the third canal act Oddershaw has proposed. He's using Parliament to line his pockets. Not"—he shook his head wryly—"that he's the only one doing it. Most, I suppose, want laws that'll help themselves. But Oddershaw is rather egregiously open about it."

"So you won't do as he wishes?"

"Oh, no," he said softly. Grimly. "I'll back his damned act. I need his vote and, more important, the votes of his cronies."

"Why?" She stopped and faced him, her brows knit faintly as if she truly wanted to know about his political mechanisms. Or perhaps it was more than that. Perhaps she wanted to know his mind.

Or his soul.

"You've been in St. Giles," he said, turning to her. "You've seen the desolation, the...the *disease* that gin causes there." He took a step closer to her without conscious thought. "There are women who sell their babies in St. Giles for a sip of gin. Men who rob and kill just to have another cup. Gin's the rot that lies at the heart of London, and it will bring her down if it's not stopped. That damned drink must be cauterized like a festering wound, *cut* clean out, or the entire body will fail, don't you see?" He stopped and stared at her, realizing that his voice was too loud, his tone too heated. He swallowed. "Don't you see?"

He stood over her almost threateningly, yet Miss Greaves merely watched him, her head slightly cocked. "You're very passionate on the matter."

He looked away, taking a careful step back. "It's my business—my duty as a member of the House of Lords—to be passionate on the matter."

"Yet men such as Lord Oddershaw aren't. You just said so." She moved closer to him, peering into his face as if all his hidden secrets were somehow made plain to her there. "I wonder why you might care so much for St. Giles?"

He swung on her, a snarl at his lips. Care for St. Giles? Hadn't he already made it plain to her that he hated the place?

It was as if icy water poured over him. His head snapped back. No. *He* hadn't told her his feelings on St. Giles before—at least not as the Duke of Wakefield.

The Ghost had.

Maximus squared his shoulders carefully and turned

back to the path. "You mistake me, Miss Greaves. It's the gin and its ungodly trade I care about—not where it's plied. Now, if you'll excuse me, I have to ready myself for the morning so that I might attend to my guests."

He whistled for the dogs and strode away, but as he did so, he was very aware of one fact:

Miss Greaves was a dangerous woman.

THAT AFTERNOON FOUND Artemis once again arm in arm with Phoebe as they strolled out the south doors of Pelham. Luncheon had been a rather tiresome affair, as she'd been seated next to Mr. Watts, who was interested only in argument and his own opinion. She was glad to spend a moment with Phoebe, not least because she *wasn't* in the habit of shouting in Artemis's ear.

Phoebe squinted at the green beyond the formal garden. "What are they doing?"

Artemis looked to the green where the guests were already gathering. "They've set up an exercise yard, I think. Your brother mentioned something about games earlier—I believe the gentlemen will be demonstrating their dueling skills. Here's where the gravel turns to grass."

They stepped carefully onto the green as Artemis described the scene for Phoebe. Several footmen stood about holding various swords while others were setting down chairs for the ladies to take as they observed the demonstration. Wakefield snapped his fingers and pointed and two chairs were instantly placed at the front for him.

Phoebe sighed. "This won't be that interesting unless someone misses and pinks their opponent."

"Phoebe!" Artemis scolded under her breath.

"You know it's true." How could Phoebe look so very innocent and have such bloodthirsty thoughts? "We'll all have to make admiring noises while the gentlemen scowl and try to look dangerous."

Artemis's amusement was dampened by the sight of Wakefield carefully helping Penelope to the seat he'd provided. Next to her, the footmen began to make a row of chairs. Penelope beamed up at the duke, her face quite impossibly beautiful in the autumn sun. Artemis remembered how ferocious he'd looked as he'd described the devastation gin wrought in London. Did he save his passions for the floor of Parliament? For he wore a mask of calm politeness now. No, she couldn't imagine him letting that mask slip even in the heat of political argument.

"Who is going first?" Phoebe asked as they took their own seats two rows behind Wakefield and Penelope.

Artemis tore her gaze away from the duke, and reminded herself that she'd already decided that there was no percentage in pining after the man. "Lord Noakes and Mr. Barclay."

Phoebe's nose wrinkled. "Really? I wasn't aware that Mr. Barclay did anything more strenuous than lift an eyebrow."

Artemis snorted softly, watching the duelists. Lord Noakes was a man in his late fifties, of medium height and with a very small paunch. Mr. Barclay was at least twenty years younger, but didn't look nearly as fit. "He seems quite serious. He's taken off his coat and is swishing his sword about in a manly manner." She winced at a particularly vehement move. "Oh, dear."

"What? What?"

Artemis leaned closer to Phoebe, for Mrs. Jellett had

cocked her head in front of them as if trying to hear their murmured conversation. "Mr. Barclay nearly took off one of the footmen's noses with his sword."

Phoebe giggled, the sound sweet and girlish, and Wakefield glanced over, his dark, cold eyes meeting Artemis's so suddenly it was almost like plunging her hand into snow. His gaze flicked to his sister beside her and the lines that bracketed his firm lips softened. Strange that here and now they were hardly acquaintances, yet in the woods they were something very close to friends.

The duelists raised their swords.

The match was utterly without surprises. All gentlemen were taught from a young age how to duel—to use swords with elegance and grace, more a dance than any real fighting. Artemis knew that there were schools in London where aristocrats went to perfect their form, exercise, and learn the rules of sword fighting. They were all trained, either well or not, and they all used the same regimented movements. She couldn't help comparing the two males' lunging in precise steps that probably had flowery French names with the Ghost's moving with deadly intent. The two gentlemen in front of her wouldn't last a minute with the Ghost, she realized. The thought sent an elated thrill of triumph through her. She really ought to be ashamed of such a bloody bias.

But she wasn't. She *wasn't.*

The duel ended with the courteous touch of a blunted sword tip to Lord Noakes's embroidered waistcoat, just over his heart.

Phoebe discreetly yawned behind her palm when Artemis related the scene.

Lord Oddershaw and Mr. Watts were next. By the

time the Duke of Scarborough took off his coat for the third demonstration, Artemis was watching the back of Wakefield's head as he bent politely once more to hear Penelope's chatter and wondering if he was as bored as she was. He was attentive to her cousin, but Artemis had a hard time believing he really found her conversation very interesting.

She grimaced and looked away. What a sour woman she was becoming! She had a sudden awful vision of herself as a crabby old lady, shuffling along in whatever house she landed in as her cousin's companion, faded, dusty, and forgotten.

"Oh, *that's* interesting."

Artemis looked up at Phoebe's soft exclamation. "What?"

"You said it was the Duke of Scarborough in front of Maximus and Penelope?" Phoebe nodded discreetly to where the older man stood in front of her brother and Penelope. Scarborough was grinning and bending over Penelope's hand. "He isn't used to that."

"What?" Artemis jerked her gaze away to stare at her companion. "*Who?*"

"Maximus." Phoebe had a fond smile on her face—an expression that Artemis had a hard time reconciling with the autocratic iceberg that was Wakefield. "With a rival. He usually just indicates what he wants and others rush to see that he gets it."

Artemis bit her lip, stifling a smile at the image of servants, family, and friends scurrying to fulfill the duke's every whim as he strode by, oblivious.

As if somehow he was aware of her amusement, Wakefield turned at that moment and glanced at her.

She inhaled, lifting her head, as she met his dark eyes.

Penelope placed her hand on his sleeve and he turned back.

Artemis looked down and only then realized her hands were trembling. She grasped them together. "Do you really think Scarborough any sort of competition for your brother?"

"Well..." Phoebe tilted her head, considering, as Artemis watched Scarborough somehow persuade the gentleman sitting on the other side of Penelope to vacate his seat. The duke promptly sat down himself. "In the normal way of things I wouldn't think his chances very good at all. Maximus is young and handsome, rich and powerful. And I've always thought he had a certain compelling air about him, don't you?"

Oh, yes.

"But," Phoebe continued, "the Duke of Scarborough seems quite taken with Lady Penelope, and really I think that might make all the difference."

Artemis frowned. "What do you mean?"

Phoebe's plump lips folded inward, her large brown eyes looking sad. "Well, Scarborough cares, doesn't he? Maximus doesn't—not really. No doubt he's a bit compelled by the chase, but if he doesn't win"—she shrugged her shoulders—"he'll simply find another suitable heiress. She—Lady Penelope herself—doesn't really matter to him. And if it comes right down to it, wouldn't you chose passion—however old—over dispassion?"

"Yes." Her agreement wasn't even considered. What woman wouldn't want interest—*real* interest—in her and her alone, no matter the physical attributes of the suitor? If Penelope ever stopped to consider the matter, the Duke of Scarborough would instantly win. Poor Wakefield didn't stand a chance.

Except…he wasn't poor, was he? He was one of the most powerful men in the kingdom, and a man personally to be wary of, if not downright feared.

She watched him, his broad shoulders fitted in fine dark green silk, his profile turned as he examined the woman he was courting as she flirted with another man. He might as well be observing a pair of beetles in a primitive mating dance. One would never know by looking at him that he wanted Penelope for himself.

What would it be like to garner this man's passion?

Artemis felt a visceral thrill go through her at the thought. Had Wakefield ever been engaged? Was he even capable of deep interest? He was so contained, so cold, save for that one moment this morning when he'd come alive over the gin trade, of all things. It seemed almost laughable to think of him bound by obsession with a female.

Yet she could imagine him so—intent, focused on his goal, his *woman*. He'd guard his chosen mate, make her both fear and long for his attention. She shivered. He would be relentless in his pursuit, unmerciful in his victory.

And she would never see him so.

She sighed, determinedly staring at her hands clenched in her lap. She longed for a man like the duke—the ache of want was a physical thing—but she would never have him, let alone a man more attainable. Her fate was to be alone.

Cursed to celibacy.

The voice of the Duke of Scarborough rose. Artemis

glanced up. The latest duelists had finished, and Scarborough was saying something to Wakefield. Scarborough's face was jovial, but his eyes were hard.

"What's happening?" Phoebe asked.

"I don't know," Artemis replied. "I think Scarborough is asking something of your brother. Oh. Oh, my. He's challenged Wakefield."

"Has he?" Phoebe looked interested.

Artemis's brows rose. "Is your brother a good swordsman?"

"I don't know." Phoebe shrugged. "He's never been much interested in fashionable pursuits—he prefers politics—but it hardly matters, does it? Scarborough must be thirty years his senior."

Penelope threw back her head in a sharp laugh that they could hear easily even three rows back. Artemis couldn't help but lean forward. Wakefield was so rigid. So proud.

Scarborough said something else and Wakefield abruptly stood.

"He's accepting."

"Oh, dear," Phoebe said with much satisfaction.

"He can't win," Artemis muttered in distress. "If he beats Scarborough, he looks a bully, if he loses—"

"He'll be humiliated," Phoebe said serenely.

Artemis felt a sudden sharp irritation with her good friend. The younger woman should be at least a *little* upset at the prospect of her brother's downfall.

Wakefield's valet, a tall, thin man, was helping the duke remove his coat. The servant appeared to murmur something in Wakefield's ear before the duke shook his head abruptly and walked away. His waistcoat was black, overworked in gold thread that sparkled in the sunshine, the full sleeves of his snowy white shirt rippling slightly in the breeze. Scarborough already had a sword and was swishing it about importantly. The older man seemed to handle the weapon expertly and Artemis's heart clenched.

Better to be thought a bully than for such a proud man to be defeated.

The duelists stood facing each other, their swords raised. Lord Noakes stood between them and held aloft a handkerchief. For a moment all was still, as if everyone had realized that there was much more to this duel than a simple demonstration of skill.

Then the handkerchief fluttered to the ground.

Scarborough lunged forward, astoundingly agile for a man his age. Wakefield caught his first thrust and retreated, moving carefully. It was evident at once that he either was a much less practiced swordsman...or he was holding back.

"Scarborough is pressing him," Artemis said anxiously. "Your brother is only defending."

Scarborough smirked as he said something so low only his opponent could hear.

Wakefield's face went completely blank.

"Your Grace," Wakefield's valet called in warning.

Wakefield blinked and cautiously stepped backward.

Scarborough's lips moved again.

And then something unexpected happened. The Duke of Wakefield transformed. He crouched low, his body flowing into an elegant threat as he attacked the older man with a kind of brutal grace. Scarborough's eyes widened, his own sword parrying blow after blow as he backed hastily. Wakefield's sword flashed in the sunlight, his movements too fast to interpret, his lean body dangerous, and controlled, and Artemis had the sudden realization that he was *toying* with Scarborough.

She was standing now, unaware of having left her seat, her heart beating unnaturally fast.

"What's happening?" Phoebe stood as well, pulling frantically at her arm.

Wakefield lunged without fear, without hesitation, at the older man using a flurry of precise, deadly blows that, had the swords been sharp...

"He's..." Artemis choked, her mouth hanging open.

She'd seen this before.

Wakefield didn't move like a dancer. He moved like a great jungle cat. Like a man who knew how to kill.

Like a man who *had* killed.

Scarborough stumbled, his face shining with sweat. Wakefield was on him in seconds, a tiger pouncing for the kill, his lip curled into almost languid dismissal of the other man as his sword descended toward—

"Your *Grace!*"

The valet's shout seemed to loop about Wakefield's neck and jerk him back like a noose. He froze, his great chest heaving, his snow-white sleeves fluttering in the breeze. Scarborough stared at him, gape-mouthed, his sword still half-raised in defense.

Wakefield deliberately touched his sword to the ground.

"What is it?" Phoebe asked. "*What is it?*"

"I..." Artemis blinked. "I don't know. Your brother has lowered his sword."

Scarborough wiped his brow, then he moved toward Wakefield gingerly as if not quite believing that he was no longer under attack. Scarborough's blunted sword tip hit Wakefield on the throat, a blow strong enough that it would bruise. The smaller man stood there for a moment, panting, almost as if he were surprised by his victory.

"Scarborough's won," Artemis murmured absently.

Wakefield spread wide his arms in surrender and opened his right hand so that his sword fell to the ground.

He turned his head to meet Artemis's gaze.

His eyes were dark, dangerous, and not at all cold. He burned with an internal inferno she wanted to touch. She stared into the gaze of a tiger and knew, even as she watched the cat retreat into the camouflage of a gentleman:

The Duke of Wakefield was the Ghost of St. Giles.

Chapter Six

A fortnight later it was King Herla's turn to attend the Dwarf King's wedding. He took the strongest and best of his men and, entering a dark cavern, rode into the depths of the earth itself, for the land of the dwarves is deep underground. They journeyed for a day and a night, traveling ever lower, until they came to a vast, open plain. Above, rock curved, craggy and jagged, like an ominous sky, and below lay the cottages, lanes, and town squares of Dwarfland. . . .
—from *The Legend of the Herla King*

Maximus woke just before dawn with a gasp, the image of his mother's white face burned into the darkness behind his eyelids, the emeralds ripped from her lifeless neck. The stink of gin seemed to linger in the air, but he knew that was merely a phantom from the dream.

Percy nosed his hand as he lay in the ancient Wakefield ducal bed. Above him, dark green drapes surrounded a gilded coronet carved into the canopy. Had any of his ancestors been plagued by dreams and doubts? Judging by the proud faces lining his gallery, he thought not. Each of those men had attained their title by the peaceful death of their father or grandfather. Not by violent murder unavenged.

He deserved his nightmares.

Percy licked his fingers with disgusting dog sympathy, and Maximus sighed and rose. The spaniel backed a step and sat, wagging his tail enthusiastically as he dressed. Percy, like the other dogs, was supposed to spend the night in the stables, but despite the fact that he wasn't nearly as clever as Belle or Starling, he somehow usually found a way past innumerable footmen and Craven into Maximus's bedroom at night. It was rather a mystery how he managed it. Perhaps providence had granted luck where it hadn't graced intelligence.

"Come." Maximus slapped his thigh and strode from the room, the spaniel trotting after.

He nodded to a sleepy maid before trekking to the stables to pick up the greyhounds. Both pushed their soft, silky heads into his palms while Percy yipped and ran a wide circle around them, skittering on the dew-damp cobblestones. Greetings done, they headed for the woods.

The sun was just rising, its pale rays lighting the leaves. It would be a beautiful day, perfect for the afternoon picnic and frivolities. Yesterday had been a success, if he judged rightly, in his planned courtship of Lady Penelope. She'd hung on his arm and giggled—sometimes at the oddest moments—and seemed altogether enthralled. If her enchantment was for his title and money rather than for his person, well, that was how it was naturally done at their rank and to be expected. The thought shouldn't bring a darkening of his mood.

Percy flushed a hare and the dogs were off, crashing

through the underbrush with all the subtlety of a regiment of soldiers. Two birds were startled by the chase and he looked up, watching their flight.

And then he was aware that he was no longer alone.

His heart certainly did *not* leap at her presence.

"Good morning, Your Grace." Miss Greaves was bareheaded, wearing her usual mud-brown costume. Her cheeks were pink from her morning walk, her lips a deep rose.

He glanced down and saw with irritation that her feet were bare again. "You ought to wear shoes in these woods. You could cut your feet."

Her lips curved in that not-smile and his irritation grew. Everyone else leaped to comply with his wishes, but not her.

Percy ran up, flush with the excitement of his hunt, and made to jump up on her.

"Down," Miss Greaves calmly commanded, and the spaniel nearly tripped over his own filthy paws to obey.

Maximus sighed.

"Did you catch that poor bunny?" she murmured sweetly to Percy as he wriggled madly with delight. "Did you tear it to shreds?"

Maximus's brows rose. "You voice a bloody sentiment for a lady, Miss Greaves."

She shrugged. "I doubt he could ever catch a rabbit, Your Grace. Besides"—she added as she straightened—"I *am* named for the goddess of the hunt."

He looked at her oddly. She was in a strange mood this morning. She'd never been deferential to him, but today she seemed almost confrontational.

The greyhounds returned, panting, along with Lady

Penelope's white lapdog, and all three greeted Miss Greaves.

He glanced at Miss Greaves in questions and she shrugged. "Bon Bon seems to like the morning rambles, and I know he loves your Percy. It's almost as if he's found a second life."

She started forward. Starling, Bon Bon, and Percy ranged into the woods, but Belle fell into step with them, nosing along the path. They walked together wordlessly in what might be deemed a companionable silence if it weren't for the tense set of her shoulders.

Maximus glanced at her sideways. "I take it your parents were of a classical mind?"

"My mother." She nodded. "Artemis and Apollo. The Olympian twins."

"Ah."

She took a deep breath, her inhalation making the bodice of her dress expand distractingly. "My brother was committed to Bedlam four years ago."

"Yes, I know."

He caught her look and didn't much like the cynical tilt of her lips. "Of course you do. Tell me, Your Grace, do you have *all* the ladies you're interested in investigated before you decided to court them?"

"Yes." There was no point in denying it. "I owe it to my title to ensure I marry the best lady possible."

She hummed noncommittally in response, which irritated him. "Your brother killed three men in a crazed, drunken rage."

She stiffened. "I'm surprised that you wish to continue courting Penelope, if you know about it. Madness is said to run in families."

It was obviously a sore point with her. Still, she proudly wore a goddess's name. One didn't coddle such as she. "Your line isn't directly connected to Lady Penelope's. Besides, murder doesn't necessarily mean madness. If your brother hadn't been the grandson of an earl, he'd have been hanged instead of committed to a hospital for the insane. No doubt it was better for all concerned—rather a member of the nobility be mad than executed."

He was watching her so he saw the pained grimace cross her face before she schooled her expression. "You're right. The scandal was awful. I'm sure it was the final straw that killed my mother. For weeks we thought he might be arrested and executed. If it weren't for Penelope's father…"

They'd come to the clearing and she stopped, turning toward him. He had an odd impulse to take her into his arms. To tell her that he'd keep the world and all its gossips at bay.

But she squared her shoulders, looking at him frankly and without fear. Perhaps she didn't need a champion. Perhaps she was well enough without him. "He isn't mad, you know, and he didn't kill those men."

He watched her. The loved ones of monsters were sometimes blind to their sins. No point in saying that fact aloud.

She inhaled. "You could get him out."

He raised his brows. "I'm a duke, not the king."

"You could," she said stubbornly. "You could free him."

He looked away, sighing. "Even if I were wont to do so, I do not think I would. Your brother was judged insane,

Miss Greaves, though I'm sure it hurts you to admit it. He was found with the bodies of three men, terribly murdered. Surely—"

"*He didn't do it.*" She was directly in front of him, one small palm placed on his chest, and though he knew it wasn't so, he seemed to feel the heat of her skin burning through his clothes. "Don't you understand? Apollo is innocent. He's been locked away in that hellish place for four years and he will never get out. You must help him. You must—"

"No," he said as gently as he was able, "I do not *have* to do anything."

For a moment her mask fell and her emotions showed through, devastating and real: rage, hurt, and a grief so deep it rivaled his own.

Stunned, he opened his mouth to speak.

But before he could, she struck, as precisely and mercilessly as her namesake.

"You *do* have to save my brother," she said, "because if you do not I will tell everyone in England that you are the Ghost of St. Giles."

ARTEMIS HELD HER breath. She'd dared to slip a bridle over a tiger's head and now she waited to see if he'd do her bidding or bat her aside with one powerful paw.

The Duke of Wakefield stood very still, his sable eyes slowly narrowing on her and she was reminded that, save for the king, this was possibly the most powerful man in England.

At last he spoke. "I think not."

Her lips firmed. "You believe I won't do it?"

"Oh, I believe that you're quite capable of such perfidy,

Miss Greaves," he said silkily as he turned to continue his walk.

She swallowed. It had been a shared walk, but it no longer seemed like one.

Heat rose in her cheeks. "My loyalty lies with my brother."

"I did save your life in St. Giles," he reminded her.

She remembered that lithe grace, the deadly skill with his swords, and she remembered the final salute he'd given her before she'd mounted the carriage. She was now certain that he'd made sure to see her to safety.

None of that mattered. "He is my *brother* and his life is at stake. I will not feel guilt."

He spared her a dismissive glance. "Nor do I expect you to, madam. I merely state the facts. No insult is intended. I believe you to be a worthy opponent."

"But?"

He sighed and stopped to face her as if dealing with a particularly trying maidservant. "I think you have not bothered to ascertain what type of opponent *I* am. I have no intention of bowing to blackmail."

She inhaled, reluctantly admiring. If she wasn't fighting for Apollo she might have conceded the field to him, for this *was* blackmail and hardly very fair.

But then again, she was no gentleman, raised on the traditions of honor. She had been a lady—a person often deemed by men such as he to have not enough intelligence to understand complicated male concepts such as honor. And now? Now she was a woman hardened by the capriciousness of fate.

This was her life. This was where the tides of fortune had landed her. She had no time or use for honor.

Artemis raised her chin. "You don't think I'll tell everyone your secret?"

"I don't think you would dare." He looked so *alone*, standing here in the merciless morning sunshine. "But even if you do so, Miss Greaves, I doubt very much that anyone will believe you."

She sucked in her breath, feeling the blow before it had been dealt, but still his voice continued, chill and uncaring.

"You are, after all, the sister of a madman and the daughter of a gentleman known for his lunatic behavior. I believe if you attempt to tell anyone my secret, you stand a very good chance of being incarcerated in Bedlam yourself." He bowed precisely, icily, every inch the impenetrable aristocrat as he threatened her with her most nightmarish fear. Had he ever let anyone past those walls? Did he even wish for the warmth of human contact? "Good day, Miss Greaves. I trust the rest of your stay at Pelham House will be satisfactory."

He turned and walked away from her.

Belle and Starling followed without a glance, but Percy stood a moment looking between Artemis and his master, hesitating.

"Go on," she muttered to the dog, and with a low whine he trailed after the duke.

Bon Bon whimpered and leaned against her ankles. The morning was suddenly cold again. Artemis curled her bare toes into the loam of the woods, watching Wakefield's arrogant back as he left her. He didn't *know* her. He was just another man under all those layers of wealth and power and solitary indifference. Just another obstacle to Apollo's freedom. There was no reason to feel as if she'd broken something very new.

And he was wrong: she *did* dare. There was literally nothing she wouldn't do for her brother.

THAT AFTERNOON THE sun shone brightly on the green on the south side of Pelham House. Maximus knew he was supposed to be enjoying the day and, more important, the lady he was wooing, but all he could think about was the infuriating Miss Greaves. To actually attempt to blackmail him—*him*, the Duke of Wakefield—was entirely beyond the pale. How she thought he might be so *weak* was a source of scorn, rage, and bewilderment within him. There was another emotion lurking there, deep inside, something perilously close to hurt—but he had no desire to examine *that* further, so he concentrated upon the rage. He'd make sure to impress upon the wench his displeasure with her actions if only she weren't being so completely childish as to ignore him all morning.

Not that her studied disregard bothered him in the slightest.

"You'll think me a braggart, Your Grace, but I vow I'm a fair hand with a bow," Lady Penelope chirped beside him.

"Indeed?" Maximus murmured absently.

Miss Greaves drifted behind them, silent as a wraith. He had the most persistent urge to turn and confront her—make her say something to him. Instead, of course, he sedately led Lady Penelope toward where footmen and maids milled about with the accoutrements of archery. Opposite, across the green, three large wooden targets had been set up, not *too* far away, for the ladies were to have their turn today demonstrating what skills they might have in archery. The gentlemen were expected to observe and praise—whether the archer deserved it or not, of course, for a lady's vanity was a fragile thing.

Maximus stifled an impatient sigh. This sort of thing—the silly games, the entire house party, come to that—was expected of him, not only for courting a lady such as Lady Penelope, but also in the regular way of things because of his rank, his social standing, and his position in Parliament, but there were times such as this when the whole thing rankled. He could be in a London coffeehouse right now, urging another member of Parliament to enact better legislation against the sale of gin. He could be in St. Giles, following any number of leads into the deaths of his parents. Damn it, for that matter he could be with his secretary managing his estates—not his favorite work, but important nonetheless.

Instead he was strolling a green like a veritable fop with a rather silly girl on his arm.

"Do you practice archery, Miss Greaves?" he found himself asking, quite out of the blue. The sunshine had probably gone to his head.

"Oh, no," Lady Penelope exclaimed before her cousin could answer. "Artemis doesn't shoot. She hasn't time for such pursuits."

Why not? he wanted to ask. Surely Miss Greaves's station as Lady Penelope's companion didn't preclude hobbies of her own—even silly ones like ladies' archery? Except it might very well do. Her position was a sort of genteel modern-day slavery, reserved solely for the most vulnerable of the gentler sex—those without family of their own. Lady Penelope could keep Miss Greaves busy from morning to night if she chose, and Miss Greaves would be expected to be grateful for the servitude.

The thought made his mood darker.

"I also enjoy riding, sketching, dancing, and singing," Lady Penelope prattled on. She tapped his sleeve with one flirtatious finger. "Perhaps I can demonstrate my voice for you—and the other guests—this evening, Your Grace?"

"I would be delighted," he replied automatically.

Behind them he heard a slight choking sound. He turned his head and glanced back to see Miss Greaves with her lips twitching. He had a sudden suspicion regarding Lady Penelope's supposedly lovely singing voice.

"Oh, look, the Duke of Scarborough is helping with the targets," Lady Penelope continued. "He told me last night that he likes to hold an annual contest at his country estate for athletics such as running and archery, so I suppose he's quite the expert. No doubt that's why he's so skilled at fencing as well." She seemed to realize her comments weren't the most politic and sent an annoyingly sympathetic glance his way. "Of course, not everyone has the time to practice fencing or indeed any other athletic endeavor."

The slight gasp that came from behind them most definitely sounded like a choked-off laugh this time.

"Oh, I'm sure His Grace has other, more cerebral skills," came Miss Greaves's voice in suspiciously dulcet tones.

Lady Penelope looked as if she were deciphering the word *cerebral*.

"I spend a great deal of time in Parliament," he replied in what even to his own ears sounded like a damnably pompous tone. "I'm glad to see that you've regained your voice, Miss Greaves."

"I never lost it, I do assure you, Your Grace," Miss Greaves responded sweetly. "But are we to understand that you don't practice fencing at all? If so, your performance yesterday—at least at the beginning of your duel with the Duke of Scarborough—must be a veritable miracle. I vow, if I didn't know better, I'd think you fought with a sword nearly every night."

He turned slowly on her. What was she about now?

Miss Greaves met his gaze, her own face serene, but there was a wicked gleam at the back of her eyes that made a chill run up his spine.

"I haven't the faintest idea what you're talking about, Artemis," Lady Penelope said plaintively after a rather awkward beat.

"May I help you don your arm guard, Lady Penelope?" Scarborough asked behind Maximus.

Maximus cursed under his breath. He hadn't noticed the ass sidling over.

Miss Greaves tutted. "I'm quite shocked by such language from a distinguished parliamentarian, Your Grace."

"I'm sure that you are anything but shocked, Miss Greaves," he snapped without thinking.

The corner of her lush mouth quirked in her not-smile, and he had a black urge to take her hand and pull her into the copse. To plunder that enticing mouth until she either smiled frankly or cried aloud in pleasure.

He blinked the erotic image away. What was he thinking? This was the gray little companion of the woman he meant to *marry*—and a blackmailer to boot. He shouldn't be feeling anything for her save revulsion.

But *revulsion* was not the word that came to mind when she leaned a little closer, ridiculously attractive in her dowdy brown frock, and whispered, "You'd better move quickly, Your Grace, or Scarborough will snatch Lady Penelope out from under your nose. He *is* the more dashing duelist, after all."

And she sauntered over to stand by Phoebe before he could make a suitable retort.

Maximus scowled and glanced at the ladies readying to shoot. Scarborough had somehow managed to position himself behind Lady Penelope, and with both arms wrapped about her, was tying on her arm guard. Maximus wanted to roll his eyes. Really, why fight for a lady so silly as to fall for such an obvious ploy?

Because it was for the dukedom.

He squared his shoulders and marched toward the couple. "If I might?" Ignoring both Scarborough's frown and Lady Penelope's sly smile, he swiftly and competently tied the arm guard on her arm. Stepping back, he couldn't help but glance to where Miss Greaves and Phoebe stood.

Miss Greaves gave a mocking salute.

He scowled and turned back to make sure his other guests were prepared to shoot.

"We gentlemen assume the role of audience today," Scarborough said jovially as they stepped aside.

Maximus drifted toward Phoebe and Miss Greaves as Lady Noakes took up her bow.

"Hiding in the back row, Your Grace?" Miss Greaves murmured as he drew near.

Lady Noakes shot her arrow.

"Oh, dear," Miss Greaves said.

"It went wide, didn't it?" Phoebe said.

"Nearly hit Johnny," Maximus said grimly.

"Your footman jumped rather nimbly," Miss Greaves mused. "Almost as if he'd been given lessons by the Ghost of St. Giles."

Maximus shot a narrow-eyed look at her.

She smiled—*really* smiled, teeth and all—back. And despite the circumstances—her blackmail, the people all around them, his anger—he caught his breath in admiration. When Miss Greaves smiled her entire face lit and became utterly beautiful.

Maximus looked away, swallowing.

Phoebe giggled. "I can see why you sought refuge back here with us, dear brother. Self-preservation is the better part of valor, I think."

They watched in silence as both Mrs. Jellett and Lady Oddershaw shot rather wildly, though Mrs. Jellett's arrow found the target through some fluke of the wind that seemed to surprise even her.

Maximus cleared his throat, loath to admit either his own cowardliness or his guests' lack of talent with a bow and arrow. "Lady Penelope has a fine form." The lady was angling herself as she drew her string back.

"Oh, indeed," Miss Greaves said earnestly. "She practices on her form quite often."

They watched in silence as Lady Penelope's arrow hit the rim of the target and bounced off.

"Her *aim* is another matter, of course," Miss Greaves murmured.

Maximus winced as Johnny crept cautiously into the field to retrieve the arrows shot so far. The footman was a braver man than he.

"She's going for another shot," Scarborough said, and indeed Lady Penelope had assumed her archer's stance again. She made a very fine figure, he noticed dispassionately: the cherry-red ribbons twined in her ebony locks fluttered in the wind, and her profile was almost Grecian.

She shot and all three footmen threw themselves prone to the ground.

"Oh, well done, my lady!" Scarborough shouted, for Lady Penelope's arrow had hit the outer blue circle of the target.

The lady beamed in pride and stepped back graciously for Miss Royale's turn.

The footmen looked besieged.

Miss Royale took up her bow and called to the footmen. "Best stand back. I've never done this before."

"Never practiced archery?" Phoebe murmured.

"Grew up in India." Mrs. Jellett had come to stand near them as she waited her next turn. "Heathen place. No doubt that explains her dark complexion."

Miss Royale's first two shots went wide, but she managed to hit the outer ring with her third one. She stepped back looking quite pleased with herself.

Fortunately, the remainder of the archery demonstration proceeded without incident, and although none of the ladies hit the inner red circle of the targets, neither did they maim one of his footmen, so, as Phoebe put it, "The afternoon must count as a victory."

Maximus held out his elbow to Lady Penelope to lead her inside for refreshments. As they walked he bent to listen attentively as she recounted her exceptional success at shooting. He murmured praise and encouragement at the appropriate moments, but all the while he was aware that Miss Greaves had lingered behind at the archery field.

"Oh, I've left my gloves behind," Lady Penelope exclaimed as they entered the Yellow Salon. The other guests were already taking seats.

"I'll go fetch them for you," Maximus said, for once trumping Scarborough.

He bowed and left before the lady—or the duke—could comment.

The halls were deserted as he strode toward the south doors. All the guests were in his Yellow Salon, and the servants were naturally in attendance there as well.

All the guests save one.

He saw her as he slipped out the south doors. She stood in profile across the green, her back straight, her stance that of some long ago warrior maiden. As he walked toward her, Miss Greaves drew back her bow briskly, aiming a tad high to account for the wind, and let her arrow fly. Before it had hit the target, she'd notched another and shot it. A third followed just as rapidly.

He glanced to the target. All three of her arrows were clustered together at the center of the red circle. Miss Greaves, who "did not shoot," was a better shot than all the other ladies—and probably the men as well.

He glanced from the target to her and saw that she stared back, proud and unsmiling. *Artemis.* She was named for the goddess of the hunt—a goddess who had slain without remorse her only admirer.

Something quickened in him, rising, hardening, reaching eagerly for the challenge. She was no soft society lady. She might disguise herself thus, but he knew better: she was a goddess, wild and free and dangerous.

And a most suitable opponent.

He picked up Lady Penelope's gloves and, unsmiling,

saluted Miss Greaves with them. She bowed to him, equally grave.

Maximus turned to the house, thinking. He had no idea how he would do it yet, but he meant to best her. He'd show her that he was the master, and when she'd admitted his victory . . . well, then he'd have her. And he'd hold her, by God. His huntress.

His goddess.

Chapter Seven

*If the Herla King's wedding had been grand, the
Dwarf King's nuptials were magnificent. For seven
days and seven nights there was feasting and dancing
and storytelling. The cavern sparkled with gold and
jewels, for a dwarf has a deep and abiding love of the
treasures that come from the earth. So when King Herla
at last presented his wedding gift there was a roar of
approval from the dwarf citizens: he offered a golden
chest, twice the size of a man's fist, spilling over with
sparkling diamonds....*
—from *The Legend of the Herla King*

"And his eyes glowed with a red fire as if he'd newly come
from Hell itself." Penelope shivered dramatically at her
own tale

Artemis, listening to the story of their encounter with
the Ghost of St. Giles for what seemed like the hundredth
time, leaned closer to Phoebe and murmured in her ear,
"Or as if he had a slight infection of the eye."

The younger woman clapped her hand to her mouth to
stifle a giggle.

"Would that I had been there to protect you from such
a fiend," the Duke of Scarborough exclaimed.

The gentlemen had just joined the ladies in the Yellow Salon after dinner, and the guests were scattered about the room. The ladies mostly lounged on the elegantly carved chairs and settees while the gentlemen stood. Scarborough had immediately crossed to Penelope and latched on to her side upon entering, while Wakefield was prowling about the perimeter of the room. Artemis wondered what his game was. Surely he should be waiting attendance on her cousin? Instead, when she looked over, his brooding gaze caught hers.

She shivered. He'd been somehow more *intent* since her little show of archery this afternoon. Perhaps that had been hubris on her part, but she'd been unable to pass up the opportunity. She wasn't another London society lady. She'd grown up in the country, had spent long days wandering woods, and she knew how to hunt. True, her game had always been birds and the odd squirrel before—not predatory dukes—but the principle was the same, surely? She would stalk him, *goad* him, until he had no choice but to save her brother. It was a delicate maneuver: she wanted to suggest she was quite ready to reveal him, but at the same time if she actually gave away his identity as the Ghost of St. Giles, she lost all her leverage. A fine game indeed, but at least she'd accomplished the first movement:

She had his attention.

"That's quite brave of you, Your Grace," Artemis said, raising her voice as she turned to the Duke of Scarborough, "offering to fight the Ghost of St. Giles. For I noted at the time that the Ghost was a rather large man. Why, he was almost exactly the same height as—" She glanced about the assembled party as if searching for a gentleman of suitable height. When her eyes landed on Wakefield, he already had a wry expression. "Why, our host, the Duke of Wakefield, in fact."

There was a fraught pause as Artemis held Wakefield's narrowed gaze, before it was broken rather prosaically by Penelope. "Don't be silly, Artemis. The Ghost was at least a foot taller than His Grace. Although I'm quite sure the Duke of Scarborough would have been able to defeat him."

The last was a lie so obvious that Artemis didn't even bother rolling her eyes.

"Certainly, His Grace would've been of better help than my brother," Phoebe said, uncaring of her treachery.

"Phoebe," Wakefield growled low in warning.

"Yes, brother dear?" Phoebe turned her blithely bright face to the duke, who was lurking like a tiger with indigestion in the corner. "You must admit that you did not show well with Scarborough yesterday."

"His Grace, the Duke of Scarborough, obviously has many more years than I practicing his fencing." Wakefield bowed to the other duke so gracefully that Artemis wondered if he'd really meant the insult to Scarborough's age. "And you, brat, should show more respect to your elders."

The teasing tone caught Artemis off guard. He truly did care for his sister, she reminded herself. He might be overprotective, but he loved Phoebe. The thought unsettled her. She was blackmailing this man. She didn't want to think about the softer, more human parts of him.

She girded her loins and readied another salvo. "Did you really find the Ghost so monstrously tall? Truly, I thought he had the height and the physical bearing of

His Grace. Indeed, were the duke a better swordsman, it might've been he we met in St. Giles."

"But whyever would His Grace traipse about St. Giles?" Penelope asked in honest confusion. "Only ruffians and the poor go there."

"Well, we were there, weren't we?" Artemis retorted.

Penelope waved a dismissive hand. "That's different. I was on a grand adventure."

"Which nearly got you both killed, by the sound of it," Phoebe whispered in Artemis's ear.

"Come, my lady," Scarborough said jovially. "Enough of this talk of scoundrels. You promised to sing for us, I remember. Will you do it now?"

"Oh, yes." Penelope immediately brightened at the prospect of being at the center of attention. "I just need an accompanist."

"I can play," Phoebe said, "if I know the piece you'll be singing."

Artemis helped her navigate across the room to the clavichord.

"What would you like to perform?" Phoebe asked as she settled gracefully at her instrument.

Penelope smiled. "Do you know 'The Shepherdess's Lament?'"

Artemis stifled a sigh and found a seat. Penelope had a very small repertoire that consisted of rather sentimental and treacly songs.

Wakefield lowered himself beside her and she couldn't help but stiffen a little.

"A miss, I think," he murmured out of the side of his mouth as they watched Penelope tilt her chin very high and extend one hand. "You can do much better than that."

"Are you challenging me, Your Grace?"

A corner of his mouth curled up, though he didn't look at her. "Only a fool would provoke his nemesis. What in hell is she doing?"

Artemis glanced back to the musician and singer. Penelope had laid one hand on her stomach, her other still extended unnaturally, and assumed a tragic look. "That's her performing stance, Your Grace. I'm sure you'll become quite accustomed to it when you marry my cousin."

The duke winced. "Touché."

Phoebe began playing with a skill and dash beyond her years.

Artemis raised her brows in delight, whispering to the duke, "Your sister is a wonderful player."

"That she is," he said softly.

And then Penelope sang. It wasn't that she was a *bad* songstress, per se, but her soprano voice was thin and on certain notes, quite sharp.

Then, too, the piece she'd chosen was unfortunate.

" 'Venture not to pet my woolly lamb,' " Penelope warbled, not quite hitting the right note on "lamb." " 'For she is shy and too gentle for a man's wicked hand.' "

"Do you know," Mrs. Jellett said thoughtfully from behind them, "I do believe this song may have a double meaning."

Artemis caught the duke's sardonic gaze and felt the heat rise in her cheeks.

"Behave, Miss Greaves," he murmured under his breath, his voice husky and deep.

"Fine words for a man who runs about St. Giles at night in a mask," she whispered.

He frowned, glancing around. "Hush."

She arched one eyebrow. "Why?"

The look he gave her was somehow disappointed. "That's the way of it, then?"

There was absolutely no reason to feel shame. Artemis lifted her chin. "Yes. Unless you wish to do as I asked you this morn?"

"You know that's impossible." He stared at Penelope and Phoebe, though she certainly hoped he wasn't paying attention to them since his upper lip was lifted in a curl of disdain. "Your brother killed three men."

"No," she said, leaning a little closer to him so that their words would not be overheard. She could smell the woods on him, incongruous in this overly ornamented room. "He was *accused* of killing three men. He didn't do it."

His face softened then in an expression she'd seen before—seen and loathed. "Your loyalty to your brother is to be commended, but the evidence was quite damning. He had blood on his person and the carving knife in his hand when found."

She sat back, eyeing him. The blood part was well known as was the knife—but that it had been a *carving* knife was not. "I see your investigations were quite detailed."

"Naturally. Did you think they would be otherwise?" He finally turned to look at her, and his face was hard and cold, as if they'd never wandered together at early dawn in a secluded wood. "Perhaps you ought to remember, Miss Greaves, that I make it my business to obtain what I set my sights on."

She couldn't very well get up and leave him without causing a scene, but she dearly wanted to. "Well, then, in the interests of fairness, perhaps *you* ought to know, Your Grace, that I have no intention of yielding the field to you."

Beside her he inclined his head a fraction of an inch. "Then en garde, Miss Greaves."

Fortunately at that moment the end of Penelope's ballad was signaled by a long, rather screeching, drawn-out high note that so stunned the audience it was a moment before anyone started clapping.

"How lovely," Artemis said loudly. "Perhaps an encore—"

"Oh, but my brother has such a wonderful voice," Phoebe interrupted, shooting Artemis an incredulous glance. "Will you sing for us, Maximus?"

Penelope looked a bit sulky at having the light taken away from her.

"No one needs to hear me," Wakefield demurred.

"I do like a sweet feminine voice better than a deep masculine one," Scarborough said.

Wakefield's eyes narrowed. "Perhaps a duet. I believe Phoebe knows several of the songs on the sheet music in the cabinet."

He stood and went to a tall, intricately carved cabinet and started drawing out music, reading each title aloud as he did so Phoebe could choose the ones she knew by heart.

But when Maximus held out a song, Penelope sniffed and pointed out the female voice was for an alto and she sang only soprano.

For a moment there was a stir of alarm in the audience at the prospect of another solo by Penelope.

Then Phoebe piped up. "Well, then, I'll just have to take the lady's part. Really, it won't do to miss out on Maximus singing, now that he's agreed." And before the duke could escape she was beginning the opening bars on the clavichord.

Artemis clasped her hands together in her lap. No doubt Phoebe had wrangled her brother into singing merely to forestall another performance from Penelope. She had no expectations of any great talent, and by the restlessness of those about her, neither did anyone else. When this duet was over she meant to corner him and make—

The first notes rang out.

The masculine voice was low but clear, capturing the senses, running along the back of her neck like a caress, making her shiver in delight. Artemis very much feared she was gaping. The Duke of Wakefield had a voice to make angels—or devils—weep. It wasn't the type of male voice currently admired—for the high, unnatural voice of the musico was the rage of London at the moment—but his was the sort of voice that would always seduce the ear. Sure and strong, with a vibrating masculinity on the low notes. She could sit and listen to a voice like this for hours.

The Duke of Wakefield seemed unaware of the stir his singing made in his guests. He leaned casually over Phoebe as he read the music he held in one hand, the other placed affectionately on her shoulder. And when they negotiated a particularly intricate passage together, he caught the grin Phoebe threw at him and smiled in return. Naturally, unself-consciously.

Almost joyfully.

If he'd never been the Duke of Wakefield, was this how he would have been? A strong man without coldness or the driving need to dominate and control? Loving and *happy*?

The thought of such a man was strangely alluring, but

even as she considered this phantom being, she caught the duke's gaze and knew: it was the man as he was now—*flawed* as he was now—that she longed for. She wanted to clash with his dominating nature, wanted to run with him in the forest, wanted to challenge him, mentally and physically, to games of their own making.

And the coldness?

Staring into his autocratic eyes, Artemis wished with all her heart. If she could, she'd take his coldness and make it her own.

Transform it into a heat to engulf them both.

APOLLO LAY IN his filthy straw and listened to the boot heels of the approaching guards. It was too late for them to be making the rounds. The inmates of this dismal place had already been served a delicate meal of moldy bread and brackish water. The lights had been dimmed. There was no earthly reason for the guards to be here save in the name of mischief.

He sighed, his chains clinking as he shifted, trying to find a more comfortable position. A new inmate had been brought in yesterday, a young woman, he thought. Due to the construction of the cells, he couldn't see any of his neighbors, except for the cell across the way from his own. That was occupied by a man whose diseased skin bore a striking resemblance to lichen on a rock.

Last night the new female inmate had sung well into the wee hours, the words of her song quite vulgar, yet her voice had been beautiful and somehow lost. Whether she was truly mad or simply the victim of relatives or a husband grown tired of her, he had no idea.

Not that it mattered here.

Light glowed in the corridor and the boot heels stopped.

"Ave ye something for me, pretty?" It was Ridley, a man both muscled and mean.

"Give us a kiss, then." And that was Leech, Ridley's favored henchman.

The woman moaned, low and hurt. Whatever they intended for her was probably quite grim. A chain rattled, as if she were trying to scurry out of their reach.

"Oi!" Apollo shouted. "Oi, Ridley!"

"Shut it, Kilbourne," the guard yelled. He sounded distracted.

"You've hurt my feelings, Ridley," Apollo shot back. "Why don't you come over here to kiss it better?"

No reply this time, save for a sob from the woman. There was the sound of rending cloth.

Damn it.

Once upon a time Apollo had thought himself a man of the world. A gentleman inured to the black sin that lurked in the depths of London. He'd drank and gambled and even purchased the favors of pretty women once in a while, for such were the pursuits of boys fresh from university and full of themselves. He'd been so innocent. So *naïve*. Then he'd come to Bedlam and found what true venality was. Here things that called themselves men preyed upon those weaker than they solely for the sport of it. Solely to laugh in the despairing faces of their victims.

He'd lain through too many nights unable to do anything about it.

But perhaps today he could divert the jackals from their chosen prey.

"Oi, Leech, are you sucking upon Ridley's prick for

him?" Apollo made rude smacking sounds with his lips, leaning as far forward as his chains allowed. "That's what you get up to when you're lazing about instead of working, isn't it? Do you like drinking his spunk? Bet he can't get enough of your pretty tongue, Leech."

"Shut his lordship's mouth for him," Ridley growled.

On cue Leech's stubby form appeared at the mouth to Apollo's cave, holding a short cudgel over his shoulder.

Apollo grinned and crossed his legs, as if lounging at some society lady's salon instead of laying on reeking filth. "A good day to you, Mr. Leech. How kind of you to stop by. Will you be taking tea with me? Or is chocolate to your better liking?"

Leech growled. He wasn't much for words, was Leech. Ridley had a tendency to do his talking for him. But Leech did have a sort of low intelligence, belied by his short, sloping brow. He didn't bother coming close to Apollo, but stayed just out of the chain's reach as he swung the cudgel viciously at Apollo's legs.

There were rumors among the inmates that Leech's cudgel had broken arms and even legs, but Apollo was more than ready. He pulled back his legs at the last minute and laughed up at Leech.

"Oh, no, no. That's not how we play nicely."

The wonderful thing about Leech was that he could be depended on. He made two more abortive swings before growing enraged and charging. Apollo caught a blow on his right arm that numbed it to the shoulder, but he was able to kick the cudgel from Leech's arm.

The guard leaped back, scowling as he nursed his hand.

The woman was moaning now, steady and awful. The

hair stood up on the back of Apollo's arms at the hurt animal sound.

"Rid-ley, oh, darling Rid-ley!" Apollo sang through gritted teeth. "Leech is sulking. Come out, come out and play with me, sweet Rid-ley!"

A foul curse came from the next cell.

"Rid-ley! We all know how tiny your prick is—can't you find it without Leech's help?"

That did it. Heavy boots stomping down the hall heralded Ridley's approach and then the big man loomed into view, his breeches only half-buttoned. Ridley was six feet of pure nastiness: broad, heavy shoulders, thick arms, and a boulder of a head squatting between. The guard's lip curled in what passed for a smile, and then Apollo realized his mistake, for behind him lurked a third man. Tyne wasn't nearly as big as Ridley—few men were—but he could be just as vicious given the chance.

Tyne and Leech spread out, circling to attack him from his sides, while Ridley smirked, waiting for his cohorts to position themselves.

Well, that wouldn't do.

"Now gentlemen," Apollo drawled, standing slowly, "you know I haven't made myself presentable. I'm not used to so many visitors this late at night. Ridley, why not send your cronies away and you and I can settle this over a nice cup of tea."

Both Tyne and Leech attacked at the same time. Tyne aimed a blow at his head from the left while Leech ducked in and went for his middle from the right. Apollo caught Tyne's fist on his upraised left arm. His right was still not working properly, but he was able to elbow Leech in the face, sending the smaller man flying into the wall.

Apollo half-turned to Tyne and backhanded the man with his left fist. Tyne staggered but remained upright, and Apollo was just about to follow with a kick when he realized his peril.

He'd lost track of Ridley.

His feet were yanked out from under him. Apollo's head smacked the stone floor and for a moment he knew nothing but ringing light. When next he looked up, he saw Ridley, still holding the chains that bound his feet.

Leech staggered over, hand cupped over his bleeding nose, and kicked Apollo in the face. Apollo raised an arm—moving far too slowly, something was wrong—but Leech kicked him again, this time in the ribs. There was pain, but it was muffled somehow, and that should be causing him alarm, he knew. Apollo tried to curl into himself, protect his vulnerable middle, but Ridley yanked on the chains again, pulling his legs straight. Leech had his cudgel now, and was lifting it—

Ridley grinned, his hands fumbling at the half-opened falls to his breeches. "We'll shut your mouth good and proper this time."

No.

True fear sparked at the back of Apollo's mind and he lurched up, butting his head into Ridley's middle. The guard fell on his arse, yelling. Apollo thrashed, kicking, hitting anything he could connect with.

Something slammed into his head.

He glared blearily up. Leech's goddamned cudgel. He'd take the thing away and beat the guard with his own weapon, by God.

Tyne stepped on his throat. Apollo's lungs heaved. Once. Twice.

No air.
Thrice...
Blackness descended.

THE MORNING SUN dappled the forest floor beneath his feet as Maximus tramped along the next day. He'd risen early, restless without his usual exercises in the London cellar. His work was in the city and he had an itch to return to it.

Courting a woman for marriage was a trying business.

Belle bumped her head under his palm as if in sympathy. Percy and Starling had already ranged ahead, but Belle liked to stay by his side.

Well, usually, anyway.

Her narrow ears suddenly perked and she was off, bounding gracefully through the underbrush. He could hear the other dogs yipping in greeting.

Ridiculously, he thought he could feel his heart beat faster. Despite their antagonism, despite her threats to his equilibrium, he wanted to see her, and right now he wouldn't examine why.

In another few steps he made the clearing with the pond and looked about. He could see the dogs milling a quarter way around the pond—even Bon Bon was there—but he couldn't yet see *her* on the path.

And then he did see her and arousal went straight to his cock.

Artemis Greaves was in the pond, as graceful as a naiad, her skirts bound up at her waist, standing thigh deep in the sparkling water.

How dare she.

He strode swiftly around the pond to stand at the shore nearest to where she was wading. "Miss Greaves."

She glanced at him and if anything looked displeased to see him. "Your Grace."

"What," he said softly but dangerously, "are you doing in the pond?"

"I would have thought that obvious," she murmured as she began moving toward the shore. "I'm wading."

He gritted his teeth. The closer she came to shore the more milky white leg emerged from the water. It was soon apparent that she was bare from just below the juncture of her thighs all the way to her narrow feet. Her skin glistened in the morning sun, pale and vulnerable, wholly, *terribly* erotic.

As a gentleman he should look away.

But damn it, it was *his* pond.

"*Anyone* could happen upon you," he hissed, aware at the back of his mind that he sounded like a prudish old woman.

"Do you really think so?" she asked, finally reaching the shore and stepping onto the mossy bank of the pond. "I doubt most of your guests usually rise before nine of the clock at the earliest. Penelope hardly ever emerges from her rooms before noon."

She stood there, head cocked, as if she truly wanted to debate the morning habits of his guests. She'd made no move to lower her skirts. He watched a bead of water slide slickly down one rounded thigh, over the pretty contours of her knee, faster down the smooth slope of her calf to drip off one delicate anklebone.

He snapped his gaze up to her face.

She still looked merely curious, as if standing half nude in front of him was a completely acceptable way to start the day.

Good God, did she think him a eunuch?

He wanted to shake her, to scold her until she hung her head in shame. He wanted to—

"*Put down your skirts*," he growled. "If this is your way of provoking me because of our disagreement, I'll have you know it won't work."

"That wasn't my intent," she said calmly. "As I told you, I was simply wading for no other reason but the enjoyment of it. However, I do think you incorrect."

"I…" He couldn't follow her with her legs so alluringly exposed. "What?"

"What makes you think I can't provoke you?" She arched an eyebrow and untied the knot that held her skirts up. They fell, shrouding her gorgeous legs to the ankle, and that *did not annoy him at all*.

"You're not to go wading in my pond again," he said.

She shrugged and picked up her shoes and stockings where they lay on the path. "Very well, Your Grace, but it's a great pity. I should've liked to go swimming."

She pivoted and glided up the path, bewitching bare ankles flashing under her skirts, leaving Maximus to imagine her swimming in his pond, gloriously nude.

All. That. White. Flesh.

For a second his mind seemed to stutter.

When he looked up again, she and the dogs were nearly into the woods again, her bottom swaying enticingly. He actually had to *trot* to catch up.

He glanced sideways at her when he did and saw her lips pressed firmly together.

"You know how to swim?"

For a moment he thought she wouldn't deign to answer. Then she sighed. "Yes. Apollo and I were allowed to run mostly wild as children. There was a little pond on a neighboring farmer's land. We'd sneak over there and after some trial and error, we both learned to swim."

Maximus frowned. Craven's report had been very factual—the date of her birth, who her parents were, her relation to Lady Penelope—but he found there was more he'd like to know about Miss Greaves. It was always prudent to learn all one could about one's enemies.

"You didn't have a governess?"

She laughed softly, though it sounded sad. "We had three. They'd stay for months or even a year or so, and then Papa would run out of money and have to let them go. Somehow Apollo and I learned to read and write and do simple sums, but not much more than that. I have no French, can't play any instrument, never learned to draw."

"Your educational lack doesn't seem to bother you," he observed.

She shrugged. "Would it make a difference if I were bothered? I have some other skills not usually seen in ladies: swimming, as I told you, and how to shoot a gun. I can bargain down a butcher to within an inch of his life. I know how to make soap and how to put a bill collector off. I can do mending but not embroidery, can drive a cart but not ride a horse, know how to grow cabbages and carrots and even make them into a nice soup, but I haven't the least idea how to trellis roses."

Maximus's hands tightened into fists at his side at this recitation. No gentleman should let his delicately bred daughter grow to womanhood without the most basic instruction of her station.

"Yet you're the granddaughter of the Earl of Ashridge."

"Yes." Her voice was terse and he knew he'd stumbled on some tender spot.

"You never mention it aloud. Is your relationship a secret?"

"It's not." She wrinkled her nose and amended her statement. "At least on my part it isn't. My grandfather has never acknowledged me. Papa had a falling out with his father when he married Mama, and apparently stubbornness runs in the family."

Maximus grunted. "You said your grandfather never acknowledged you. Did he acknowledge your brother?"

"In his way." She strode along, the greyhounds at her side. It struck him that had she a bow at her back and a quiver of arrows, she could've posed for a painting of the goddess she'd been named for. "As Apollo was his future heir, apparently Grandfather thought it important he be properly educated. He paid for Apollo's schooling at Harrow. Apollo says he's even met Grandfather once or twice."

He sucked in a breath. "Your grandfather has never even *met* you?"

She shook her head. "Not to my knowledge."

He frowned. The idea of abandoning family was anathema to him. He couldn't conceive of doing it for any reason.

He looked at her closely, a thought striking him. "Did you try contacting him when...?"

"When my mother was dying and Apollo had been arrested and we were quite desperate?" She snorted. "Of course I did. He never replied to the letters I sent. If Mama hadn't written to her cousin, the Earl of Brightmore, I don't know what I would've done. We were penniless, Papa had been dead less than a year, Mama was on her deathbed, and Thomas called off our engagement. I would've been on the street."

He stopped short. "You were engaged."

She took two more strides before she realized that he was no longer beside her. She looked over her shoulder at him, that not-smile on the bow of her lips. "I've found a fact you didn't know about me?"

He nodded mutely. Why? Why hadn't he considered this? Four years ago she would've been four and twenty. *Of course* she'd had suitors.

"Well, I shouldn't feel too bad," she replied. "We hadn't announced it yet, which was a good thing: it made it so much easier for him to call it off discreetly without seeming like a cad."

Maximus glanced away so she couldn't examine too closely the expression on his face. "Who was he?"

"Thomas Stone. The son of the town's doctor."

He sneered. "Beneath you."

Her gaze hardened. "As you so kindly pointed out, my father was notorious for his flights of fancy. Too, I had no dowry to speak of. I couldn't very well be choosy. Besides"—her tone softened—"Thomas was quite sweet. He used to bring me daisies and violets."

He stared, incredulous. What sort of imbecile brought such common flowers to a goddess? Were it him, he'd shower her with hothouse lilies, peonies overflowing with perfumed bloom, roses in every shade.

Bah, *violets.*

He shook his head irritably. "But he stopped bringing those flowers, didn't he?"

"Yes." Her lips twisted. "As soon as the news of Apollo's arrest got out, in fact."

He stepped closer, watching her face for any minute signs, wanting to see what would break her. Had she fancied herself in love with the doctor's son? "I detect a trace of bitterness."

"He did say he loved me more than the sun," she said, her voice as dry and brittle as ashes.

"Ah." He looked up as they emerged from the woods at the brightly shining sun. The man had been an idiot and a cad, no matter if he'd managed to save his own good name. Besides. Anyone could see she was tied to the moon, not the sun. "Then I wish I had it in my power to make him live without the sun for the rest of his pitiful life."

She stopped and glanced at him. "That's a romantic thing to say."

He shook his head. "I'm not a romantic man, Miss Greaves. I don't say things that I don't mean. I find it a waste of time."

"Do you?" she looked at him oddly for a moment, then sighed and glanced toward the house. "We're no longer in the woods, are we? The day is about to begin."

He bowed. "Indeed it is. Don your helmet, Lady Moon."

She lifted her chin. "And you yours."

He nodded and strode away without looking back. But he couldn't help wishing it were different. That they could lay aside their armor and find a way to have the woods around them always.

A far too dangerous thought.

Chapter Eight

❧⸱❧

*The Dwarf King was very pleased with King Herla's
wedding present, and when at last the feasting ended and
his guests were leaving, he bid farewell to his friend with
the gift of a small, snow-white hound.*
*"I know your love of the hunt," said the Dwarf King. "With
this hunting dog in your saddle, your arrow will never miss
the quarry. But mind that you do not dismount before the
dog leaps down of its own accord. In this way you shall
always be safe." ...*
—from *The Legend of the Herla King*

Artemis entered Penelope's room just before eleven of the
clock to find her cousin seated before her vanity mirror,
turning her head one way and then another as she scruti-
nized her coiffure.

"What do you think of this new style?" she asked.
Curled tendrils framed her face, artfully interwoven with
seed pearls. "Blackbourne suggested it, but I'm uncertain
if it truly complements the roundness of my face."

Blackbourne was at the far end of the room tidying Penelope's stockings and could clearly hear their exchange—not
that Penelope seemed to care. "I like it," Artemis said truthfully. "It's quite elegant, yet very modern, too."

Penelope flashed one of her lovely smiles—the real one that not many people saw. For a moment Artemis wondered if Wakefield had ever seen that smile. Then she shook the thought aside. "Do you want your shawl?"

"I suppose you've already been out." Penelope touched a curl.

"Yes. I had a ramble with Bon Bon."

"I had wondered where Bon Bon had got to." Penelope nodded at herself in the mirror, apparently satisfied with her hair. "No, I'll leave the shawl and then if I get cold I'll send Wakefield or Scarborough to fetch it for me."

She grinned over her shoulder at Artemis.

Artemis shook her head, amused at the thought of her cousin using dukes as her errand boys. "Then if there's nothing else, shall we go down?"

"Yes." Penelope gave a last careful pat to her hair. "Oh, wait. There was something…" She began rummaging in the mess of jewelry, fans, gloves, and other debris that in the short time they'd been at Pelham House had taken up residence on the vanity. "Here 'tis. I knew I forgot something. This arrived for you this morning by special rider 'round about eight. Ridiculous. Who sends notes so early?"

She held out a rather tattered letter.

Artemis took it, prying off the seal with her thumbnail. There was no use chiding Penelope about the lateness in delivering the letter. Her cousin was perennially absentminded—especially in matters not her own. Hastily, she scanned the cheap paper, words suddenly jumping out at her as she realized that the letter was from the guard at Bedlam that she'd bribed long ago to send word if anything terrible ever happened.

Your brother … dying … come soon.

Dying.

No, this couldn't be true. Not when she'd finally found a way to get him out.

But she couldn't take that risk.

Dying.

"Penelope." Artemis carefully folded the letter, creasing it between her fingertips. Her hands were trembling. "Penelope, I must return to London."

"What?" Penelope was peering at her nose in the mirror now. She dabbed on a bit of rice powder. "Don't be silly. We've another week and a half at the house party."

"Apollo is ill. Or"—Artemis drew in a shuddering breath—"he's been beaten again. I must go to him."

Penelope sighed deeply, in the same manner as she would if she'd been presented with a new gown and found the lace edging the sleeves not quite up to what she'd expected. "Now, Artemis, dear. I've told you again and again that you must learn to forget your … brother." She shuddered delicately as if even the mere word somehow acknowledged the relationship more than she wished. "He's quite beyond your help. It's Christian, I know, to wish to give comfort to him, but I ask you: can one comfort a beast maddened by disease?"

"Apollo is not diseased, nor is he a beast," Artemis said in a tight voice. Penelope's lady's maids were still in the bedroom. They acted as if they had no ears, but Artemis knew full well that servants could hear. She would not succumb to humiliation. Apollo needed her. "He was accused falsely."

"You know that's not true, darling," Penelope said in what really was an attempt to be gentle, Artemis was sure. Unfortunately it only made her want to scream at her cousin. "Papa did all he could for your brother—and you, for that matter. Really, this harping on about that poor, insane thing isn't very grateful of you. I do think you can do better."

Artemis wanted to stomp out of the room. To fling Penelope's rote words back in her face and finally— *finally*—have done with all this artifice.

But that, in the end, would not serve Apollo.

She still needed her uncle's help. If she left now, abandoned Penelope and the Earl of Brightmore's protection, then she might reach Apollo, but she'd have no way of getting him out of Bedlam. Only a powerful man could do that.

Perhaps, in fact, *only* the Duke of Wakefield.

Yes. That was what she must do. Stay here at the house party—though it near killed her not to fly to Apollo's side—and *make* the duke help her. Help Apollo. If she had to, she'd scream the Ghost of St. Giles's secret identity from the rooftops.

She truly had nothing to lose now.

THAT AFTERNOON MAXIMUS took luncheon with his guests. He sat at the head of the long mahogany table in the great hall at Pelham House and wished for perhaps the first time in his life that one did not have to dine in order of precedence. For what gave dukes the right to sit at the upper end, also decreed that lowly lady's companions were seated so far away at the bottom of the table that one might as well send a carrier pigeon if one wanted to communicate with said lowly lady's companion. Not that he did, of course. Whatever had caused the hectic flush in

Miss Greaves's cheeks, the almost manic gesturing, the nearly desperate light in her fine gray eyes…all of that was of no concern to him.

Or shouldn't be in any case, for he found himself quite unable to keep his attention on his table companion's chatter.

Not that it was easy at any time to understand Lady Penelope.

That lady fluttered her eyelashes as she said, "And as I told Miss Alvers, one might *suggest* chocolate after four of the clock, but to actually drink it—and with pickled cucumbers, no less!—can never be correct. Don't you agree, Your Grace?"

"I haven't formed an opinion about chocolate, before or after four of the clock," Maximus replied drily.

"Hadn't you, Wakefield?" Scarborough, sitting to his left, looked shocked. "I find that deplorable, though no offense is meant—"

"And none taken," Maximus murmured as he took a sip of his wine.

"But all persons of manners must have an opinion on chocolate," the older man continued, "and indeed other beverages, and when they ought to be taken, how, and with what other suitable foodstuffs. Lady Penelope shows great sensitivity to have such a pretty turn of mind on the matter."

Maximus arched a brow at his rival. Really, the man had certainly won this round by the simple expedient of having been able to articulate such nonsense with a perfectly straight face. What was more—he checked Lady Penelope's expression closely, sighing silently when he found the expected—the lady had swallowed the sweetly wrapped offal, hook, line, and sinker. Maximus discreetly tipped his wineglass to the older man.

Scarborough winked back.

But Lady Penelope was already leaning forward, nearly dipping her abundant cleavage in her fish, to say earnestly to Scarborough, "I'm so thankful you agree, Your Grace. You would not credit it, but Artemis just last week said she didn't care one way or the other if her tea was taken with *blue* figured china or *red*!"

Scarborough inhaled sharply. "You don't say!"

"Indeed." Lady Penelope sat back, having delivered this terrible breach of etiquette. "I have both, naturally, but wouldn't dream of serving anything but coffee in the red, although sometimes"—she peeked coquettishly at Scarborough through her eyebrows—"sometimes I *do* serve chocolate in the blue."

"Naughty thing," the elderly duke breathed.

Maximus did sigh aloud at that, though no one seemed to notice. Was this truly the type of conversation he would have to endure once married? He stared broodingly into his wineglass and then glanced down the table to where Miss Greaves was laughing too loudly at something Mr. Watts had said. Somehow he doubted he would ever grow weary of her conversation. The thought was disturbing. He shouldn't even be meditating on Miss Greaves—there was no room for her in his carefully ordered life.

"I suppose I ought not to blame poor Artemis," Lady Penelope said with a thoughtful air. "She hasn't my refinement—nor my sensitivity."

Maximus nearly snorted. If refinement was quibbling over the type of china to serve chocolate in, then he supposed that Miss Greaves did indeed lack it—and he for one regarded her the better for it.

He looked down the table again and felt an irrational urge to push poor Mr. Watts out of his chair when Miss Greaves tilted her head toward him to hear something he'd said. He caught her eye briefly and she stared back in defiance, her mouth twisting tragically before looking away again.

Something was wrong. She was leaking emotion.

He sipped his wine, contemplating the matter. It was barely a few hours since he'd seen her in the woods this morning. Then she'd been as defiant as ever, no trace of weakness. The preluncheon entertainment had divided the ladies from the gentlemen. The latter had gone grouse hunting—with dismal luck—while the former had engaged in some sort of party game. Had something disturbed her during the games?

The arrival of dessert caught him by surprise, but he was glad to finish the luncheon. As the guests rose he took an abrupt leave of Lady Penelope and started down the room toward Miss Greaves.

But she was already making her way toward him.

"I trust your hunting went well, Your Grace," she said when they met in the middle of the dining room, her tone brittle.

"It was awful, as I'm sure you've already heard," he replied.

"I am so sorry," she said quickly. "But then I suppose you're not used to hunting in a rural setting."

He blinked, slow to realize the direction she was taking. "What—?"

"After all," she said, as smooth as a striking adder, "you do most of your hunting in London, don't you?"

Mr. Watts who'd been lingering nearby, smiled uncertainly at her words. "Whatever do you mean, Miss Greaves?"

"Miss Greaves is no doubt referring to my duties in Parliament," Maximus said through gritted teeth.

"Oh." Mr. Watts's brow crinkled in thought. "I suppose one could term some parts of a parliamentarian's efforts as hunting, but truly, Miss Greaves—and I hope you'll forgive my frankness—but it is an awkward way to characterize such—"

"Then it's a good thing I wasn't referring to the duke's role in Parliament," Miss Greaves said. "I said London and I meant London—the streets of London."

Mr. Watts stiffened, his uncertain smile disappearing altogether. "I'm sure you did not mean to insult the duke by insinuating that he frequents the *streets* of London"—here a ruddy blush rose in Mr. Watts's cheeks, presumably at the word *street* and all its connotations—"but you must be aware—"

It was Maximus's turn to cut the poor man off. "Miss Greaves misspoke, Watts."

"Did I, Your Grace?" Her chin was raised challengingly, but there was a desperate, vulnerable glint in her eyes. A glint that made him simultaneously want to shake her and protect her. "I'm not at all sure I misspoke. But then if you would like to have me quit this discussion, you know full well what you can do to stop me."

He inhaled and spoke without thinking, ignoring their audience. "What has happened?"

"You know full well, Your Grace, for what—*who*—I fight." Her eyes were glittering and he couldn't believe it, but the evidence was clear.

Tears. His goddess should never weep.

He took her arm. "Artemis."

Cousin Bathilda was there, suddenly, beside them. "We've a ramble planned to see the Fontaine Abbey ruins, Maximus. I'm sure Miss Greaves would like to ready herself."

He swallowed, strangely loath to release her. His guests were turning to look, Lady Penelope had a slight frown between her eyebrows, and Mr. Watts seemed quite perturbed. He made himself unclench his fingers, take a step back, and nod. "Miss Greaves. Cousin Bathilda. In half an hour, shall we say? On the south terrace? I look forward to escorting you both to the ruins."

And he made himself turn and stride away.

ARTEMIS COULD FEEL Miss Picklewood's worried gaze on her as the house party tramped across a field toward the ruins of the old abbey. The older lady had made sure to pair Artemis with Lady Phoebe on the walk. Ahead of them, Lady Penelope was bracketed by the Duke of Wakefield on her right and the Duke of Scarborough on her left. Artemis squinted in the sunshine, watching Wakefield's broad back. She sympathized with Miss Picklewood's attempt to deflect a potential scandal, but she couldn't let the other woman's unease dissuade her from her own mission.

Apollo was *dying*.

The thought vibrated through her limbs with every casual step. She wanted to run to him. To hold her brother in her arms and reassure herself that she'd have at least one more moment with him.

She couldn't. She had to hold to her purpose.

Penelope tossed her head and laughed, the ribbons on her bonnet fluttering in the wind.

"She's got them both on a string, hasn't she?" Phoebe said quietly.

Artemis blinked, brought back from her own dark thoughts. "Do you think so? I've always thought Wakefield a man to himself. If he wants to walk away, he'll do so without a backward glance."

"Perhaps," Phoebe said, "but at the moment what my brother wants is *her*. I wish sometimes that he'd pause a while and truly consider what it is he's pursuing."

"What makes you think he hasn't?" Artemis said.

Phoebe glanced at her. "If he had, wouldn't he have realized how ill-matched he and Penelope are?"

"You make the assumption that he cares."

For a moment Artemis thought she'd caused insult with her blunt words. Then Phoebe slowly shook her head. "You forget. He may have a crusty exterior, but truly my brother isn't as cold as the world thinks him."

Artemis already knew that. She'd seen his face as he'd looked at Phoebe, watched his mouth as he'd sung with that beautiful voice. Let him show her his mother's folly, walked with him in his woods accompanied by his sweet dogs. She knew he was a living, breathing man beneath the ice.

But she couldn't think of him that way now. She must push aside the affinity she felt for him and sway him to her goal.

If she could only find a way.

She quickened her pace just enough that she and Phoebe began to overtake the trio in front of them. They were almost at the abbey ruins now—a row of gray stone arches that held up empty sky.

"Do you know," she said to Phoebe as they got within earshot of the three, "I met another such cold man the other day. The Ghost of St. Giles struck me as a man with a heart like an icicle. Very like your brother, in point of fact. I'm surprised that the comparison has never been made before, for they are quite similar. Well, nearly. The duke seems rather cowardly next to the Ghost of St. Giles."

Wakefield's back stiffened in front of them.

"Artemis...," Phoebe began, her voice both puzzled and horrified.

"Ah! Here we are, then," Miss Picklewood boomed.

Artemis turned to find Miss Picklewood right behind them. Her eyes narrowed. The lady moved very quietly for her age.

"Now, Your Grace," Miss Picklewood said brightly, speaking to Scarborough. "I believe I once overheard you telling my dear cousin, the late duchess, some terribly interesting ghost stories about the abbey. Perhaps you'll refresh my memory."

"Your memory, Miss Picklewood," Scarborough said, bowing gallantly, "is as sharp as a razor."

"Oh, but do tell us a story," Penelope said, clapping her hands.

"Very well, but my tale is a long one, my lady," the duke said. He drew out a large handkerchief from a pocket and dusted off one of the big tumbled stones that must have at one time made up the abbey's walls. He laid the square of linen down and gestured. "Please. Take a seat."

All the ladies found places to sit—save Artemis, who preferred to stand—and the footmen who had trailed the party began serving wine and minuscule cakes pulled from wicker baskets.

"Now then," Scarborough began, assuming a dramatic pose—feet braced wide apart, one hand comfortably tucked between the buttons of his waistcoat, his other hand gesturing toward the ruins. "Once this was a grand and mighty abbey, erected and inhabited by monks who had taken a vow of silence..."

Artemis paid little attention to Scarborough's words. She watched the assembled group dispassionately, and then began slowly moving around the outer edge of the guests. She slipped behind Mrs. Jellett, paused a moment, then moved again. Her object was to circle around to where Wakefield stood beside Penelope.

"...and when the maiden woke up, she was served a most wonderful meal by the monks, but of course none of them spoke because they'd all taken their vow of silence..."

Artemis glanced down to maneuver around a crumbling stone with its base obscured by weeds, which was why she didn't see him until it was too late.

"What the hell do you think you're doing?" Wakefield growled in her ear. He clamped his hand on her upper arm.

Wisely, she kept silent.

He drew her toward where part of the wall still stood. They were at the back of the group and thus few noticed them. Miss Picklewood raised her head, a bit like a guard dog with its hackles high, but Wakefield shot her a rather filthy look.

And then they were out of sight of the others.

But the duke didn't stop. He hustled her through the ruins and into the stand of trees that edged one side of the abbey. Only when they were sheltered by the cool branches of the great trees, did he stop.

"What"—he turned and seized both her arms—"has gotten into you?"

"He's dying," she whispered furiously, trembling within his grasp. "I didn't receive the letter until almost noon—because Penelope didn't think it *important* enough to give it to me earlier. Apollo is lying in that hell-hole dying."

His jaw set as he searched her face. "I can have a carriage readied for you to return to London within the hour. If the roads are—"

She slapped him, quick and hard.

His head turned slightly with the blow, but other than that his only reaction was the narrowing of his eyes.

Her chest was heaving as if she were running. "No! *You* must go to London. *You* must get him out. *You* must save my brother because if you don't, I swear upon everything I hold holy that I'll ruin both you and your illustrious name. I'll—"

"Little bitch," he breathed, his face turned fiery red, and he slammed his mouth against hers.

There was no softness in him. He claimed her lips like a marauder: hard and angry. If she'd once thought him cold as ice, well, that ice was burned away now by the fire of his rage. He shoved his tongue into her mouth, his breath a hot exhalation against her cheek. He tasted of wine and power, and something within her trembled in answer. His chest was pressed to her, and each frantic breath she took shoved her breasts into his waistcoat. He wasn't gentle and he wasn't at all romantic, and despite that she almost lost her way. Almost found herself wandering in the wildness of his lips. In the passion of his anger. She almost forgot everything.

She remembered the brother who needed her just in time.

She pulled back, gasping, trying to find words as his hands tightened, preventing her from escaping entirely.

He ducked his head to look her in the eye. "I don't *have* to do anything you order me to do, Miss Greaves. I am a *duke*, not your personal lapdog."

"And here, *now*, I am *Artemis*, not Miss Greaves," she blazed. "You'll do as I say because if you don't I'll make sure you're the laughingstock of London. That you're banished from England forever."

His eyes flared wide with anger, and for a moment she was sure he was going to strike her down. He shook her roughly instead, sending her fichu slithering to the ground.

"Stop demanding. Stop trying to be something you're not."

The pain bloomed in her breast, so sharp, so cold, that for a wild moment she thought he'd stabbed her with a dagger rather than words.

He yanked her close, his mouth against her exposed neck. She could feel the scrape of his teeth, sharp with warning.

Artemis let her head fall back, her eyes closed, her lips suddenly trembling. Apollo *dying*. "Please. *Please*, Maximus. I'll refrain from provoking you anymore. I'll stay in the shadows with my stockings and shoes on and never swim in your pond again, never disturb you again, only *please* do this one thing, I beg you. Save my brother."

His lips left her throat. She could hear Scarborough's voice somewhere back at the ruins, still telling his silly children's stories. She could hear a bird trilling a series of high, bouncing notes, suddenly cut off. She could hear the rustling of the eternal trees. But she couldn't hear him.

Perhaps he wasn't there anymore. Perhaps he was merely a figment of her imagination.

She opened her eyes in panic.

He was staring at her with a face entirely expressionless, as if made from cold stone. Nothing showed at lips or brow or cheek. Nowhere save in his eyes. Those burned with an impassioned fire, reckless and deep, and her breath caught at the sight as she waited for her—and her brother's—fate.

A GODDESS SHOULD never have to beg. It was the one thought, clear and simple, that ran through Maximus's mind. Everything else—his rank, the party, their conflict, seemed to fall away from that one truth. *She* should never have to beg.

He still tasted her mouth on his tongue, still wanted to crush her breasts against his chest and bend her until she bared her throat to him, but he made himself let her go.

"Very well."

Artemis blinked, her sweet lips parting as if she didn't believe what she'd heard. "What?"

"I'll do it."

He turned to go, his mind already making plans, when he felt her fingers clutch at his sleeve. "You'll take him from Bedlam?"

"Yes."

Perhaps his decision had already been made from the moment he'd seen tears in her eyes. He had a weakness, it seemed, a fault more terrible than any Achilles's heel: he couldn't stand the sight of her tears.

But her eyes shone as if he'd placed the moon itself into her hands. "Thank you."

He nodded, and then he was striding in the direction of Pelham before he could linger and be drawn again into the seduction of her mouth.

He emerged into the sunshine and was almost surprised by the sight of his guests. His tête-à-tête in the woods with Artemis had seemed like an interlude in another world, a journey of days, when it had in reality been only minutes.

Cousin Bathilda looked up with a crease between her brows. "Maximus! Lady Penelope was wondering if you might show us the famous abbey well. Scarborough has been telling us that some poor girl flung herself into it centuries ago."

"Not now," he muttered as he brushed past her.

"Your Grace." Bathilda had never been mother to him. His own mother had died when he'd been fourteen— old enough to no longer need a parental hand. Yet when Bathilda—rarely—used that tone and the courtesy of his title, he always paid attention.

He turned to face her. "Yes?"

They stood a little apart from the group. "What are you about?" she whispered, frowning. "I know Lady Oddershaw and Mrs. Jellett have spent the last five minutes muttering between themselves over you and Miss Greaves, and even Lady Penelope must be wondering what you can have had to say to her lady's companion that necessitated dragging the poor woman off into the woods." Bathilda took a deep breath. "Maximus, you're on the very brink of causing a scandal."

"Then it's a good thing that I have cause to go to

London," he replied. "I've had word that a business matter cannot wait."

"What—?"

But he had no time to make further ridiculous excuses. If Artemis was right and her brother was truly dying, he must get to London and Bedlam before the man perished.

The thought prompted him to start into a jog as soon as he was away from sight of the abbey. Maximus was panting by the time he made Pelham. He detoured by the stables to order two horses saddled, then ran inside the house. He wasn't surprised to see Craven eyeing him askance at the top of the stairs.

"Your Grace seems out of breath. I do hope you're not being chased by an overly enthusiastic heiress?"

"Pack a light bag, Craven," Maximus snapped. "We're going to London to help a murderous lunatic escape from Bedlam."

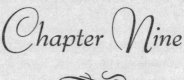

Chapter Nine

King Herla and his men traveled back to the land of humankind, but what a surprise met them when at last they saw the sun. Brambles hid the entrance to the cave, and where once there had been fertile fields and plump cattle, now a strange, thorny forest had grown, and in the distance they saw the ruins of a great castle. They rode until they found a peasant to question.

"We have no king or queen here," stuttered the peasant. "Not since noble Herla King disappeared and his queen died of grief—and that, my lords, was nigh on nine hundred years ago." ...

—from *The Legend of the Herla King*

Artemis could hear voices as the duke met his guests at the abbey ruins. The tones rose and then fell, and then it was nearly quiet enough that she might imagine that she was by herself in the little wood. Alone and safe.

But she was no longer a girl with fanciful dreams. She knew she must face the real world—and the rest of the guests.

She took a deep breath, smoothed down her hair, and before she could waver, made for the abbey.

It wasn't very bad—not nearly as bad as the morning after Apollo was arrested. Then she'd had to walk through the village green to fetch a bit of beef from the butcher. He'd closed his doors and pretended not to see her outside and she'd had to walk home empty-handed, with the loud whispers of people she'd thought her friends in her ears.

The guests turned and stared as she emerged from the woods, and Lady Oddershaw and Mrs. Jellett put their heads together, but Phoebe smiled at the sight of her.

One genuine smile of friendship was worth a thousand false faces.

"Where have you been?" Penelope asked when she reached her. "And where is your fichu?"

Artemis felt the heat rise in her cheeks—and her too-bare throat—but there was nothing for it but to brave it out. Casually she put her hand to her neck—and discovered the chain with the emerald drop and Maximus's ring was exposed as well. *Had Maximus seen his ring?* If he had, he'd given no indication. She tucked them both back into her bodice as casually as she could. The ring was merely a signet ring—like many others in England. Hopefully it wouldn't be recognized.

"Artemis?" Penelope was waiting for her answer.

"I saw a bearded titmouse and wished for a closer look."

"With the Duke of Wakefield?"

"He has an interest in nature," she said, entirely truthfully.

"Hmm." Penelope looked suspicious, but was distracted by a whispered word from Scarborough. The guests were gathering their things in preparation for returning back to Pelham House.

Phoebe started for Artemis, but Miss Picklewood laid her hand on her charge's arm and directed her to accompany Miss Royale.

A confused expression flitted over Phoebe's sweet face, but then she smoothed it into social politeness and took Miss Royale's arm.

"Miss Greaves, will you walk with me?" Miss Picklewood asked in a tone that suggested an order rather than a request. "The path is so uneven."

"Of course," Artemis murmured as she linked arms with the older lady.

"We haven't had a chance to speak in quite some time," Miss Picklewood said softly. They were at the back of the line of returning guests, a position that Artemis felt sure the other lady had maneuvered them into. "I hope you've been enjoying the country party?"

"Yes, ma'am," Artemis answered warily.

"Good, good," Miss Picklewood murmured. "So often I'm afraid people come to these country parties and leave their, shall we say, *higher principles* behind in London. You wouldn't believe, I know, my dear, but such scandalous goings-on I've heard about!"

"Oh?" Artemis thought herself inured to innuendo, but the problem was that she rather liked Miss Picklewood and so cared for her opinion. The older lady's words made her ears burn.

"Oh, yes, my dear," Miss Picklewood said ever so gently. "And of course it's always the most innocent who become entangled in gossip's net, as it were. Why, a married lady—especially if she's titled—can get away with all sorts of things. I won't enumerate them, for they aren't for innocent ears. But a respectable young matron who might not be titled or have any weight in society must be very, very careful."

Miss Picklewood paused as they picked their way around an outcropping of rock, then said, "And of course, it's quite beyond the pale for an *un*married lady to engage in any sort of behavior that might seem *untoward*. Especially if such behavior might make her lose what was otherwise her only position."

"I understand," Artemis said tightly.

"Do you, dear?" Miss Picklewood's tone was gentle, but underneath there was iron. "It's the way of the world that the ladies in such cases are always to blame, never the gentlemen. And it's also the way of the world that dukes—however honorable they might be otherwise— have no reason but the nefarious to take young, unmarried ladies of little means into secluded places. You must have no hopes there."

"Yes." Artemis breathed in quietly, making sure her voice did not shake. "I do realize."

"I wish it were otherwise," Miss Picklewood exclaimed quietly, "truly I do. But I think it doesn't do for ladies such as we to be anything but utterly practical. Too many have stumbled into disaster thinking otherwise."

"Ladies such as we?"

"Of course, dear," Miss Picklewood said comfortably. "Do you imagine I was born with gray hair and wrinkles? I once was a comely young girl like you. My dear papa loved to play at cards. Unfortunately he was never very good at it. I *did* have several offers from gentlemen, but I felt we wouldn't get on well, so I went to live with my Aunt Florence. Quite a persnickety old lady, I'm sad to report, but a good heart underneath it all. After Aunt Florence I

went to my brother's house. You would *think* the closeness of blood would make the connection dearer, but such
was *not* the case between my brother and me. Possibly our
mutual antagonism was made worse by my sister-in-law,
a dreadful penny-pincher who resented another mouth to
feed in their household. I was forced to return to my aunt.
And then…"

They were within sight of Pelham House, and here
Miss Picklewood stopped and looked wistfully up at
the magnificent mansion. "Then you know the rest.
Poor Mary died along with the duke, her husband.
Well. Our relation was distant, you know. Quite distant.
But Mary and I were bosom bows as girls, and when I
heard about the tragedy I came at once. There was a
time at the beginning when the lawyers and men of
business were swarming 'round, when I thought someone would throw me out. Find another to bring up Hero
and Phoebe. But then Maximus started speaking again
and that was that. Even at fourteen he had the bearing
of a duke. I showed him the letters his mother and I had
exchanged, and he made up his mind that I should raise
his sisters."

Miss Picklewood stopped to draw breath and for a
moment both ladies stood staring up at Pelham House.

Artemis turned to the older lady. "You said he 'started
speaking again'?"

"Hmm?" Miss Picklewood blinked. "Oh, yes. I suppose not many remember now, but Maximus was so shat-
tered by the deaths of his parents that he went mute for a
full fortnight. Why, some of the quacks that came to look
at him said his brain was addled by the tragedy. That he'd
never speak again. Rubbish, of course. It simply took him

time to come to rights again. He was quite sane. Just a sensitive boy."

A boy who, when he came to himself again, was no longer a boy but the Duke of Wakefield, Artemis thought. "It must have been horrible for him."

"Yes, it was," Miss Picklewood said simply. "He witnessed their murders, you know. A terrible shock for such an emotional lad."

Artemis looked thoughtfully at the older lady. *Emotional* wasn't a word she'd ever use to describe the duke.

But perhaps he'd been a different person before the tragedy.

"Goodness!" Miss Picklewood exclaimed. "I *have* gone off track. Your pardon, my dear. I'm afraid sometimes my words run away from me. I simply wanted to let you know that you and I aren't that different, after all—we're merely at dissimilar stages of life. I, too, can understand the temptations of our position. But you must learn to resist them—for your own good."

"Thank you," Artemis said gravely, for she knew the advice was meant kindly.

Miss Picklewood cleared her throat. "I do hope this little talk won't come between us?"

"Not on my part," Artemis assured her.

The elder lady nodded, evidently satisfied. "Then let us see if refreshments have been laid out for us."

Artemis nodded. Tea sounded good, and after that she meant to run Penelope to ground.

She needed to return to London and Apollo. And Maximus.

For though Miss Picklewood's advice was wise, she had no intention of following it.

*   *   *

BETHLEM ROYAL HOSPITAL—OR, as it was more commonly called, Bedlam—was a monolithic monument to charity. Newly built since the Great Fire, its long, low silhouette was all that was modern and grand. Almost as if the governors meant to put icing on the rot within.

Or advertise their wares, Maximus thought cynically as he slipped through the magnificent front gates just as the clock struck midnight. He wore his Ghost of St. Giles costume tonight, for though he had no doubt he could affect Lord Kilbourne's release as the Duke of Wakefield, it would take time.

Time the madman evidently didn't have.

Over his head, twin stone figures writhed on the arched gate, one representing Melancholia and the other Raving Madness. Before him was a vast, open courtyard, made monochrome in the moonlight. On holidays the courtyard and building within was flooded with sightseers—all of whom paid a tithe to see the amusements of deranged madmen and madwomen. Maximus had never been himself, but he'd sat listening distastefully often enough as some fashionable lady described the titillating horrors she'd seen with her bosom bows. Over one hundred poor souls were incarcerated here—which meant that if he were to find Kilbourne amongst them, he'd need a guide.

Maximus glided toward the massive front doors and found them, not surprisingly, locked. All the windows were barred to keep the patients safely inside, but there were several side doors for the delivery of food—and perhaps the inmates themselves. He selected one and tried the handle. It, too, was locked. So he tried the next obvious choice.

He knocked.

There was an interminable period of waiting before shuffling could be heard and the door swung open.

Inside, staring at him with wide eyes, was a guard.

Maximus immediately thrust his short sword against the guard's throat. "Hush."

The attendant's mouth opened in an oval of surprise, but he didn't make a sound. The man was dressed in breeches, waistcoat, and a very ragged coat, his head covered by a soft hat. He'd probably been asleep. No doubt Bedlam was not used to receiving visitors in the middle of the night.

"I wish to see Lord Kilbourne," Maximus whispered. He was unlikely to ever meet this man again, but it never hurt to be cautious.

The attendant blinked. "'E's in th' Incurables ward."

Maximus cocked his head. "Then take me to him."

The man started to turn, but Maximus pressed the sword tip against his throat warningly. "And don't go alerting any of your fellow guards, mind. You'll be the first to fly this life should I find myself in a sword fight."

The attendant swallowed with a small clicking sound and turned with exaggerated care to lead Maximus into Bedlam. He'd brought a lantern with him when he'd answered the door, and this gave a feeble light as they entered a long corridor.

To the left were tall, barred windows overlooking the courtyard. To the right, a row of doors led away into the darkness. A square window was cut into the upper part of each door and inset with crossed bars. Faint sounds came from the inhabitants of this place: rustling and sighs, moans, and an odd, eerie humming. Somewhere a voice was raised in argument, but no other voice answered back. The air was thick with a miasma of smells: urine and cooked cabbage, lye and tallow, wet stone and feces. Something about the corridor and the place gave Maximus a sense of déjà vu, but he could not remember why.

They were almost halfway down the corridor when footsteps echoed behind them. "Sully? Is that you?"

The attendant—apparently, Sully—stopped and turned, his eyes widening in alarm. Maximus ducked his face into his shoulder so the nose of his mask couldn't be seen in profile and peered behind.

A figure was at the other end of the corridor, but surely he couldn't tell at this distance who they were.

Maximus poked Sully with his sword under cover of his cloak. "Remember what I told you."

"J . . . just me, Ridley," Sully stuttered.

"Oo's that you got with you?" Ridley asked suspiciously.

"My brother, George, come to have a bit of tipple with me," Sully said nervously. "He'll be no bother."

"Keep walking," Maximus whispered.

Ridley started down the corridor.

"I . . . I'll just show George to my rooms," Sully called in a high voice, and then they were around the corner and running up a central flight of stairs.

"Will he follow us?" Maximus demanded.

"I don't know." Sully sent him a nervous glance. "'E's a suspicious one is that Ridley."

Maximus glanced back when they reached the upper floor, but he couldn't make out if anyone was trailing them in the darkness. He turned back to Sully. "Show me Kilbourne."

"This way."

To the left was a door. Beside it stood a stool and a key hanging on a hook.

"Leech's turn for the night guard," Sully muttered as he took the key and fit it into the lock on the door. "'E's probably drunk in 'is bed, though."

As Sully held high his lantern to open the door, Maximus could see the sign that hung over the lintel: *Incurable*.

Beyond lay a long corridor like the one below, save that here the cells opened on both sides. The rooms had no doors to either shield the occupants or protect the visitor. The inmates within lay upon straw like stabled animals, and the stink of their manure was enough to make Maximus's eyes water. Here was a white-haired, bearded venerable, his nearly colorless eyes staring sightlessly into the light as they passed. There, a young woman, pretty, save for the savage lunge she made at them when they crossed her doorway. A chain rattled and she fell back, exactly like a bitch choked by a collar. The youth in the next stall laughed, high and hysterical, scrabbling at his own face as he did so.

Sully crossed himself and hurried to the last stall. He stopped and held his lantern high, illuminating a massive male body lying in the straw.

Maximus frowned, stepping closer. "Is he alive?"

Sully shrugged. "Was when we brought dinner 'round to the others. 'Course 'e didn't eat it seein' as 'ow 'e's been asleep."

Not so much asleep as insensible, Maximus thought grimly. He went to one knee beside the man in the filthy straw. Viscount Kilbourne looked nothing like his sister. Where she was slim he was huge—wide shoulders, massive hands, legs that sprawled across the cell. Whether he was a handsome man or not was impossible to tell: his face was swollen and caked with dried blood, both eyes blackened, his bottom lip split and grown to the size and color of a small plum. This close Maximus could hear an odd, whistling wheeze as the big man's chest struggled to draw air into his lungs.

Kilbourne appeared near death. Would he even survive the move out of this place? He also looked as if he'd received no doctoring at all—even the blackened blood on his face hadn't been wiped away.

Maximus's lips thinned grimly. "Do you have the key to his manacle?"

"It'll be hanging by the door." Sully made to turn, but Maximus grabbed him.

The guard quailed.

"You come back within the minute or I find you. Understand?"

Sully nodded frantically.

Maximus let him go.

Sully was back in less than a minute with an iron ring of keys. "Should be one o' these—"

"What're you doing in here?"

Maximus rose and whirled at the voice, both swords out.

Sully squeaked and froze, his hands clutching the keys before him like a shield.

The man who stood in the doorway to the cell paused with Maximus's sword at his throat, his eyes wide. Maximus recognized the voice now as Ridley's. He was a big man—nearly as big as the one sprawled at their feet—and he had the look of a bully.

"Sully, take off the manacles," Maximus ordered, careful to keep his eyes on Ridley.

He heard the clank of the manacle falling to the floor.

"You"—Maximus gestured to Ridley with his sword—"pick up his feet."

"What d'you want with 'im?" Ridley sounded sullen, but he bent to grab Kilbourne's feet. "'E's near enough dead as 'tis."

"Give me the lantern and take his head," Maximus said to Sully, ignoring Ridley.

The first attendant looked doubtful, but he surrendered the lantern readily enough. With a grunt and a bit of swearing, both men lifted Kilbourne's limp form.

"Weighs a bloody ton, 'e does." Ridley spat into the straw.

"Less talk," Maximus said softly. "If another guard comes, I won't be needing you, will I?"

That shut up the second attendant. They made their way back down the hallway and—with more difficulty—down the staircase. Maximus watched carefully that they didn't drop Kilbourne, but otherwise didn't help, preferring to keep his hands free in case more guards showed up.

"Would've finished the job if'n I knew you was coming for 'im anyway," Ridley muttered as they finally made the ground floor.

Maximus slowly turned his head. "You did this?"

"Aye," Ridley said with satisfaction. "Always were mouthin' off, th' whoreson. 'E 'ad it comin' to 'im, 'e did."

Maximus looked at Kilbourne, lying near death, his face unrecognizable, and thought: *No one deserved that.*

"Surprised 'e lived through that first night," Ridley

mused, apparently under the impression that they were now fast friends.

"Really?" Maximus asked in a flat tone. He looked at the rows of cells they passed, the long, wide corridor, perfect for viewing the inmates, and suddenly knew what this place reminded him of: the Tower Menagerie. The humans within this place were used for the entertainment of others, exactly like the exotic animals of the menagerie...excepting that the animals were better kept.

"We gave it to 'im good, we did," Ridley said in a voice that made Maximus's skin crawl. "An' if 'e 'adn't passed out so quick, we woulda give it to 'im better, if'n you know what I mean."

"Oh, I think I do," Maximus growled. They were at the end of the long ground floor corridor now. "Put him down by the door."

Sully looked at him warily, while Ridley was puzzled. "'Ere? 'Ow're you going to get 'im out the door?"

"Don't worry your head about it," Maximus said gently, and smashed him on the temple with the butt of his sword.

Ridley slumped to the floor.

Sully threw up his arms. "Please, sir!"

"Did you take part in this?"

"No!"

Sully might've been lying, but Maximus hadn't the heart to hit him in any case. The gore on Kilbourne made him sick. He bent, took Kilbourne's right arm, and hauled the big man over his shoulder with a grunt. The man was heavy, but not as heavy as his stature should make him. Maximus could feel the bones of Kilbourne's wrist, stark and hard. No doubt he'd lost weight in this place.

The thought made Maximus's mood darker. "Open the door for me."

Sully ran to do his bidding.

Maximus stepped out, but paused to look over his shoulder at Sully. "Tell Ridley and all the other guards: I'll be back. At night, when you're sleeping, when you least expect it. And if I find any more inmates treated as Lord Kilbourne was, then I'll not ask questions. I'll simply deal justice with the point of my sword. Understand?"

"Aye, sir." Sully looked absolutely terrified.

Maximus stepped into the night.

He trotted to the gates with his burden, and slipped through. Outside lay the gardens of Moorfields and, a little way down from the main gates, a waiting horse and cart.

"Go," Maximus muttered as he heaved Kilbourne into the bed of the cart and climbed in after.

"Are we being followed?" Craven asked as he slapped the reins.

"No, not yet, at any rate." Maximus panted, trying to catch his breath while watching for pursuers.

"A successful job then."

Maximus grunted, glancing at the madman. He still breathed at least. What in hell was he going to do with a fugitive from Bedlam?

Maximus shook his head at the thought and replied to Craven, "Only if Kilbourne lives."

ARTEMIS WOKE TO a soft tap at her door. She blinked and looked around the room, for a moment, confused, until she remembered that she was in her guest room at Pelham House.

The tapping came again.

She struggled out of the warm bedcovers and shrugged into a wrapper. A glance at the window showed that it was just dawn.

Artemis cracked the door open to find a maid, already dressed for the day. "Yes?"

"Beg pardon, Miss, but there's a messenger for you at the back door. Says he's to speak to you and no other."

Apollo. It must be. Trembling, Artemis found her slippers and followed the maid down the stairs and back toward the kitchens. Had Maximus found her brother? Did he still live?

The kitchens were already abustle with preparations for the day. Cooks and maids were rolling out pastry, footmen carrying silver, and a young girl carefully tended the hearth. A great table lay in the middle of the kitchens, the center of much of the food preparation, but at one end a lad sat, a cup of tea and a plate of freshly buttered bread before him. He stood as she neared, and Artemis saw that his clothes were still dusty from the road.

"Miss Greaves?"

"Yes?"

He fumbled in his coat pocket before drawing out a letter. "His Grace said I was to place this in your hands and no other's."

"Thank you." Artemis took the letter, staring for a moment at the embossed seal.

"Here, Miss," the lad said, holding out his butter knife. He had a fresh, country face, though he must've come from London. "To break the seal."

She smiled her thanks—rather tremulously, she was afraid—and hastily broke the seal. The letter held only one sentence, but it meant the world:

He is alive at my house.

—M

Artemis exhaled a breath she hadn't known she'd been holding. *Oh, thank God. Alive.*

She must go to him at once.

About to leave the kitchen, the letter clutched in her fist, she remembered the messenger with a pang. She turned back to him. "I'm afraid I forgot to bring my purse down, but if you'll wait here, I'm sure I have a shilling for you."

"No need, Miss." The lad grinned in a friendly way. "His Grace is a generous master. He said as how I wasn't to accept coin from you."

"Oh." Artemis said. That Maximus had thought to spare her the embarrassment of having no money for the messenger made her heart warm. "Well, I thank you, then."

The lad nodded cheerfully and went back to his breakfast.

Artemis hurried back to the stairs. She'd half-convinced Penelope yesterday that there wasn't much point in staying if their host had left for "business" in London. Perhaps she could get her cousin to arise a bit earlier than usual.

The upper hall was dim when she made her door, but she could hear a footman hurrying away further down the corridor. Artemis pushed open the door and went to the dresser to begin a hasty toilet. She'd learned long ago how to dress herself without help, as Papa had been able to afford a maidservant only irregularly. So she dressed in her usual brown serge and sat to put up her hair, and only then noticed something odd: her hairbrush had been placed bristle side down. She always left it up—the back was made of common wood, and the boar's bristles were the most delicate part of the brush.

Had the maid moved it?

But the fire hadn't yet been made. The maid hadn't been to her room this morning.

Artemis pulled out the top drawer of her dresser. Her paltry collection of stockings lay inside and seemed as usual. But the next drawer...

The corner of one of her chemises was caught in the drawer, the edge sticking out. She couldn't be entirely certain—perhaps she had shut the drawer hastily herself—but she thought not.

Someone had been in her room. Someone had gone through her things.

Artemis recalled the sound of retreating footsteps as she'd neared her door. Had Maximus sent orders for one of his footmen to search her room whilst she was called to the kitchen to see his messenger? It seemed an odd thing for him to do, and she couldn't think why he'd do it. Perhaps to get back his ring without asking for it?

She drew out the chain from the fichu she'd donned and examined again the ring and pendant. They winked silently in her palm. She shook her head and tucked the pendant and ring back into her bodice. The ring belonged to Maximus, and she would give it to him as soon as she saw him in London.

As soon as she saw Apollo.

The rest of her toilet took minutes, and then she was hurrying to Penelope's room.

Her cousin was naturally still abed, but after an interminable two-hour wait, Penelope was ready to go down for breakfast.

"I don't know why we must rise so early," Penelope grumbled. "After all, if Wakefield has flown off to London, there's no one to see me, is there?"

"What about Scarborough?" Artemis asked absently and then felt like groaning. The last thing she needed was to encourage Penelope to stay for the elderly duke.

"Scarborough is charming enough." Penelope's cheeks actually pinkened despite her casual words. "But he's not as rich as Wakefield, nor as powerful."

"He's a duke," Artemis said softly as they entered the long room at the back of the house where breakfast was served. "And he *likes* you."

"Oh, do you think so?" Penelope stopped and glanced at her, her expression shy.

"Of course." Artemis nodded to where the elderly duke had stood at their entrance. "Just look at his expression."

Scarborough was smiling so widely, Artemis was afraid something might crack in his face. It was odd, really, but the duke *did* seem to like her cousin—not just her youth or beauty, but Penelope herself.

"But he's so old," Penelope said, for once lowering her voice. She had a slight frown between her brows as if honestly distressed.

"Does that really matter?" Artemis said softly. "He's the type of man who will shower his wife with all manner of expensive gifts. It's said that his first wife had a veritable treasure chest of jewels. Think how nice that would be."

"Humph." Penelope bit her lip, looking indecisive. "We'll be returning to London in any case."

They'd neared Scarborough as they spoke and his face fell almost comically as he heard Penelope's last words. "Never say you're deserting me, Lady Penelope?"

Penelope made a moue as she sat in the chair Scarborough held for her. "Since it seems our host has deserted *us*, I think it the thing to do."

"Ah, yes." Scarborough frowned down at the gammon steak on the plate before him. "Wakefield did take off yesterday like a startled hare. I've never seen the like. I do hope," he said jovially, glancing at Artemis, "that he didn't take your teasing about the Ghost of St. Giles badly, Miss Greaves."

"I do not think the duke is so easily frightened," Artemis replied.

Scarborough raised his eyebrows and spread wide his hands. "And yet Wakefield has fled his own country home."

Artemis's heartbeat picked up. The last thing she wanted was suspicion being cast Maximus's way *now*.

"But the duke said he had urgent business in London," Penelope said, her brows drawn together in a puzzled frown. "I don't see how that can have anything to do with something Artemis said."

"No doubt you're right," Scarborough said at once. "Yet his abrupt departure has left his younger sister to travel alone to London."

"But surely Miss Picklewood will be accompanying her?" Artemis pointed out.

"Not as I understand it," Scarborough said to her. "Apparently Miss Picklewood received news this morning of a friend in Bath who has been struck by a sudden illness. She's already left to go to her side."

"Then Lady Phoebe will simply have to make do with her lady's maid on the trip to London," Penelope said dismissively.

"A servant is hardly the same as a companion, especially for a lady in Lady Phoebe's condition," Scarborough mused. "As I said, it's a pity that Wakefield found his business more urgent than his blind sister."

Artemis winced at the blunt words. Yet, the duke's insistence on the subject might be used to her advantage. Penelope usually only gave her a half day once a week to do as she pleased. Even if Apollo were gravely injured, Artemis very much doubted that Penelope would let her go to the Duke of Wakefield's London home for more than a couple of hours. But if she thought it was her own idea...

Artemis cleared her throat. "I know that Wakefield is very fond of Lady Phoebe."

"Of course, of course," the duke rumbled.

"In fact, I suppose he would be very grateful if someone were to volunteer to travel with his sister."

Penelope wasn't a complete widgeon. She immediately understood Artemis's hint—understood and didn't much like it. "Oh, I couldn't. Why, with you and my maids and all my luggage, we barely fit in the carriage on the way here. It's simply impossible."

"That is too bad," Artemis murmured. "Of course, Phoebe could take her own carriage and only you could travel with her."

Penelope looked horrified.

"...Or I could go."

"You?" Penelope squinted, but it was a calculating squint. "But you're *my* lady's companion."

"No, you're right," Artemis hastily demurred. "Such an extravagant gesture of kindness would be too much."

Penelope frowned. "You really believe Wakefield would think me extravagantly kind?"

"Oh, yes," Artemis said, wide-eyed with sincerity. "Because you *will* be. And if you lend me for the time that Miss Picklewood is away, why, Wakefield will hardly be able to thank you enough."

"Oh, my," Penelope breathed. "What a very good idea."

"You are beneficence itself, my lady," Scarborough announced as he bent over Penelope's hand, and winked at Artemis.

Chapter Ten

At the peasant's words, one of Herla's men leaped from his horse, but when his feet touched the ground, he crumbled into a pile of dust. King Herla stared and remembered the Dwarf King's warning: none of them could dismount before the little white dog or they, too, would turn to dust. He gave a terrible cry at the realization, and as he did so, both he and his men faded into ghostly forms. Then he spurred his horse and did the only thing left to him: he hunted.
Thus King Herla and his retinue were doomed to ride the moonlit sky, never quite of this world or the next....
—from The Legend of the Herla King

"Will he awake?" Maximus stared down at the madman later that morning.

Viscount Kilbourne was hidden away in the cellar under Wakefield House, having been smuggled in along the secret tunnel. Maximus and Craven had set up a cot down here, close to a brazier of glowing coals to keep him warm.

Craven frowned at his motionless patient. "'Tis uncertain, Your Grace. Perhaps if we were able to take him to a more salubrious place above ground..."

Maximus shook his head impatiently. "You know we cannot risk Kilbourne being found."

Craven nodded. "'Tis said on the streets that Bedlam's governors have already sent for soldiers to hunt down the Ghost. Apparently they are quite embarrassed at the escape of one of their inmates."

"They ought to be embarrassed by the entire place," Maximus muttered.

"Indeed, Your Grace," Craven replied. "But I still fear for our patient. The noxious fumes from the brazier, not to mention the damp of the cellar—"

"Aren't the best conditions for an invalid," Maximus cut in, "but discovery and a return to Bedlam would be much worse. He wouldn't survive another beating."

"As you say, Your Grace, this is the best we can do, but I don't like it very much. If we could but send for a physician more learned in the healing arts—"

"The same objection applies." Maximus paced restlessly to the opposite wall of the cellar. Damn it, he needed Kilbourne to wake for Artemis's sake. He remembered her shining, grateful face, and he couldn't help but think she wouldn't be so grateful now if she could see her brother's condition.

"Besides," Maximus continued, returning to Craven's side, "you're as good as if not better than most of the university-educated doctors I've seen. At least you haven't a peculiar fondness for disgusting miracle draughts."

"Hmm," Craven murmured. "While I am of course gratified by Your Grace's confidence in me, I must point out that most of my doctoring has consisted of tending to *your* gashes and bruises. I've never had to deal with a patient with a head wound and broken ribs."

"Even so, I trust you."

Craven's face went completely blank. "Thank you, Your Grace."

Maximus gave him a look. "Don't let's get maudlin, Craven."

Craven's craggy face twitched. "Never, Your Grace."

Maximus sighed. "I must make an appearance upstairs, else the servants will begin to wonder where I've gone. Come at once, though, should he regain his senses."

"Of course, Your Grace." Craven hesitated, studying the unconscious man's face. "I think, though, we will have to find another place to conceal Lord Kilbourne when he wakes."

"Don't imagine I haven't already thought of that problem," Maximus grunted. "Now if I only knew *where* to secrete him more permanently."

With that dispiriting thought he turned and made his way to the upper floors. Craven would stay and nurse Kilbourne in the cellar while Maximus would return periodically as he was able throughout the day. He'd spoken only the truth: there was no one else to trust with the task save Craven.

As Maximus made the upper hall he was waylaid by his butler, Panders, who, fortunately, was too well trained to ever ask awkward questions. Panders was an imposing man of middling years with a round little belly who normally never had so much as a hair of his snowy white wig out of place, but today he was so perturbed his left eyebrow had shot up.

"Begging your pardon, Your Grace, but there is a soldier in your study who is quite *insistent* that he see you. I have informed him that you are not receiving, but the fellow will not be sent away. I had thought to call Bertie and John, but though they are stout lads, the soldier is naturally armed and I should not like to see blood upon your study carpet."

At the beginning of this recitation Maximus had felt a thrill of alarm, but by the end of it, he had begun to have an idea who his visitor was. So it was with calm aplomb that he told Panders, "Quite right. I'll see to the man myself."

His study was at the back of the house—situated so that he might not be disturbed by the hubbub of the street or the frequent callers whom Panders usually dealt with quite adequately.

Today's visitor was another matter.

Captain James Trevillion turned as Maximus opened the door to his study. The dragoon officer was tall with a long, lined face that lent him an air of austerity, even though he was much the same age as Maximus.

"Your Grace." Trevillion's nod was so curt that in any other man Maximus might have taken insult. Fortunately he was long used to the dragoon's lack of obsequiousness.

"Trevillion." Maximus murmured and took a seat behind his massive mahogany desk. "To what do I owe the pleasure of your visit? We met just a fortnight ago. Surely you haven't managed to stop the gin trade in London in that short a space of time?"

If the dragoon captain felt any resentment at Maximus's sarcasm, he hid it well. "No, Your Grace. I have news regarding the Ghost of St. Giles—"

Maximus interrupted the officer by waving an irritable hand. "I've told you more than once that your obsession with the Ghost of St. Giles does not interest me. *Gin* is the evil in St. Giles, not some lunatic in harlequin's motley."

"Indeed, Your Grace, I am well aware of your thoughts on the Ghost," Trevillion said with composure.

"Yet you persist in ignoring them."

"I do what I think best for my mission, Your Grace, and between the Ghost and this new fellow, Old Scratch—"

"*Who?*" Maximus knew his voice was too sharp, but he'd heard that name before: the drunken aristocrat in St. Giles who had been robbed—he'd said his attacker was Old Scratch.

"Old Scratch," Trevillion replied. "A rather vicious highwayman who has been hunting in St. Giles. He's much newer than the Ghost."

Maximus clenched his jaw as he glared at the man. A little over two years ago he'd caused the 4th Dragoons to be outfitted and brought to London to assist in the veritable war on gin in London. He'd handpicked Trevillion himself, for he wanted an intelligent, brave man. A man capable of making important decisions on his own. A man resistant to both bribes and threats. But the problem was that the same qualities that made the dragoon captain excellent at his job also made him damnably stubborn when he saw what he perceived to be a lawbreaker in his territory. Trevillion had been near obsessed with the Ghost almost from the start of his mission.

The irony of having his own nemesis in his pay was not lost on Maximus.

Trevillion shifted, clasping his hands behind his back. "You may not be aware, Your Grace, that the Ghost of St. Giles broke into Bedlam last night, assaulted a guard, and effected the escape of a murderous madman."

Ah, of course Trevillion would be interested in the matter. Maximus leaned back in his chair, steepling his fingers before him. "What do you propose I do about it?"

Trevillion looked at him for a long moment, his face perfectly impassive. "Nothing, Your Grace. It is my job to capture and detain the Ghost of St. Giles so that he doesn't do further harm in St. Giles or, indeed, the rest of London."

"And this latest event will somehow help you capture him?"

"Naturally not, Your Grace," the captain said with grave respect. "But I find it interesting that a footpad that usually is to be seen only in the same place he is named after ventured so far east as Moorfields."

Maximus shrugged, feigning boredom. "The Ghost has been, I believe, sighted at the opera house near Covent Garden. That is outside St. Giles."

"But very close to St. Giles," Trevillion replied softly. "Moorfields is clear across London. Besides, that particular Ghost retired two years ago."

Maximus stilled. "I beg your pardon?"

"I have made a study of the Ghost of St. Giles, Your Grace," Trevillion said with the calmness of a man announcing that it looked like rain. "By examining the movement, actions, and minute physical dissimilarities, I have come to a conclusion. There are at least *three* men who play the Ghost of St. Giles."

"How…" Maximus blinked, aware that the captain was silently watching him. The man Trevillion sought— the man who could expose Maximus's secret—lay four floors below them at this very moment. He pulled himself together and frowned. "Are you sure?"

"Quite." Trevillion clasped his hands behind his back. "One of the Ghosts was much deadlier than the other two. He often wore a gray wig beneath his floppy hat, and he had a tendency to not worry about his own safety—more so even than the others. I believe that man retired this summer. One Ghost never killed, as far as I am aware. His hair was his own, a dark brown, and he wore it clubbed back. I have not seen him for two years. Most probably, given his occupation, he is dead. The third is still quite active. He wears a white wig and he's ferociously adept with the sword. I consider him the original Ghost since he was the first I ever saw—on the night that the old Home for Unfortunate Infants and Foundling Children burned to the ground, he helped with the apprehension of the madwoman known as Mother Heart's-Ease."

Good God. For a moment Maximus could only stare at the man. *He'd* been the one to capture Mother Heart's-Ease.

Fortunately Trevillion seemed to take no note of his speechlessness and was continuing. "It is my theory that it is this last Ghost—the original Ghost—who broke into Bedlam last night. The madman the Ghost liberated must be someone very important to him."

"Or the Ghost is a madman himself." Maximus pulled a stack of papers forward as if ready to dismiss the other man. "Again, I don't see how this matter is of importance to me."

"Don't you?"

Maximus looked up sharply at the dragoon captain. "Explain."

It was Trevillion's turn to shrug. "I mean no offense, Your Grace. I merely observe that the Ghost appears to have much the same interests as you. He patrols St. Giles, often accosting thieves, footpads, and those engaged in the gin trade. He seems to have the same obsession with the gin trade that you yourself have."

"He's also rumored to be a murderer and a ravisher of women," Maximus said drily.

"And yet just a few months ago I interviewed a woman who said the Ghost *saved* her from ravishment," the dragoon captain said.

"What's your point, Trevillion?"

"No point, Your Grace," the captain said smoothly. "I simply seek to keep you apprised of my intentions."

"Consider your report complete, then," Maximus said and began thumbing through his papers. "If that is all, I have business to attend to."

The dragoon captain bowed and limped to the door, closing it softly.

Maximus immediately dropped the papers and eyed the door. Trevillion was treading too close for his taste. The polite but pointed questions, the intelligent remarks, all led to a man near to discovering his secret.

Always supposing Trevillion didn't already know that Maximus was the Ghost.

Maximus sighed in irritation and pushed the thought from his mind to focus on his papers, for he hadn't lied: he did have business to attend to. His secretary had left several letters to be read and signed as well as a report on his land in Northumberland to be read and considered.

Those matters took up the rest of the morning before Philby, his secretary, arrived for further consultation. Maximus ordered luncheon brought to his study so that they could continue to work with the maps spread over the desk and floor. Craven appeared at the study door midafternoon to give a single shake of his head before disappearing again. Maximus bent over his work, trying not to brood on the man lying unconscious in his cellar below.

Supper was a makeshift meal as well, since Philby and he had run across a complicated bit pertaining to the inheritance of a tiny tract of land hardly worth the bother at all if it didn't give access to a coal mine.

It wasn't until nearly nine of the clock that he looked up again, and that was because of a commotion in the hall, boisterous enough to be heard even at the back of the house.

Maximus stood and stretched. "That's done for the day, I think, Philby."

The secretary nodded wearily and began gathering the maps as Maximus strode out of the study.

He could hear Phoebe chattering before he saw her and rounded the corner to find her piling her hat and gloves in Panders's arms as Belle, Starling, and Percy milled about her feet. Maximus eyed the dogs with a raised brow. Usually they stayed at Pelham.

"I trust your trip was uneventful," Maximus said in greeting as Percy attempted to knock him down.

Phoebe turned from pulling off her gloves. She was an affectionate little thing and she flung herself at once into his arms. "Oh, Maximus, it was quite fun with Artemis along!"

And he looked over his sister's shoulder to see Artemis Greaves with Bon Bon the dog in her arms, regarding him gravely.

*   *   *

"MISS GREAVES," THE Duke of Wakefield said as Phoebe stepped back from his arms. "What a surprise."

It'd only been little more than a day since she'd last seen him, yet the shock of his presence before her shook her physically. He was so commanding. So vital. This man—*Maximus*—had gripped her and kissed her with such an intense passion she'd felt as if she were drowning, helpless and wanton and wanting more. Now he stood before her and she had so many questions to ask—and she could utter none of them.

"Your Grace," Artemis murmured, dipping into a curtsy as Bon Bon wriggled in her arms. "I trust the surprise is not an ill one."

She set the elderly dog down on the floor and he ran to nip affectionately at Percy's legs.

"Don't be silly, Artemis." Phoebe laughed. "And you, Maximus. You mustn't be quite so stern. You'll scare Artemis away and I won't have that. She's only just come to stay."

"Stay?" Maximus arched one intimidating brow.

"*Yes.*" Phoebe linked her arm with Artemis. "Lady Penelope said that as Cousin Bathilda had to go tend her ill friend, she would lend me Artemis as companion. Wasn't that awfully nice of her?"

"Unusually so," Maximus murmured with a sharp glance at Artemis. "And she sent her little lapdog as well?"

"I'm the one who usually looks after Bon Bon," Artemis said, smoothing her skirt. Did he want her gone? The thought brought an unexpected pang of hurt to her breast. "I thought he could do with a change of scenery and Penelope agreed."

"It would seem so." He inclined his head, his expression neutral. "And whose decision was it to bring up the greyhounds and Percy?"

"Mine, of course," Phoebe said brightly. "I think they get lonely when we leave them at Pelham."

"Mmm." Maximus murmured noncommittally.

"We've made all sorts of plans on the drive home," Phoebe chattered on. "I thought we could attend the theater at Harte's Folly and go shopping and perhaps see the fair."

Maximus's mouth thinned at that. "I'll accompany you on the first two, but the last is out of the question."

"Oh, but—"

"Phoebe."

The single word seemed to signal defeat to the girl. Her bright smile wobbled a bit before she caught it and continued, "Anyway, we'll have a wonderful time while Artemis is here. I just sent the maid upstairs to have the pink room freshened for her, and I ordered tea. Would you like to join us?"

Artemis half-expected Maximus to decline—Phoebe had indicated in the carriage that he often kept much to himself even though they shared the same house in London.

But Maximus inclined his head. "I'd be delighted."

He offered his arm to Artemis and she laid her hand on his sleeve, taking advantage of Phoebe turning to talk to the butler to lean close and whisper, "Where is he?"

He shook his head minutely. "Later."

She bit her lip. The drive up to London had been near agony, trying to be bright and cheerful with Phoebe, and all the while worried and wondering about Apollo.

"Please."

His deep brown eyes met hers. "As soon as I can. I promise."

It was illogical, but his words of assurance warmed her. She knew that if Apollo's health were dire, he'd take her straight to her brother. As it was, they needs must endure tea and cakes first.

Maximus held out his other elbow to his sister, and he led them both up a curving flight of stairs with a gilded rail with the dogs following merrily behind. At the top, immediately facing the stairs, was a grand salon. Pink painted doors were ornamented with bas-relief-carved vines picked out in gold. The salon itself had a soaring ceiling, intricately painted with gods floating foreshortened on billowy clouds. Artemis tipped back her head, studying the scene.

"The education of Achilles," Maximus murmured in her ear.

Well, that explained the centaur.

"Must we have tea in here?" Phoebe was muttering on the other side of him. "I always feel like I'm on a stage. The blue sitting room is much more comfortable."

Maximus ignored his sister's complaints. "Mind the table there. Mrs. Henrys had it moved whilst we were in the country."

"Oh." Phoebe carefully skirted the low, marble table with his help before sitting on a rose settee. Bon Bon jumped up to sit beside her, his mouth open in a wide, doggy grin.

Artemis took the seat opposite her, and the greyhounds settled at her feet.

"I do hope your business in London was very important," Phoebe said severely. "It quite spoiled the party at

Pelham when you left so abruptly. Everyone was calling for their carriages this morning."

"I'm sorry if I caused you distress," Maximus replied, looking rather more bored than sorry as he leaned against the ornate black marble mantle near them. Percy wandered over and flopped down on the hearth with a gusty sigh.

Phoebe rolled her eyes. "It's not my distress you should be worried about. Lady Penelope was quite put out, wasn't she, Artemis?"

"She did seem a little, er, miffed," Artemis said cautiously.

"Was she?" Maximus looked at her, his eyes sardonic and intimate.

"Well, she was until the Duke of Scarborough took it upon himself to console her," Phoebe said. "You ought to watch out for him, dear brother. Scarborough will snatch her out from under your nose."

"I'll worry about that when Scarborough's income increases by another tenth."

"Oh, Maximus," Phoebe said, her mouth turning down.

The maids entered at that moment, so Phoebe was forced to swallow whatever she was about to say.

Artemis watched as the tea things were set on a low table between them, along with trays of cakes and small, savory treats.

"Will that be all?" the head maid asked Phoebe.

"Yes, thank you," Phoebe replied and, as the maids trooped out again, turned to Artemis. "Would you like to pour?"

"Of course." Artemis leaned forward and began assembling the tea.

"I know it isn't my place, Maximus," Phoebe began slowly as she offered a piece of cake to Bon Bon, "but I can't help but think that you deserve better than a wife who weighs your worth down to the ha'penny."

"Shall I have a wife who values not the importance of money—particularly *my* money?" Maximus asked lightly as he accepted his dish of tea from Artemis. His hands made the dainty dish look like a thimble.

"I would you had a wife who valued *you* instead of your money," Phoebe snapped back.

Maximus waved an impatient hand. "It matters not. My money is from the dukedom and while I live I am the duke. One might as well sever my heart from my chest as separate me from my title. We are one and the same."

"Do you truly believe that?" Artemis asked low.

Both Phoebe and Maximus looked at her as if startled by her voice, but it was only Maximus that Artemis concentrated on. Maximus and his unfathomable deep brown eyes.

"Yes." He answered without hesitation—without even stopping to think about it, as far as she could see.

"And if you didn't have the title?" she asked. She shouldn't talk to him like this in front of Phoebe—it revealed too much about their peculiar relationship— yet she needed to know his answer. "Who would you be then?"

His mouth flattened impatiently. "Since I *do* have the title, it doesn't matter."

"Humor me."

He opened his mouth, shut it, frowned, and then said slowly, "I do not know." He glared at her. "Your question is silly."

"But telling, nonetheless," Phoebe said. "Both in the answer and in the inquiry."

"I will take your word for it," Maximus said, placing his dish of tea on the tray. "But I have more important matters to attend to. If you'll allow me to borrow Miss Greaves, I'll show her the house and instruct her on her duties as your companion."

Phoebe looked startled. "I thought I'd do that in the morning."

"You may show Miss Greaves your rooms and whatever personal things you want done tomorrow, but I have a few special instructions I want to make clear tonight."

"Oh, but—"

"Phoebe."

The girl slumped. "Oh, all right."

Maximus's lips twitched. "Thank you." He looked at the dogs sternly. "You lot *stay*."

Artemis rose at his nod and bid Phoebe good night before following him from the room. He immediately mounted the stairs to the third floor.

"Was that necessary?" Artemis asked low as she trailed him.

"You do want to see your brother, don't you?" he inquired rhetorically.

"Of course," she said tartly, "but you needn't have made it sound as if I were Phoebe's keeper and that you have special instructions about her."

He turned at the top of the stairs, so suddenly that she nearly ran into him. She halted a bare inch away, aware of the heat of him, the anger that seemed to always boil just beneath the surface.

"But I do have special instructions for you," he said

with simple clarity. "My sister is all but blind. Since you have inveigled your way into being her companion, you might as well act as one. I expect you to keep her safe. To deter her from her more dangerous outings, to make sure she doesn't exceed what she can do without her sight, to always take at least one footman, preferably two, whenever you venture forth from my doors."

Artemis tilted her head, studying him. His concern was real, but it also must be nearly stifling for Phoebe. "You find an afternoon at the fair too dangerous?"

"For one such as she, yes," he said. "She might be easily lost in a crowd, easily shoved or jostled. There are pickpockets, thieves, and worse at the fair. A gently bred lady of means who cannot see is an obvious and easy target. I will not have her hurt."

"I see."

"Do you?" He didn't move, but his sheer size seemed suddenly intimidating. "My sister is very dear to me. I would do anything to keep her from harm."

"Even if your measures to keep her safe become a cage?" she asked gently.

"You speak as if she were like any other young girl her age," Maximus growled. "She's not. She's *blind*. I brought in every doctor, every man of science, every learned healer from near and far, no matter the expense or trouble. I let them torture her with noxious medicines, all in the hope they could help her. None could keep her from going blind. I couldn't save her *sight*, but I'll be thrice damned before I see her further hurt."

Artemis inhaled, his fervor both exciting and slightly frightening. "I understand."

"Good." He turned and led her down the hall. "These are

my sister's rooms." He indicated a pale green door. "And here is the pink room where Phoebe wants you to stay." He gestured to the next door down, which stood ajar. A maid hurried out, pausing only to curtsy deeply to Maximus.

Artemis peeked inside. The walls were covered in a deep rose-watered silk, lending the room its name. A canopied bed was bracketed by two carved tables topped by yellow marble, and the fireplace was surrounded by rose-veined marble.

"It's delightful," Artemis said truthfully. She glanced over her shoulder to the duke. "Are your rooms on this floor as well?"

He nodded. "Down this corridor."

They turned into a passage and walked toward the back of the house.

"Here's the blue sitting room—the one that Phoebe likes to use. And these are my rooms."

The doors to his rooms were a rich forest green detailed in black.

"Come." He led her to a small door paneled to look like the surrounding wainscoting. Behind it was a narrow staircase, obviously a servant's stairs. They went down, spiraling into the dark, but Artemis followed him without fear.

Two floors below, and through a door cut into a stone stairs, he paused before a second door and looked at her intently. "No one must know he is here. I had to take him out as the Ghost. They're looking for him."

She nodded, her throat clogging. Four years. Four years he'd been locked up in Bedlam.

Maximus unlocked the door and opened it, revealing a long, low subterranean room.

"Your Grace." It was the servant that Artemis had

noticed at the dueling demonstration. He'd risen from a chair set beside a cot. And on the cot—

Artemis rushed forward, ignoring everything else. Apollo lay so still, his dear face made almost unrecognizable by dark bruises and swelling. What flesh that wasn't maimed was very pale.

She fell to her knees beside him, reaching out one trembling hand to push the shaggy hair from his forehead.

"Craven," Maximus spoke behind her. "This is Miss Artemis Greaves, the sister of our patient."

"Ma'am." The servant nodded.

"Have you called a doctor?" she asked without taking her eyes from Apollo's face. She slid her hand over his unshaven cheek to his neck and searched. There. A flutter. The blood still beat within his veins.

"No," Maximus answered.

She turned at that, her eyes narrowed. "Why not?"

"I told you," he said patiently, his voice even. "No one must know."

She held his gaze a moment longer before turning back to Apollo. He was right. Of course he was right. They mustn't risk Apollo being discovered and possibly being forced to return to Bedlam.

And yet to see him like this and offer no care near killed her.

Craven cleared his throat. "I've been looking after his lordship, Miss. There's not much else a doctor could do."

She glanced at the man quickly. "Thank you." She meant to say more, but something was caught in her throat. Her eyes stung.

"Weep not, proud Diana," Maximus murmured. "The moon will not allow it."

"No." She agreed, swiping fiercely at her cheeks. "There's no need for tears yet."

For a moment she thought she felt a hand on her shoulder. "You may stay here with him for a while. Craven needs a respite in any case."

She nodded without turning. She didn't dare.

The men's footsteps retreated and she heard the door shut behind them. The candle flames wavered and then stood still again.

Still, like her brother.

She laid her head on his arm and remembered. They'd been children in a family broken by madness and genteel poverty, left to run wild by parents with other cares. She recalled wandering the woods with him, watching him catch frogs in the tall grass by the pond. She'd searched for bird nests in the reeds as he fought dragons with fallen branches. The day he'd been sent away to school had been the worst of her young life. She'd been left with Mama, an invalid, and Papa, who was usually off on "business"—one of his wild schemes to repair their fortunes. When Apollo had returned for the holidays she'd been relieved—so relieved. He hadn't left her forever.

She watched his chest rise and fall and remembered and reflected. All her life things had been taken from her: Apollo, Thomas's affection, Mama and Papa, her home, her future. No one had ever asked her opinion, garnered her thoughts on what she wanted or needed. Things had been done to her, but she'd never had the chance to *do* things. Like a doll on a shelf, she'd been moved about, manipulated, flung aside.

Except she wasn't a doll.

What she might've once had: a home, husband, and

family of her own was gone now. She would never have them. But that didn't mean that she couldn't decide to have something else.

That she couldn't live her life as best she could. As best she *wanted*.

She could either spend the rest of her life being manipulated and quietly mourning what she'd lost, or she could create a new life. A new reality.

The candles had burned low when Craven opened the door to the chamber again. "Miss? It's late. I can sit with Lord Kilbourne for the night while you go to bed."

"Thank you." She rose, stiff from sitting on the cold stone floor, and looked at the man. "You'll let me know if he changes?"

"Yes, I will," he said, and his voice was kind.

Artemis touched Apollo's cheek and then turned to make her way up the stairs.

Up out of stagnation and despair.

Chapter Eleven

*For one hundred years King Herla led his wild hunt,
and all those who had the misfortune to see the
shadowy riders in the moonlit sky crossed themselves
and muttered a prayer, for death often followed such a
sighting. On one night of the year, and one night only,
King Herla and his hunt became corporeal: the night of
the autumn harvest when the moon was full. On that night
everyone who could hid in terror, because King Herla
sometimes caught up mortals into his wild hunt, dooming
them for eternity.
It was on such a night that King Herla captured a young
man. His name was Tam....*
—from *The Legend of the Herla King*

Maximus was just sealing a letter in his sitting room when he heard the door to his bedroom open. Craven had already gone down to tend to Kilbourne, and the other servants had strict instructions not to bother him between the hours of ten at night and six in the morning. Maximus rose and crossed to look in his bedroom.

Artemis stood by his bed, her beautiful dark gray eyes calmly inspecting it.

Something within his veins began to heat. "These are my private rooms," he said as he strolled toward her.

"I know." She watched him without any fear. "I've come to give you back your ring."

She unwrapped the fichu from about her neck, revealing the plain square neckline of her dress and the chain that disappeared into the valley between her breasts. Dipping a finger into the shadowy recess, she pulled out the chain and drew it off over her head. He just caught sight of something else on the chain—something green—and then she took the ring off before tucking the chain into a pocket and giving the ring to him. He stepped closer to her and took the ring between his fingers. It was warm from her body heat, as if she'd brought the ancient metal to life. Holding her gaze, he screwed the ring onto his left little finger. As he stared into her eyes she seemed to stop breathing and the color rose, delicately pink, in her cheeks, giving the illusion of vulnerability. Something in him wanted to seize her and lick the tenderness from her sweet skin.

He swallowed. "Why are you here?"

She shrugged one delicate shoulder. "I told you: to bring you your ring."

"You come to a bachelor's rooms—bedroom—well after dark all by yourself to give him a trinket you could just as easily hand him in the morning." His voice was mocking. He wanted to break her suddenly. To make her feel the rage he did at the situation they had been placed in. Were it not for her history—and his—he might've courted this woman. Might've made her his *wife*. "Have you no care for your reputation?"

She stepped toward him until she was so close he fancied he breathed the same air as she and when she tilted her face up to look at him he saw that she wasn't nearly as calm as he'd imagined.

"No," she murmured, her voice a siren's song, "none at all."

"Then I'll be damned if I will," he muttered and kissed her.

THERE. THERE IT was again: that whirlpool pulling her in, sweeping away all the doubts and fears and sorrow, all her thoughts. Leaving in their place only *feeling*, pure and searing. He licked into her mouth with a hot, conquering tongue. Artemis stood on tiptoe, trying to get closer to him, spreading her fingers wide against the silk of his banyan. If she could, she would've crawled right into him, made a home for herself in his broad, strong chest, and never emerged again.

This man, she wanted *this* man, despite his wretched title, his money, his land, his history, and all his myriad obligations. Maximus. Just Maximus. She'd take him bare naked if she could—and be the gladder for it.

The man without the trappings was what she craved, but since his trappings came with him, she'd take them perforce as well.

He pulled back, his chest heaving, and looked at her angrily. "Don't start something you mean to stop."

She met his gaze squarely. "I don't mean to stop."

His eyes narrowed. "I cannot give you marriage."

She'd *known*. She'd never thought he could—she would've sworn so had she been asked a minute earlier—but his blunt words were an arrow of pain piercing her heart nonetheless. She bared her teeth in a smile. "Have I asked you to?"

"No."

"And I never shall," she vowed.

He still wore his white wig and she snatched it off, flinging the expensive thing aside. Underneath, his dark brown hair was shorn close to his head. She ran her hands over it, reveling in the intimacy. *This* was the private man beneath. This was the man without his public persona.

Suddenly she wanted all his disguises stripped away. She began working frantically at the buttons of his banyan, almost tearing the beautiful shot silk in her haste.

"Hush," he murmured to her, catching her hands with his own. He looked at her, and although his voice was gentle his face was not kind. "Are you experienced, my Diana?"

She scowled. The very last thing she wanted was for him to send her away because of some ridiculous scruples. On the other hand, she didn't want any more lies between them. "No."

His expression didn't change, save for a small, satisfied curve of his lips. "Then by your leave, we'll take this slow, both for your sake and because I have a mind to savor you."

If she'd wanted to protest, she wouldn't have been able to. He spread her hands wide and bent to take her mouth again. She felt the press of his thumbs, rubbing in slow, sensuous circles on her palms even as his lips parted hers. The kiss lingered achingly, as if they'd all the time in the world. He licked across her upper lip, pulling back teasingly when she opened for him.

"Maximus," she moaned.

"Patience," he chided, and angled his head before pressing his mouth against hers again.

She tried to pull her hands from his, but his grip was too strong. He chuckled low in his throat and pressed into her, still holding her hands wide. She was distracted by a nip at the corner of her mouth and then she found herself falling backward.

For a split second alarm made her frame stiffen... and then she bounced on a soft, feathered mattress. Artemis looked up and saw Maximus standing over her that satisfied little smile on his lips again.

He reached down and traced the line of her throat, his touch light, nearly tickling as his fingers trailed to where her bodice cut across her breasts.

She shivered.

"Don't think I've forgotten when your fichu slipped from your dress," he murmured. "Strange, for I've seen more immodest décolletages at every ball I've ever attended, yet I've been entirely unable to remove the thought of your breasts from my mind." His gaze flicked up to hers, dark and enigmatic. "Your breasts and other parts of you. Perhaps it's the very fact that you usually cover yourself so modestly in public that makes the unveiling that more anticipated. Or perhaps"—he bent and whispered in her ear—"it's you. Merely you."

She swallowed even as he licked around the rim of her ear, pausing to tug on her earlobe with his teeth before trailing his open, wet mouth down her neck and to the slopes of her breasts.

"I've never before been so obsessed with a woman," he said, his warm lips brushing against her flesh with each word. "I wonder if you've ensorcelled me, Diana?"

His tongue probed between her breasts and she inhaled sharply. He'd at last let go of her hands and she moved both to his head, holding him against her as he made love to her still-clothed bosom. Surely if anyone were bespelled it was she? In moments she would be giving up any hope of marriage. Of the future she'd taken for granted before Apollo's arrest.

She felt nothing but exultation at the prospect. To finally *live*. To take the reins of her own life, however hobbled. This was what she wanted.

If she were bespelled, she wanted the spell to never end.

Artemis blinked and saw that Maximus was watching her. "Second thoughts?"

"The exact opposite." She pulled him down and this time it was she who kissed him. Fiercely, if not expertly.

"Roll over, then, my goddess of the moon," he murmured against her lips. "Let me free you from these earthly weights."

She moved to her belly, then, and felt the tiny tugs as he unhooked her bodice, untied her skirts, unlaced her stays. He was right: each layer of cloth removed from her body made her lighter. More free.

He gently nudged her to her back and drew her stays over her head, then he plucked the pins from her hair, putting each one carefully in his banyan pocket, until her hair fell down in a great, heavy loop.

"Artemis," he whispered as he drew her hair to her breast, "goddess of the hunt, of the moon, and of childbirth." His lips quirked wryly. "I've never understood the last, as she's a virgin goddess."

"You forgot wild things," she whispered back. "She guards all the wild animals and the places they live, and I suppose childbirth is, at base, the closest a woman comes to becoming an animal, isn't it?"

He pulled back, examining her face, and then grinned, quick and mercurial. "I adore the turnings of your mind."

The word *adore* made her heart leap foolishly, but she knew that sort of declaration meant very little in the bed-chamber. She would be content with what she *could* have, not what she really longed for.

She wound her arms about his neck. "You still wear your banyan."

"Mmm," he hummed, but his attention was once again on her bosom. Her chemise was old and worn, and she had no doubt at all that her breasts could be seen quite clearly through the thin material.

He slid his hand over one breast, pulling the material taut. "Did you do this?"

He rubbed a thumb over a small, neat square patched over a hole worn into the linen. The patch happened to sit right above her left nipple.

"Yes," she said. "Who else?"

"A practical woman." He fitted his mouth over her nipple.

She arched into his sucking warmth, her fingers flexing against his scalp. "A woman without any other options."

He looked up, his face suddenly grim. "Have you come to me because of your lack of options?"

"No." She frowned at him because she resented the abrupt absence of his lips. "I've come to you because I *want* to." She arched up to him, scraping her teeth against the edge of his jaw before falling back. "I come of my own free will. I have the right to do as I wish."

He nodded slowly. "So you do."

And he caught her chemise between his hands and ripped it from top to bottom.

She was bare before him now, everything from her

nipples to the place between her legs. She should be ashamed. Embarrassed and confused.

Instead she felt wonderfully free. She stretched her arms over her head, arching her back, and looking through her eyelashes up at him. "Will you take off that banyan now?"

His eyelids had half-lowered, his gaze a burning brand upon her naked skin as he stared at her legs. "Yes, I believe I will."

He straightened and she watched as he carelessly flicked open the buttons lining the front of his banyan. Beneath he wore merely a shirt and breeches. He shrugged off the shirt easily, the muscles on his shoulders bunching and relaxing as he moved.

She caught her breath as his torso was revealed. She hadn't seen many a male chest unclothed—a rustic or two when she was a child, once a drunken soldier in the streets of London, and of course the marble chests of statues—but she had a mind that most aristocratic men didn't have such muscled bodies. She was reminded abruptly that this man was not only the Duke of Wakefield but also the Ghost of St. Giles. What exertions had built such massive shoulders, such bulging upper arms, and such a deep chest? This body had been honed to fight. This was the body of a dangerous warrior.

His eyes narrowed as if he knew her thoughts and he shucked his breeches and hose quickly before climbing into the bed.

"Now we two are as God made us," she said as he settled over her again.

He arched an eyebrow. "And you prefer me thus?"

"Always," she said. "There's nothing between us

now—neither your past nor mine. Your rank and titles mean nothing here."

He bent to kiss the tip of her breast, making her wiggle. "Most ladies prefer my ducal finery, I think."

"But then I am not most ladies," she said sternly.

"That is true. You are like no other lady I know," he breathed and took her nipple into his mouth.

Heat enveloped her, making her moan. She could feel his tongue against her sensitive breast, the curling hairs on his chest tickled her belly, and one hard thigh was suddenly pressed against the apex of her legs.

She caught her breath. She might not be ashamed of her nudity—or his—but that did not mean that there wasn't a bit of trepidation about what would come. She'd never done this. Never even come close. While her peers had been marrying and learning the joys of motherhood, she'd been cataloging Penelope's embroidery thread.

But she wanted this—wanted *him*. She ran her fingers through his shorn locks, fascinated by the bristles. He had speckles of gray at the sides, making him look both more commanding and more human. Her hands dropped to his broad shoulders and their warmth, their tensile strength, made her bite her lip in anticipation. He was so vital. So alive. And soon he would be her lover.

He moved abruptly to her other breast, sucking strongly even as his fingers teased the first damp nipple. The twin points of pleasure made her restless. She clenched at his sides with her fingers, wanting more.

He reared back, watching her. "All right?"

"Yes?" She frowned and bit her lip, shaking her head against the pillow.

The corner of his lips quirked, but he looked far from

amused. A dark flush had moved up his high cheekbones and the lines beside his mouth had deepened. She could feel that part of him—his male part—pressed into her leg. It seemed to throb against her, a living thing wanting sacrifice.

He petted down her side, soothing her as if she were a fractious mare.

She glared at him, prompting him to kiss her, hot and quick, on the mouth. "Patience."

"I don't want to be patient anymore." She stared at him defiantly. She wanted to find out what this was about. What would happen and how it would feel and if she would be a different woman afterward.

He smiled down at her just as his fingers reached the tiny curls at the top of her slit. She could feel him parting them, carefully, probing, and she went very still, waiting to see what he would do.

One finger trailed to her valley and he looked up into her eyes and smiled. "You're wet."

She frowned because she didn't like not knowing if that was good or bad.

He bent, brushing his mouth against hers, growling so deeply his words were nearly unintelligible. "Wet for me."

Good, then.

He slid his thumb between her folds and found that nub at the top, pressing down as he watched her face. She arched involuntarily, the sensation singing through her limbs.

A muscle ticked on his jaw, his face stern and ruthless, as he pressed again, his finger finding her entrance and slipping in.

She bit her lip, staring back at him, refusing to break their gaze, wanting him to continue.

"God," he whispered. His nostrils flared suddenly, and seemingly against his will, he kissed her.

She opened hungrily beneath him, trying to press up with both her head and her pelvis. But he held her still, pleasuring her with his fingers, taunting her with his tongue.

She tore her mouth from his, panting. "Faster."

"Like this?" he asked, and flicked with his thumb.

"Yes." She closed her eyes, her words slurred as she felt the lovely warmth. "Yes, oh, yes."

His long fingers explored her intimately, each touch sparking her passion higher as he kissed her with leisurely thoroughness. She felt something building beneath her surface, like water over a fire just before it comes to a boil. She closed her eyes, lost in the sensations, feeling wanton.

Feeling free.

He broke their kiss and suddenly took her nipple between his lips just as he sped up his flicks against her clitoris, and she felt as if something inside her detonated. She shuddered, arching into his mouth, his hand, waves of fiery bliss spreading to her toes and fingertips.

It was like finding a new world.

She opened her eyes to see him delicately licking the tip of her nipple as he watched her. "Did you like that?"

She nodded, voiceless with pleasure.

He suddenly closed his own eyes, his hips tilting into her as if involuntarily, and he ground against her. "God. I cannot wait any longer."

He shifted and suddenly his thick cock was between her over-sensitive folds, sliding exquisitely, making her gasp.

"Just…" He grunted and took hold of her knees, bringing them up on either side of his hips, making a wider space between her legs. He was hot and heavy against her, bearing her into the mattress with his solid bulk. He propped himself up on one arm and reached between their bodies. She felt his fingers on her belly and then the nudge of something wide at her entrance.

She held her breath.

His eyes flicked open to look at her. "Be brave."

She raised an eyebrow, waiting.

He grinned.

There was a pinch, a growing pressure. She tensed. It hurt. He was so big and she felt suddenly small and fragile. Was this truly meant to be?

He leaned down and brushed his lips against her nose. "Sweet Diana."

Then he shoved hard.

She inhaled. It burned, but that didn't matter. She was called Artemis, and a huntress could withstand pain. More importantly he was a part of her now, *in* her now. This intimacy, this closeness with him, was something she would remember forever. All her life seemed to turn upon this point, here, now. She lay very still, but couldn't help running her hands over his back. He was so powerful and at this moment, he was only hers, pain or no.

Then, still watching her, he shifted, pulling out before slowly shoving back into her again.

His movement lit a spark within her. Not the fire of before, but something warm and nearly sweet. She framed his face with her palms, widening her legs.

He grunted as if pained. "Wrap your ankles about me, Diana."

She did, the different position making him sink deeper into her. She stroked his high cheekbones, liking the lines on his brow, the sweat that gathered at his hairline. He was moving faster now, the thud of his body against hers on each of his downstrokes firm and strong.

"Diana," he whispered. "My Diana."

She touched the corner of his lips, and he opened, taking her thumb into his mouth, biting tenderly on her flesh.

She felt his belly rubbing against hers, the wet slide of his hard flesh in hers, the brush of his chest against her nipples, and she liked it. There was no pain now, only a feeling of closeness. Of animal intimacy. Perhaps she'd been wrong: perhaps *this* was the moment a woman was nearest to the wild animal: when she was without constraints or thought, no society telling her what she must do and what she must not. Free from civilization.

They were bound together in this primitive act.

He shuddered, like a horse at the point of collapse, his head thrown back, his strong throat working, and she watched his face as he thrust into her one last time, holding himself deep within her as she felt the hot spill of his seed.

Whatever else came tomorrow and for the rest of her life, she would have this moment: this one point in time when she was intimately linked to Maximus.

Maximus the man.

When he first woke, Apollo thought he had died.

For just a moment.

He was warm. His arms and legs and face and indeed

his entire body seemed to ache, but the wonder of the warmth and, now that he considered it, some type of soft material beneath him, made him think he might—he just might—be in a better place.

Then he remembered Ripley.

The turnkey's eyes as he'd unbuttoned his fall, the unmerciful smirk twisting his lips. The bolt that shot through Apollo's chest was part fear, part horror, and overlaying both was a cast of shrinking shame.

He rolled and heaved over the side of whatever he lay on. Or at least his stomach attempted to heave. Bile, green and disgusting, drooled from his mouth as his belly cramped, trying to expel what wasn't there.

A voice exclaimed nearby, and then gentle hands took his shoulders.

Apollo flinched. The hands were male.

He turned fast, shoving them off, and glared at the offender.

The man threw up his hands in a gesture meant to placate. He was tall and rather stringy. Not someone Apollo would fear in the normal way, but this wasn't normal.

Perhaps nothing would ever be normal again.

"My lord," the man said gently, "I am Craven, the Duke of Wakefield's valet. You're in his home and you're safe."

He said the words as if trying to calm a wild animal—or a madman.

Apollo was quite used to the tone, so he disregarded it as he glanced about him. He lay on a low bed or cot in a vast, dim room. Besides the cot and Craven's chair was an iron brazier, filled with burning coals. A few flickering candles sent shadows dancing over ancient arched stone and pillars. There was the distinct smell of damp.

If this place was part of Wakefield's home, then Apollo was much mistaken in how he imagined dukes lived.

He turned back to the valet to ask how he'd come to be here, what had happened, and where the duke was... but other than a very sharp pain in his throat, nothing happened.

Which was when he realized that he couldn't speak.

Chapter Twelve

*Now Tam was an ordinary lad in all respects save one:
he'd been born a twin, and he and his twin sister, Lin,
were as close as two petals furled inside a rosebud. When
Lin heard how her brother had been caught by the Herla
King on harvest night, she screamed with grief. Then she
sought out all who knew anything about King Herla and
his hunt until eventually she sat before a strange little
man who lived all by himself in the mountains. And from
him she learned what she must do if she were to save her
beloved Tam....*
—from *The Legend of the Herla King*

"Your Grace."

The voice was low and deferential—the voice of a
supremely trained manservant. The voice that meant that
Craven was incandescently angry.

Maximus opened his eyes to see the valet standing
by his bedside, holding a candle and very obviously *not*
looking at the woman in the bed beside him.

"What?"

"Viscount Kilbourne has awakened, Your Grace."

Both men had kept their voices low enough that a normal person shouldn't have been disturbed.

But then Artemis had long proved that she was no normal woman. "How long?"

Maximus's head snapped around at her voice. A *normal* woman would've been blushing, looking scared or shamefaced or appalled at having been discovered in the bed of a man she was not married to. Some women of his acquaintance would've swooned—or at least had had the grace to *pretend* to swoon. Artemis merely looked at Craven as she waited for an answer.

Even Craven seemed a bit startled. "Miss?"

Artemis blew out an impatient breath. "My brother. How long has he been awake?"

Craven actually blinked before regaining his aplomb. "Only a few minutes, ma'am. I came at once."

"Good." She nodded and sat up, the coverlet clutched to her magnificent bosom.

Maximus scowled.

"Would you please turn, Craven?" she asked and then barely waited for the valet to give his back before tossing aside the covers and emerging naked. "Is he well?" she asked as she bent, presenting her delicious arse to Maximus's gaze as she picked up her stockings from the floor. She sat on the edge of the bed to quickly roll them on.

Craven cleared his throat. "Lord Kilbourne appears to be in some pain, ma'am, but he understood when I told him I was going to fetch you."

She nodded. "Thank you." She bent for her stays, struggling into them, before trying to tighten the laces.

Maximus muttered an ugly oath and rose from the bed, ignoring the disapproving set of Craven's back. "Let me."

She turned her head to the side, giving him her profile,

before stilling as he touched her shoulders. She pulled her hair over one breast so he could see the laces. This wasn't how he'd meant to spend their morning together. She'd been a virgin—a virgin goddess, of course, but even the most brave of females must feel a bit delicate the morning after her deflowering. He glanced at the windows, still barely gray with predawn. They hadn't even been able to share a breakfast.

He cleared his throat as he swiftly pulled her laces tight, trying not to let himself think too deeply about the tender, curling hairs at the back of her neck. "What time is it, Craven?"

"Not yet six of the clock, Your Grace," the valet said with perfect, stony politeness.

Maximus's mouth tightened, but he said not a word as he tied the laces. He threw on his breeches, shirt, waistcoat, and coat. Artemis was dressing just as swiftly, and he wondered if she did this every day: dressed without help. She must, though. She hadn't a lady's maid unless Penelope lent her hers. The thought made him more irritable. His own mother and most ladies he knew couldn't dress themselves without the aid of another. They weren't supposed to have to do it themselves.

That was the chore of the lower classes.

He snatched up a candlestick and led the way from his rooms. He'd made the trek to his hidden cellar so many times he could've done it without the light, but Artemis would need it. His heels clacked loudly on the steps as he descended, and it wasn't until he stood before the door to the crypt that it occurred to him:

Kilbourne was a murderer thrice over.

They hadn't bothered to chain the madman because

he'd been insensible. Now Maximus bitterly damned his own stupidity. Who knew what waited beyond the door?

"Stay here," he told Artemis curtly.

She frowned, watching him put the key to the door. "No."

His head reared back, his eyes narrowing. He simply wasn't used to anyone disobeying his orders. He took a breath to still his immediate impulse to order her back to his rooms. "We don't know what his disposition is like."

Her look was withering. "Which is why I'm coming inside."

Maximus darted a look at Craven. The valet was examining the ancient graffiti on the wall as if he'd never seen it before and was considering writing an academic paper on it.

"He might be dangerous."

She arched an eyebrow. "Not to me."

"Artemis."

She simply reached out and covered his hand with hers to turn the key and push open the door. Artemis started to enter the room, but Maximus was damned if he'd let her go in first. He might not be able to stop her from seeing her lunatic brother, but he could protect her at the very least.

He ducked his head and went inside ahead of her.

The cellar was very quiet. The brazier still glowed with the embers of the coals and a single candle flickered, casting light on the man in the cot. He was still, lying on his side, facing away from the door.

Maximus approached cautiously. Artemis might think

her brother harmless, but he'd been found with the bloody bodies of three of his friends. A man capable of that was capable of anything.

He was within a stride of the bed when its occupant reared up like a sleeping giant awakened. Maximus had been aware that Viscount Kilbourne was a big man— he'd carried his dead weight out of Bedlam after all—but somehow Kilbourne seemed to have gained bulk along with his senses. His shoulders were as broad and thick as those of a smith, his head shaggy with untrimmed hair. His beard had grown, and now Kilbourne looked like nothing so much as a green man. Something big, feral, and ancient that haunted gloomy woods and knew not the language of men.

Maximus had thought the tales of the murder scene exaggerated, but the beast before him looked quite capable of tearing a man's head from his shoulders.

"Apollo." Artemis started around Maximus.

He caught her arm and drew her to his side.

She shot him an irritated glance.

The one her brother gave him was much more murderous. He stared at Maximus's hand tight about his sister's wrist and then raised angry eyes to meet Maximus's gaze. Maximus was relieved to see that Kilbourne didn't share his sister's eye color. His eyes were a muddy brown. The madman opened his mouth and made a choking sound before closing his lips. A low rumble came from deep in his chest and it was a moment before Maximus realized that Kilbourne was *growling* at him.

The hairs stood up on the back of his neck.

"Let me go to him," Artemis said, pulling against his grip.

"No." One thing to let her into the room when he thought her brother still weak. Quite another to let her near this animal.

"Maximus." Both Craven and Kilbourne swiveled their heads to stare at her when she used his Christian name. She ignored them. "You may come with me, but I *will* touch and talk to my brother."

Maximus swore beneath his breath, earning himself a disapproving stare from Craven. "You are the most stubborn woman I know."

She merely stared at him with an implacable look that would've done justice to the most severe of society dowagers.

He sighed and turned to the madman. "Show me your hands."

Maximus half-expected no response at all, but Kilbourne immediately shoved his great paws in front of him.

Maximus lifted his eyes to the animal's and saw sardonic anger in the muddy brown.

Not such a beast after all then.

"I am Wakefield," Maximus said directly to the man. "I don't believe we've met before. On the request of your sister I took you out of Bedlam and brought you to my own house."

Kilbourne lifted one eyebrow and glanced about the long, low cellar.

"You're under the house," Maximus said. "I was forced to take you out at sword point. The governors of Bedlam would very much like to have you back."

Kilbourne's eyes narrowed speculatively, then he looked at Artemis.

"You're safe here. He won't make you return to Bedlam," she said. Maximus felt a tug on the grip he still had on her arm. "Will you?"

He didn't dare take his eyes off the viscount. "No. My word of honor: if you're committed to Bedlam again, it won't be from any action of mine."

The sardonic expression had returned to Kilbourne's eyes. He hadn't missed the implication that Maximus thought him quite capable of doing something that would have him apprehended and returned to the madhouse.

Another tug on his hand and a reproachful "Maximus." Her next words were for her brother, though. "You can trust him, darling. Truly."

Kilbourne didn't take his gaze off Maximus, but he nodded. He took a breath and opened his mouth. A terrible, wrenching noise issued from Kilbourne's lips and Maximus's eyes widened as he realized.

"Stop!" Artemis tore herself from his hand and hurried to her brother. "Apollo, you must stop."

Kilbourne grimaced horribly, his hand clutching his throat.

"Let me see." Artemis placed her small hand on his great paw. "Craven, would you be so kind as to bring us some water, wine, and a few cloths?"

"Right away, ma'am." The valet turned.

"Bring foolscap and a pencil as well," Maximus said.

Craven hurried from the room.

"Darling," she crooned to the monster, and Maximus couldn't stop the stab of jealousy, even if it was her brother. "You must let me have a look."

The great paw dropped.

Artemis drew in a sharp breath.

Even from his stance behind her, Maximus could see the black bruise stamped upon Kilbourne's throat.

It was in the shape of a boot.

She turned to look at Maximus, her beautiful gray eyes stricken.

He took her hand again, this time to comfort rather than to restrain. Kilbourne watched with narrowed eyes as his sister curled her fingers about Maximus's hand. For a madman he seemed uncommonly aware.

Artemis turned to help her brother to lie down upon the cot. He might've regained consciousness, but he obviously was still injured. She smoothed the blanket over his chest and murmured softly to him as they waited interminably for Craven's return.

It seemed like hours later when Craven reentered the cellar, bearing the requested items.

Artemis immediately took one of the cloths the valet held and dipped it in the jug of water he'd brought. She wrung out the cloth and laid it on her brother's throat, her movements exquisitely gentle.

Maximus waited until she was done before handing the pencil and paper to Kilbourne.

The man looked at him, then propped himself on one elbow to scratch out words on the paper.

Maximus bent to read the bold, scrawled hand:

When can I leave?

APOLLO WAS ALIVE. That was the main thing, Artemis reminded herself late that afternoon as she trailed Phoebe from shop to shop. Even if he still—distressingly— couldn't talk, even if Maximus seemed to think her darling brother mad—despite her protests and Apollo's own quite sane manner this morning—at least he was *safe*.

Everything else could be managed as long as he was alive and safe. Apollo would heal and speak again, and she would somehow persuade Maximus of what an idiot he was being.

Apollo would be all right.

"Artemis, come see."

She brought herself back to the present at Phoebe's eager urging. Shopping with Phoebe was nothing like shopping with Penelope. Penelope shopped like a general planning a major campaign: she had objectives, strategies for assault and retreats—though she hardly ever retreated—and the ruthless eye of a woman ready to slaughter her enemy—in this case the shopkeepers of Bond Street. Despite Penelope's great wealth, she seemed to consider it her duty to bargain down the price on everything she bought.

Artemis had once witnessed a shopkeeper acquire a tic under his eye after two hours of waiting upon Lady Penelope Chadwicke.

In contrast, Phoebe shopped like a honeybee in a field of wildflowers: erratically and with no clear purpose in mind. So far they'd stopped at a stationer's, where Phoebe had flitted from bound books to blank sheets of foolscap, caressing the papers and bindings with sensitive fingers. She'd finally alighted on a darling little blank notebook bound in dyed green calfskin and embossed in gold bumblebees—rather fitting, that. Afterward they'd wandered into a perfume shop, where Phoebe had sniffed delicately at a bottle and sneezed for the next ten minutes, complaining under her breath about the overuse of ambergris. That had been a relatively short stop. Phoebe had tried another few bottles and then left, whispering that the proprietor hadn't the proper nose for perfumes.

Now they stood in a tobacconist's as Phoebe poked into different jars. Behind the jars of finely ground tobacco were twists of leaf tobacco for smoking.

Artemis wrinkled her nose—she'd never particularly cared for the aroma of tobacco smoke. "Does your brother imbibe from a pipe?"

"Oh, Maximus never smokes a pipe," Phoebe said absently. "Claims it makes his throat dry."

Artemis blinked. "Who are you buying the tobacco for, then?"

"No one," Phoebe said dreamily, inhaling. "Did you know that even the unscented tobacco has different, distinct odors?"

"Erm, no." Artemis hesitantly peered over the smaller woman's shoulders. Although she could see a slight variation in the color of the tobacco powder in the rows of open jars, they all looked virtually the same to her.

The proprietor of the shop, a man with a long, sloping face and a belly to match, beamed. "My lady has a wonderful sense for the leaves."

Phoebe's cheeks pinkened. "You flatter me."

"Not at all," the man said. "Would you like to sample the snuff? I just received a new shipment from Amsterdam. Would you believe it's scented with lavender?"

"No!" Apparently lavender was an unusual scent. Phoebe looked quite excited.

Half an hour later they exited the shop with Phoebe clutching a small pouch of the precious snuff. Artemis eyed it doubtfully. Many fashionable ladies took snuff, but Phoebe seemed a little young for such a sophisticated hobby.

"Artemis!"

She looked up at the call, in time to see Penelope hurrying toward them, a beleaguered maid trailing behind, laden with packages.

"There you are," her cousin exclaimed as she drew close, rather as if she'd somehow misplaced Artemis. "Hullo, Phoebe. Are you shopping?" Phoebe opened her mouth, but Penelope continued on without pause. "You wouldn't believe the dreariness of my journey back to London. Nothing to do but embroider, and I pricked my thumb three times. I did try to have Blackbourne read to me, but her voice is quite sputtery, not at all like yours, Artemis, dear."

"That must've been very trying for you." Artemis hid a smile, feeling quite fond of her cousin suddenly.

"Well, of course I don't mind lending you to Phoebe *at all*," Penelope said carefully, and then rather spoiled the intent of her statement by adding, "Did the duke notice my generosity?"

Artemis's lips parted, but no sound emerged, for her mind had come to a halt. The duke. *Maximus*. Penelope was still determined to have him as husband—of course she was! She didn't know—nothing had changed for Penelope in the last two days.

While everything had changed for Artemis.

She'd lain with the man her cousin wanted as a husband, and she had a sudden urge to weep. It wasn't fair—either to Penelope or herself. Life shouldn't be this complicated. She should've stayed far, far away from the duke. Except that while she might've been able to hold the duke at length, Maximus the man was another matter entirely.

And despite the guilt that seeped through her veins like poison, she couldn't help but feel that *Maximus*, if not the duke, belonged to *her*, not Penelope.

At least that was the way the world *should* be.

"...so grateful," Phoebe was saying when Artemis became aware that the other two women were still talking. "I do appreciate you lending her to me."

"Well, just as long as I get her back eventually," Penelope said, sounding like she was regretting her beneficence, and Artemis realized with another horrid pang that she might never go back to Penelope. What did Maximus want with her? Would she become his mistress, or was he interested in only one night?

Blackbourne shifted, and one of the boxes in her arms began to slide.

"But I'd better go," Penelope said, eyeing her purchases like a hawk. "The crowds are awful today, and I was forced to leave the carriage two streets over."

They said their farewells, and Artemis watched Penelope retreat, chiding poor Blackbourne over the packages all the while.

"We'd best hurry," Phoebe said, laying her hand on Artemis's arm.

Artemis raised her eyebrows as she carefully guided the younger woman away from the noisome street. "To where?"

"Didn't I tell you?" Phoebe grinned up at her. "We're meeting Hero for tea at Crutherby's."

"Oh." Artemis couldn't help a small jolt of pleasure. She quite liked the elder of the Batten sisters, though she didn't know her as well as she knew Phoebe.

Another block further, just past an elegant millinery

shop, Crutherby's ornate sign loomed up ahead. A smiling maid opened the door, and Artemis immediately caught sight of a flaming head of hair sitting in the corner of the little shop.

"Miss Greaves!" Lady Hero Reading looked up at their approach. "What a lovely surprise. I hadn't known you'd be accompanying Phoebe here today."

"Lady Penelope has lent her to me," Phoebe said as she felt for a chair and lowered herself into the seat. "We've been shopping."

Hero rolled her eyes at Artemis. "She didn't take you to that terrible tobacconist, did she?"

"Well..." Artemis tried to think of how to answer.

"It's not terrible," Phoebe said, rescuing her. "Besides, how else am I to surprise Maximus with snuff?"

"Maximus has quite enough snuff as it is," Lady Hero said as two girls began placing tea things on the little table between them. "And I can't help but think 'tisn't quite respectable for an unmarried lady to be seen in such an establishment."

Phoebe's brows drew together ominously. "That's the very shop you buy Lord Griffin's snuff at."

Hero looked smug. "And *I'm* no longer a maiden."

"Shall I pour?" Artemis hastily cut in.

"Please," Lady Hero said, distracted. "Oh, there are fairy cakes. I always like fairy cakes."

"I did get something for you as well," Phoebe said and fished the little bumblebee notebook from her pocket.

"Oh, Phoebe, you are a dear!" Lady Hero's face shone with genuine delight.

Artemis felt a twinge of sadness. Of course the notebook wasn't for Phoebe herself—she wasn't sure the girl could see to read or write anymore. She looked down, careful to steady her hand as she poured. It wouldn't do to spill the hot tea.

"It looks just like the one Mother used to have," Hero murmured, still examining the notebook.

"Really?" Phoebe leaned forward.

"Mmm." Her elder sister looked up. "Do you remember? I showed you it when you were in the schoolroom. Mother used it to remember names. She was dreadful at it, you know, and she hated to admit it, so she always had the notebook and a small pencil with her..." For a moment Lady Hero's voice trailed away, and she stared into space as if looking at something far distant from the cozy teahouse. "She forgot it that night, for I found it in her rooms months later." Lady Hero frowned at the small notebook. "It must've vexed her—they'd gone to the theater, you know."

"I didn't know," Artemis said, though she wasn't sure Lady Hero had been speaking to her. "I thought they were killed in St. Giles."

"They were," Lady Hero murmured, tucking the little notebook away before accepting a dish of tea. "But why they were there no one knows. St. Giles is quite the opposite direction home from the theater they'd attended. What's more, they were on foot. The carriage was left streets away. Why they left the carriage and why they headed into St. Giles is a mystery."

Artemis knit her brows as she poured a second dish. "Doesn't the duke know why they went that way on foot?"

Lady Hero glanced at Phoebe before staring into her tea. "I don't know if he can remember."

"What?" Phoebe looked up.

Lady Hero shrugged. "Maximus doesn't like to talk about it—you know that—but over the years I've gleaned bits and pieces here and there. As far as I can tell, he won't talk about anything that happened that night after the last act of the play."

For a moment they were silent as Artemis poured herself the last dish of tea.

"He saw them killed, I have no doubt," Lady Hero whispered. "When the coachman and footmen found them, Maximus was lying over their dead bodies."

Artemis blinked at the terrible image and carefully set down her teacup. "I didn't know he was wounded."

Lady Hero looked up, her eyes weary with an old sorrow. "He wasn't."

"Oh." Unaccountably, Artemis's eyes blurred. The thought of Maximus, so strong, so sure, broken as a boy and huddling over the bodies of his parents...it was simply too awful to contemplate.

"I wish I could've known them." Phoebe broke the silence. "And Maximus, too, before...Well, he must've been different."

Lady Hero smiled, as if at a fond memory. "I remember he had a terrible temper and was quite spoiled. Maximus once threw a plate of roasted pigeons at a footman because he had wanted beefsteak for his dinner. The plate hit the footman's face—his name was Jack—and broke his nose. I don't think Maximus had meant to hurt the footman—he simply hadn't thought before he acted—but Father was furious. He made Maximus apologize to poor Jack, and Maximus wasn't allowed to ride his horse for an entire month."

Phoebe wrinkled her brows in thought. "I can believe

the temper—Maximus is quite frightening when he loses his calm—but I can't even imagine him acting that impulsively. He must've been very different as a boy."

"He was different before Mother and Father were killed," Lady Hero said pensively. "Afterward he was so quiet—even when he started speaking again."

"Strange how people can change," Phoebe said. "It's disconcerting, isn't it?"

"Sometimes." Lady Hero shrugged. "I personally find it stranger how often people *don't* change—no matter what happens around them."

Artemis lifted her brows. "Have you a particular person in mind?"

Lady Hero sniffed. "Certain males can become quite ridiculously protective. Can you imagine? Griffin thought I should stay abed today just because I felt a little ill this morning. You would think he'd never seen..."

Lady Hero swallowed the rest of her sentence, but she seemed unable to stop her hand drifting to her middle.

Artemis raised her eyebrows.

"Never seen what?" Phoebe asked.

"Well..." Lady Hero actually blushed.

Artemis cleared her throat, a smile tugging at the corner of her mouth. "I may be wrong, but I believe you are about to become an aunt, Phoebe. Again."

A good deal of squealing ensued.

Artemis signaled the maid for another pot of tea.

When Phoebe had at last quieted and Artemis had poured everyone a fresh dish of tea, Lady Hero sat back. "It's just that he becomes so *brooding*."

Artemis mentally thought that Lord Griffin—a rakish man who often had a grin on his face—could never touch the brooding of Hero's brother, but she forbore pointing this out.

Phoebe piped up. "Your confinement with sweet William went well. Surely he'll remember that?"

"I think he may have some type of wasting brain disease," Lady Hero said darkly. "He's been *hovering*."

Phoebe bit her lip as if quelling her amusement at her brother-in-law's worry over his wife's condition. "Well, in any case, this explains why you were so insistent that we visit the modiste this afternoon."

Lady Hero immediately brightened. "Yes, I ordered a dress before I knew and that will have to be altered, but besides that I've seen some lovely new gowns from Paris especially for ladies in an interesting way. And of course we'll have to get something for Miss Greaves."

Artemis blinked, nearly dropping her dish of tea. "What?"

Phoebe nodded, looking unsurprised by her sister's non sequitur. "Maximus already instructed me this morning to make sure she had at least three new gowns as well as everything else she might need."

"But..." A lady could never accept a gift of clothing from a gentleman. Even with her spotty education and upbringing, that one rule had been drummed into her. Only a mistress accepted such financial obligation from a gentleman.

But wasn't that what she already was?

"It's only right," Phoebe was saying stubbornly. "You came to stay with me without any thought for your own schedule."

Artemis crimped her lips, trying not to laugh. *What* schedule? She lived at the beck and call of Penelope. She had no plans of her own.

"Besides," Phoebe said more bluntly, "I'm tired of looking at that brown thing."

Artemis smoothed a hand over her lap. "What's wrong with my brown dress?"

"It's *brown*," Phoebe said. "Not coffee or fawn or that delicious shade of dark copper, but brown. And not your color at all, in any case."

"No," Lady Hero said thoughtfully, "I think some shade of blue, or perhaps green, would be quite interesting."

Phoebe looked startled, then thoughtful. "Not a light pink?"

"Definitely not." Lady Hero shook her head decisively. "Mind, I saw a lovely cream with red, pink, and dark green embroidered flowers we might look at, but no pastel colors overall. Her own coloring is too delicate. Light shades would simply wash her out. Dark and really rather dramatic, I think."

Both ladies swiveled to examine her, and Artemis suddenly realized what a lump of dough might feel like under the scrutiny of a master baker. She knew from this morning that though Phoebe had trouble discerning shapes, she had no trouble with colors if the object were large enough.

"I see what you mean," Phoebe said, squinting.

For just a second, Lady Hero's face revealed a deep sadness, then she straightened with determination. "Yes, well, I do think we ought to get started, then."

Nodding, Phoebe sipped the last of her tea and set her teacup down.

Artemis watched the ladies as they rose. They thought they were simply giving her a present as friends, but the money for the dresses would come from Maximus, that much was clear.

She'd slept with Maximus.

Her mind caught on the thought, here in this respect-able tea shop. She'd run her hands over his bare back, wound her legs over his hips, and clenched deep inside when he'd thrust his penis into her.

He was her lover.

To take a gift from him now was to make her no bet-ter than a bought woman. A bought woman was the low-est of the low. Little more than a whore. For a moment the breath stopped in her throat in panic. She'd become everything she'd been warned against. Everything she'd struggled not to be in the last four years. She'd succumbed both to her own weakness and the perils of her position.

She'd fallen.

And then she drew breath again, almost in a gasp. Because there was something liberating in reaching the depths. It was a strange place, true, new and foreign, the way murky with hidden perils, but she found she could breathe here. They'd been wrong all along, all those who'd warned her of this place. She could live here well enough.

Perhaps even flourish.

Artemis lifted her chin and rose from her seat, meeting the curious stares of her friends. "Yes, please, I would like a new dress. Or even three."

Chapter Thirteen

❦

On the night of the next autumn harvest, Lin ventured
out into the dark bramble wood. She stood in a
clearing, shivering, and waited until the moon rose,
huge and round, in the sky. She heard a rushing, like a
thousand voices sighing in lament, and when next she
looked, there were ghostly riders urging their silent
mounts through the clouds. Leading them was a giant
of a man, intent, strong, his crown a silvery glow in the
moonlight. She just had time to catch the flash of his pale
eyes before the Herla King reached down with one great
hand and took her....
—from *The Legend of the Herla King*

The full moon lounged in the black velvet sky as Maximus crept into St. Giles that night disguised as the Ghost. He glanced up and watched as she draped herself in the wisps of white clouds, mysterious and coy and everything he could never have.

He snorted derisively to himself and stole into a dark alley, ears and eyes alert to danger. What kind of fool longed for the moon? The kind that forgot his duty, his obligations, the things that he *must* do if he were to continue to call himself a man.

No, not just a man, but the Duke of Wakefield. Romantic fools didn't qualify for the job.

Better to concern himself with the present. Which was why he was haunting St. Giles tonight. It had been far too long since he'd seen to his duty: the hunt for the man who had killed his parents. Night after night, year after year, he'd stalked these stinking alleys, hoping to find some trail, some clue to the identity of the footpad who had robbed and killed them. The man was probably dead by now, yet Maximus couldn't give up the chase.

It was the least he could do for the parents he'd failed so fatally.

Maximus froze as the scent of gin hit his nostrils. He'd emerged from the alley. A man lay in the channel of the larger street the alley emptied into. Broken barrels gushed the nauseous liquid as the man groaned next to his weary nag, an overturned cart still hitched to the horse.

Maximus's lip curled. A gin seller—or perhaps even a distiller. He started forward, pushing down the roiling of his stomach at the stench of gin, when he saw the second man. He sat a great black horse just inside an alley kitty-corner to Maximus's own, which was why Maximus hadn't seen him at once. His coat was a dark blue, gilt or silver buttons glinting in the dark, and in both hands he held pistols. As Maximus emerged, his head turned, and Maximus could see he wore a black cloth over the lower part of his face, his tricorne hiding the upper part.

The highwayman cocked his head, and somehow Maximus knew he was grinning beneath the black cloth. "The Ghost of St. Giles, as I live and breathe. I'm surprised we haven't met before, sir." He shrugged indolently. "But then I suppose I've only just returned to these parts. No matter—even if I've been gone for decades, you should know I still rule this patch of London."

"And who might you be?" Maximus kept his voice to a whispered rasp—as did the highwayman.

They might disguise their voices, but the cadence of a gentleman was impossible to conceal.

"Don't you recognize me?" The highwayman's tone was mocking. "I'm Old Scratch."

And he fired one of his pistols.

Maximus ducked, the brick beside his head exploded, and the gin cart horse bolted up the street, dragging the broken cart behind.

The highwayman wheeled his own horse and galloped away down the alley. Maximus hurdled the gushing barrels and raced after Old Scratch, his heart banging against his chest as his boot heels rang on the filthy cobblestones. The alley was darker than the street they'd left. He might be running headlong into a trap, but he wouldn't have been able to *not* give chase even if the real Old Scratch had stood in his way.

There'd been a glint at the highwayman's throat. Something pinned to his neck cloth. It had almost looked—

A shout, then the clear boom of a gunshot.

Maximus hit the end of the alley at a dead run, nearly barreling into the flank of Captain Trevillion's mount. The captain was fighting as his horse attempted to rear. One of his dragoons was down on the ground, blood welling from a wound on his stomach. The wounded man gasped, eyes wide and uncomprehending. Another dragoon, a pale young lad, was still mounted, his face white and shocked.

"Stay with him, Elders!" Trevillion shouted at the boy. "Do you hear me, Elders?"

The young soldier's head snapped up at the tone of command. "Yes, sir! But the Ghost—"

"Let me worry about the Ghost." Trevillion had control of his horse now and Maximus braced himself for his attack.

Instead, Trevillion gave him a sharp look and said, "He was heading north, in the direction of Arnold's Yard."

With that he wheeled his horse and set spurs to the beast's sides.

Maximus leaped to a crumbling house, swarming up the side. The way to Arnold's Yard was a maze of twisting, narrow lanes, and if Old Scratch was truly headed in that direction, then Maximus could move more quickly over the rooftops.

Above, the moon had deigned to reveal her pale face, casting his shadow ahead of him as he scrambled over tiles and rotting wooden shingles, while below...

Maximus caught his breath. Below, Trevillion was riding like a demon, skillfully guiding his horse around obstacles and leaping the ones he couldn't avoid. It had been so long since Maximus had hunted like this, in tandem with another. Once, long, long ago there had been the others, young men, one just a boy. They'd sparred and fought, joked and wrestled. But somehow he'd grown apart, forever stalking the stinking streets of St. Giles alone. His quest hadn't room for others.

It was good, he realized as he panted and ran. Good to have someone at his back.

He heard a shout from below and slid to the edge of the roof to peer over. Trevillion had come to an alley entirely blocked by an empty cart.

The dragoon captain looked up, a shaft of moonlight catching the gleam of metal on his tall hat and illuminating the pale oval of his face. "I'll have to find a way around. Can you go ahead?"

"Yes," Maximus shouted down.

Trevillion nodded curtly without another word and backed his horse.

Maximus ran. The rooftops were jumbled here. The buildings were from before the Great Fire. They listed, tired and crumbling, waiting for another fire or merely a strong wind to send them crashing to the ground. He leaped between two buildings so close that a grown man would have to turn sideways to sidle between them. He made the second roof, but his boot slipped. He fell, sliding on his hip nearly off the edge. He caught himself just as his boots flew into space. He could hear the clatter of hoofbeats now. Trevillion couldn't have found a way around so fast.

It must be Old Scratch.

Maximus twisted, peering beyond his dangling feet, and saw as the shadow entered the alley below. He didn't give himself time to think.

He let go.

Whether by instinctive timing or simple good luck, he landed on Old Scratch. The highwayman just had warning enough to raise his arm in defense. Maximus caught an elbow to the side of his face, and then he fell to the horse's haunches as the horse reared beneath both of them. Maximus slid, his booted toes brushing the ground before he kicked back up to straddle the horse. His weight pulling on the highwayman's upper body, combined with the horse's movement, should have dragged Old Scratch from the saddle. Somehow, the highwayman hung on with unnatural strength and skill. The horse's front hooves met the cobblestones again with a teeth-crunching jolt, nearly throwing Maximus from his prey. Maximus punched at the man's head, missing as the highwayman twisted like a snake. Maximus grabbed for his hat, trying to reach the scarf. If he could only see Old Scratch's features.

The highwayman turned almost all the way around in the saddle, gold and green glinting at his throat. A knife flashed. Maximus hit out with a gloved hand, felt a tug, and the knife clanged against the bricks on the nearby building. But he'd had to let go to defend himself. The horse lurched forward as the highwayman put spurs to its side and at the same time Maximus felt a hard shove.

He tumbled to the ground, heavy hooves flying close to his head. Instinctively, he ducked and rolled as the sound of hoofbeats retreated.

For a moment he lay against a wall gulping air.

"You let him get away." The voice was Trevillion's and slightly out of breath.

Maximus looked up with a glare. "Not on purpose, I assure you."

The dragoon captain grunted, looking tired. He was leading his horse, having entered the alley from a very narrow lane.

Maximus rose, glancing from the narrow lane to Trevillion's rangy mare. "I'm surprise you didn't get stuck in there."

The other man raised a sardonic eyebrow. "I think Cowslip's surprised, too." He gave the mare an affectionate pat on the neck.

Maximus blinked. "*Cowslip*?"

Trevillion glared. "I didn't name her."

Maximus grunted noncommittally. He supposed he hadn't any leg to stand on, considering the names his sister had given his dogs. He bent to examine the ground close to the wall of the opposite building.

"What are you looking for?"

"He dropped his dagger. Ah." Maximus bent and picked up the knife with satisfaction, stepping closer to the dragoon and the better moonlight.

The dagger was a two-edged blade, a simple, narrow triangle, with hardly any guard and a leather-wrapped handle. Maximus turned it in his hands, peering for any sort of mark without result.

"May I?"

Maximus looked up to see the dragoon captain holding out his hand. His hesitation was only a split second long, but he saw Trevillion's knowing glance anyway.

Maximus handed over the dagger.

The dragoon examined it and then sighed. "Common enough. It could belong to almost anyone."

"Almost?"

A corner of Trevillion's thin lips cocked up. "He's an aristocrat. I'd bet Cowslip on it."

Maximus slowly nodded. Trevillion was an intelligent officer, but then he'd always known that.

"Did you get a look at his face?" the captain asked, handing him back the dagger.

Maximus grimaced. "No. Slippery as an eel. He made sure I couldn't catch hold of that scarf."

"Outwrestled by a man older than you?"

Maximus glanced up sharply.

Trevillion shrugged at his look. "He had a small bit of paunch about his middle and he sat his saddle a bit stiffly. He's athletic, but I wouldn't be surprised if he were older than forty." He considered a moment as if thinking over what he remembered of the highwayman, then nodded to himself. "He might even be older than that. I've seen men on the far side of seventy riding to the hounds without problem."

"I think you're right," Maximus said.

"Was there anything else you noticed about Old Scratch?"

Maximus thought about that glint of green at the high-wayman's throat and decided to keep that hint to himself. "No. What do you know of the man?"

"Old Scratch is without fear—or morals, as far as I can see." Trevillion looked grim. "He not only robs both rich and poor, he doesn't hesitate to harm or even murder his victims."

"How broad is the area he frequents?"

"Only St. Giles," Trevillion said promptly. "Perhaps because he meets little resistance or because the people here are more vulnerable and not as protected."

Maximus grunted, staring at the knife in his hands. A highwayman who hunted only in St. Giles and said he'd not been back for many years. Could he be the man who'd murdered his parents so long ago?

"I have to return to my men." Trevillion placed his boot in Cowslip's stirrup and swung himself up into the saddle.

Maximus nodded, tucking the highwayman's dagger into his boot, and turned.

"Ghost."

He stopped and looked at the captain.

The other man's face gave nothing away. "Thank you."

IF ONLY APOLLO could talk. Artemis frowned as she crept down the darkened hall that night, Bon Bon trotting at her heels. It was past midnight, so everyone ought to have been asleep in Wakefield House—well, everyone save Craven, who she'd left guarding her brother. The valet never seemed to sleep. One presumed he must be fulfilling his duties to Maximus, yet he somehow managed to care for Apollo as well.

Artemis shook her head. Craven was a capable nurse—though she didn't like to think how he'd come by his experience—yet Apollo still couldn't speak. Otherwise her brother seemed to be getting better, but every time he tried to utter a word, his throat only produced strangled sounds. Sounds that quite obviously caused him a great deal of pain. She just wished he could tell her he was better in his own words instead of scrawled handwriting.

Then she might believe him.

The corridor outside Maximus's door was deserted. Still she looked nervously around before she tapped at the door. She might have decided to embrace her path as a fallen woman, but it seemed it was hard to quell the fears of a lifetime.

Artemis waited, shifting from one foot to another, disappointment seeping through her breast as the door remained silently closed. Perhaps he hadn't meant to see her again. Perhaps he'd thought it only a one-time event. Perhaps he was bored with her now.

Well. She wasn't yet finished with *him*.

She tried the handle and found the door unlocked. She quickly pushed it open and entered, closing it just as quickly behind her.

Then she looked around.

She hadn't the time to examine his rooms last night—she'd been otherwise distracted. Artemis went to the connecting door through which Maximus had emerged the night before. It led to a sitting room-cum-study. Percy stood from where he'd been lying before the banked fire and stretched before coming over to greet both her and Bon Bon.

Artemis patted his head absently as she examined Maximus's sitting room. Books lined the walls and overflowed into neat stacks on the floor; an enormous desk was completely covered with papers, also in neat, cornered stacks. The only thing, in fact, that looked at all out of order was a globe on a stand, which appeared to be draped with Maximus's banyan. Artemis bit her lip to quell their upward curve at the sight. She wandered to the globe, giving it a gentle spin, banyan and all, before setting her candlestick on the desk and trailing her fingers across the papers. She saw a news sheet, a letter from an earl mentioning a bill before parliament, a letter in a much less refined hand pleading for monies to send a boy to school, and a scrap of paper with what looked like the beginnings of a speech in a bold hand—Maximus's, presumably. For a moment Artemis studied the speech, tracing the words and feeling warm as she followed the clear points he laid out in making his argument.

She laid aside the paper and saw the corner of a thin

book peeking out from under one pile. Carefully, she pulled it out and looked at the title. It was a treatise on fishing. Artemis raised her brows. No doubt Maximus had scores of streams on his properties, but did he ever have time to fish? The thought sent a pang of melancholy through her. Did he sneak peeks at his fishing book in between all his duties? If so, it shed a curiously vulnerable light upon the Duke of Wakefield.

Artemis picked up the fishing book and, curling into one of the deep chairs before the fireplace, began to read. Both dogs came to settle at her feet, curled together, and then quiet descended on the room.

The book was surprisingly entertaining and she lost track of the time. When next she looked up and saw Maximus lounging in the doorway to his bedroom watching her, she didn't know whether it had been five minutes or half an hour.

She stuck a finger in the book to save her place. "What time is it?"

He tilted his head to the side, peering at the fireplace, and she saw that a clock sat on the mantelpiece. "One in the morning."

"You were out late."

He shrugged and pushed away from the doorway. "I often am."

He turned to walk back into his bedroom and she set aside the book, rose, and followed him, leaving the sleeping dogs behind in the sitting room. He wore the same coat and waistcoat that he'd worn to the supper at home with Phoebe.

She found another chair and sat to watch as he peeled off the coat. "Were you out as the Ghost?"

"What?"

She nearly rolled her eyes. As if she couldn't guess where he'd been all this time. "Were you running about as the Ghost of St. Giles?"

He doffed his wig and placed it on a stand. "Yes."

He took a small dagger from his boot and set it on the dresser.

Her eyebrows rose. "Do you always carry that?"

"No." He hesitated. "It's a souvenir from tonight."

Had he fought then? Rescued some other poor woman attacked in St. Giles?

Had he killed tonight?

She examined his expression, but she found him impossible to read at the moment. His face was closed as tight as a locked room.

The waistcoat came off next and was thrown carelessly over a chair opposite to where Artemis sat. She wondered if he usually had Craven help him undress—most aristocrats did, but then he seemed very comfortable in his movements. She remained silent and at last he glanced over at her.

He sighed. "I was hunting a particular footpad—the one who killed my parents. I thought I might've finally found him..." He trailed off, shaking his head bitterly. "But I failed. I failed as I have every other night I've hunted. I wasn't even able to get close enough to see if it was the right man."

Artemis watched as he stripped his shirt off with a violent movement, revealing those broad shoulders. How many nights had he returned to his house alone, having lost what had seemed a promising trail to his parents' murderer?

He picked up a pitcher of water from his dressing table and poured into a wash basin. "No words of sympathy?"

She watched him splash water on his face and neck. "Would anything I say make a difference?"

He froze, water dripping from his chin as he leaned over the basin, his back still toward her. "What do you mean?"

She shivered and tucked her feet into the chair beside her, pulling the edge of her wrap over her bare ankles. "You've hunted for years now, in secret and alone. Done so without praise or censure. You are a force unto yourself, Your Grace. I doubt anything I said or do would move you."

He shifted finally, swiveling his head to look at her over his shoulder. "Don't call me that."

"What?"

"Your Grace."

His reply made her want to cry, and she didn't know why. He was . . . something to her now, but it was all so complicated, made more so by his title and all it entailed. If only he'd been a pleasantly poor man—a solicitor or merchant. Penelope wouldn't have been interested in him then. Artemis wouldn't bear the guilt that she was hurting her dear cousin. They could've married and she would tend his house and cook their meals. It would've been so much more simpler.

And then, too, she would've had him all to herself.

He turned back to the dresser without a word, picked up a flannel cloth, and rubbed it with soap. He raised one arm, the muscles flexing on his back in a rather spectacular show, and washed himself along that side and under his arm.

He dipped the cloth into the basin and repeated the

performance on the right side as well before finally glancing over at her just as she shivered again.

Maximus scowled and dropped the cloth into the water. He stoked the fire, making it flame high. Then he strode to his wardrobe and plucked out a lap rug, came to her, and arranged the plush folds over her legs.

"You should've told me you were cold." His hands were infinitely gentle.

"Your water is cold," she murmured. "Doesn't it bother you?"

He shrugged. "I find it bracing."

"Then bring your cloth here."

He looked at her curiously, but did as she bade.

She took the wet cloth from him. "Turn around and kneel."

He arched one brow, and she remembered that she was ordering a duke to kneel before her. But he wasn't just that anymore, was he? He was Maximus now.

Maximus, her lover.

He turned and lowered himself. The fire burnished his broad back, highlighting muscle and sinew.

Slowly she drew the wet cloth between his shoulder blades.

He bowed his head and arched his back.

She took the hint and rubbed the cloth gently over the damp hair at the top of his neck before drawing the cloth down his spine.

He drew in a breath. "I was fourteen when they died."

She hesitated only a fraction of a second before she smoothed the cloth back up his spine.

"I…" His shoulders moved restlessly. "I didn't know what to do. How to find their killer. I was angry."

She thought about a boy deprived of his parents in such a shocking way. "Angry" was probably a great understatement.

"I spent the next two months doing what I had to. I was the duke." His shoulders bunched and flexed. "But every night I thought about my parents—and what I would do to their murderer when I found him. I was fairly tall for my age—nearly six feet tall—and I thought I could defend myself. I started going into St. Giles at night."

Artemis shuddered at the thought of any boy—for a fourteen-year-old youth was still a boy to her mind—going into St. Giles after dark, no matter how tall he might be.

"I had a fencing master and I considered myself quite good," Maximus continued. "Still, it wasn't enough. I was badly beaten and robbed by a footpad one night. I got two black eyes. Craven was quite angry."

"You had Craven even then?"

He nodded. "Craven had been my father's valet. I suspect he made inquiries. The next day as I lay in bed, I had a caller."

She drew the cloth gently over his shoulders. "Who?"

"His name was Sir Stanley Gilpin. He was a business partner and friend of my father's—not a particularly close one, actually, as I found out later."

"Why did he visit?" She'd finished washing his back, but she was loath to stop touching him. Gingerly she stroked a bare finger over the bunched muscle at his neck. It was so hard.

"That's what I wondered," he said, swiveling his head a bit. She couldn't tell if he disliked her touch or not, but he didn't protest, so she laid her hand against his skin, feeling the heat. "I'd never met him before. That first day he stayed an hour, talking about Father and other, more inconsequential things."

"First day?" she questioned softly, daring to place both hands on his back. "He came back?"

"Oh, yes." He bowed his head and arched his back into her hands, like a giant cat urging her to stroke. "He came back every day for the week that I was abed. And then at the end of that week he told me he could train me so that I wouldn't be beaten the next time I went to St. Giles to look for my parents' murderer."

Her hands stilled for a moment as she heard his words. On the one hand, she was glad someone had cared enough—been strong enough—to train him so he wouldn't be hurt. On the other, he'd been only fourteen.

Fourteen and already preparing for a life of hunting.

It seemed wrong somehow.

He pushed back against her hands in silent command, so she began rubbing over his shoulder blades, feeling the thick flesh bound over strong bone.

He sighed and his shoulders seemed to relax a bit. "I went with him and found that he had a sort of training place—a big room in his house where there were saw-dust dummies and swords. He showed me how to use the swords not as a gentleman, but as the footpads might. He taught me not to fight fair, but to fight to win."

"How long?" she asked, her voice choked.

"What?" He started to look over his shoulder, but she dug her thumbs into the ropes of muscle on either side of his spine. Instead he groaned and let his head fall.

"How long did you train like this with Sir Stanley?" she whispered.

"Four years," his voice was almost absent. "Mostly by myself."

"Mostly?"

He shrugged. "At the beginning, when I first came, there was another boy, a sort of ward of Sir Stanley's. Actually I suppose he was a young man—he must've been eighteen at the time. I remember that he fought ferociously—when he wasn't reading—and he had a dry sense of humor. I rather liked him."

Maximus's admission was almost whispered to himself. Artemis felt tears prick at her eyelids. Had he had any friends of his own age after his parents' death—or had he spent all his time training for revenge? "What happened to him?"

Maximus was silent so long she thought he might not answer, but then he rolled one shoulder. "Went off to university. I remember I got a package from him once—a book. *Moll Flanders*. It's rather risqué. I think I still have it around here somewhere. Later, after I'd left, Sir Stanley trained a third boy. I've met him once or twice. I suppose we three were sort of Sir Stanley's legacy. Strange. I haven't spoken to either about that time—about any of it—in years." He sounded troubled.

She swung her legs down from the chair and settled them on either side of his shoulders, spread wide, so that she might more comfortably rub his arms. They were so strong—simply corded with muscle—and yet he was only a man. Didn't all men need companionship? Friendship? Love?

His head lolled against her right thigh, a heavy weight that made her aware that she wore only a chemise and wrap. For many moments they were quiet together as she stroked his arms and back and the fire crackled.

She was rubbing her thumbs in circles on the ball of his shoulder joints when she asked, "When did you become the Ghost?"

She thought he might refuse to talk more, but he answered readily enough, "When I was eighteen. Sir Stanley and I rather fought about it. I wanted to go into St. Giles by myself earlier, but he hadn't wanted me to. By eighteen, though, I made my own decisions."

She knit her brows. There was something she was missing. To go into St. Giles was one thing...

"Why did you wear a harlequin's costume?"

He chuckled, tilting his head back so he could see her eyes. "That was Sir Stanley's idea. He had rather an odd sense of humor, and he was quite excited by the theater. He had a costume made for me and said that a man in a mask can hide not only his identity, but the identity of his family. He can move about like a ghost."

She brought her hands up on either side of his lean, upside-down face. "But what a strange idea."

He shrugged. "I've sometimes wondered if Sir Stanley hadn't been the Ghost of St. Giles in his youth. The legend is older than my tenure."

"Your tenure?"

"The boys who sparred with me. They were Ghosts as well. All three of us, at different times, and sometimes at the same time."

"Were?" She swallowed. "Are they dead?"

"No," he said lazily. "Merely retired. I'm the only Ghost of St. Giles remaining."

"Mmm." He sounded so lonely. She bent over him, nearly near enough to kiss. "Maximus?"

His eyes were watching her lips. "Yes?"

"Why were you in St. Giles when your parents died?"

There was a second when she knew she'd pried too far. When his gaze froze and his sable eyes iced over.

Then he was pulling her head down. "I don't remember," he murmured against her lips just before he kissed her.

Chapter Fourteen

*For a year Lin rode pillion behind King Herla in his awful
wild hunt. The phantom horse between her legs labored
and strained but did not make a sound. She saw King Herla
bring down great stags and mighty boars, but he never
once celebrated his success. Only sometimes, after she had
bagged a hare or small hart, did he turn his head and she
felt the weight of his gaze upon her. Then she would see
that he watched her, his pale eyes cold and bleak and so
very, very lonely....*
—from *The Legend of the Herla King*

It was odd kissing a man upside down—odd, but also
oddly erotic. Artemis could feel Maximus's lips slanted
across hers, the shadow of his beard on his chin scratch-
ing faintly against her nose. In this position, their lips
didn't quite fit together properly, so to compensate she
had to open her mouth wide, as did he. It wasn't elegant,
this strange twisting of tongues, this driven mingling of
mouths. This was passion made elemental, even though
there was no hurry at all.

She felt his hand reach up, grasping her head to hold
her in place for the ravishment of her mouth. He broke
away for a second and she saw a flash of determined sable

eyes, then he twisted his torso to face her. He leaned into her widespread legs and wrapped one arm about her waist as the other brought her face back to his. She thought she heard him murmur, "Diana," and then he was kissing her again.

Slowly, thoroughly.

She let her lips fall apart on a gasp and felt the sure thrust of his tongue into her mouth. He didn't hurry, as if he had all the time in the world to hold her thus and explore her inner depths. She made a sound, a sort of low groan that in any other circumstances would've caused her embarrassment, but she was so drugged, so heady with the wine of his kiss, that she didn't even think about it. Nothing existed but his mouth, his lips, the thick intrusion of his tongue. She couldn't imagine wanting anything else ever.

But he broke from her, withdrawing his tongue, his lips, though she whimpered and made an aborted move to follow him.

She opened her eyes to find him watching her like a predator. Calculating, waiting.

He held her gaze, and she saw a faint smirk curl one corner of his mouth. The rug was suddenly gone from her lap, and then she felt the slide of her skirts up her legs.

"Do you remember that morning?" he asked, his voice impossibly deep. "You emerged from the pond like a goddess triumphant. You'd flaunted your ankles the day before"—he brushed warm fingers over her left ankle, making her shiver—"but that morning I saw the tender curve of your inner thigh, the sweet bend of your knee, the shy sweep of your calf. You revealed them as coyly as a siren singing a man to his ecstatic death—and you didn't even know it, did you? By the time you reached the shore I was hard as iron."

She blushed at his words, remembering that morning. She had no idea she'd affected him so. To think that they'd talked calmly and all the time his penis had been engorged with want for her.

The very thought made her wet.

Her gaze darted down to his hands on her thighs and then back up to meet those knowing, watchful eyes. He smiled as if he could hear her thoughts. He was bunching the skirts of her wrap and thin chemise in his big fists, slowly drawing the fabric up, revealing her legs—and if she didn't protest, much more.

And this time she knew exactly what the sight of her legs did to him.

He silently cocked an eyebrow in challenge.

But if he was a predator, all masculine danger, then she was his rightful mate. She'd roamed the forest alone as a child. Had swum the pond, stalked squirrels, climbed trees like a wanton. Deep inside, hidden by the bland costume of a lady's companion, she was just as dangerous as he.

Just as daring.

So she let her own mouth curl as she leaned back in the chair. If he expected maidenly fear or outrage from her, he'd be disappointed.

She wasn't a maiden anymore.

His eyes lit with almost boyish mischief, his usually stern mouth curling further, and he inclined his head, just slightly, as if in approval.

And then he pushed her skirts up over her hips in one movement, baring everything below her waist to his gaze.

She swallowed a gasp. He wouldn't frighten her into crying off.

He held her gaze, not even looking at what was spread just below his chin, as he turned his body completely, slowly thrusting his long legs under the chair so he sat on the floor facing her, her lap like a feast before him. His thumbs rubbed slow circles on her hipbones as if to gentle her or maybe to keep her relaxed. Although if that were his purpose, it wasn't working. She still held his gaze in defiance, but her breath was quickening as if she were climbing a staircase.

Abruptly he looked down.

He stilled, simply staring at her. He made no movement, but there was a wild possessiveness in his eyes that made something inside her stretch and purr in response. He wanted *her*. Wanted this part of her. She was suddenly jealous of any other woman he'd ever looked at like this. He hadn't the right—*they* hadn't the right. This look, his expression, this *moment* was only between them and no one else.

They were a universe of two.

It was almost unbearably intimate, but she made herself watch as he spread wide his fingers and drew his hands down over her hipbones, over that tender spot where thigh met hip, until his forefingers brushed her curling hair. His thumbs continued down under her leg until he held each of her upper thighs in his hands. He pushed, slowly, inevitably, making her widen her legs further, helping her to hook one leg over the arm of the chair, until she lay open before him, a lewd offering.

He bowed before her then, like a priest worshipping at an altar, and she watched, her breath catching and breaking in her lungs, as he licked her.

The touch of his hot, moist tongue against her there was so exquisite that she trembled and shut her eyes. It was the most amazing feeling, both terrible and right, and she knew that she would never be the same after this moment. Here, now, he was tearing down the walls of her facade, crumbling the stone, dissolving the mortar. Laying bare the woman within, and the most frightening thing was she wasn't completely sure who that woman was.

She'd never met her.

He spread her folds with his thumbs and licked into her crevasse, and she arched her neck and groaned. Loudly. Deeply. Without any way to stop the sound.

She felt him open his mouth against her flesh as if he would inhale her, and her heart beat so fast she thought she might die. He laid the flat of his tongue against her nub and pressed and kissed and sucked, and she swore her heart stopped beating completely. It was like a seizure, like a spasm of the soul. Her body quaked, and she caught his head between her palms to hold him there against her. Her hips moved gently, beneath his mouth, rising and falling to meet his relentless kiss. She threw her head back, her back arching, as he flicked his tongue against her, fast and hard and obscene, wet noises filling the room. She didn't know if she would survive if he went on, but she knew she would die if he stopped.

And when the culmination hit her, she rose. Like an eagle spreading her wings, catching a hot, percussive wave from an explosion below.

She flew and was reborn.

When she at last opened her eyes, she saw him watching her, his mouth still between her thighs, the heat of his gaze enough to scald her newborn skin.

She swallowed, caressing his cheek, and tried to think of some way to express her gratitude, but she'd lost the art of language.

He lifted his head then, and she couldn't even find the stamina to resent the self-satisfied curl of his lips. He put his hands on her waist and pulled her, gently helping her to fall into his lap, her legs straddling his. He placed one hand at the back of her head and kissed her and when she tasted a kind of tang on his lips, she knew where it had come from.

Without speaking he kicked the chair away so that they sat together in front of the fire all alone.

He leaned into her, softly kissing the tender skin under her ear, and whispered, "Wrap your legs about me."

She shifted languidly, for there was no reason as far as she could see to hurry this. But when her softness was open and exposed by her position, she could feel how hard he was. How insistent. He might not have the same mind as she about the urgency of the matter.

When he slid a hand between them, she twined her arms around his neck for balance and leaned back to watch. He was working at the falls to his breeches. She cocked her head as he fumbled one handed, his other hand braced against the floor to keep them both upright.

She looked back up at him from beneath her lashes. "Would you like some help?"

He punished her for her amusement by nipping at her mouth. For a moment she became lost in their play, in the impatient kisses he gave her.

She leaned away and unbuttoned his falls with calm deliberation.

He, sadly, was not as calm as she.

"Diana," he growled, cutting off his own words with an oath as she worked his penis free of his falls and breeches. It was the first time she'd held him—held any man—and she took the opportunity to examine the prize in her hands. His skin was soft, and it surprised her that this most masculine part of him was so velvety. She stroked him with her fingers, marveling at the hardness under the skin, the thick ropes of veins climbing the length. His foreskin had retreated back from the broad head, and a bead of liquid pearled at the tiny slit. She delicately touched her finger to the drop, stroking the liquid over his ruddy head. The column in her hand flexed at her touch and she wanted to laugh. To sing, though her voice wasn't anything wonderful. This was so special, so curious, how he was built. That he would let her play with him.

She shot him a look from under her brows and saw that he had an extraordinary expression on his face—a kind of fond hunger.

"Diana," he breathed, and caught her lips with his.

Suddenly she no longer wanted to play. There was a coiling within her, drawing her body tight again, building to what she now knew was unbearable pleasure.

She shifted closer, rucking her skirts up and bringing the tip of his hard penis against her folds. They still kissed as she rolled her hips, her breath stuttering when she used him to rub herself.

He opened wide his mouth and kissed her deeply, shoving his own hips up. She knew what he wanted—what he probably *needed* at this point—but she, too, needed.

Just a little more.

She caught her breath, writhing as she slid him through

her slippery folds. He was so hard, so wide, so absolutely perfect, he might've been made expressly for her.

Well, in a way he was, wasn't he?

But his patience broke.

He grasped her waist and raised her, looking her in the eye fiercely. "Hold me there."

So she reluctantly put him to her entrance, holding him steady as he let her weight bear down.

As he joined with her.

He watched her even as she gasped at the intimate intrusion. She was still a little sore from the day before, and she stiffened.

He paused, his fingers stroking the small of her back through the frail materials of her chemise and wrap. "Easy."

She nodded as her flesh accepted him, and he seemed to understand it as the permission it was. Slowly he impaled her on his cock. She was aware of the fluttering of her heart, of the short, staccato pants of her breath, of the way his face was set and grim as if it took all of his considerable control to keep from simply thrusting up into her.

But the soreness was fading now, being replaced by the lovely feeling of being stretched full. She bit her lip, arching her head back, staring at the ceiling as she rotated her hips gently, screwing herself down on him until she felt the smooth silk of his breeches against her bottom.

He groaned, deep and very male, and bowed his head against her for a moment, his hot breath panting across the slopes of her breasts. She ran her hands over his upper arms soothingly and felt when they bunched beneath her fingers.

That was her only warning.

He shoved her up, his cock sliding exquisitely through her tunnel as he withdrew, then he set his feet flat on the floor and drove his hips into her. Fast and hard, he set a punishing pace.

She'd once imagined lovemaking as a sweet joining of souls, a gentle wave surging and retreating. An act both respectful and honored.

What Maximus was doing to her was anything but sweet. He gasped, his great chest working as if he fought off demons. Sweat beaded on his brow and shone in the fine hairs on his chest. His movements were sharp and abrupt as he drove himself into her again and again. He was nothing like the sophisticated aristocrat he was in front of others. One corner of his mouth twisted in a sneer, his eyes a glaring furnace. He used her body for his own pleasure, for his own need, working her up and down on his cock. He was little more than an animal now.

And she gloried in it. She—*she*—had driven him to this. Had made a man who captured kings and foreign diplomats with the surety of his eloquence quite simply lose his mind.

He pushed up with all his might, shoved to the hilt within her, and froze, head thrown back in an agony of pleasure.

She leaned forward and delicately licked the salt sweat from his lips as his seed flooded her.

THE NEXT MORNING Craven attended Maximus in his rooms and was excruciatingly correct until Artemis left to dress herself in her own rooms.

The door had hardly closed behind her lovely bottom

when the valet turned slowly to Maximus and pinned him with a gaze that would've done justice to the King in one of his fouler moods. "Pardon me, Your Grace, but I hope you'll not mind if I speak bluntly—"

"Would it matter?" Maximus muttered under his breath, wishing he'd at least had his morning cup of tea before his own valet raked him over the coals.

Craven didn't bother acknowledging the interruption. "I wonder if you've quite lost your bloody mind?"

Maximus began soaping his face in a rather vicious manner. "If I wanted your opinion, I would've—"

"Much as it *pains* me to speak to you in this manner," Craven said, "I feel I must. Your Grace."

Maximus snapped his mouth shut and snatched up his razor, making sure his hand was steady before setting the blade to his jaw. He could feel Craven behind him and he knew without turning that the valet would be standing at attention, shoulders back, head held high.

"A gentleman does not ravish a lady," Craven said. "A lady, moreover, living under his own roof and therefore in his protection."

Maximus banged the razor against the wash basin, feeling irritated at both Craven and himself. "I've never ravished a woman in my life."

"What else to call the seduction of an unmarried lady of gentle birth?"

It was a well-aimed volley and Maximus felt the hit. She'd already told him that she'd been hurt previously by her ass of a fiancé—was he, in the end, any better? No, of course not. At least that doctor's son hadn't gone so far as to *seduce* her.

As Maximus had.

Was he hurting her, his goddess? Did she hide a heart bruised from his careless actions? The mere thought made him want to punch walls. No one should hurt her so, least of all him. Craven was right: he was a cad and a rogue, and if he were any sort of gentleman at all, he'd give her up. Break off the thing and set her free.

And yet he wouldn't. Quite simply, he *could not* bear to let her go.

He took a deep breath and said tightly, "Craven, what is between Miss Greaves and myself is of no concern of yours."

"Isn't it?" The other man's voice had an edge Maximus had rarely heard in it before. "If not my business, then whose? Do you listen to your sisters, Miss Picklewood, the men you call friends in Parliament?"

Maximus turned slowly to look at the valet. No one spoke to him thus.

Craven's face was sagging and he looked every inch of his years. "You are a law unto yourself, Your Grace. You always have been. It's what helped you to survive the tragedy. It's what made you a great man in Parliament. But it also means that when you are wrong there is no one to make you pause."

Maximus's eyes narrowed. "And why should I pause?"

"Because you know what you have done—what you are *doing*—is not right."

"It was she who came to my bed, not the other way 'round," Maximus muttered, feeling heat flush his neck even as he gave the feeble excuse.

"A gentleman has full control over his urges—*all* his urges," Craven said with just a hint of sarcasm. "Would you blame the lady for your own fault?"

"I blame no one." Maximus turned back to his dresser, unable to meet his valet's eyes. He scraped the stubble from his right cheek.

"And yet you should."

"Craven."

Craven's voice sounded old. "Tell me you mean to marry the lady and I'll gladly celebrate."

Maximus froze. What he wanted and what was best for the dukedom was entirely separate. "You know I cannot. I plan to marry Lady Penelope Chadwicke."

"And you know, *Your Grace*, that Lady Penelope is a frivolous fool not worth half of you. Not worth half of Miss Greaves, for that matter."

"Have care," Maximus said, frost dripping from his lips. "You malign my future duchess."

"You haven't asked her."

"*Yet*."

Craven held out pleading hands. "Why not make this right? Why not marry the lady you've already bedded?"

"Because, as you well know, her family is diseased with madness."

"So are half the aristocratic families of England." Craven snorted. "*More* than half if we count the Scots. Lady Penelope herself is related to Miss Greaves and her family. By your estimation she is not fit to be your duchess, either."

Maximus gritted his teeth and breathed out slowly. Craven had been there at his christening. Had taught him how to shave. Had stood behind him when he'd laid his mother and father in a cold crypt. Craven wasn't just a servant to him.

Which was why Maximus made sure to keep his voice level as he discussed something so utterly private with the man. "Lady Penelope doesn't have a *brother* who is a murderous madman. To take Miss Greaves as my duchess would taint the dukedom. I owe it to my forebears, to my father—"

"*Your father* would never have made you marry Lady Penelope!" Craven cried.

"Which is *why* I shall marry her," Maximus whispered.

Craven simply looked at him. It was the same look he'd given Maximus when he'd snapped at one of his sisters as a youth, when Maximus had drunk too much wine for the first time, when he'd refused to speak for that fortnight after his parents' death. It was the look that said, *This is not behavior becoming of the Duke of Wakefield.*

That look had always stopped Maximus.

But not this time. This time *he* was the one who was right and Craven who was in the wrong. He could not marry Artemis—his debt to his father's memory, to what he must be as the duke in order to make *something* right, did not allow it—but he could have her and keep her and make her his most secret desire.

Because he wasn't sure at this point that he could live without her.

He looked at Craven and he knew his face had assumed the cold, stony mask that made other men glance away. "I will marry Lady Penelope, and I will continue bedding Miss Greaves as I see fit, and if you are unable to reconcile yourself to those facts you may leave my employment."

For a moment Craven merely looked at him and Maximus was reminded suddenly of his first sight the day he woke after his parents' murder: it had been Craven's face as he'd slept in a chair by Maximus's bedside.

Craven turned away and left the bedroom, shutting the door gently behind him.

It might as well have been a gunshot to Maximus's soul.

Chapter Fifteen

*Now Tam rode behind the Herla King, and though she
tried to talk to him, never in that year did he speak to her
or make a sign that he knew her. Still, when the night of
the autumn harvest next came, Lin took a deep breath and
did as the little man in the hills had bid her: she reached
back and dragged her brother from his ghostly horse,
gripping him tightly. Immediately Tam turned into a
monstrous wildcat....*
—from *The Legend of the Herla King*

The steps to Maximus's cellar were damp. Artemis
climbed down carefully, for she held Apollo's breakfast in
her hands: tea, bread thickly spread with butter and jam,
and a huge dish of coddled eggs. The maid had looked at
her a little oddly when she'd requested such a large breakfast but was obviously too well trained to inquire about
her unladylike appetite.

Now Artemis balanced the wooden tray on one hip
as she fumbled with the key to the door. It seemed rather
odd to lock Apollo in like this—surely no one would dare
investigate the duke's cellar—but both Maximus and Craven had insisted it was for the best.

Inside, nothing seemed to have changed since she'd bid

Apollo good night only hours before. The brazier still cast a dull light and Apollo sat upon the narrow cot. But as she drew nearer she saw there was one very large difference: Apollo had a ball and chain around one ankle.

She stopped short only feet from him. "What's this?"

He might be half-starved, beaten near to death, and for some reason still unable to speak, but her brother had never had any trouble expressing his thoughts to her.

He rolled his eyes.

Then he looked down and started theatrically at the ball as if he'd never seen it before. The skittish movement was quite silly when made by such a large man.

Her lips twitched, but she stilled them. This was a serious matter.

"Apollo," she said warningly, setting the tray on the bed next to him. The chain was long enough that he could easily reach a covered commode not that far away and the brazier, but nothing else. "Who did this? Maximus?"

He didn't deign to reply, tearing into the bread before halting for a moment and then beginning to eat again almost daintily.

Artemis frowned at his odd behavior, but was distracted by the chain clinking against the stone floor as he shifted to reach for the teacup. "Apollo! Answer me, please. Why would he chain you?"

He gazed at her over his teacup's rim as he sipped before shrugging and putting down the cup. He picked up the notebook that had been left on the floor by the cot and scratched something out with a pencil before handing it to her.

Artemis glanced at what he'd written.

I'm mad.

She scoffed, thrusting the notebook back at him. "You know you're not."

He paused, his fingers upon the little book, to flick his eyes at her, and she saw them soften. Then he pulled the notebook from her hands and wrote something else.

She sat beside him to read.

Only you, sister dear, think me sane. I love you for it.

She swallowed and leaned over to buss him on the cheek. At least he'd shaved. "And I love you, too, though you drive me half mad."

He snorted and dug into the eggs.

"Apollo?" she asked softly. "What happened in Bedlam? Why were you beaten so badly?"

He took another bite, refusing to meet her eyes.

She sighed and watched him. Even if he was too stubborn to recount what had caused a boot to be thrust into his throat, she was glad that he was safe and had enough food.

She glanced again at the chain on his ankle. He might be safe, but he was chained like an animal again, and that simply wouldn't do. "I'll talk to Maximus. He'll understand that you were wrongly accused and not mad at all." She said it confidently, even though she was beginning to doubt that Maximus would ever change his mind. And if he didn't? She couldn't leave her brother chained here—it was little better than Bedlam.

He chewed, looking at her narrowly, and for some reason his expression made her nervous.

He picked up the notebook and wrote one word: *MAXIMUS?*

She could feel heat climbing her cheeks. "He's a friend."

He cocked a sardonic eyebrow as he scribbled, the pencil hitting the paper with an audible thump when he made the period. *He must accord you a very good friend indeed to rescue me from Bedlam on your word.*

"I suppose he thought it a good deed."

He arched an incredulous eyebrow before writing, *I've lost my voice, not my power of reason.*

"Well, of course not."

But he kept writing. *I don't like such closeness with a duke.*

She lifted her chin. "Would you have me only associate with earls and viscounts, then?"

He bumped her shoulder with his, and wrote, *Very funny. You know what I mean.*

He was the dearest person in the world to her, and she hated to lie to him. Still, the truth would do nothing but anger him. "Don't worry about me, darling. A duke would never be interested in a lady's companion. You know Lady Phoebe is my friend. I'm here to act as her companion while her cousin, Miss Picklewood, is away. Nothing more."

He stared at her suspiciously until she pointed out that his tea would grow cold if he didn't finish his breakfast. After that they sat together in companionable silence as she watched him eat.

But she couldn't shake her own words, for without meaning to she'd spoken the truth: a duke truly didn't have any reason to consort with her. Maximus had never said anything about making their arrangement more permanent. What if he only wished to bed her for a few nights and nothing more? What would she do then? What they'd done made it impossible for her to live again as

Penelope's companion—even if her cousin never found out the truth. Artemis simply couldn't deceive Penelope in such an awful manner.

Her actions had laid waste to her former life.

MAXIMUS FELT HIS heart beat faster that night as he made his way through the shadows of London dressed as the Ghost of St. Giles. It was as if he could no longer keep a raging beast inside. Nearly twenty years—more than half his life—he'd spent in this hunt. He'd not married, not sought out friendship or lovers. All his time, all his thought, all his *soul* was bent on one thing:

Avenging his parents. Finding their killer. Making the world somehow *right* again.

And tonight, now, he was as close as he'd ever been to failure.

It began to rain as if the heavens themselves wept at his weakness.

He paused, tilting his face to the night sky, feeling the drops run cold down his face. *How long?* Lord, how long must he search? Was Craven right? Had he done penance enough or would he forever toil?

A shout came from nearby, and without turning he ran into the night. The cobblestones were slippery beneath his boots, and his short cape whipped away behind him as if mocking his attempt at flight. The rain was relentless, but that didn't stop the denizens of London from coming out. He passed two dandies mincing their way along, holding their cloaks over their heads. Maximus merely ducked to the side when one pointed and yelled. A horse shied as he passed, as if the animal knew the blackness blown over his soul.

More people up ahead. He'd come out too early.

Maximus darted to the right and grasped a pillar supporting an overhanging second story. He pulled himself up only to find himself face-to-face with a fair-haired child in a nightgown at the window. He paused, startled, as the child stuck a finger in her mouth and simply stared, then he began climbing again. The tiled roof was slippery, but he hoisted himself up and over the edge and began running. The rain beat down, soaking his tunic, making the shingles slippery, turning the world into a house of mourning.

Below, the people streamed through the rain, miserable and wet, while above he leaped from rooftop to rooftop, soaring through the air, risking with each jump a fatal fall to the ground.

He neared St. Giles. He knew because he could smell it: the stink of the channel, the rot of bodies living on nothing but despair and gin—always gin. He fancied he could smell the stench of the liquor itself, foul and burning, with the sweet note of juniper. Gin pervaded this entire area, drowning it in disease and death.

The thought made him want to vomit.

He stalked the night, running through the rain, haunting the rooftops of St. Giles for minutes, days, a lifetime, perhaps even forgetting what he'd come here for.

Until he found it—or rather *him*.

Below, in a yard so small it had no name, he saw the highwayman called Old Scratch. The man was mounted and had a whimpering youth cornered, his pistol aimed at the boy's head.

Maximus acted on instinct and entirely without plan. He half-slid, half-climbed down the side of the building, dropping between the boy and Old Scratch.

Without hesitation Old Scratch turned his pistol on Maximus and fired.

Or tried to.

Maximus grinned, rain sliding into his mouth. "Your powder's wet."

The boy scrambled to his feet and fled.

Old Scratch tilted his head. "So 'tis."

His voice was muffled by the wet scarf bound around the lower half of his face. He seemed entirely unafraid.

Maximus stepped closer and, though the light was dim, he finally got a clear look at the emerald pinned at the other man's throat. Saw it and recognized it.

He stilled, his nostrils flaring. *Finally.* Dear God, *finally.*

His gaze flicked up to the obscured eyes of the man on the horse. "You have something that's mine."

"Do I?"

"That," Maximus said, pointing with his chin. "That emerald belonged to my mother. The last of two. Do you have the other one still as well?"

Whatever he'd expected from Old Scratch, it wasn't the reaction he got: the man threw back his head and bellowed with laughter, the sound echoing off the tilting brick walls that surrounded them. "Oh, Your Grace, I should've recognized you. But then, you're not the sniveling boy you were nineteen years ago, are you?"

"No, I'm not," Maximus said grimly.

"But you're just as foolish," the Devil taunted him. "If you want the last of your mother's emeralds, I'd suggest searching within your own house."

Maximus had had enough. He drew his sword and charged.

Old Scratch yanked on the reins and his horse reared, iron-shod hooves flashing in the night. Maximus ducked, trying to edge around the great beast to reach its master, but the highwayman wheeled his horse and gave it spur, galloping down the only alley leading out of the yard.

Maximus whirled and leaped to a corner where two walls met. He jumped and climbed, his fingers hurriedly searching for holds in the dark. He could hear the hoof-beats retreating, the sound fading. If he didn't make the roof soon, he'd lose the man and horse in the maze of narrow streets that made up St. Giles.

Desperately, he reached for a fingerhold over his head. The brick gave without warning, coming entirely off the wall and with it his hold on the building. He fell backward, scrabbling like a rat, his fingernails scraping against the brick.

He hit the muddy ground with a thump that sent sparks flying across his vision.

And then he lay there, flat on his back in the filthy yard, his hands and back and shoulders aching, with the rain falling coldly in his face.

The moon had disappeared from the midnight sky.

ARTEMIS WOKE TO the feel of strong arms grasping her tight and lifting her from her bed. She should've been alarmed, but all she felt was a strange rightness. She looked up as Maximus carried her into the corridor outside her room. His face was set in grim lines, his eyes drawn and old, his mouth flat. He wore his banyan, its silk smooth beneath her cheek. She could hear his heart beating, strong and steady.

She reached up and traced the groove beside his mouth.

His gaze flicked down to hers, and the naked savagery she saw there made her gasp.

He shouldered open his door and strode to his bed, placing her there like a prize of war.

He stood over her and tore the clothes from his body. "Take it off."

She sat up to pull her chemise over her head.

Only just in time. Naked, he crawled over her, his body hot and hard. "Never sleep anywhere but in my bed."

She might have protested, but he turned her roughly so that she lay on her stomach, her cheek pressed into his pillow.

He lay on top of her, his upper body braced on his arms but his hips and legs weighing her down. Trapping and holding her.

"You're mine," he said, laying his cheek against hers. "Mine and no one else's."

"Maximus," she warned.

"Yield, Diana," he whispered, parting her legs. She could feel the thick heat of his cock pressed hard on her bottom. "Yield, warrior maiden."

"I'm not a maiden. You took that."

"And I would again," he growled. "I'd steal you away and keep you in a castle far from here. Far from any other man. I'd guard you jealously and every night come to your bed and put my cock into your cunny and fuck you until dawn."

The crude words, the near-mad sentiment, should've frightened her. Perhaps there was something amiss with her makeup, for they merely made her warm. No, hot. Near burning. It was all she could do to stop herself from squirming beneath him.

"Do you want that, Diana?" he muttered into her ear, his breath humid on her skin. "Do you want to be mine and only mine, away from this cursed world, in a place inhabited by just we two?"

"Oh, yes," she said, her voice fierce.

He levered himself up. "I'd go a-hunting in the day and kill a fine stag. I'd bring it back to our hidden castle and dress it and cook it over a fire and then I'd sit you on my lap and feed you, morsel by morsel. All your sustenance would be by my hand and mine alone."

She laughed then, for she knew he didn't truly want such a biddable doll. She squirmed and turned in a sudden movement so that she lay facing him.

"No, I'd hunt with you by your side," she said as she reached up to pull his face down to hers. "I am your equal, my lord. Your equal and mate."

"So you are," he breathed, and bit her lip.

She tasted rain on his mouth. Rain and wine and something much darker. Something was driving him, and she needed to talk to him—about her future and about releasing Apollo. But right now, in this moment, she wanted none of reality. Reality was a screeching harridan who never could be made happy.

If she couldn't have happiness, then she could at least have this.

She opened her mouth wide and bit her mate back, digging her nails into the nape of his neck as if to hold him as fiercely as he held her.

His chest rubbed against her nipples, and he felt warm and male. His arms braced on either side of her head, a welcome cage. And between her legs he worked his cock against her, making her slick.

He pulled back. "Like this."

And he flipped her again.

She growled a protest and he actually *laughed*.

"Magnificent Diana," he murmured into her ear, rubbing himself against her like a great tiger. "I'm going to fuck you now."

She arched against him, part in protest at being used so cavalierly, part in sheer excitement. She felt his cock sliding into her crevasse, seeking, prodding. One day she wanted to see him—all of him. Wanted to touch and taste and explore this magnificent body, but at the moment, all she wanted was to have him in her.

She got her wish.

He thrust deep, breaching her in one violent movement, his hips coming to rest right against her bottom. She groaned, biting her lower lip.

She could hear him panting in her ear. In this position, pressed into the bed, she could hardly move, much less get the leverage to push back.

He seemed to realize her predicament. He laughed low in this throat, the sound vibrating against her back, and ground into her. She could feel him, full and rock hard, inside her, and his small deliberate movements seemed to press against something deep inside her. She felt herself growing impossibly wet, swelling with tension. She shifted her hips as much as she could, and the tiny movement prompted a growl from him. He caught her ear between his teeth as he ground deeper.

"Yield, sweet, sweet Diana," he whispered in her ear. "You are so hot, so wet for me, I would stay here within you forever, holding you, compelling your submission."

She tried to get her arms beneath her, to somehow

push herself back against him, but he only chuckled, pulling back just enough for her to feel the head of his penis stretch her entrance before shoving back into her again. He suddenly thrust his arms under her, holding her tight as he found one breast and cupped it. His long legs braced on either side of hers, squeezing and immobilizing her.

"Diana," he murmured in her ear, licking. "Diana, you are everything I've ever wanted and shall never have."

Tears pricked at her eyes and she opened her mouth to sob.

"That's it," he said. "Weep for me. Bear my pain. Take my come. For I can give you nothing else."

And he thrust into her in hard, sharp punches, each movement striking against that place within her. She gritted her teeth and bowed her head into the pillow. It was too much. Too little. A continual assault against her senses.

He laid his cheek against hers and she felt something wet between their skin. "Come, o Diana. Wash me in your passion."

She tensed and shuddered. Once. Twice. Thrice. Like a seizure. Like a piercing of the soul.

Like the death of hope.

He sagged onto her, heavy as lead, but she was loath to make him move. Something had happened tonight to make him so wild. Something dreadful.

She turned enough so that she could stroke the back of his head, feeling the shorn hair brush her palm. "What is it? What has happened?"

He rolled off of her, but wrapped his arms around her as if he couldn't stand not to touch her. "I met him tonight, the man who killed my parents. Met him and lost him."

Her heart stopped. "Oh, Maximus..."

He laughed, a dry, awful sound. "He's a highwayman who calls himself Old Scratch. My mother..." She heard him swallow before he tried again. "My mother was wearing the Wakefield emeralds the night she died—a fabulous necklace with seven emerald drops that hung off a central diamond and emerald chain. He must've broken it up after he stole it, for it was several years after her death before I saw the first emerald drop—on the neck of a courtesan. It's taken me years, but I've collected the pieces one by one: the central chain and five of the seven drops. Last night I saw something emerald pinned to Old Scratch's neck cloth, but I couldn't get close enough to be sure. Tonight I did. He wears one of my mother's emerald drops. I asked him about the other, and do you know what he said?"

"No," Artemis whispered, a dreadful feeling welling in her chest.

Maximus's lips twisted. "He told me to look within my own house."

Artemis sat up. "Oh, dear God."

Chapter Sixteen

> *Lin held fast to her brother even as the wildcat clawed*
> *her, for she'd been told by the strange little man in the*
> *hills that if she let go of her brother before the cock's*
> *first crow, they would both be doomed to the wild hunt*
> *forever. So Lin grasped Tam as they rode through the*
> *night sky, and the Herla King gave no word that he saw*
> *the struggle right behind him, but his fist tightened on his*
> *horse's reins.*
> *Then Tam turned into a writhing serpent....*
> —from *The Legend of the Herla King*

Maximus stared at the single emerald drop in Artemis's palm. She'd hastily donned her chemise before running back to her room without telling him why, only to appear moments later with her hand fisted around something.

Now he wondered if he should feel betrayed. "Where the *hell* did you get that?"

"I..." Her hand clutched the pendants protectively. "Well, it certainly isn't what you may be thinking."

He blinked and raised his gaze to her face at her indignant tone. Her beautiful gray eyes were wary. They'd made love not moments before, and yet the bed felt cold now. "What am I thinking?"

She raised her eyebrows haughtily. "That I'm somehow involved with the murderer of your parents."

Stated baldly like that, it was obviously preposterous. He shook his head. "I'm sorry. Tell me."

She cleared her throat. "My brother gave it to me on our fifteenth birthday."

He stiffened. "Kilbourne?"

"Yes."

Maximus looked down, thinking. The murderer had been cautious. Maximus had only discovered the first drop nearly ten years after the murder. By tracing back through the sale of the drop, he'd realized that the jewel had only been originally sold months before. Unfortunately, that drop had been a dead end—quite literally. The owner of the original pawnshop where the emerald drop had been sold was found lying in a pool of his own blood.

Maximus had bought the last pendant over three years ago. Likely the murderer had begun to realize that Maximus was collecting the jewels—and that they might provide a link back to the murderer.

But if Artemis was correct, then the jewel she wore had come into the possession of her brother *before* the other drops had begun to be sold.

Before the murderer knew how dangerous the jewels were to him.

Kilbourne might have the clue to help him find the murderer. He might even know the murderer himself.

Maximus's head snapped up. "Who did your brother get it from?"

"I don't know," she said simply. "He never said. I didn't realize it was a real emerald until I tried to pawn it a couple of months ago."

He stared at the emerald for a long moment before rising from the bed and going to the iron box on his bedside table. He took the key from a hidden drawer in the table and opened the box. The top held a shallow tray, perfectly fitted to the inside. He'd had it lined in black velvet. On it lay what remained of his mother's most prized possession: the Wakefield emeralds.

He felt Artemis come up beside him to look, and then she took his hand and pressed the emerald pendant into his palm. He wrapped his fingers about her hand for a moment before letting go, suddenly realizing what she'd given him: the missing piece to Old Scratch. With this he might be able to find who the man really was. Maximus swallowed, reluctant to look at her, for it wasn't only gratitude that swelled within his chest.

Gratitude was the least of the emotions he felt for her.

He laid the pendant in its place beside her sisters.

"There's one still missing," she said, leaning her head on his arm.

The pendants lay in an arc around the central chain with one noticeable gap.

"Yes. The one Old Scratch wears at his throat." He closed the box and locked it again. "When I have it, I intend to have them all reattached."

"And then you'll give it to Penelope," she said quietly.

He flinched. Truly, he'd never thought that far ahead. Finding and restoring the necklace, bringing his parents' murderer to justice, and achieving some kind of redemption occupied all his thoughts. He hadn't considered what—if anything—came afterward.

But she was right. The necklace belonged to the Duchess of Wakefield.

He turned to look at her, this woman who had given her body and perhaps her soul to him. This woman who knew him like no other on earth. This woman he could never, *never* honor as he should.

As he wanted to. "Yes."

"Penelope will like it," Artemis said, her voice very calm, her beautiful eyes wide and unblinking. She was always brave, his Diana. "She loves jewels, and the emeralds are magnificent. She'll look gorgeous in them."

Her very bravery broke something inside of him. She showed no trace of jealousy, no rage that he might bed another woman, and somehow that made him want to break her, too. To make her say how obscene this was. To make her put her rightful claim on him.

"She'll be magnificent," he said cruelly. "Her black hair will make the emeralds glow. Perhaps I'll buy her emerald earbobs to match."

She watched him steadily. "Will you?"

And he knew somehow, no matter what happened, that he'd never buy Penelope Chadwicke emerald earbobs. "No."

He shut his eyes, breathing. If she could withstand this, then so could he. At least he'd *have* her—no matter that it would be only partially and badly. He could not give her up, so he vowed to take what he could of her.

Maximus closed and locked the box before taking Artemis's hand and pulling her gently down beside him in the bed. He arranged the covers over her as tenderly as if she were a queen and he a lowly cavalier. "I'll ask your brother in the morning."

She huffed and laid her head on his shoulder. "I know you think Apollo is a murderer, but he couldn't have been part of your parents' murder. He was much too young."

He reached to pinch out the candle. "I know. But he may know the murderer—or someone who does. In any case I must question him."

"Mmm," she murmured sleepily. "Maximus?"

"Yes?"

"Did you have my room searched at Pelham House?"

He tilted his head to peer at her face in the dark. She seemed perfectly serious. "What?"

She traced a circle on his chest with her finger. "The morning you sent the messenger to inform me you'd rescued Apollo, someone searched my rooms." She knit her brows and looked at him. "When I realized that the emerald was real, I started wearing it all the time. I just didn't know what else to do with it, it was so expensive. And then when I got your signet ring I strung it on the same chain."

He remembered the chain she'd been wearing when she'd given him back his signet ring. He frowned. "Then why haven't I ever seen the emerald on you?"

A blush rose in her cheeks. "I took it off before we'd... *Anyway.* I left the woods at the abbey, after you'd already raced off, and I forgot to put my fichu back on. My necklace was visible for a moment, with both the emerald drop and your signet ring on it."

He understood at once. "Any of the guests could've seen it."

She nodded. "Yes."

"If one of them saw the emerald on you," he said slowly, staring into the darkness about the bed, "and then searched your room looking for it, then the murderer

might have been at Pelham. Might've eaten at my table."
The mere thought filled him with hot rage.

She stroked his chest as if to soothe him. "Then it
could be any of the men?"

He considered. "Watts is younger than I."

"Surely it isn't he, then."

He nodded. "That leaves Oddershaw, Noakes, Barclay,
and Scarborough." Scarborough, who had been a friend
of his parents'.

For a moment they were quiet, contemplating the
possibilities.

Then he stirred. "Thank you."

"What for?"

He shook his head, for a moment unable to speak.
Finally, he cleared his throat and said huskily, "For
believing me. For telling me all this, even when I was ini-
tially foul to you. For being here."

She didn't answer, but her hand moved on his chest
until it lay exactly over his heart.

And there it stayed.

MAXIMUS OPENED HIS eyes the next morning to the warm
scent of Artemis in his arms. For the first time in a very
long while he'd neither dreamed nor woken in the night,
and he felt, in body and soul . . . content.

He leaned forward to nuzzle his lips against the nape
of the sleeping woman he held. She was so warm, so soft,
in sleep, with none of the prickling edges of the maiden
warrior she showed when awake and alert. He loved that
maiden warrior—the woman who looked him in the eye
and told him they were equals—but this sweet, vulnerable lady made his heart ache. Like this he could imagine

that she would yield to him, come softly into his arms, and agree to all that he said.

The mere thought made him huff a breath of laughter against her hair.

She stirred, making a small moaning sound. "What time is it?"

He glanced at the window—bright with the sharp, new light of day—and made an estimate. "Not more than seven of the clock."

She exclaimed and tried to move away from him.

He hugged her tighter.

"Maximus," she said, her voice gruff with sleep. "I have to leave at once. The servants will be up."

He bent and licked her neck. "Let them be up."

She stilled, her face turned away so he couldn't see her expression. "They'll see me. We'll be discovered."

He pulled back a little to try and see her face, but her hair had fallen over it, making her look like a naiad in mourning. "Does it matter?"

She turned then to lie on her back, looking up at him. Her dark brown locks fanned out around her serious face, and a bold nipple peaked from beneath the sheets. He noticed that she had a triangle of tiny moles just below her right collarbone.

Her dark gray eyes were lovely looking up from his pillow. "Then you don't care if everyone knows?"

He bent to taste those moles.

"Maximus."

He swallowed and raised his head. "I'll buy you a house."

She lowered her eyes so that he could no longer see their gray depths, but didn't speak.

His contentment was leaching away, an urgent need to

make her agree taking its place. Something very like fear was freezing his heart. "Either here in London or in the country, though if you're in the country I won't be able to see you as often."

From without the room he could hear the padding of servants.

He ducked his head, trying to catch her gaze. "Or I can buy both for you."

Silence. He could feel himself beginning to sweat. Many a parliamentarian could learn something of the art of negotiation from her.

He'd never wavered in Parliament, but he wavered here in his own bed with her. "Artemis..."

Her eyes flicked up, entirely dry and completely free from emotion. "Very well."

It should have been a moment of triumph—he'd snared his goddess—but instead he felt an odd sense of sorrow, even loss. Suddenly he knew: he'd never have her, not truly.

Not like this.

Perhaps that was what made his kiss so harsh, almost desperate.

But her lips parted beneath his as easily as if she were a biddable wench, merely here for his own pleasure. Her very passivity made him more frantic, for he knew it wasn't real. He rolled onto her, his body caging hers as if he could cage her heart as well. This woman. *His* woman. He'd make it all up to her, give her anything she'd wish for, if only she'd never leave him.

Behind them, the door to his bedroom opened.

"Get out," he growled to whichever servant had dared disturb him.

There was a squeak and the door was hastily shut.

Below him, Artemis cocked an eyebrow. "That was ill done."

He scowled. "Would you like her to witness our coupling?"

"Don't be crude." She pushed against his chest and he reluctantly gave way—only because he knew he was behaving like a churlish knave. She rose gloriously nude from the bed. "Besides, they'll all know soon enough, won't they? That I'm your mistress?"

He snorted, hitting the bed with one arm as he sprawled.

She raised a delicate eyebrow. "That *is* what you want, isn't it?"

"I can't have what I want."

"Can't you?" Her voice was light, nearly careless. "But you're the Duke of Wakefield, one of the most powerful men in England. You sit in Parliament, you own many estates, you have so much money you could *bathe* in it, and if that weren't enough, you go into St. Giles at night to risk death." She bent to pick up her chemise, discarded from the night before, and when she rose she pinned him with a challenging stare. "Isn't that right?"

He sneered. "You know that it is."

"Then, Your Grace, it follows that you can have anything and anyone you like even, apparently, me. Please don't insult me by telling me otherwise."

He closed his eyes. This wasn't how it was supposed to be. Shouldn't there be a little bit of joy in making her his? "What do you want?"

There was silence, broken only by a faint rustling. When he opened his eyes she was buttoning his banyan over her chemise.

"Nothing, I think," she said to her hands. Then, "My freedom, perhaps."

Freedom. He stared. What did freedom mean to such a wild creature? Did she want to be entirely quit of him?

"I'll not let you go," he snapped.

She glanced up at him and her look was sardonic. "Did I ask you to?"

"Artemis—"

"At the moment," she said, suddenly brisk, "the only thing I want is my brother's release. You've put chains upon him."

"Of course I put a chain on him—he's recovering fast and he's quite muscular." He frowned on a thought. "You shouldn't be visiting him now that he can move about—he might grab you."

She gave him an incredulous look.

He grimaced. "I can find a suitable place for him, perhaps a room with a barred door—"

"You mean a *cage*."

"We've already discussed this: I'll not let a madman near you."

She sighed and came to sit on the bed beside him. "He woke up in a tavern four years ago with the bodies of three of his friends around him. He didn't kill them. The most he can be blamed for is drinking too much."

Maximus cocked an eyebrow. "Then why was Kilbourne committed to Bedlam?"

She reached over and stroked his uplifted eyebrow. "Because no one believed him when he said he didn't remember what had happened or how his friends came to be killed. Because my uncle thought it better to hurry him into Bedlam rather than risk a trial."

"Yet you expect me to believe him innocent?"

"Yes." Her lips twisted. "Or rather I expect you to believe me when I say that I *know* my brother and he would never kill any man, let alone his friends, in a drunken rage."

He looked at her, so fiery, so brave in her defense of her brother and he felt jealousy that she might feel such strong emotion for anyone but him. "I'll think on it."

She frowned. "You can't keep him locked up—"

"I can and I will until such time as I am satisfied in my own mind that he won't do someone a harm. I promise to consider it. Don't ask more of me now." He saw her hurt and tried to grasp her hand, but she stood and her fingers slid away from him.

"I hope you'll not bar me from seeing Apollo once he's well," she said stiffly.

He didn't like her near anything that might harm her.

She must've seen his hesitation in his face. "You do know I've been visiting him in Bedlam by myself for years?"

He sighed. "Very well."

She inclined her chin, as haughty as any queen. "You're too kind."

His blew out a breath in exasperation. "Artemis…"

But she'd already gone out the door.

He threw a pillow at it anyway.

Maximus sighed and quickly dressed before exiting his rooms in search of an answer.

Kilbourne was lying on the cot when Maximus entered the cellar, and at first he couldn't tell if the man were awake or not, but as he drew near he saw the shine of open eyes.

"My lord," he said, making sure to stop outside the

reach of the chain he'd attached to the man's right ankle. "Where did you get the emerald pendant you gave to your sister on her fifteenth birthday?"

Kilbourne simply stared.

Maximus sighed. The man might be insane, but somehow he didn't think him unintelligent. "Look, Artemis says—"

That got a reaction—a growl. Kilbourne rose, a monolith of shifting rock, and reached for the notebook and pencil on the floor beside his cot. He scribbled something and held out the notebook.

Maximus hesitated.

The other man smirked as if aware of Maximus's wariness, his eyes daring him to come closer.

Maximus stepped forward and took the notebook, stepping back before dropping his eyes to read.

You haven't the right to call my sister by her Christian name.

Maximus looked the other man in the eye. "She herself has given me that right."

Kilbourne sneered and lounged back on his cot, staring defiantly.

Maximus frowned. "I haven't the time for your sulking. I need to know who you truly got the pendent from. I rescued you from Bedlam. Is this not a small fee for your freedom?"

Kilbourne cocked one eyebrow and looked pointedly down at the chain on his ankle.

Maximus remained unmoved. "You killed three men. Do not expect me to let you run free in a house with my sister—and yours, for that matter."

The look the viscount sent him was filthy, but he took up

the notebook again to write. Then he once again extended his arm.

Maximus looked at the offered notebook. This man was accused of a horrific crime, had been incarcerated in Bedlam for over four years, and had shown him no friendship. Then again Kilbourne hadn't shown him violence, either. And he *was* Artemis's brother.

Maximus stepped forward to take the notebook and this time he didn't back away again as he read:

I would never hurt my sister. You insult me to insinuate it. I got the pendant when I was a boy at school. Another boy, in the same house as I, bet it in a game of dice and I won. The boy was John Alderney. I know not how he had it. Even though I thought the necklace was paste, it was pretty, so I gave it to Artemis on our birthday. Have you seduced my sister?

Maximus looked up to find that the other man had leaned near, his muddy brown eyes glittering with threat. Maximus held his gaze and began backing away.

Something changed in the other man's eyes.

He lunged, fast for such a big man, his whole weight hitting Maximus in his middle. Maximus went down, Kilbourne on top of him, as the chain screeched across the floor. The viscount heaved himself up, his right arm pulled back, rage masking his features. Maximus thrust with his right palm while at the same time kicking out. He missed the other man's balls but kneed him in the belly. Kilbourne's breath whooshed out and Maximus shoved him off as hard as he could.

He scrambled back, out of the reach of the chain.

For a minute the only sound in the cellar was the panting of both men.

Maximus looked up.

Kilbourne was glaring at him, and there was no need for words or writing to know what the other man meant. For a moment Maximus wondered if this was the last thing those three men had seen that bloody night: Lord Kilbourne with a feral look of violence on his face.

He stood. "Whatever happens, be assured that I'll take care of your sister."

Kilbourne lunged. He was already almost at the end of his chain, so the additional movement merely brought him to his hands and knees. Still, he glared at Maximus steadily and Maximus knew that if the other man had been free, he'd be fighting for his life right now.

He turned away. He couldn't blame the viscount. If it had been Phoebe and someone had seduced her...His hands clenched. He ought to feel guilt, he knew, but all he felt was an odd, poignant sorrow. If only things were different. If only he weren't the Duke of Wakefield.

He straightened his shoulders. But he was the Duke of Wakefield. He'd assumed the title because of his own stupidity and cowardliness. To give up his duties, his *standards*, as the duke would be to let his father's death mean nothing.

His father had died for him, and he owed him the best stewardship of the dukedom possible.

Maximus shook his head and concentrated on the matter at hand. Kilbourne claimed that Alderney had lost the pendant to him.

Obviously he needed to question Alderney.

ARTEMIS HADN'T SEEN Maximus since she'd left his bed this morning. She couldn't help brooding on that fact even as she made her way to a table laden with tea and cakes that afternoon. Overhead the sun was brightly shining as ladies mingled and drank tea in Lady Young's garden. Lady Young was holding a small party, presumably to show off her autumn garden—though the only flowers Artemis saw were some rather bedraggled daisies.

The sad fact was that there wasn't much reason for her and Maximus to be together during the day. Not if they didn't want to arouse suspicion, that is. She supposed that if she became his official mistress then he might spend more time with her during the daylight hours. Maybe. And in return she would no longer be welcome in places like this.

Well, that was depressing.

"Miss Greaves!"

The hearty voice of the Duke of Scarborough made her turn around. He strolled toward her with Penelope on his arm. "Well met, well met indeed!"

"Your Grace." Artemis sank into a curtsy.

"Whatever are you doing here, Artemis?" Penelope looked around eagerly. "Is Wakefield here as well?"

"Ah, no." Artemis could feel guilty heat flooding her cheeks. "It's just Phoebe and me."

"Oh." Penelope pouted, seemingly unaware that the elderly duke beside her had wilted a bit.

"Er, I was about to retrieve a dish of tea for Lady Penelope," Scarborough said. "Would you like one as well?"

Artemis made sure to smile at the man. "That's very kind of you, but I was going to get two dishes—one for me and one for Phoebe. I'm sure you can't carry all that—"

"But of course I can." Scarborough puffed out his chest. "Please wait here, ladies."

And he was off as eagerly as a knight errant.

Penelope watched him go affectionately. "He really is the most charming gentleman. It's just too bad..."

Artemis sighed. If only Penelope would see Scarborough as a worthy suitor. He seemed perfect for her cousin in every respect save age. If Penelope turned her sights on Scarborough, then maybe she wouldn't be nearly so hurt when the inevitable happened and Artemis's own liaison with Wakefield came to light. Of course that wouldn't solve Artemis's own problem—Maximus would just find another heiress of noble birth and *sane* family to wed.

She was pulled from her depressing thoughts by Penelope leaning forward as if in confidence. "I can't think what the Duke of Wakefield has been about. No one seems to have seen him since his return to London. I know he has his silly parliamentarian duties, but the man must have social rounds to make as well." Penelope bit her lip, looking vulnerable. "Do you think he's lost interest in me? Perhaps I ought to do something daring again. I've heard Lady Fells rode in a *horse* race last week—*astride*."

"No, darling," Artemis said, her throat clogged with tears. She swallowed. She'd never forgive herself if she let Penelope think that she needed to break her neck racing a horse in order to win Maximus. "I'm sure he's as interested as ever. It's just that he's so very busy." She ventured a tremulous smile. "You must get used to that when you marry—his duties in Parliament and the like. He'll often be away." Oh, dear God, she loathed her own perfidy at the moment!

Penelope had brightened during this painful speech and now she beamed. "Well, *that* won't be a chore— I'll simply use his money to shop." She placed her hand almost shyly on Artemis's arm. "Thank you for telling me so. I don't know what I would do without your advice."

Her simple declaration nearly made Artemis's knees buckle. How could she have wronged Penelope so terribly? In the bright sunshine it seemed an insurmountable sin: to have put her own wants before the girl who had offered her sanctuary when Artemis had been so desperate. No matter how silly Penelope sometimes acted, Artemis knew, deep down, that her cousin truly had a heart.

And it would break when she'd realized Artemis's betrayal.

Artemis looked down at her hands, drawing a steadying breath. She very much feared that if she stayed with Maximus, this awful taint—this terribly wrong act— would, day by day, year by year, wear at her until she was no more than a ghost of her former self. She saw need when she looked into his eyes, but was there any love as well? Had she discarded Penelope's friendship for a man who didn't, in the end, truly care for her?

For she loved him, she realized now, in this brightly lit garden, of all places, with his future wife, her *cousin*, by her side. She loved Maximus totally and completely, with all of her bitter, broken heart, and she did not know if it was enough for the two of them.

Scarborough bustled up at that moment, his hands full of steaming dishes of tea. Artemis quickly took two cups and thanked the duke before turning away to bring the tea to Phoebe.

She was within sight of Phoebe when she was hailed again.

"I had not thought to see you again so very soon, Miss Greaves."

Artemis turned at the voice, surprised to find Mrs. Jellett looking at her with interest.

"Erm, how nice to meet again," Artemis replied, wondering if she was expected to curtsy even though she held a dish of tea in each hand. She glanced to the right where Phoebe was seated at an arbor waiting for Artemis's return. Her friend had her face tilted up to catch the sunlight.

"You left Pelham House so precipitously," Mrs. Jellett continued, linking arms with Artemis before she could defend herself. Artemis watched the full dish of milky tea hovering over the fine blond lace adorning Mrs. Jellett's sleeve and hoped the lady wouldn't hold her at fault if it soon became tea stained. "Just after Wakefield hurried back to London in fact. Such a pity! My dear friend Lady Noakes was quite put out at the early end to the house party. She has so little occasion to dine well. Not since Noakes lost most of her dowry. He was quite penniless before he married Charlotte. All his wealth came from her and now it's gone." Mrs. Jellett leaned close in confidence. "*Gambling*, you know. Such a terrible affliction."

Artemis eyed the older woman warily. "I'm just taking this tea to Lady Phoebe if you'll—"

"Oh, is Phoebe here, too?" cried Mrs. Jellett. She glanced in the direction in which Artemis had been walking and smiled.

Artemis did not like that smile.

"Well, we shouldn't keep her waiting," Mrs. Jellett announced, and Artemis found herself standing in front of Phoebe still linked with the other woman.

"I had no idea you'd be here, dear," Mrs. Jellett said in an overly loud voice, rather as if Phoebe's poor sight had affected her hearing as well.

"It's a lovely day for a garden party, isn't it?" Phoebe said.

"Here's your tea," Artemis said, carefully placing the cup into the girl's hand. "I was just discussing your brother's house party with Mrs. Jellett."

Phoebe's eyes cleared with the mention of Mrs. Jellett's name and Artemis suspected that she hadn't known who exactly had greeted her until just then. "Will you sit with us, ma'am?"

"Oh, thank you, my dear." The older lady immediately sat beside Phoebe, forcing Artemis to take Mrs. Jellett's other side. "I was just telling Artemis that we all missed her when she left the house party in such a rush."

"But she left with me," Phoebe said sweetly. "So if Artemis was in a rush, I suppose I was as well."

Mrs. Jellett looked a trifle put out by this simple statement before her expression smoothed over and she leaned forward. "But then, Phoebe dear, you didn't wander off with a bachelor gentleman into the woods before you left." She tittered with horrible gaiety. "We did so *wonder*, Miss Greaves, what you might have been doing with His Grace out there in the woods."

"As I said before, His Grace was merely looking at a bird I'd spotted." Artemis was careful to keep her voice even.

"Indeed? Why, I wish I were as daring as you, Miss Greaves! No wonder he immediately installed you in his town house."

"Actually, Artemis is acting as my lady's companion," Phoebe said quietly.

Mrs. Jellett patted her hand. "Yes, dear. I'm sure she is."

Artemis inhaled, but Phoebe was quicker than she. "I

think we'll take a turn about the garden. If you'll excuse us, ma'am?"

She stood and Artemis hastily offered her arm. They were quiet as Artemis led her down one of the less crowded paths, until Artemis spoke. "I'm sorry about that."

"Don't you dare apologize," Phoebe said fiercely. "Spiteful old witch. I don't know how she can stand herself. I'm just sorry that helping me has laid you open to such gossip."

Artemis looked away, her throat closing in guilt. Soon—very soon, if Mrs. Jellett's attitude was any indication—her secret with Maximus would be revealed. She'd known from the start that there was no way to keep it for long, but she hadn't guessed it would happen so abruptly. She was about to enter a different level of society.

One reserved for ladies who had fallen.

Chapter Seventeen

*Lin had never liked serpents and the one in her hands was
very big, but she gripped it firmly nonetheless, for she knew
it was her beloved brother, Tam. The serpent reared back
and sunk its awful fangs into the soft flesh of her arm, yet
still Lin held him fast. The Herla King turned his head,
staring at her with hollow eyes, his attention finally torn
from the hunt.*
Then Tam turned into a burning coal....
—from *The Legend of the Herla King*

John Alderney was a thin man with wide blue eyes and
a nervous blink that seemed to be made worse by the
presence of the Duke of Wakefield in his London sitting
room.

"I've sent for tea," Alderney said, beginning to lower
himself to a chair before popping back up again. "That's
all right, isn't it? Tea? Or...or there's brandy about somewhere, I think." He peered around his little sitting room
as if expecting the brandy to appear of its own accord.
"French, of course, but then I suppose most brandy is."

He blinked rapidly at Maximus.

Maximus fought back a sigh and sat. "It's ten of the
clock."

"Oh, er?"

They were both saved by the arrival of the tea. An awe-struck maid stared at Maximus the entire time she was pouring, and he couldn't help but think it was a miracle she didn't spill the tea on the carpet. She backed from the room, revealing as she opened the sitting room door a bevy of servants and Alderney's pink little wife gawking in the hallway before reluctantly closing it.

Clutching a steaming cup in both hands seemed to settle Alderney enough that he was at least able to sit and form a coherent thought. "Quite the honor, of course— don't have dukes comin' to visit before noon all that often—and I can't say enough how...how grateful we are, but I...I was wonderin'..."

But that seemed to be as far as Alderney's courage took him. He broke off to gulp half his dish of tea and then winced as he apparently burned his mouth.

Maximus took the emerald pendant from his waistcoat pocket and put it on the table between them. "I'm told that this used to belong to you. Where did you get it?"

Alderney's mouth dropped open. He blinked several times, staring at Maximus as if he expected some further explanation, and when none was forthcoming, at last stretched out his arm to pick up the pendant.

Maximus growled.

Alderney snatched back his hand. "I...er...what?"

Maximus took a breath and deliberately let it out slowly to try and release some of the tension in his body—a move that seemed to alarm Alderney. "Do you remember this pendant?"

Alderney wrinkled his nose. "Ah...n-no?"

"It would've been some years ago," Maximus said,

holding his patience with both hands. "Thirteen years or so."

Alderney calculated, his lips moving silently, and then suddenly brightened. "Oh, Harrow! That's where I was thirteen years ago. Pater hadn't the money himself, of course, but Cousin Robert was kind enough to send me. Jolly place, Harrow. Met quite a lot of fine fellows there. Food wasn't what you might call elegant, but there was lots of it and I remember a sausage that was simply..." Alderney looked up at this point and must've read something on Maximus's face that alarmed him for he started. "Oh, er, but that's perhaps not what you want to know?"

Maximus sighed. "Lord Kilbourne said that he had this pendant from you."

"Kilbourne..." Alderney laughed, high and nervous. "But everyone knows the man's mad. Had an attack of some kind and killed three fellows." Alderney shuddered. "I heard that one man's head was nearly severed from his body. Bloody. Never would've thought it of Kilbourne. *Seemed* a nice enough fellow at school. Remember he once ate an entire eel pie. Not something you see every day, I can tell you that. The eel pies were quite large at Harrow and usually—"

"So you did know Kilbourne at Harrow?" Maximus asked to clarify.

"Why, yes, he was in my house," Alderney said at once. "But there were many other quite sane fellows in my house as well. Lord Plimpton, for instance. Quite a bigwig in Parliament now, as I understand. Though"— Alderney's brow knit on a thought—"he *wasn't* a very nice fellow at school. Used to gobble rare beefsteak with his mouth half open." Alderney shuddered. "Surprised *he* didn't turn out to be a bloody raving madman, now that I think of it. But there you are: can't predict these things apparently. Perhaps it was all that eel pie."

Maximus stared at Alderney for a moment, trying to decide if the man were lying or really as foolish as his words seemed to paint him.

Alderney appeared to brighten at his confusion. "Was there anything else?"

"Yes," Maximus gritted out, making the man cringe back. "Think: when could you have given that pendant to Kilbourne?"

"Why..." Alderney knit his brows. "Never, as far as I know. I don't remember even talking that much with Kilbourne beyond the usual 'Good morning' and 'Are you eating your portion of sausage?' We weren't really friends. *Not*," Alderney hastened to add at Maximus's growing scowl, "that I wasn't friendly or anything, but he was the sort who actually *read* things in Latin, and I was more interested in sweets and smuggling tobacco into the house."

Alderney stopped abruptly and stared at Maximus rather helplessly.

Maximus closed his eyes. He'd been so sure that here at last was the trail he could follow to find the murderer—only to be stopped by a fool's faulty memory. Of course, that was supposing that Kilbourne had even been telling the truth. He was a madman, after all.

Maximus opened his eyes, scooped up the pendant, and stood. "Thank you, Alderney."

"That's it?" The other man didn't hide his relief. "Oh, well, glad to be of help. Don't have such illustrious visitors, as I said, only Cousin Robert, and he hasn't been by since Michaelmas of last year."

Maximus halted on his way to the door and slowly turned on a sudden thought. "Who is your cousin Robert, Alderney?"

His host grinned, looking quite idiotic. "Oh! Thought you knew. He's the Duke of Scarborough."

ARTEMIS HAD JUST sat down to dinner that night with Phoebe and Maximus at Wakefield House when her world came tumbling down about her ears.

She'd only taken in the dear sight of Maximus frowning over his fish when the commotion began. Armageddon was heralded by voices in the corridor outside the dining room and the hurried footsteps of the servants.

Phoebe cocked her head. "Who could that be at this time of night?"

They hadn't long to speculate.

The door was flung open to reveal Bathilda Picklewood. "My dears, you should've seen the roads! Simply awful, all of them. I thought we would be stuck forever in a mud hole at the turnpike near Tyburn. Wilson actually had to get down from the box and lead the horses out, and I won't even repeat the language he used."

Belle, Starling, Percy, and Bon Bon all trotted over to greet Miss Picklewood, while Mignon rumbled from her arms at the other dogs.

"Hush, Mignon," Miss Picklewood scolded. "Goodness, you sound like a bumblebee! Where did all these dogs come from? Surely you didn't bring them from Pelham?"

"We thought they'd like the change of scenery," Phoebe said brightly. "I'm so glad you've arrived! We didn't expect you back for another fortnight or so."

"Well, I thought I'd pop in to see how you all were doing," Miss Picklewood said, exchanging a look Artemis couldn't interpret with Maximus.

The duke's expression had shut down as surely as a door closing. "I trust your friend is doing better?"

"Oh, much," Miss Bathilda said as she sat. Footmen scurried under the eagle eye of the butler to set another place for her. "And dear Mrs. White was so sweet. She told me I must come at once, just for a small visit, so that I wouldn't tire of Bath."

"That was kind," Maximus replied flatly.

"Now, dear." Miss Picklewood turned to Phoebe. "You must tell me what you did today."

Artemis was quiet, poking the tines of her fork gently into her fish as she listened to Phoebe prattle. Once she glanced up and caught Maximus staring at her broodingly. She couldn't help a shiver of premonition. It seemed very strange that Miss Picklewood would leave her friend's sickbed just to "pop in."

It wasn't until after a lovely apple tart that Artemis could only pick at that she found out Miss Picklewood's true intent.

She and Phoebe rose to retire into the sitting room for tea, but the older lady spoke up, halting them. "Artemis, dear, won't you stay here? I do wish to discuss something with you and His Grace." Phoebe's brows knit, and Miss Picklewood addressed her, "Phoebe, Agnes can help you to the sitting room. We'll be along in a bit."

Phoebe hesitated, but in the end accepted the arm of Agnes the maid and left the room.

Artemis slowly retook her seat.

"Panders," Miss Picklewood addressed the butler, "can

you leave His Grace's brandy? We shan't have need of you for the next half hour, I think."

"Yes, ma'am," Panders said without a speck of curiosity.

"Oh, and Panders? I do know you'll make sure we're not overheard."

At that subtle hint about the eavesdropping of servants, Panders stiffened imperceptibly. "Of course, ma'am."

And then, he, too was gone.

Maximus sat back in his chair, looking like a particularly dangerous cat lounging. "What is this about, Bathilda?"

Artemis was rather admiring of Miss Picklewood's courage. She didn't even hesitate as she looked at her powerful relative. "You've seduced Miss Greaves."

Maximus didn't move. "Where did you hear that?"

Miss Picklewood waved a hand and reached over to take the decanter of brandy. She spoke as she poured herself a slight inch into the empty wineglass before her. "Where I heard it from doesn't matter. What matters is that it is true and it is now, or very soon will be, public knowledge."

"What I do in the privacy of my own home is no business of anyone's but mine," Maximus said with all the arrogance of a man with a thousand years of aristocratic ancestors.

Miss Bathilda took a delicate sip of her brandy. "I'm sorry, but I must disagree, Your Grace. What you do, even in the privacy of your own home, affects many other people, including Phoebe." She set down her glass firmly. "You cannot keep your mistress in the same house as your maiden sister. Even you must bow to the dictates of society."

Artemis's gaze dropped to the table. She noticed absently that her hands, laid sedately on the wood before her, were trembling. Carefully, she balled her fingers and let her hands drop to her lap.

Maximus waved his hand as if he were swatting a fly. "Artemis won't corrupt Phoebe, you're aware of that."

"You know as well as I that a reputation is based purely upon what is perceived rather than any reality. You've made Miss Greaves a fallen woman. By her very presence she soils all ladies around her."

"Bathilda!" Maximus's warning was a growl.

Artemis couldn't help a small gasp at the same time. She'd known what she was now, but to have it so bluntly stated by someone she'd considered a friend was still shocking.

Miss Picklewood turned to Artemis for the first time. Her face was determined, but her eyes were sympathetic. "I'm sorry, but I did warn you, my dear."

Artemis nodded, ignoring Maximus's glower. "So you did."

"You need to leave."

Artemis held the other woman's gaze. "And I will. But tomorrow night Phoebe has her heart set on seeing the opera at Harte's Folly with the other ladies from the Ladies' Syndicate. She'll be upset if I don't attend."

Miss Picklewood frowned.

"Oh, for God's sake, Bathilda," Maximus ground out. "One day more won't taint Phoebe."

Miss Picklewood's lips pursed. "Very well. I expect one day won't make any difference. Attend Harte's Folly and then, my dear, it *must* be over."

Artemis glanced at Maximus. He had his face turned, his teeth clenched so tightly she could see the muscle flex in his jaw. Their affair wouldn't be over—he'd offered her a house—but she supposed as far as Miss Picklewood was concerned it didn't matter as long as she was hidden away.

Artemis rose from the table, not looking at Maximus again. "You needn't say anything more, Miss Picklewood, for you're quite right. I can't stay here with Phoebe. If you'll both excuse me, I'll go begin packing."

She walked to the door of the dining room with her head held high, but she still couldn't help the small sob when she closed the door without anyone protesting.

IT WAS LATE when the door to the cellar opened. Apollo didn't bother turning. He'd already been served his supper by the valet. Now he simply lay on his back, his arm thrown across his eyes and dozed.

But the footsteps that approached his bed were lighter than a man's.

"Apollo."

Artemis stood over him with a cloth bag in her hands.

He sat up.

"We have to hurry," she said as she dropped the bag to the ground beside his cot. The bag clanked.

She bent and took out a mallet and a chisel. "You wouldn't believe how long it took me to find these. I finally asked one of the stable boys and voila."

She looked inordinately pleased for a woman who was risking herself for him. He scowled and wished he could swear. *God damn it.* Wakefield had seduced her—he *knew* it—and now she was going to risk the duke's wrath. Where would that leave her if that bastard decided to throw her out?

"Well?" She set her hands on her hips. "*I* certainly can't do it."

He grabbed his notebook and wrote in it before thrusting it at her. She took the notebook, and he picked up the chisel and set it on the first link in the chain that dropped to the floor from the circlet around his ankle.

"*Won't the duke punish you?*" Artemis read aloud.

He struck the chisel with a ringing *clang.*

Artemis lowered the notebook to look at him with exasperation. "No, of course not. You've been reading too many of those lurid pamphlets I used to bring you in Bedlam. I'm not even sure the stories they report are real. In any case, Maximus might be quite cross with me, but he'd hardly punish me. *Really.* The thought."

He hit the chisel again before giving her a speaking glance and mouthed, pointedly, *Maximus?*

"I've already told you he's a friend."

He rolled his eyes. Artemis was lying to him for that bastard. He wished the duke's skull was beneath the mallet. He struck the chisel for a third time as hard as he could. The link broke open.

"Oh, well done!" Artemis exclaimed and bent to help him work the broken link from the two still attached to the manacle around his ankle. "You'll have to wrap that with a cloth or something so it doesn't clink. I brought clothes." She gestured to the bag.

He took the notebook from her and wrote, *Why now?*

She read his words and her face went carefully blank just before she smiled and looked back up at him. "I'll be leaving Wakefield House soon and I wanted to make sure you were free before I go."

Why was she leaving? What else was going on? Silently he mouthed, "Artemis."

She pretended not to see. "Hurry up and get dressed."

Troubled by her haste and his unanswered questions, he obeyed. He'd been given breeches and a shirt by the valet. Now he changed into the fresh clothes, which also included a waistcoat, coat, and shoes.

Everything was just a bit too small, including the shoes.

Artemis looked at him apologetically. "I got them from one of the footmen. He had the largest feet in the household."

Apollo shook his head, smiling for her, and bent to kiss his sister. He had nothing save what she'd given him. He grabbed up the notebook and wrote, *How will I contact you?*

She stared at the notebook for a moment, and he could tell by her expression that she hadn't thought of that.

He took back the notebook. *Artemis. We must stay in touch. You're all that I have now and I don't trust your duke. At all.*

"Well that's just silly, the part about Maximus," she said when she'd read what he'd written. "But you're right—we mustn't lose each other. Do you know where you can go from here?"

He'd been thinking on the matter as he lay in the cot for days and he had a ready answer of sorts. He wrote carefully, *I have a friend by the name of Asa Makepeace. You may send a letter in care of him to Harte's Folly.*

He gave the notebook to her and saw when her eyes widened in astonishment. "Harte's Folly? I don't understand. Is that where you'll go?"

He shook his head, gently taking the notebook from her hands. *Better you don't know.*

She was reading over his shoulder. "But—"

Take care of yourself.

He thought he saw her smile waver when she read it, then she was hugging him tightly. "You're the one who needs to take care of yourself. Your escape is still all the news. They'll be searching for you." She drew back to look at him, and to his consternation he saw that she had tears in her eyes. "I couldn't bear to lose you again."

He bent and kissed her forehead. Even if he could speak there was nothing he could say to comfort her.

He turned to go.

"Wait." She laid her hand on his arm, forestalling him. "Here." She thrust a smaller bag into his hands. "There's three pounds sixpence. It's all I have. And some bread and cheese. Oh, Apollo." Her brave speech ended on a little sob. "Go!"

She gave him a shove just as he was about to bend to her again.

So without looking at her, he turned and ducked into the cramped tunnel he'd seen Wakefield take earlier that night.

He had no idea where it would lead him.

MAXIMUS DIDN'T KNOW how long he'd been searching St. Giles that night when he heard the pistol shot. He dived around a corner and ran flat out down an alley, heading toward the sounds. Overhead the moon guided him, his fair mistress, his unattainable lover.

The hoarse shouts of men and the clatter of hooves on cobblestones came from ahead.

He spilled into a cross street and saw to his right Trevillion riding hell for leather straight toward him. "He's headed toward the Seven Dials!"

Maximus ran across in front of the horse, so close he fancied he felt the horse's breath upon his cheek as he passed. On foot he could duck down one of the many tiny alleys too small for a man on horse and head Old Scratch off. For he knew, deep in his soul, that it was Old Scratch that Trevillion hunted tonight. Old Scratch, the man who wore his mother's pendant at his throat.

Old Scratch, who'd murdered his parents nineteen years ago on a rainy St. Giles night.

A jog to the left, a duck to the right. His legs were aching, the breath sawing in and out of his lungs. The Seven Dials pillar loomed ahead, in the circular junction of seven streets. Old Scratch sat his horse casually under the pillar, as if waiting for him.

Maximus slowed and slunk into the shadows. The highwayman didn't have his pistols out, but he must have been armed.

"Your Grace," Old Scratch called. "Tsk. I'd thought you'd grown out of hiding long ago."

He felt the coldness invade his chest, the fear that he was too small, too weak. The powerlessness as he'd watched this man shoot his mother. There had been blood on her breast, splattering scarlet over the white marble of her skin, running in the rain into her spilled hair.

He wanted to vomit. "Who are you?"

Old Scratch cocked his head. "Don't you know? Your parents knew—it's why I had to kill them. Your mother recognized me, even beneath my neck cloth, I'm afraid. Pity. She was a beautiful woman."

"Then you *are* an aristocrat." Maximus refused to rise to the bait. "And yet you've sunk to thieving in St. Giles."

"*Robbing*, I'll have you know." Old Scratch sounded

irritable, as if he thought robbery somehow above thievery. "And it's a pleasant hobby. Gets one's blood flowing."

"You expect me to believe that you do this for *excitement*?" Maximus scoffed. "Acquit me of stupidity. Are you a poor younger son? Or did your sire gamble your inheritance away?"

"Wrong and wrong again." Old Scratch shook his head mockingly. "I grow weary, Your Grace. Don't be such a coward. Come out, come out to play!"

Maximus stepped from the shadows. He was no longer a cowering boy. "I have all of them but that one, you know."

Old Scratch clucked as his big black horse shifted from one foot to another. "The emerald drops like this?" He touched his gloved fingers to the emerald pin at his throat. "That must've cost a pretty penny, for I know I sold them for such. Your mother's necklace kept me in wine and wenches for many years."

Maximus felt his ire rise and tempered it. He wouldn't be drawn out so easily. "I only need that one to have it remade."

Old Scratch crooked one finger. "Come and take it."

"I intend to," Maximus said as he circled the horse and man. "I'll take it and your life as well."

The highwayman threw back his head and laughed. "Am I the reason for that?" He gestured to Maximus's costume. "La, sir, I confess myself flattered. To've driven the Duke of Wakefield into madness so deep that he donned the guise of a common *actor* and runs the streets of St. Giles. Why, I—"

It happened so fast Maximus had no time to think, let alone act. He heard the clatter of hoofbeats behind him, saw the glint of metal as Old Scratch raised his left hand from where he'd kept it hidden in his coat.

And then there was the flash and the bang.

The terrible, *terrible* bang.

An equine scream. Maximus jerked and whirled. Behind him, a horse was falling, writhing on the ground. He turned back to Old Scratch. The highwayman was spurring his horse into one of the seven radiating streets.

Maximus started after him.

The horse screamed again.

This time when he looked he saw the man trapped beneath the horse. *Christ.* The horse had fallen on its rider.

He ran back to the wounded horse. The horse's legs were stiffened and the entire big body shuddered.

A dragoon rode up and stopped, simply gaping.

"Help me get him out!" Maximus shouted.

He glanced into the bloodied face of the man on the ground and saw it was Trevillion. Beneath the blood, his skin was bone-white. The dragoon captain was silent, his teeth clenched, his lips pulled back in a grimace of agony.

"Take his other hand," Maximus ordered the young soldier. The man grasped his captain's arm and together they heaved.

Trevillion gave a deep, awful groan as his legs came free of his horse. Maximus saw that the dragoon captain's lip was bloody from where he'd bitten it through. He knelt by Trevillion and winced when he looked at his right leg—the same leg that Trevillion limped on from some previous injury. It was bent in an unnatural angle, the bone quite obviously broken—and broken badly.

Trevillion reached up and grasped Maximus's tunic front with surprising strength, pulling him down close enough that the other soldier couldn't hear. "Don't let her suffer, Wakefield."

Maximus glanced at the mare—Cowslip, he remembered now. A silly name for a soldier's horse. He looked back at Trevillion, his chin bloody with his attempt to silence his own pain.

"Do it," the captain grunted, his eyes shimmering. "God damn it, just *do* it."

Maximus rose and stepped over to the mare. She'd stopped thrashing and lay, her great sides heaving. Her right front foreleg was held oddly, either broken or very badly hurt. An ugly hole marred the mare's smooth chocolate hide at her chest, and her mane trailed, wet with blood, on the cobblestones. For a moment he saw his mother's hair trailing bloodily in the wet street channel.

He shook his head and stepped closer. Cowslip rolled her eye as he neared, afraid and hurt.

He drew his short sword.

Maximus knelt, covered her eye, and slit her throat.

Chapter Eighteen

Lin screamed as the red-hot coal singed her palms, but she
did not let go of Tam. King Herla flinched at her cry and
made as if to tear the burning coal from her hands.
"No!" Lin said, holding the burning coal away from the
king. "He is my brother and I must save both him and me."
At her words his eyes saddened, but he nodded and
withdrew his hand.
And the cock crowed....
—from *The Legend of the Herla King*

Artemis woke in the early hours of morning to the sound
of splashing. She rolled over in Maximus's great bed and
saw him standing by his dresser lit by a single candle. He
was bare to the waist and splashing water on his chest and
hands...water that was running down his chest in red
rivulets.

She sat up. "You're hurt."

He paused, then continued sluicing himself, apparently
without regard for his carpet. "No."

She frowned. Something was the matter, he was too
quiet. "Then whose blood is that?"

He looked at his dripping hands. "Captain Trevillion's
and a horse named Cowslip."

She blinked, wondering if she'd heard right. But as she stared at him he said nothing more. She wrapped her arms around her bent knees. She remembered, vaguely, meeting the dragoon captain years ago in St. Giles. He'd seemed a stern man. She shivered. "Is Captain Trevillion dead?"

"No," he whispered. "No, but he's very badly injured."

"What happened?"

"I found him."

"Who?"

He finally looked up at that, and though his face was drawn, his eyes burned. "Old Scratch. The man who killed my parents."

She let out a sigh. "Then you captured him?"

"No." He threw down a washcloth he'd been using and braced his arms on the dresser. "We chased Old Scratch to the Seven Dials pillar in St. Giles. There he shot Trevillion's horse and the horse fell on the captain."

Artemis drew in a breath. Such accidents happened and they could easily be fatal to the rider. "But you said he's alive."

Maximus at last looked at her. "His leg is badly broken. I had to put down the horse and then I brought Trevillion here."

Artemis began to rise. "Does he need nursing?"

"Yes, but I've seen to that." Maximus held up his hand, forestalling her. "I sent for my doctor as soon as I arrived. He set the leg as best he could. He wanted to take it off, but I forbade it." Maximus winced. "The leg is bandaged and the doctor says if it doesn't putrefy Trevillion may live. I have one of the footmen sitting with him. There's nothing more to be done tonight."

Artemis stared. She was half on, half off the bed, stopped by his command. "But the captain may still die?"

Maximus turned away. "Yes."

"I'm so sorry," she whispered.

He nodded as he stripped his breeches off. "I've lost my only ally."

She looked at him sharply. "And a friend, I think."

He paused for a split second before he began unbuttoning his smalls. "That, too."

"Will you send more soldiers out to capture Old Scratch?"

He kicked off his smalls and straightened, nude. "I'll go after him myself."

"But…" She frowned, glancing away from his distracting body. "Wouldn't it be better to have help?"

He threw back his head and barked with laughter. "Better, yes, but I have no one to ask for help."

She stared. "Why not? You mentioned before the two other boys—men now—that you trained with. Surely one of them—"

He made a cutting motion with the blade of his hand. "They've left off dressing as the Ghost."

"Then someone else. You're the *Duke of Wakefield.*"

He shook his head impatiently. "This is a dangerous chase—"

"Yes, it is," she interrupted. "I can see the bruises on your ribs and you have a cut on your shoulder."

"All the more reason to do this by myself," he said. "I don't want anyone else hurt in my service."

"Maximus," she said softly, trying to understand, trying to find what would move him. "Why must you do this at all? If he's a highwayman the soldiers will capture and hang him sooner or—"

He whirled, sudden and violent, and kicked one of the chairs in front of the fireplace. It flew across the room and hit the wall, splintering. He stood, chest heaving, and stared at the battered chair, though she very much doubted he saw it.

"Maximus?"

"I killed them." His voice was raw.

"I don't understand."

"On the night they were murdered. It was because of me that they were in St. Giles." He finally looked up, his eyes dry and stark and so wounded she wanted to cry the tears he couldn't.

Instead she lifted her chin and commanded, "Tell me."

"We were at the theater that night." He held her eyes as if afraid to look away. "Only Father, Mother, and I, for Hero was too young and Phoebe was just a baby. It was something of a privilege for me—I wasn't that long out of a governess's care. I remember we saw *King Lear* and I was dreadfully bored, but I didn't want to show it, for I knew it would make me seem naïve and young. Afterward, we got in the carriage, and I don't know how, I can't remember, though I've been over and over it in my mind, but Father was talking about guns. I'd received a pair of fowling pieces for my birthday, and I'd taken them out and shot some birds in the garden in London the week before, and he'd been quite angered. I'd thought he was done scolding me, but it came up again and this time he said he'd take my guns away from me until I learned to handle them properly. I was surprised and angered and I shouted at him."

He inhaled sharply as if he couldn't catch his breath.

"I shouted at my father. I called him a bastard, and my

mother began to weep and then to my horror I felt tears at my own eyes. I was fourteen and the thought of crying in front of my father was too terrible to bear. I threw open the carriage door and ran out. Father must've stopped the carriage then and come after me, and I suppose Mother followed. I ran and ran. I didn't know where we were, and I didn't much care, but the houses were tumbling down and I could smell spilled gin and corruption. I heard my father's shouts as he neared, and in a moment of malicious stupidity I ducked around a corner, behind some barrels—gin barrels—and hid. The smell of gin was overwhelming, filling my nostrils, my lungs, my head until I wanted to vomit. I heard a shot."

He stopped, his mouth opening wide, as if he were screaming, but no sound emerged.

He bared his teeth and flung back his head, still holding her gaze with those awful eyes. "I peered around the barrel and my father . . . my *father* . . ." He closed his eyes and opened them again as if unable to look away. "He saw me, as he lay there with the blood upon his chest. He saw me hiding and he . . . he moved his head, just a bit, in a small shake, and he *smiled* at me. And then the highwayman shot my mother."

He gulped. "I don't remember what happened then. I'm told they found me over my parents. All I recall is the stink of gin. That and the blood in my mother's hair."

He looked down at his hands, fisting them and opening his fingers again as if they were foreign appendages.

He glanced up at her and somehow he'd come back to himself, contained all that terrible sorrow and anger and fear, enough to make ten strong men fall down like babes. Maximus held it all inside of him and straightened his shoulders, his chin level, and Artemis couldn't understand it—where he got the strength to hide that awful, bloody wound in his soul—but she admired him for it.

Admired him and loved him.

She felt an answering wound open within her own soul, a kind of faint reflection of all the pain he'd endured, just because she cared for him.

"So you see," he said quietly, in full possession of himself, even standing completely naked. He was the Duke of Wakefield now as much as when his stood and gave a speech in the House of Lords. "I have to do it myself. Because I caused their deaths, I have to avenge them—and my honor."

She held out her hands to him, and he approached the bed and sank to one knee before her. "Can you look at me now, knowing what kind of coward I am?"

"My darling," she said, cupping his face in her hands, "You are the bravest man I know. You were but a boy, then, surely someone else has told you this?"

"I was the Marquess of Brayston, even then."

"You were a *child*," she said. "A willful, silly child who lost his temper. Your father didn't blame you. He protected you as he lay dying, telling you not to leave your hiding place. Think, Maximus. If you had a child—a son—wouldn't you give your life for his? Wouldn't you be glad, even if you died, that *he* lived?"

He closed his eyes and laid his head in her lap. She ran her palms over his head, feeling the soft bristles beneath her fingers.

After a while she bent and softly kissed his forehead. "Come to bed."

He rose then and climbed beneath the sheets, pulling her close. She faced away from him, his heavy arm across her waist, and stared into the darkness and waited for sleep.

"YOUR GRACE."

For a moment, as Maximus swam to consciousness, he thought he'd imagined Craven's voice. He blinked. Craven was hovering next to his bed.

"Craven," he said stupidly. "You're back."

Craven arched an eyebrow, looking miffed. "I never went away, Your Grace."

Maximus winced. By the amount of "Your Grace's" Craven was tossing around, he was still on the outs with his valet. "I didn't see you about the house."

"Your Grace doesn't know all that goes on in this house," Craven pointed out acidly. "There is a gentleman waiting for you downstairs. He says his name is Alderney."

"Alderney? At this hour?"

Craven raised both eyebrows at once. "It's just before noon, Your Grace."

"Oh." Maximus sat up, careful not to disturb Artemis. His mind felt muddy, but whatever Alderney had come for must be important.

"I've provided your visitor with luncheon and he seems quite content, so I believe you have time to perform your ablutions and make yourself presentable before entertaining him."

"Thank you, Craven," Maximus said a little wryly as he rose, nude, from the bed. "You know about Captain Trevillion?"

"Indeed," Craven replied, back still turned. "I have looked in on the captain and he appears to be resting peacefully. The doctor has sent word he will return this afternoon to see to his patient."

"Good." Maximus felt better knowing the captain had survived the night.

Craven cleared his throat. "I couldn't help but notice that Viscount Kilbourne was no longer in the cellar."

Maximus stilled, water dripping from his face. "What?"

"He appears to have somehow freed himself from his chain with the help of a mallet and chisel and escaped." Craven very carefully didn't look at Artemis, still burrowed beneath the covers.

Maximus had no such qualms, and he noticed that her breathing was too light for sleep. "Craven, I wonder if you might leave us for a moment?"

"Of course, Your Grace."

Maximus eyed his valet as he turned to the door. "Were you aware that Miss Picklewood returned unexpectedly from the country? She seemed to have information that could only have come from inside this house. You wouldn't know anything about that, would you?"

Craven widened his eyes. "Whatever are you insinuating, Your Grace?"

Maximus gave him a wry look and closed the door behind him.

When he turned back, Artemis was watching him. There was a sorrow in her eyes that sent a chill through his bones.

Perhaps that was why his voice was overloud when he demanded, "You let him out, didn't you?"

"Yes." She sat up. "Did you truly expect anything else?"

"I expected you to obey me when I told you that he must remain locked up."

"Obey." Her face had gone white and blank, save for the blaze within her eyes.

She was withdrawing and he couldn't let her. "*Yes.* I would've found a safe place for him—a place away from people he might hurt. You—"

She made a scoffing sound and threw back the covers. Underneath she was nude, her skin rosy and delicious from sleep. "You want me to obey like all your other minions. To fit neatly in the box in which you decide to place me. Can't you see? I'll rot in that box. I cannot be contained by your expectations of me."

He felt the argument spiraling out of his control. He was adept at debate within the House of Lords, but this was no logical political argument—this was emotions laid raw between a man and a woman.

He looked at her helplessly, knowing somehow that this argument encompassed far more than the difficulty of what to do with her brother. "Artemis—"

"No." She rose, as martial as any Greek goddess, and grabbed her chemise. "This is my brother we're talking about, Maximus."

"You'll take his part before mine?" Oh, he knew it was a mistake even before the words left his lips.

Her shoulders squared. "If I must. We shared a womb. We're flesh and blood, tied together forever, both physically and spiritually. I *love* my brother."

"As you don't me?"

She stopped, her chemise in her hands before her. For a moment her shoulders slumped and then she raised her head. His goddess.

His Diana.

"When you've tired of me," she said softly, precisely, "Apollo will still be my brother. Will still be there for me."

"I'll never tire of you," he said, knowing with every thread of his soul that he spoke the absolute truth.

"Then prove it."

He knew what she asked with such an open and vulnerable face. Something within him shriveled and died. She deserved this. Deserved a husband and a home and *children*. His children. But he'd been on the rack too long for a penance he wasn't sure he could ever entirely pay. The dukedom...his father.

"You know..." His voice was hoarse, the croaking of a dying man. He licked his lips. "You know why I cannot. I owe him my life, my service, the duty of being the duke."

She shrugged one delicate, bare shoulder. "Well, I do not owe your father's memory anything."

He staggered as if she'd slapped him. "You cannot—"

"No," she said. "I *cannot*. I thought I could do this, truly I did, but I'm not brave enough, you see. I can't hurt everyone around me, can't hurt Penelope, can't hurt *me* any longer." She held out a trembling hand. "I don't fit into the pretty little box you've made for me. I can't watch you rise from my bed knowing you'll visit another woman's. I'm not a saint."

"Please."

He was pleading. He who had never bowed before anyone before.

She shook her head and he broke, grasping her hand, pulling her body against his. "Please, my Diana, please don't go."

She made no spoken answer, but she tilted her face

up to his, parting her lips so sweetly when he pressed his mouth to hers. He cradled her face in his palms, holding her like the precious thing she was as he sipped from her lips. She was *his*, in this world and the next, and if he could only convince her of that one, immutable fact, then he could still save this.

Could still live and breathe with her by his side.

So he slid his fingers into her hair, resting his thumbs at her temples as he licked into her mouth. He claimed her, gently, slyly, using all the sexual wiles that he'd ever learned.

She moaned and arched her neck and he crowed inside, even as he moved his mouth to her throat, licking down that slim column, tasting woman and need.

She tried to break away, to turn her head, groaning. "Maximus, I can't—"

"Hush," he whispered, his hands shaking as he slid them down to her waist. "Please. Please let me."

He walked backward, making no sudden, jarring movement as he drew her with him, until he found a chair and lowered himself into it.

"Oh, Maximus," she sighed as he pulled her down, holding her tenderly across his lap.

"Yes, sweet," he murmured as he opened his mouth over her nipple.

"Darling," she said and caught his face between her hands, making him meet her eyes.

He didn't want to. He didn't like the look in her eyes— a grim determination.

"I love you," she whispered and his soul soared until she uttered her next words. "But I must leave you."

"No." He clutched at her hips as if he were a child of three refusing to give up his toy sword. "No."

"*Yes,*" she replied.

Something cruel rose in him then, born of grief and rage. He caught the back of her head and brought her mouth to his. Would she deny *this*? How could she find it possible?

She twined her arms about his neck and let him ravish her mouth, sighing as he parted her legs, settling them on either side of his hips. His cock pounded, a crude symbol of his desires, between them. He thumbed the head, pressing it toward her until he rubbed against her pretty cunny with the base thing. She was wet on the back of his fingers, open and hot, and his soul sang with vicious joy when she moaned helplessly.

He'd have this, by God, if nothing else of her.

She arched, a graceful bow of eroticism, and ground her hips against him.

He ran his hand up over her soft belly to her lovely breasts, tweaking each in turn, mindful of any way to drive her to her point.

But she foiled his intentions. She rose up above him and opened determined gray eyes before tangling her fingers with his on his cock. Even that small touch made him grit his teeth. He watched with half-lowered lids as she brought him to herself, his crown wet and sensitive, and notched him in her cunny.

"Maximus," she whispered, all moonlight and strength. "I love you. Never forget that."

And she impaled herself on him.

Ah! He closed his eyes. It was sweet to the point of agony. He grabbed her hips, preventing any movement so that he might not spill too soon. Her depths were hot and tight and *home*.

He opened his eyes. "Never leave me."

She shook her head, breaking free from his rein and rising like the huntress she was. She let his poor cock slip to the very mouth of her before slamming herself back down. She rode him. Her thighs were strong and lithe, her brows drawn down in resolute purpose, and her lips were parted wide in something very like wonder.

It was the last that made him move. Dear God, if he couldn't have anything else, if she was determined to hollow him out and leave him a husk, then he would remember this:

Artemis riding him like the goddess of the hunt.

He drew her face to his and covered that wondrous mouth, seeking her heat with his tongue, and tried not to break like a green lad. And he held out, until her rhythm faltered, until she gasped against his lips, until her sheath clutched at his cock in the throes of release. He let himself go then, bringing her damp and limp body into his embrace, holding her hips as he lunged up once, twice, as deep as possible.

As if he could stay within her forever.

He spilled his seed.

She lay against him, sweet, sweet weight, until she turned her head a little. He rose then, with her cradled in his arms, and brought her to the bed, gently laying her there.

"I need to see what Alderney has come about," he murmured to her. "I won't be a moment. Stay here until I return."

She merely closed her eyes, but he took that as assent, quickly dressing and running down the stairs.

Alderney was bent nearly in half, examining a curio

on an Italian marble table, but he straightened with a jerk when Maximus entered the sitting room.

"Oh! Ah, good morning, Your Grace."

"Good morning." Maximus gestured to a settee. "Will you sit?"

Alderney lowered himself to the settee and sat fidgeting for a moment.

Maximus raised an eyebrow impatiently. "You wanted to see me?"

"Oh! Oh, yes," Alderney said as if startled out of a reverie. "I thought it best to come and tell you at once because you seemed to think it so important before."

Here he stopped and blinked expectantly at Maximus.

"Tell me what?"

"That I'd remembered," Alderney replied. "Who gave me that pendant you showed me. Well, he didn't really *give* it, now did he? More like I won it from him. You see, he said that the tabby cat that came 'round the kitchens of our house would have three kittens and I said rubbish, there were at least *six* in there, and when the cat finally let us see her kittens—wary little thing she was, she'd hidden them under the porch—it turned out that I was quite right, there were six and so he had to give me the pendant."

Alderney took a deep breath at the end of this recitation and beamed.

Maximus inhaled very carefully. "*Who* gave you the pendant?"

Alderney blinked as if surprised that Maximus hadn't worked it out for himself. "Why, William Illingsworth, of course. Now, where he'd gotten it, I haven't a clue. Came back from the hols with the thing and was showing all the boys and the next night after I got it off Illingsworth, well, then I went to play a game of dice with several of the boys and that's when I lost it to Kilbourne." Alderney looked sad. "Poor Kilbourne. I quite liked him at school, don't you know, though we called him Greaves back then as his father was still alive and he hadn't yet inherited the courtesy title."

Maximus stared. "Illingsworth."

"Yes," Alderney said brightly. "It only came to me last night because my wife said that the ginger cat our children keep in the nursery is expecting, and then naturally I thought of that wager I made with Illingsworth."

"Do you know where William Illingsworth is now?" Maximus said without much hope of a positive answer.

"Right now, no." Alderney shook his head gravely. "But if you go 'round to his house his servants might have an idea."

"His house," Maximus repeated.

"Why, yes," Alderney replied. "Lives over on Havers Square. Not the nicest address, but then he lives off a limited income. His pater was something of a gambler."

"Thank you," Maximus said, rising at once.

"What? What?" Alderney looked startled.

"My butler will see you out. I've an appointment."

Maximus barely waited until the man had left the room before bounding back up the stairs. There was still time. If he could just make her listen to him...

He opened the door to his bedroom and saw at once that he'd run out of time after all.

Artemis was gone.

Chapter Nineteen

*The burning coal in Lin's hands turned into her own
dear brother, Tam. He jumped from the phantom horse
he rode and as his feet touched the earth he once more
was mortal.*
*Tam grinned up at Lin. "Sister! You've saved me, but
now you, too, must leave the wild hunt in order to live
once again."*
*Lin looked from her brother's joyful face to that of
the Herla King, but he avoided her gaze, his eyes
already set on a ghostly horizon, resigned to his
eternal chase....*
—from *The Legend of the Herla King*

Artemis slipped out the back door of Wakefield House,
what few belongings she had clutched in a pathetic soft
bag in her hands. She hesitated, panic beating at her
breast. She had to leave—leave right now while she could,
when Maximus wasn't before her, tempting her with
everything she hoped for and could never have—but she
had no idea where to go. It didn't seem right to seek Penelope out—not after what she'd done with Maximus. And
she certainly couldn't ask Lady Hero or Lady Phoebe.

The door opened behind her and she braced herself.

Not again. Oh, dear God, she wasn't sure she could go through this all over again with Maximus. She felt as if a part of her soul had been torn out, the wound bleeding, slow and steadily, somewhere internally.

But the voice that addressed her was feminine.

"My dear."

She turned to see Miss Picklewood regarding her with deep compassion. "Can I be of help?"

And for the first time in her life Artemis Greaves burst into tears.

MAXIMUS STRODE FROM the front of his house and called for a horse. This was all he had left, it seemed: revenge. Well if that was so, then he intended to complete his task quickly and with the most amount of blood possible.

In minutes he was trotting down the street.

Havers Square was indeed not in a very fashionable area of London. The house itself was an old half-timbered affair, though not nearly as broken down as something found in St. Giles. Maximus dismounted and gave a small boy a shilling to watch his horse. Illingsworth apparently rented only the top two floors of the house, and luckily he was at home. Maximus was shown up the stairs and into a cramped sitting room by an elderly maid who simply left him there without a word.

Maximus turned, inspecting his surroundings. The room had been furnished with a mishmash of furniture, some of which had been expensive at one time. The dirty grate wasn't lit, probably as a cost-saving measure, and the two framed engravings upon the wall were cheap.

The door to the sitting room opened.

Maximus turned to see a man in a frayed green banyan, stained on the front with something that might be egg yolk. He wore a soft cap on his head and was unshaven, a patchy ginger beard straggling up a thin face with cheekbones so sharp it looked like the skin of his face was pulled too tight over them.

"Yes?" Illingsworth asked warily.

Maximus held out his hand. "I'm Wakefield. I wonder if I might ask you a few questions?"

Illingsworth stared at his hand, perplexed, before taking it. His palm was damp.

"Yes?" he repeated.

Evidently his host wasn't going to offer him a seat.

Maximus reached into his pocket and took out the pendant. "Thirteen years ago you lost this in a wager to John Alderney. Where did you get it?"

"What...?" Illingsworth leaned forward to peer at the pendant. He reached for it, but Maximus closed his fist without thinking.

Illingsworth looked up at that. "Why do you want to know?"

"Because," Maximus said, "this pendant was part of a necklace that belonged to my mother."

"Ah." Illingsworth had a knowing look that Maximus didn't like. "Pawned it, did she?"

"No. She was robbed of it the night she was murdered."

If he hadn't been watching, Maximus might've missed it: a subtle shifting, a slight widening of the eyes. In a second it was gone and all Illingsworth's face revealed was wariness. "I was a fifteen-year-old schoolboy thirteen years ago. I assure you, Your Grace, that I had nothing to do with your mother's lamentable death."

"I never said you did," Maximus said. "I merely want to know the man you got this from."

But Illingsworth shook his head, pacing quickly to the fireplace. "I've never seen that gem before in my life."

His manner was too casual—the man was lying. "John Alderney says otherwise."

Illingsworth laughed, but it was a brittle, cawing sound. "Alderney was a fool at school. I can't imagine age has improved him any."

He turned and faced Maximus, his gaze frank and steady.

Maximus contemplated him. Illingsworth knew something—Maximus could feel it in his bones—yet if the other man refused to tell what he knew, there wasn't much he could do. He made a decision and pocketed the pendant. "You're lying."

Illingsworth started to protest.

Maximus cut him off with a sharp movement of his arm. "I could beat it out of you, the name of the man who gave this to you, but I have a certain dislike of violence. So I'll make you a bargain: I'll give you a day and a night to tell me who it is. If, at the end of that time you haven't given me what I want, I'll ruin you. Take what little you have from you. This house, your clothes, whatever else you might hold dear. By the end of the week you'll be begging in the gutter if you don't tell me what I need to know."

Maximus turned on the sputtered protests of innocence and outrage. They were a waste of time.

He descended the stairs again without the guidance of the elderly maid.

Outside, the boy was patiently waiting with the horse. "Good lad," Maximus said to him. "Would you like to earn a little more today?"

The boy nodded eagerly.

"I need you to run a message for me." Maximus gave the boy his address and the message to tell Craven, making him repeat it back word for word. Then he sent the boy out.

Maximus mounted his horse and made a show of riding away.

When he was out of sight of Illingsworth's house, he dismounted and led the horse back around to an alley that had a view of Illingsworth's front door.

There he settled down to wait and see what Illingsworth would do with his ultimatum.

"I KNEW THAT lovely shade of hunter green would exactly suit you," Lady Hero said that night as they walked toward the theater at Harte's Folly.

"Thank you." Artemis glanced distractedly around the pleasure garden before reminding herself that Apollo would hardly be out in the open here. No doubt he'd found some place to hide behind the scenes.

She smoothed down the skirts of her new dress sadly. It had been originally started for Lady Hero, but when Hero had realized that she would be needing dresses of an entirely different cut very soon, she'd insisted that Artemis have it. The modiste had delivered it to the Home for Unfortunate Infants and Foundling Children that afternoon, along with the two other dresses made specifically for her. Miss Picklewood had decided that the orphanage was the best place for Artemis to stay, just until she could journey to Miss Picklewood's dear friend Miss White. It seemed that Miss White was in need of a lady's companion.

Artemis sighed. She was grateful—truly she was—but the prospect of returning to her old life, even with a different mistress, simply made her depressed.

Or perhaps it was leaving Maximus that left her so despondent.

She looked down at the wonderful dress. Wherever would she wear it when she was accompanying an elderly lady in Bath? Perhaps she could sell it. She stroked it again, rather longingly. Of silk damask, the dress had a low, round neckline, edged with a tiny border of exquisite lace. The lace also decorated the full ruffles at the end of the elbow-length sleeves. The whole was simply sublime, and Artemis thought wryly that she'd never worn such a lovely thing in all her life.

She wished Maximus could see her in it.

Artemis looked around the sparkling pleasure garden in something like despair. Lights in tiny blown-glass globes had been strung from the fantastically shaped bushes and trees, creating a magical effect. She could already hear strains of stringed instruments floating in the air. The footmen were dressed whimsically in yellow and purple suits, some with lavender flowers or ribbons in their ornate wigs.

It was such a wonderful place, Harte's Folly, and after tonight it would be lost to her.

Besides her, Phoebe, Lady Hero and her husband, Lord Griffin Reading, and Miss Picklewood, there was also Isabel and Winter Makepeace, her hosts at the orphanage, and Lady Margaret and her husband, Godric St. John. She didn't know the gentlemen very well, but the ladies she'd considered her friends. They were all members of the Ladies' Syndicate for the Benefit of the Home for Unfortunate Infants and Foundling Children. Penelope was a member as well, of course, but she hadn't yet arrived.

But then Penelope was almost always late, Artemis thought a little wistfully.

Phoebe was chattering with her sister as they reached the theater and waited for everyone to come up from the dock—for Harte's Folly was just off the south bank of the Thames, and the best way to reach it was by way of hired barges. Miss Picklewood caught Artemis's eye and seemed to know her mood, for she had a look of understanding on her face as she inclined her head.

On impulse, Artemis bent her head to the elder lady's as they entered the theater's wide doors. "Thank you."

"Oh, my dear, you have no need to thank me." Miss Picklewood blushed. "I hope you know that I've never condemned you for your choices. Well do I know the peculiar loneliness of ladies such as ourselves."

"Yes." Artemis looked away. "I wish it could be otherwise."

Miss Picklewood snorted. "It could if Maximus made it so."

Artemis was about to reply when they were hailed by Lord Noakes, just entering the theater with his wife. "Miss Picklewood, Miss Greaves, well met. I wasn't aware you were back already from the country, Miss Picklewood." He glanced speculatively at Phoebe.

Lady Noakes's pinched face looked nervous this evening as she clutched her husband's arm.

Miss Picklewood, an old hand at social innuendo, merely smiled. "I'm simply stopping for a bit before returning to my friend. I do so love Harte's Folly, don't you, my lord, my lady?"

"Oh, indeed," Lady Noakes twittered before glancing at her husband and abruptly falling silent.

Lord Noakes nodded easily. "But isn't the duke escorting you ladies tonight?"

"We've no lack of escort," Miss Picklewood said, gesturing to Lord Griffin and the other gentlemen now joining them with their ladies. "I fear that the duke had other things to attend to tonight."

An odd, twisted smile crossed Lord Noakes's face. "I hope he isn't off chasing phantoms."

Artemis glanced at him sharply. Was he somehow referring to the Ghost? Surely he had no way of knowing Maximus's secret?

"If you'll excuse me, ladies, we must to my box." Lord Noakes bowed and ushered his wife away.

"What an odd thing to say," Miss Picklewood murmured, her forehead crimped. "What do you think he meant by 'chasing phantoms'?"

Artemis cleared her throat. "I've no idea."

"Oh, here's Lady Penelope at last," Isabel Makepeace drawled in amusement. "Wretched creature to keep us all waiting."

Penelope was making an entrance, naturally. She wore a dress of gold tissue and was escorted by the Duke of Scarborough. As she entered the crowded theater, she flipped open her fan, gazing languidly about.

Artemis felt a burst of fondness for her cousin. She was so vain, so mannered, but underneath she could be quite sweet at times. And Artemis had hurt her so badly without Penelope ever knowing. Well, at least she'd decided to leave Maximus. Pray Penelope never discovered the truth. Artemis smiled and held out her hand to Penelope as she approached. They hadn't seen each other in days.

Penelope gathered her skirts and quickened her pace, nearly rushing at her.

Still, Artemis was surprised when the slap came.

"Whore!" Penelope shouted, her voice echoing around the theater's lobby as Artemis staggered back from the blow, gasping.

Lady Hero and Isabel Makepeace caught her.

Miss Picklewood bravely stepped between her and Penelope, but there was no need. The Duke of Scarborough had moved very quickly to catch up with Penelope. He grabbed her arm roughly, pulling her back. His normally genial face was wearing a frown. "What is this about?"

Penelope kept her eyes on Artemis as she said, "You know I want Wakefield, yet you spread your legs for him like a common strumpet."

Artemis stared, her hand at her cheek as a kind of icy numbness seemed to spread through her limbs.

"You had no right!" Penelope cried, tears in her eyes. "No right at all. He'll never marry you, not with Apollo's madness. You'll be tossed into the streets and I'll be glad! Glad, I tell you, for—"

She was abruptly interrupted in her diatribe by Scarborough turning her about and shaking her once. As Penelope had been yelling his face had gone completely blank. Now, it was dark with anger.

"Stop this! Stop it at once!" Scarborough snapped.

Penelope looked up at him and gasped, "But—"

"No. Whatever your imagined slights, you may not bellow about them in a public place like a mad fishwife. And to hit your defenseless cousin! This was badly done, Penelope. Badly done indeed." He turned to Artemis and bowed. "Miss Greaves, I hope you are not hurt. If you'll excuse me, I'll be escorting her ladyship home."

Artemis blinked, able only to nod jerkily.

Penelope's eyes widened and tears sparkling in them. "But, Robert—"

"No." The duke frowned sternly. "I have much patience, my dear, and I think I have demonstrated my affection, but I have my pride as well. I simply will not have you bawling over another man like this. I fear I may have to reevaluate my courtship of you."

"Oh," Penelope said in a very small voice, and for the first time Artemis saw apprehension in her face.

"Come." Scarborough took her arm and marched Penelope out of the theater.

There was a moment of absolute silence.

Artemis's heart felt small and sore. She gently disengaged herself from Isabel and Hero and turned to face her former friends.

WHEN ILLINGSWORTH LANDED at Harte's Folly, Maximus was disappointed. An entire day watching the man only to have him traipse off to the theater come night. It seemed he'd wasted his time. All at once he realized that if he'd given up the hunt, just for this once, he might've spent the evening with Artemis and his sisters. They were probably themselves already seated at the theater. Perhaps Artemis would even let him speak to her.

He hung back as Illingsworth murmured something to one of the brightly dressed footmen, then disembarked only after his quarry had gone ahead.

"What did Mr. Illingsworth want?" Maximus asked the same footman as he pressed a coin into the man's hand.

"He asked if Lord Noakes was attending tonight," was the reply.

Maximus raised his brows. "And is he?"

"Yes, Your Grace," the footman said. "Both Lord and Lady Noakes are in attendance tonight. They're at the theater now, as I told Mr. Illingsworth."

Maximus looked at the footman—a sharp-looking young man. He took out a larger coin, this one gold. "Do you know Lord Noakes?"

"Oh, yes, Your Grace." The footman eyed the gold coin. "He and his nephew attend the theater often."

"His nephew?"

The footman raised his brows. "Didn't you know, Your Grace? Mr. Illingsworth is Lord Noakes's nephew."

Maximus absently pressed the coin in the lad's hand. No, he hadn't known. Noakes wasn't a particularly close acquaintance. He'd been mainly a friend of his father's, although Maximus remembered now that his mother had never cared for the man, and he'd overheard her speak disparagingly of Noakes's gambling. He had a sudden memory of Noakes at his parents' funeral wearing a new suit.

Maximus whirled and strode up the path leading to the pleasure gardens and theater. Until now he'd mainly suspected Scarborough, but both Noakes and Scarborough were of an age. Too, they had—now that he considered the matter—a similar type of body. Average height, a very slight paunch, but athletic for their ages. The same build as Old Scratch.

Surely it couldn't be that easy.

Maximus broke into a jog.

Someone shouted.

Maximus stopped and listened. There was music in the distance and the murmur of voices and laughter. This place had a myriad of paths, artistically lit so that there were darkened places perfect for romantic assignations. A man could very easily get lost here.

Something thrashed in the bushes to his right.

Maximus ran in that direction.

A man came rushing out, his head down, and hurried away without seeing Maximus. Maximus ran three steps after him before he was stopped by a cry.

"Help me!"

He turned and followed the voice, nearly tripping over a body.

He knelt and felt with his hands, finding a man. His chest was wet with a warm liquid.

"He's killed me," Illingsworth said. "He's killed me."

"Who?" Maximus demanded.

"I . . ." Illingsworth coughed with an awful dragging sound just as Maximus found the knife protruding from his chest.

"I told him you'd come to see me, that I'd tell you about finding that pendant in his desk drawer when I was a boy. I only needed a little money, not much. It isn't fair . . ."

"Illingsworth, who was it?" Maximus demanded.

The other man's voice was being overtaken by his wheezing breaths. "Not . . . fair. I'm family. He owed . . ."

Illingsworth shuddered and went still.

Maximus swore, holding his open hand over the other's nose.

He couldn't feel anything.

He stood, looking around. Illingsworth hadn't said so in so many words, but it must be his uncle who'd killed him. If it had been Noakes, would he flee the pleasure garden or go to his theater box as if nothing had happened?

Maximus started for the docks.

Behind him there was a popping sound. He turned. A woman screamed.

He was already running toward the theater when he smelled it.

Smoke.

Artemis.

Chapter Twenty

❧

The wild hunt was turning, preparing to race away into the clouds, but Lin had made up her mind. She leaned around the Herla King and stole the little white hound sitting before him on his saddle. King Herla grabbed for her and the dog, but his fingers caught only air. Lin had already leaped to earth, the little dog clutched to her breast....
—from *The Legend of the Herla King*

"Is it true?" Phoebe asked Artemis, her sweet hazel eyes worried.

Phoebe had somehow managed to get Artemis away from the others, despite Miss Picklewood's eagle eye. They were walking now in the lower corridor of the theater.

Artemis had been shocked when, instead of refuting her, the other ladies had seemed to come to a tacit agreement to simply forget the whole scene with Penelope. Indeed, Isabel Makepeace had made it a point to link her arm with Artemis's as they'd walked to the theater box. Although, now that Artemis thought about it, Lady Hero had had a rather determined gleam in her eye.

A determined gleam very like the one in Phoebe's

face. Most of the time the two sisters looked dissimilar. Right now, though, anyone could see that they were
related.

"I knew it," Phoebe exclaimed when Artemis didn't
immediately answer her question. "My brother has
seduced you."

"I shouldn't be talking about this with you," Artemis
said hastily. "In fact, after tonight, I doubt I'll ever be
allowed to have a private conversation with you."

"Ridiculous!" Phoebe looked like a small, fierce
nuthatch. "You have nothing to be ashamed of. This is
entirely *Maximus's* fault."

"Well...," Artemis began, because truth be told, it had
been *she* who'd gone to Maximus's bed, not the other way
'round.

Not that she could tell his sister that.

"I could throttle him, I really could," Phoebe said. "He
never even offered for you, did he?"

"No," Artemis said starkly. "He didn't. But I didn't
expect him to. I chose this, dear. I really did."

"Did you?" Phoebe looked up with unfocused eyes, as
if trying—and failing—to see Artemis's expression. "Did
you really? So you'd turn down my brother if he offered
you marriage, is that what you want me to believe?"

"It's just such a mess," Artemis whispered.

"Do you love him?"

"What?" Artemis stared at Phoebe. "Yes, *of course*.
Yes, I love him."

"Then I really don't see the problem," Phoebe said
with determination. "For it's obvious he loves you."

"I..." Artemis frowned, distracted. "How can you
tell?"

Phoebe looked at her as if she were a half-witted schoolgirl. "My brother is the most contained man I know. He keeps the books in his library ranked by language, then age, then author, *then* alphabetically. He prepares his speeches for Parliament weeks in advance and makes sure to know exactly which lords will be attending and how they will be voting in advance. He's never, as far as I know, kept a mistress—and before you comment, even a virginal younger sister like myself has ways of finding these things out. He's fanatical about family and is so worried about my safety that he had bars put on my bedroom windows, presumably so that I wouldn't, in a fit of absentmindedness, blunder into them and fall out."

Phoebe took a deep breath and fixed Artemis with a gimlet eye. "And yet he dragged you into the woods in front of his entire country party, loses his tight rein on his temper with you, and has seduced you in his *own home*— a home he shares with me. Either my brother has a brain fever or he's fallen hard in love with you."

Artemis couldn't help smiling, even though it didn't matter. Maximus wasn't marrying for love, after all. He was marrying to please his long-dead father.

She opened her mouth to gently tell Phoebe as much when there was a woman's scream.

And then she smelled smoke.

A pale wisp innocently curled into the corridor where they stood.

Artemis's heart started beating fast. The theater was an old one, made of wood and plaster.

"I smell smoke," Phoebe said.

"Yes." Artemis took her hand. "We must leave here."

Where was Apollo? Was he even at Harte's Folly? He'd been so cryptic as to where exactly he'd go. In any case there was no time to search for him. She could only hope that he could make it out of the theater if he were indeed here.

Artemis pulled Phoebe toward the entrance. Of course everyone else had the same idea of escape. People began crowding into the corridor, pushing in their panic. A stout gentleman shoved Artemis hard into the wall as he hurried past.

Her fingers slipped and lost Phoebe's.

"Phoebe!" Her shout was swallowed by the melee. She fought her way back through the crowd, elbowing people with utter disregard for propriety. "Phoebe!"

She caught sight of the other woman's face, unseeing eyes wide with panic. Artemis grasped her hand, squeezing tight.

"Artemis!" Phoebe cried. "Please don't leave me here."

"I won't, dear." There were too many people between them and the main entrance. "Come this way—I thought I saw a side door here."

The smoke was thickening at a frightening pace. Artemis found herself coughing as she pulled Phoebe in the direction of the door she'd seen. A loud crackling came from the direction of the stage, followed closely by a shrill scream. Artemis found the door and shoved.

It stayed obstinately shut.

"It's locked," she shouted at Phoebe as she felt around the edge of the door. "Help me find the bolt."

Tears caused by the smoke were streaming down her face, blinding her, and she felt the beginnings of panic. If they couldn't get the door open...

Her fingers brushed metal. Quickly she shoved back the bolt and stumbled with Phoebe into the fresh air.

She turned, looking back, and froze.

"What is it?" Phoebe cried.

"The entire gardens are alight," Artemis whispered, awed.

Flames leaped from the top of the theater, even as the garden guests, actors, footmen, and servants streamed from the building. A bucket brigade had formed under the command of a man with a mane of tawny hair, but Artemis could see that it was already a lost cause. The flames had leaped to the artfully planted trees and shrubs and were racing through the open gallery where the musicians usually performed. Soon everything would be aflame.

"Come on," Artemis shouted. "We have to get to the docks!"

"But Hero!" Phoebe pulled back. "And Cousin Bathilda."

"The gentlemen were with them," Artemis said, praying she was correct. "They'll get your sister and cousin and everyone else to safety."

She began pushing her way through the brush, for the paths were full of streaming people. Her beautiful new hunter-green dress was streaked with soot and torn by branches, but that hardly mattered.

"Ah, Lady Phoebe," a voice drawled, strangely calm.

Artemis looked up to see Lord Noakes standing in their way. He held a pistol in one hand and the other...

The other was covered in blood.

"Are you hurt, my lord?" Artemis asked stupidly, for she knew at once that something entirely different was amiss.

"Oh, not I," Lord Noakes said cheerfully. "Now, if you don't mind, I'd like you to step aside, for I have need of Lady Phoebe. I'd like to leave England and I think it prudent to bring Wakefield's sister should he try to detain me."

If she let Phoebe be hurt, Maximus would never forgive her. She'd never forgive *herself.*

"My lord," Artemis said carefully, backing a step to shield Phoebe, "Lady Phoebe has twisted her ankle and can hardly walk. I'm sure you'll understand that she can't come with you."

"D'you know I can't tell if you're lying or not," Lord Noakes said conversationally. A male shout came from their left. Lord Noakes's eyes hardened. "But I suppose it hardly matters whether I take Wakefield's sister or his whore. You'll do just as well."

Artemis had started to push Phoebe back as she ducked away from the madman but Lord Noakes was very fast for a man his age. He caught her wrist and yanked her against him, his grip as hard as steel.

She struggled but Lord Noakes pointed the pistol at Phoebe. "Stop that or I'll shoot her."

Artemis immediately stilled.

"Artemis!" Phoebe shouted, standing arms outstretched. Her face was white and Artemis knew she would be completely blind in the dark.

"Go toward the voices, darling," Artemis said, but before she could say anything more she was pulled roughly through the bushes.

He set a fast pace, nearly running toward the docks. They emerged to find a scene of chaos. Gentlemen and ladies were standing on the dock, screaming for the boats, some piling into already full barges. Footmen ran back and forth, while others were clearly still trying to keep up the futile bucket brigade to put out the fire. Artemis saw Hero, Miss Picklewood, and Isabel, and breathed a sigh of relief that they had escaped.

Lord Noakes shoved to the front of the docks and pointed his pistol to a gentleman about to hand a lady into a boat. "Move aside."

"Are you insane?" sputtered the gentleman.

Lord Noakes grinned. "Probably."

The gentleman's eyes widened as his lady shrieked.

"Get in," Lord Noakes ordered Artemis.

Gingerly she got into the boat. The boatman was watching, wide-eyed.

Lord Noakes descended and pointed his pistol at Artemis's head. "Head for Wapping," he told the boatman.

They were pulling into the river when a shout came from the dock. Maximus was there and by his side was Phoebe. Artemis smiled, her sight blurring. At least Phoebe was safe.

Maximus shouted obscenities at a boatman. She'd never seen him so angry. He had a pistol pointed at the boat they were in, but since Lord Noakes had made sure to sit Artemis in front of him, Maximus couldn't fire without fear of hitting her.

"Do you think it's driving him mad?" Lord Noakes asked with clear amusement. "To've spent his entire adult life hunting me, to come so close to catching me, and then to see me simply sail away?" He chuckled in her ear. "I should've killed him that night along with the duchess and duke, but he was *hiding*, see. Like a little rabbit. The great Duke of Wakefield. Oh, you needn't shiver, my dear." He stroked a hand over her arm because she had indeed shuddered. "There's no need to be afraid, for I doubt I'll hurt you. Much."

"You," Artemis said very quietly through gritted teeth, "are a loathsome man who will never be even one-hundredth the man Maximus is, and besides that, you don't know me at all."

And so saying she dived over the side of the boat and into the black waters of the Thames.

THE MOMENT ARTEMIS'S body disappeared under the murky waters of the Thames all thought stopped for Maximus. He was aware in a dim sort of way of shouts, of the fire still raging behind him, of his sisters screaming, and the boat carrying Noakes away, but that was all at the back of his mind.

He dropped the pistol he held. He reached into his coat pocket for the dagger he'd taken off Old Scratch and placed it between his teeth. He tore off his coat and shoes.

Then he dived into the Thames.

A small, calm voice at the back of his brain was counting off the seconds since she'd disappeared, was pointing out that she hadn't resurfaced, and was calculating how fast the river was moving.

He struck out, heading to a spot a little downstream from where she'd gone in.

A shot rang out, followed closely by another.

He dove into darkness.

At arm's length he couldn't see his hand. He felt about frantically. Nothing. Nothing. Nothing.

His lungs began spasming.

He kicked to the surface and drew his lips back from his teeth clenched around the dagger to gasp.

He dived again.

Nothing. Nothing.

Nothing.

His eyes stung.

He tasted death on his tongue.

She couldn't end like this. He wouldn't allow it.

He went deeper.

Nothing.

His chest was screaming.

He saw no point in rising to the surface.

He looked up a last time and saw a white hand.

One beautiful white hand.

He clutched at her and pulled until she was in his arms and they began sinking under the weight of her sodden skirts. He took the knife from his mouth and inserted it under the neckline at the back of her dress, yanking out hard. The thin silk split under his knife all the way to the waist. He slit the sleeves and tore them from her lifeless arms, before dragging the dress over her hips. Then he kicked hard, and as they rose, she slipped free from the garment, like a selkie shedding its skin.

They rocketed to the surface.

He broke the water, gasping, and looked at Artemis. Her face was white, her lips blue, and her hair trailed lifelessly in the water. She looked dead.

Arms suddenly seized him and he nearly fought them off before he realized that it was Winter Makepeace and Godric St. John hauling him into a boat.

"Take her first," Maximus managed.

The men pulled Artemis into the boat without a word

and Maximus clambered in after, falling gracelessly to the bottom of the boat. He immediately took her in his arms and cut off her stays. She didn't move.

He shook her. "Artemis."

Her head flopped back and forth limply.

Makepeace laid a hand on his arm. "Your Grace."

He ignored the other man. "*Diana*."

"Your Grace, I'm sorry—"

He swung back his arm and slapped her face, the sound echoing across the water.

She choked.

Immediately he flipped her so that her face was over the gunwale of the boat. She coughed and a great stream of dirty water fountained out of her mouth. He'd never seen such a wonderful sight in his life. When she'd stopped coughing, he hauled her back into his arms. St. John took off his coat and handed it over.

Maximus gently pulled it over her shoulders, wrapping his arms around her. He was never going to let her go after this. "What in bloody hell were you thinking?"

Makepeace cocked an eyebrow, but Maximus ignored it. He never, ever wanted to go through such agony again. He glared sternly down at the woman in his arms.

"I was thinking," she rasped, "that you couldn't get a clear shot with me in the way."

He tucked her head under his chin, running his palm over her wet hair. "And so you decided to sacrifice yourself? Madam, I had not taken you for a halfwit."

"I can swim."

"*Not* in water-logged skirts."

She frowned impatiently. "*Did* you shoot him?"

"I had much more important matters to consider," Maximus snapped.

At that she tilted back her head and glared at him. "You've been hunting him for nearly *two decades*. What could possibly be more important than killing your parents' murderer?"

He scowled at her. "*You*, you maddening woman. Whatever possessed you to..." Just the memory of watching her dive into the Thames made his throat close up. When he spoke again, his voice was rough. "Do not think to ever do that to me again, Diana. Had you not lived I would've joined you at the bottom of the Thames. I cannot survive without you."

She blinked and her militant expression softened. "Oh, Maximus." She laid her palm against his cheek.

And there in that wretched boat, dripping and shivering, with black smoke darkening the sky and ashes floating on the wind, Maximus thought that he'd never been so happy.

"I'll find him again someday," he murmured into her hair. "But once lost to me, I cannot find life without you, my Diana. Please, my love. Don't ever leave me. I promise, on my mother's grave, that I'll never cleave to another but you."

"I won't leave," she whispered back, her sweet gray eyes glowing, "though it is a pity you missed your chance with Lord Noakes."

Makepeace cleared his throat. "As to that..."

"I shot him," St. John muttered almost apologetically.

Maximus looked at him in astonishment.

St. John shrugged. "It seemed the thing to do, what with that gun to Miss Greaves's head business and his subsequently shouting after she'd gone in that he'd started the fire and wasn't sorry. Oh, and also, he shot at you, Wakefield, when you were in the water. Didn't seem very gentlemanly, and although he wasn't a very good shot, there was always the possibility that he wouldn't miss with a second one. He was aiming another pistol when I shot him."

"It was a good action." Makepeace nodded. "And a good shot. Must've been near seventy feet."

"Closer to fifty, I think," St. John corrected modestly.

"Even so."

"But…" Both men looked over inquiringly when Maximus spoke. "But I never asked you to help me with Noakes."

Makepeace nodded, his expression grave. "You didn't have to."

"You never had to," St. John concurred.

THAT NIGHT ARTEMIS lay nude in Maximus's huge bed and watched as he shaved. She'd already had a lovely, hot bath and washed her hair twice. They'd dined in his rooms, a simple supper of chicken and gravy with carrots and peas and a cherry tart for dessert.

Nothing had ever tasted better.

"It's rather a miracle that no one was killed," she said. She'd been very glad of that news, even after spotting a very familiar set of broad shoulders among the crowd at the dock. "Do you think anything remains of Harte's Folly?"

"Last I heard it was still smoldering," Maximus replied without turning. He frowned at his reflection in his dresser mirror. "But I understand that the theater is completely gone as well as the musician's colonnade. They might be able to save some of the plantings, but whether Harte will rebuild..." He shrugged. "The gardens are probably a lost cause."

"It's too bad," she murmured. "Phoebe loved Harte's Folly, and I rather liked it, too. It was such a magical place. Why do you think Lord Noakes set it alight in the first place?"

"Presumably to cover the fact that he'd just murdered his nephew," Maximus replied.

"What?" She thought about the blood on Lord Noakes's hands. "Poor man!"

"Well, he was trying to blackmail his uncle," Maximus said drily. "If he'd just told me that he'd gotten the pendant from his uncle's house in the first place, he'd be alive right now."

"Mmm." She picked at the coverlet. "Well, I suppose I wouldn't have been going to Harte's Folly again in any case."

"Why not?" he asked absently. "Was the play not to your liking?"

"We didn't get that far." She sighed. "Penelope had rather a fit when we first arrived and caused a scene. I'm surprised no one told you."

He turned slowly. "What?"

She looked at him. "She called me a whore."

"Damn it." He scowled at his hands. "That rather destroys my plans."

"Plans for what?"

"When I was swimming through that foul water, I decided." He went to his lockbox and opened it. "I was going to have it remade before I asked you. It seemed symbolic somehow." He glared at her. "Now I'll just have to do without."

She raised her eyebrows. "I'm sorry?"

Then Maximus did something very strange: he went on one knee before her.

"This isn't right at all," he said, continuing to glare as if he found it all her fault.

She sat up. "What are you doing?"

"Artemis Greaves, will you do me the honor of—"

"Are you insane?" she demanded. "What of your father? Your conviction that you must marry for the dukedom?"

"My father is dead," he said softly. "And I've decided the dukedom can go hang."

"But—"

"Hush," he snapped. "I'm trying to propose to you properly even without my mother's necklace."

"But why?" she asked. "You think my brother is mad."

"He seemed sane enough to me the last time I saw him," Maximus said kindly. "He tried to attack me."

She goggled. "Most would take that as confirmation of his madness."

He shrugged, reaching into the lockbox for the pendant she'd worn about her neck for so long. It lay next to the other six emeralds, all recovered now that the last had been taken from Noakes's dead body. "He thought I'd seduced his sister."

"Oh." She blushed, still uncomfortable with the thought of Apollo knowing about...that.

"I know that this is rather disappointing," he said as he slipped off his signet ring and threaded it on the chain the pendant still hung on. "But I intend to make you respectable."

"Not because of what Penelope said?" she protested.

"No." He put the necklace over her head, settling the

ring and the pendant between her breasts with care. The brush of his warm fingers made her nipples peak. "Well, yes, in a way. I don't want you to think that I would allow anyone to call you such. I vowed it to myself when I was searching for you underwater. That if I could get you out alive..." He cleared his throat, frowning. "Anyway, you can wear the necklace at the wedding."

"Maximus." She took his face, making him look up at her. "I don't want to marry you simply because you want to protect my name. If—"

Her heartfelt protest was interrupted by him lunging at her and taking her mouth. He kissed her thoroughly, openmouthed, until she had trouble remembering what exactly they'd been talking about.

When he broke the kiss, he still held her tight, almost as if he were afraid to let her go. "I love you, my Diana. I've loved you, I think, since I discovered you walking barefoot in my woods. Even when I thought I couldn't marry you, I fully intended to keep you by my side forever." He pulled back to look at her and she saw to her absolute astonishment that there was a trace—a very *small* trace—of uncertainty in his expression. He smoothed a thumb down the side of her face. "You mustn't leave me. Without you there's no light in the world. No laughter. No purpose. Even if for some silly reason you don't wish to marry me, promise me at least—"

"Hush." She cupped his face in her hands. "Yes, I'll marry you, you foolish man. I love you. I suppose I'll even wear your mother's extravagant necklace—though it won't look nearly as good on me as it would've on Penelope. I'll do anything you want, just so that we can remain together. Forever."

He surged up over her at that, capturing her mouth, surrounding her with his strong, possessive arms.

When at last he allowed her to draw breath she saw that he was frowning sternly at her. "We'll marry in three months. You'll wear the Wakefield emeralds and the ear-bobs I'll have made, but mark me well, you are confused. *No one* would look better in those emeralds than you. Your cousin might be a pretty face, but *you*, my darling, courageous, maddening, seductive, mysterious, *wonderful* Diana, *you* are the Duchess of Wakefield. *My* duchess."

Epilogue

*Tam cried out his sister's name, expecting Lin to turn
to ash before his eyes. But a strange thing happened
when Lin touched the earth: nothing at all. She bent her
head and whispered something into the ear of the little
white dog, whereupon the animal leaped from her arms
to the ground and stood wagging his tail. Immediately
the wild hunt's horses and riders fell from the sky, each
one assuming his mortal shape as he landed on the
earth. The last to descend from the sky was King Herla
himself. He stepped from his horse and as his booted foot
touched the ground he drew a deep, shuddering breath,
tilting his head back to feel the rays of the dawning sun
upon his face.*

*Then he smiled and looked down at Lin, his eyes no
longer pale. Now they were a warm brown. "You've saved
me, brave little maiden. Your courage, cleverness, and
unwavering love has broken the curse set on me, my men,
and your own brother."*

*At his words the men of his retinue threw their hats into the
air, cheering.*

*"I owe you everything I have," King Herla said to Lin.
"Ask what you will for your reward and it is yours."*

"Thank you, my king," Lin said, "but I want for nothing."

"Not jewels?" asked King Herla.

"No, my king."

"Not land?"

"Indeed not, my king."

358   ELIZABETH HOYT

"Not horses or cattle?"

"No, my king," Lin whispered, for King Herla had stepped closer as he had questioned her and she had to tilt back her head to look him in the eye now.

"Nothing I have will tempt you?" King Herla murmured. Lin could only shake her head.

"Then perhaps I should offer myself," Herla said as he sank to his knees before her. "Wonderful girl, will you have me as your husband?"

"Oh, yes," Lin said and all about her the King's men cheered again.

Then King Herla married Lin in a ceremony that was quite nice but not nearly as grand as his first wedding so many centuries before. After that, he cleared the dark wood of brambles, tilled the fields again, rebuilt his crumbling castle, and caused fat cattle to graze upon his lands. The people were once again content and well-fed. And if King Herla ever felt the urge to go a-hunting, he ignored it and turned to see the smile of his wise queen instead, for he'd already found and captured the best quarry of all.

True love.

—from *The Legend of the Herla King*

MEANWHILE...

"Nine *fucking* years."

Apollo sat on an overturned tin pail and watched as his good friend, Asa Makepeace, thrust the bottle of wine gripped in his fist into the air, a defiant salute.

"D'you hear me, 'Pollo?" Asa demanded, waving the bottle so wildly he nearly boxed Apollo's ear with it. "*Nine* fucking years. I could've been whoring or drinking or pottering about the continent, *seeing* places, and instead

I was working, nay, *slaving* on this very pleasure garden, building and planting and coddling fickle actresses and more fickle *actors* and now, *now* it's nothing but a smoldering pile of *shit*. I say again: nine fucking *years*!"

Apollo sighed and drank from his own bottle as Asa continued to repeat his profane refrain. Apollo's bottle was half gone, which was good since he no longer cared that the wine stank of smoke. They sat in the only part of Harte's Folly still standing: the actor's dressing rooms behind the stage.

Or what had once been the stage. That part of the theater, and indeed the rest of it, was a still-smoldering blackened mess of fallen beams and debris, too hot to sift through to see if anything could be recovered, although Apollo was very doubtful on that score.

It might have been nine years of Asa's life lost tonight, but it was also the last bit of capital Apollo had to his name gone, too. Just before he'd woken that dreadful day to find three of his acquaintances bloodily slaughtered around him, he'd taken that capital—a tiny legacy from his father—and invested the lot in Harte's Folly. At the time it had seemed a sound financial move: he was terrible with money while Asa seemed on the verge of wealth and prosperity with the pleasure garden. Apollo hadn't expected too much—maybe enough made in interest to keep himself and Artemis.

That dream had just turned to ash.

"'Spect I'll have to live on the street now," Asa was saying mournfully to his bottle. "My family isn't too fond of me, you know. And I haven't any talent or trade save the ability to talk people into things—like I talked you into giving me all your savings, 'Pollo."

Apollo would've corrected Asa's misconception—he'd made the investment decision of his own free will—but he still couldn't speak, and he wasn't sure it mattered anyway. Asa seemed to be almost enjoying wallowing in his own tragedy.

"Hullo?"

They looked at each other at the call from without.

Asa's eyebrows rose comically high on his forehead. "Who d'you think that is?" he asked in a very loud whisper.

"Ah, there you are." The prettiest man Apollo had ever seen picked his way through the trash strewn around their little shelter. He was exquisitely dressed in a silver waist-coat and a pink satin coat and breeches, but it was his hair that drew the eye: shining golden curls drawn back by a huge black bow.

Fop, thought Apollo.

"Who the hell are you?" Asa asked belligerently.

The fop smiled and Apollo's eyes narrowed. He might be pretty, but this wasn't a man to be underestimated.

"I?" The fop fastidiously laid a lace handkerchief on the remains of a bench and perched on it. "I am Valentine Napier, the Duke of Montgomery, and I have a proposition for you, Mr. Makepeace."

SEE HOW THE STUNNING
MAIDEN LANE SERIES BEGAN!

Please turn this page
for an excerpt from the first book
in this series,

Wicked Intentions.

Chapter One

*Once upon a time, in a land long forgotten now, there lived
a mighty king, feared by all and loved by none. His name
was King Lockedheart....*
—from *King Lockedheart*

LONDON
FEBRUARY 1737

A woman abroad in St. Giles at midnight was either very
foolish or very desperate. Or, as in her own case, Temperance Dews reflected wryly, a combination of both.

"'Tis said the Ghost of St. Giles haunts on nights like
this," Nell Jones, Temperance's maidservant, said chattily
as she skirted a noxious puddle in the narrow alley.

Temperance glanced dubiously at her. Nell had spent
three years in a traveling company of actors and sometimes had a tendency toward melodrama.

"There's no ghost haunting St. Giles," Temperance
replied firmly. The cold winter night was frightening
enough without the addition of specters.

"Oh, indeed, there is." Nell hoisted the sleeping babe
in her arms higher. "He wears a black mask and a harlequin's motley and carries a wicked sword."

Temperance frowned. "A harlequin's motley? That doesn't sound very ghostlike."

"It's ghostlike if he's the dead spirit of a harlequin player come back to haunt the living."

"For bad reviews?"

Nell sniffed. "*And* he's disfigured."

"How would anyone know that if he's masked?"

They were coming to a turn in the alley, and Temperance thought she saw light up ahead. She held her lantern high and gripped the ancient pistol in her other hand a little tighter. The weapon was heavy enough to make her arm ache. She could have brought a sack to carry it in, but that would've defeated its purpose as a deterrent. Though loaded, the pistol held but one shot, and to tell the truth, she was somewhat hazy on the actual operation of the weapon.

Still, the pistol looked dangerous, and Temperance was grateful for that. The night was black, the wind moaning eerily, bringing with it the smell of excrement and rotting offal. The sounds of St. Giles rose about them—voices raised in argument, moans and laughter, and now and again the odd, chilling scream. St. Giles was enough to send the most intrepid woman running for her life.

And that was without Nell's conversation.

"*Horribly* disfigured," Nell continued, ignoring Temperance's logic. "'Tis said his lips and eyelids are clean burned off, as if he died in a fire long ago. He seems to grin at you with his great yellow teeth as he comes to pull the guts from your belly."

Temperance wrinkled her nose. "Nell!"

"That's what they say," Nell said virtuously. "The ghost guts his victims and plays with their entrails before slipping away into the night."

Temperance shivered. "Why would he do that?"

"Envy," Nell said matter-of-factly. "He envies the living."

"Well, I don't believe in spirits in any case." Temperance took a breath as they turned the corner into a small, wretched courtyard. Two figures stood at the opposite end, but they scuttled away at their approach. Temperance let out her breath. "Lord, I hate being abroad at night."

Nell patted the infant's back. "Only a half mile more. Then we can put this wee one to bed and send for the wet nurse in the morning."

Temperance bit her lip as they ducked into another alley. "Do you think she'll live until morning?"

But Nell, usually quite free with her opinions, was silent. Temperance peered ahead and hurried her step. The baby looked to be only weeks old and had not yet made a sound since they'd recovered her from the arms of her dead mother. Normally a thriving infant was quite loud. Terrible to think that she and Nell might've made this dangerous outing for naught.

But then what choice had there been, really? When she'd received word at the Home for Unfortunate Infants and Foundling Children that a baby was in need of her help, it had still been light. She'd known from bitter experience that if they'd waited until morn to retrieve the child, it would either have expired in the night from lack of care or would've already been sold for a beggar's prop. She shuddered. The children bought by beggars were often made more pitiful to elicit sympathy from passersby. An eye might be put out or a limb broken or twisted. No, she'd really had no choice. The baby couldn't wait until morning.

Still, she'd be very happy when they made it back to the home.

They were in a narrow passage now, the tall houses on either side leaning inward ominously. Nell was forced to walk behind Temperance or risk brushing the sides of the buildings. A scrawny cat snaked by, and then there was a shout very near.

Temperance's steps faltered.

"Someone's up ahead," Nell whispered hoarsely.

They could hear scuffling and then a sudden high scream.

Temperance swallowed. The alley had no side passages. They could either retreat or continue—and to retreat meant another twenty minutes added to their journey.

That decided her. The night was chilly, and the cold wasn't good for the babe.

"Stay close to me," she whispered to Nell.

"Like a flea on a dog," Nell muttered.

Temperance squared her shoulders and held the pistol firmly in front of her. Winter, her youngest brother, had said that one need only point it and shoot. That couldn't be too hard. The light from the lantern spilled before them as she entered another crooked courtyard. Here she stood still for just a second, her light illuminating the scene ahead like a pantomime on a stage.

A man lay on the ground, bleeding from the head. But that wasn't what froze her—blood and even death were common enough in St. Giles. No, what arrested her was the *second* man. He crouched over the first, his black cloak spread to either side of him like the wings of a great bird of prey. He held a long black walking stick, the end tipped with silver, echoing his hair, which was silver as well. It fell straight and long, glinting in the lantern's light. Though his face was mostly in darkness, his eyes glinted from under the brim of a black tricorne. Temperance could feel the weight of the stranger's stare. It was as if he physically touched her.

"Lord save and preserve us from evil," Nell murmured, for the first time sounding fearful. "Come away, ma'am. Swiftly!"

Thus urged, Temperance ran across the courtyard, her shoes clattering on the cobblestones. She darted into another passage and left the scene behind.

"Who was he, Nell?" she panted as they made their way through the stinking alley. "Do you know?"

The passage let out suddenly into a wider road, and Temperance relaxed a little, feeling safer without the walls pressing in.

Nell spat as if to clear a foul taste from her mouth.

Temperance looked at her curiously. "You sounded like you knew that man."

"Knew him, no," Nell replied. "But I've seen him about. That was Lord Caire. He's best left to himself."

"Why?"

Nell shook her head, pressing her lips firmly together. "I shouldn't be speaking about the likes of him to you at all, ma'am."

Temperance let that cryptic comment go. They were on a better street now—some of the shops had lanterns hanging by the doors, lit by the inhabitants within. Temperance turned one more corner onto Maiden Lane, and the foundling home came within sight. Like its neighbors, it was a tall brick building of cheap construction. The windows were few and very narrow, the doorway unmarked by any sign. In the fifteen precarious years of the foundling home's existence, there had never been a need to advertise.

Abandoned and orphaned children were all too common in St. Giles.

"Home safely," Temperance said as they reached the door. She set down the lantern on the worn stone step and took out the big iron key hanging by a cord at her waist. "I'm looking forward to a dish of hot tea."

"I'll put this wee one to bed," Nell said as they entered the dingy little hall. It was spotlessly clean, but that didn't hide the fallen plaster or the warped floorboards.

"Thank you." Temperance removed her cloak and was just hanging it on a peg when a tall male form appeared at the far doorway.

"Temperance."

She swallowed and turned. "Oh! Oh, Winter, I did not know you'd returned."

"Obviously," her younger brother said drily. He nodded to the maidservant. "A good eventide to you, Nell."

"Sir." Nell curtsied and looked nervously between brother and sister. "I'll just see to the, ah, children, shall I?"

And she fled upstairs, leaving Temperance to face Winter's disapproval alone.

Temperance squared her shoulders and moved past her brother. The foundling home was long and narrow, squeezed by the neighboring houses. There was one room off the small entryway. It was used for dining and, on occasion, receiving the home's infrequent important visitors. At the back of the house were the kitchens, which Temperance entered now. The children had all had their dinner promptly at five o'clock, but neither she nor her brother had eaten.

"I was just about to make some tea," she said as she went to stir the fire. Soot, the home's black cat, got up from his place in front of the hearth and stretched before padding off in search of mice. "There's a bit of beef left from yesterday and some new radishes I bought at market this morning."

Behind her Winter sighed. "Temperance."

She hurried to find the kettle. "The bread's a bit stale, but I can toast it if you like."

He was silent and she finally turned and faced the inevitable.

It was worse than she feared. Winter's long, thin face merely looked sad, which always made her feel terrible. She hated to disappoint him.

"It was still light when we set out," she said in a small voice.

He sighed again, taking off his round black hat and sitting at the kitchen table. "Could you not wait for my return, sister?"

Temperance looked at her brother. Winter was only five and twenty, but he bore himself with the air of a man twice his age. His countenance was lined with weariness, his wide shoulders slumped beneath his ill-fitting black coat, and his long limbs were much too thin. For the last five years, he had taught at the tiny daily school attached to the home.

On Papa's death last year, Winter's work had increased tremendously. Concord, their eldest brother, had taken over the family brewery. Asa, their next-eldest brother, had always been rather dismissive of the foundling home and had a mysterious business of his own. Both of their sisters, Verity, the eldest of the family, and Silence, the youngest, were married. That had left Winter to manage the foundling home. Even with her help—she'd worked at the home since the death of her husband nine years before—the task was overwhelming for one man. Temperance feared for her brother's well-being, but both the foundling home and the tiny day school had been founded by Papa. Winter felt it was his filial duty to keep the two charities alive.

If his health did not give out first.

She filled the teakettle from the water jar by the back door. "Had we waited, it would have been full dark with no assurance that the babe would still be there." She glanced at him as she placed the kettle over the fire. "Besides, have you not enough work to do?"

"If I lose my sister, think you that I'd be more free of work?"

Temperance looked away guiltily.

Her brother's voice softened. "And that discounts the lifelong sorrow I would feel had anything happened to you this night."

"Nell knew the mother of the baby—a girl of less than fifteen years." Temperance took out the bread and carved it into thin slices. "Besides, I carried the pistol."

"Hmm," Winter said behind her. "And had you been accosted, would you have used it?"

"Yes, of course," she said with flat certainty.

"And if the shot misfired?"

She wrinkled her nose. Their father had brought up all her brothers to debate a point finely, and that fact could be quite irritating at times.

She carried the bread slices to the fire to toast. "In any case, nothing did happen."

"*This* night." Winter sighed again. "Sister, you must promise me you'll not act so foolishly again."

"Mmm," Temperance mumbled, concentrating on the toast. "How was your day at the school?"

For a moment, she thought Winter wouldn't consent to her changing the subject. Then he said, "A good day, I think. The Samuels lad remembered his Latin lesson finally, and I did not have to punish any of the boys."

Temperance glanced at him with sympathy. She knew Winter hated to take a switch to a palm, let alone cane a boy's bottom. On the days that Winter had felt he must punish a boy, he came home in a black mood.

"I'm glad," she said simply.

He stirred in his chair. "I returned for luncheon, but you were not here."

Temperance took the toast from the fire and placed it on the table. "I must have been taking Mary Found to her new position. I think she'll do quite well there. Her mistress seemed very kind, and the woman took only five pounds as payment to apprentice Mary as her maid."

"God willing she'll actually teach the child something so we won't see Mary Found again."

Temperance poured the hot water into their small teapot and brought it to the table. "You sound cynical, brother."

Winter passed a hand over his brow. "Forgive me. Cynicism is a terrible vice. I shall try to correct my humor."

Temperance sat and silently served her brother, waiting. Something more than her late-night adventure was bothering him.

At last he said, "Mr. Wedge visited whilst I ate my luncheon."

Mr. Wedge was their landlord. Temperance paused, her hand on the teapot. "What did he say?"

"He'll give us only another two weeks, and then he'll have the foundling home forcibly vacated."

"Dear God."

Temperance stared at the little piece of beef on her plate. It was stringy and hard and from an obscure part of the cow, but she'd been looking forward to it. Now her appetite was suddenly gone. The foundling home's rent was in arrears—they hadn't been able to pay the full rent last month and nothing at all this month. Perhaps she shouldn't have bought the radishes, Temperance reflected morosely. But the children hadn't had anything but broth and bread for the last week.

"If only Sir Gilpin had remembered us in his will," she murmured.

Sir Stanley Gilpin had been Papa's good friend and the patron of the foundling home. A retired theater owner, he'd managed to make a fortune on the South Sea Company and had been wily enough to withdraw his funds before the notorious bubble burst. Sir Gilpin had been a generous patron while alive, but on his unexpected death six months before, the home had been left floundering. They'd limped along, using what money had been saved, but now they were in desperate straits.

"Sir Gilpin was an unusually generous man, it would seem," Winter replied. "I have not been able to find another gentleman so willing to fund a home for the infant poor."

Temperance poked at her beef. "What shall we do?"

"The Lord shall provide," Winter said, pushing aside his half-eaten meal and rising. "And if he does not, well, then perhaps I can take on private students in the evenings."

"You already work too many hours," Temperance protested. "You hardly have time to sleep as it is."

Winter shrugged. "How can I live with myself if the innocents we protect are thrown into the street?"

Temperance looked down at her plate. She had no answer to that.

"Come." Her brother held out his hand and smiled.

Winter's smiles were so rare, so precious. When he smiled, his entire face lit as if from a flame within, and a dimple appeared on one cheek, making him look boyish, more his true age.

One couldn't help smiling back when Winter smiled, and Temperance did so as she laid her hand in his. "Where will we go?"

"Let us visit our charges," he said as he took a candle and led her to the stairs. "Have you ever noticed that they look quite angelic when asleep?"

Temperance laughed as they climbed the narrow wooden staircase to the next floor. There was a small hall here with three doors leading off it. They peered in the first as Winter held his candle high. Six tiny cots lined the walls of the room. The youngest of the foundlings slept here, two or three to a cot. Nell lay in an adult-sized bed by the door, already asleep.

Winter walked to the cot nearest Nell. Two babes lay there. The first was a boy, red-haired and pink-cheeked, sucking on his fist as he slept. The second child was half the size of the first, her cheeks pale and her eyes hollowed, even in sleep. Tiny whorls of fine black hair decorated her crown.

"This is the baby you rescued tonight?" Winter asked softly.

Temperance nodded. The little girl looked even more frail next to the thriving baby boy.

But Winter merely touched the baby's hand with a gentle finger. "How do you like the name Mary Hope?"

Temperance swallowed past the thickness in her throat. "'Tis very apt."

Winter nodded and, with a last caress for the tiny babe, left the room. The next door led to the boys' dormitory. Four beds held thirteen boys, all under the age of nine—the age when they were apprenticed out. The boys lay with limbs sprawled, faces flushed in sleep. Winter smiled and pulled a blanket over the three boys nearest the door, tucking in a leg that had escaped the bed.

Temperance sighed. "One would never think that they spent an hour at luncheon hunting for rats in the alley."

"Mmm," Winter answered as he closed the door softly behind them. "Small boys grow so swiftly to men."

"They do indeed." Temperance opened the last door—the one to the girls' dormitory—and a small face immediately popped off a pillow.

"Did you get 'er, ma'am?" Mary Whitsun whispered hoarsely.

She was the eldest of the girls in the foundling home, named for the Whitsunday morning nine years before when she'd been brought to the home as a child of three. Young though Mary Whitsun was, Temperance had to sometimes leave her in charge of the other children—as she'd had to tonight.

"Yes, Mary," Temperance whispered back. "Nell and I brought the babe home safely."

"I'm glad." Mary Whitsun yawned widely.

"You did well watching the children," Temperance whispered. "Now sleep. A new day will be here soon."

Mary Whitsun nodded sleepily and closed her eyes.

Winter picked up a candlestick from a little table by the door and led the way out of the girls' dormitory. "I shall take your kind advice, sister, and bid you good night."

He lit the candlestick from his own and gave it to Temperance.

"Sleep well," she replied. "I think I'll have one more cup of tea before retiring."

"Don't stay up too late," Winter said. He touched her cheek with a finger—much as he had the babe—and turned to mount the stairs.

Temperance watched him go, frowning at how slowly he moved up the stairs. It was past midnight, and he would rise again before five of the clock to read, write letters to prospective patrons, and prepare his school lessons for the day. He would lead the morning prayers at breakfast, hurry to his job as schoolmaster, work all morning before taking one hour for a meager luncheon, and then work again until after dark. In the evening, he heard the girls' lessons and read from the Bible to the older children. Yet, when she voiced her worries, Winter would merely raise an eyebrow and inquire who would do the work if not he?

Temperance shook her head. She should be to bed as well—her day started at six of the clock—but these moments by herself in the evening were precious. She'd sacrifice a half hour's sleep to sit alone with a cup of tea.

So she took her candle back downstairs. Out of habit, she checked to see that the front door was locked and barred. The wind whistled and shook the shutters as she made her way to the kitchen, and the back door rattled. She checked it as well and was relieved to see the door still barred. Temperance shivered, glad she was no longer outside on a night like this. She rinsed out the teapot and filled it again. To make a pot of tea with fresh leaves and only for herself was a terrible luxury. Soon she'd have to give this up as well, but tonight she'd enjoy her cup.

Off the kitchen was a tiny room. Its original purpose was forgotten, but it had a small fireplace, and Temperance had made it her own private sitting room. Inside was a stuffed chair, much battered but refurbished with a quilted blanket thrown over the back. A small table and a footstool were there as well—all she needed to sit by herself next to a warm fire.

Humming, Temperance placed her teapot and cup, a small dish of sugar, and the candlestick on an old wooden tray. Milk would have been nice, but what was left from this morning would go toward the children's breakfast on the morrow. As it was, the sugar was a shameful luxury. She looked at the small bowl, biting her lip. She really ought to put it back; she simply didn't deserve it. After a moment, she took the sugar dish off the tray, but the sacrifice brought her no feeling of wholesome goodness. Instead she was only weary. Temperance picked up the tray, and because both her hands were full, she backed into the door leading to her little sitting room.

Which was why she didn't notice until she turned that the sitting room was already occupied.

There, sprawled in her chair like a conjured demon, sat Lord Caire. His silver hair spilled over the shoulders of his black cape, a cocked hat lay on one knee, and his right hand caressed the end of his long ebony walking stick.

This close, she realized that his hair gave lie to his age. The lines about his startlingly blue eyes were few, his mouth and jaw firm. He couldn't be much older than five and thirty.

He inclined his head at her entrance and spoke, his voice deep and smooth and softly dangerous.

"Good evening, Mrs. Dews."

SHE STOOD WITH quiet confidence, this respectable woman who lived in the sewer that was St. Giles. Her eyes had widened at the sight of him, but she made no move to flee. Indeed, finding a strange man in her pathetic sitting room seemed not to frighten her at all.

Interesting.

"I am Lazarus Huntington, Lord Caire," he said.

"I know. What are you doing here?"

He tilted his head, studying her. She knew him, yet did not recoil in horror? Yes, she'd do quite well. "I've come to make a proposition to you, Mrs. Dews."

Still no sign of fear, though she eyed the doorway. "You've chosen the wrong lady, my lord. The night is late. Please leave my house."

No fear and no deference to his rank. An interesting woman indeed.

"My proposition is not, er, *illicit* in nature," he drawled. "In fact, it's quite respectable. Or nearly so."

She sighed and looked down at her tray, and then back up at him. "Would you like a cup of tea?"

He almost smiled. Tea? When had he last been offered something so very prosaic by a woman? He couldn't remember.

But he replied gravely enough. "Thank you, no."

She nodded. "Then if you don't mind?"

He waved a hand to indicate permission.

She set the tea tray on the wretched little table and sat on the padded footstool to pour herself a cup. He watched her. She was a monochromatic study. Her dress, bodice, hose, and shoes were all flat black. A fichu tucked in at her severe neckline, an apron, and a cap—no lace or ruffles—were all white. No color marred her aspect, making the lush red of her full lips all the more startling. She wore the clothes of a nun, yet had the mouth of a sybarite.

The contrast was fascinating—and arousing.

"You're a Puritan?" he asked.

Her beautiful mouth compressed. "No."

"Ah." He noted she did not say she was Church of England either. She probably belonged to one of the many obscure nonconformist sects, but then he was interested in her religious beliefs only as they impacted his own mission.

She took a sip of tea. "How do you know my name?"

He shrugged. "Mrs. Dews and her brother are well-known for their good deeds."

"Really?" Her tone was dry. "I was not aware we were so famous beyond the boundaries of St. Giles."

She might look demure, but there were teeth behind the prim expression. And she was quite right—he would never have heard of her had he not spent the last month stalking the shadows of St. Giles. Stalking fruitlessly, which was why he'd followed her home and sat before this miserable fire now.

"How did you get in?" she asked.

"I believe the back door was unlocked."

"No, it wasn't." Her brown eyes met his over her teacup. They were an odd light color, almost golden. "Why are you here, Lord Caire?"

"I wish to hire you, Mrs. Dews," he said softly.

She stiffened and set her teacup down on the tray. "No."

"You haven't heard the task for which I wish to hire you."

"It's past midnight, my lord, and I'm not inclined to games even during the day. Please leave or I shall be forced to call my brother."

He didn't move. "Not a husband?"

"I'm widowed, as I'm sure you already know." She turned to look into the fire, presenting a dismissive profile to him.

He stretched his legs in what room there was, his boots nearly in the fire. "You're quite correct—I do know. I also know that you and your brother have not paid the rent on this property in nearly two months."

She said nothing, merely sipping her tea.

"I'll pay handsomely for your time," he murmured.

She looked at him finally, and he saw a golden flame in those pale brown eyes. "You think all women can be bought?"

He rubbed his thumb across his chin, considering the question. "Yes, I do, though perhaps not strictly by money. And I do not limit it to women—all men can be bought in one form or another as well. The only trouble is in finding the applicable currency."

She simply stared at him with those odd eyes.

He dropped his hand, resting it on his knee. "You, for instance, Mrs. Dews. I would've thought your currency would be money for your foundling home, but perhaps I'm mistaken. Perhaps I've been fooled by your plain exterior, your reputation as a prim widow. Perhaps you would be better persuaded by influence or knowledge or even the pleasures of the flesh."

"You still haven't said what you want me for."

Though she hadn't moved, hadn't changed expression at all, her voice had a rough edge. He caught it only because he had years of experience at the chase. His nostrils flared involuntarily, as if the hunter within was trying to scent her. Which of his list had interested her?

"A guide." His eyelids drooped as he pretended to examine his fingernails. "Merely that." He watched her from under his brows and saw when that lush mouth pursed.

"A guide to what?"

"St. Giles."

"Why do you need a guide?"

Ah, this was where it got tricky. "I'm searching for...a certain person in St. Giles. I would like to interview some of the inhabitants, but I find my search confounded by my ignorance of the area and the people and by their reluctance to talk to me. Hence, a guide."

Her eyes had narrowed as she listened, her fingers tapping against the teacup. "Whom do you search for?"

He shook his head slowly. "Not unless you agree to be my guide."

"And that is all you want? A guide? Nothing else?"

He nodded, watching her.

She turned to look into the fire as if consulting it. For a moment, the only sound in the room was the snap of a piece of coal falling. He waited patiently, caressing the silver head of his cane.

Then she faced him fully. "You're right. Your money does not tempt me. It's a stopgap measure that would only delay our eventual eviction."

He cocked his head, watching as she carefully licked those lush lips, preparing her argument, no doubt. He felt the beat of the pulse beneath his skin, his body's response to her feminine vitality. "What do you want, then, Mrs. Dews?"

She met his gaze levelly, almost in challenge. "I want you to introduce me to the wealthy and titled people of London. I want you to help me find a new patron for our foundling home."

Lazarus kept his mouth firmly straight, but he felt a surge of triumph as the prim widow ran headlong into his talons.

"Done."